THE
COLONISTS

═══

COMING SEPTEMBER 1995

An American Family Portrait Book Three:
THE PATRIOTS

An American Family Portrait

B O O K T W O

The Colonists

Jack Cavanaugh

ChariotVICTOR
PUBLISHING
A DIVISION OF COOK COMMUNICATIONS

Copyediting:
Greg Clouse

Cover Illustration:
Chris Cocozza

Cover Design:
Paul Higdon

Maps:
Andrea Boven

The song "The Little Mohee" is reprinted with permission from *Annals of America*, © 1968, 1976 Encyclopedia Britannica, Inc.

Victor Books is an imprint of Chariot Victor Publishing,

a division of Cook Communications, Colorado Springs, Colorado 80918

Cook Communications, Paris, Ontario

Kingsway Communications, Eastbourne, England

Library of Congress Cataloging-in-Publication Data

Cavanaugh, Jack.
    The colonists / by Jack Cavanaugh.
      p.   cm.
    ISBN 1-56476-346-3
    1. Boston (Mass.)—History—Colonial period, ca.
1600–1775—Fiction.   2. Family—Massachusetts—Boston—Fiction. I. Title. II. Series: Cavanaugh,
Jack. American family portrait; bk. 2.
    PS3553.A965C65   1994
    813'.54—dc20   94–32469
                                       CIP

6 7 8 9 10 Printing/Year 99

Chariot VICTOR
PUBLISHING
A DIVISION OF COOK COMMUNICATIONS

To my wife, Marni, and my children, Elizabeth, Keri, and Sam. When I was young I never dreamed being the father of a family would be so much fun. Sometimes it seems unnatural that we enjoy each other so much.

ACKNOWLEDGMENTS

This is the second book in the series and the second time some of the names below have appeared on this page. Their work is no less appreciated the second time around. I'll never tire of thanking them.

To Barbara Ring and Carol Rogers who read and offered invaluable criticisms of the early draft—thank you, your comments always hit the mark.

To John Mueller who was a serendipitous source of knowledge in all things nautical as well as a valued story critic—I'm glad that some good has come from your Navy experience.

To Judith Deem Dupree—your poetry never fails to inspire me; thank you for the use of "Oh Child." The poem is a wonderful expression of Anne Pierpont's character.

To Elizabeth Cavanaugh—I'm amazed at your grasp of words, structure, and literary devices at such a young age. Thank you for writing Anne's love poem. You make me proud.

To Greg Clouse and the staff at Victor Books—with every contact to your offices you make me feel like family. A man can never have too many friends like you.

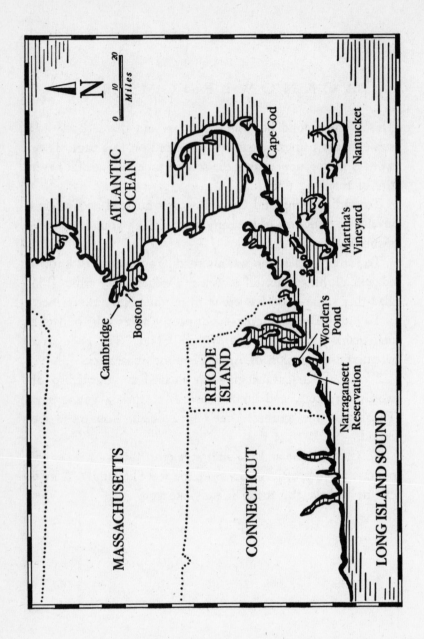

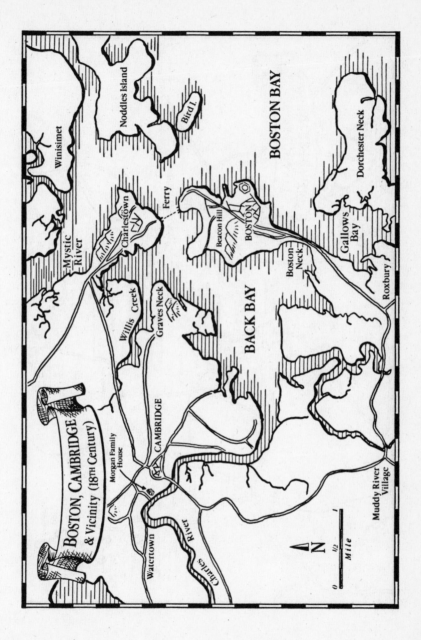

BOSTON, CAMBRIDGE & Vicinity (18TH Century)

Winisimet

Noddles Island

Bird I.

BOSTON BAY

Mystic River

Charlestown

Ferry

Beacon Hill

BOSTON

Dorchester Neck

Gallows Bay

Boston Neck

Roxbury

Willis Creek

Graves Neck

BACK BAY

Morgan Family House

CAMBRIDGE

Watertown

Charles River

Muddy River Village

N

0   1/2   1
        Mile

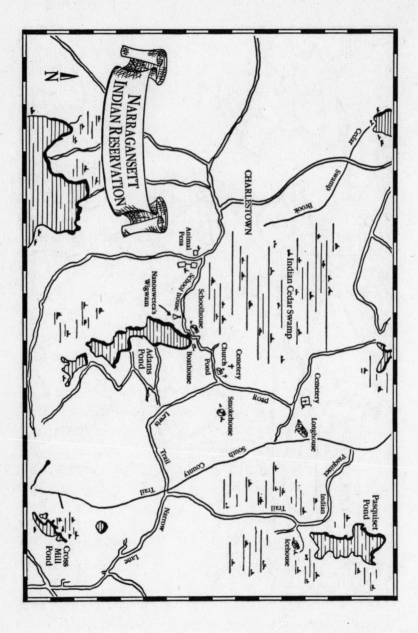

IN 1727 Benjamin Morgan fulfilled his lifelong dream, but he had to die to do it. Although the Harvard College instructor didn't live long enough to see the fruit of his sacrifice, there was little doubt in his children's minds that his death was the seed that produced the harvest.

The sitting room in which his coffin lay was in an unnatural order. The large circular table which had always occupied a prominent place in the center of the room was pushed into a corner. In its place was the draped bier upon which the open coffin rested. Odd-shaped pieces of paper were randomly fastened to the black cloth—laudatory verses and sentences offered on behalf of grieving friends and family. The room's chairs, normally grouped informally for intimate conversation, were backed against the walls in rigid ranks. A gaping entryway door allowed a chilly wind from the Charles River to intrude into the normally cozy interior, causing Priscilla Morgan to shiver involuntarily.

She stood alone, her back to a wall. Brushing aside a few wayward strands of shocking red hair, she watched as her father's friends and colleagues drifted in with the breeze to pay their last respects.

Imbeciles and half-wits all, she groused. *I daresay not a one of them has ever had an original thought in his life.*

As if to confirm her evaluation of them, each man passing

through the door followed an identical routine. Upon entering the house he removed his hat with his left hand, smoothed down his hair with his right, approached the coffin, gazed upon the corpse, made a crooked face, passed on to the liquor table, took a glass of his preferred liquor, then went back outside to talk of things less disturbing—like politics, or the new road, or summer crops, or swapping horses.

Father's death means nothing to them, Priscilla murmured. *What do they care that his body is boxed up like freight; that his mouth is clamped shut in a grim line; that his arms are stiff and unfeeling; that his fingers lay cold and still on his chest?*

Priscilla bit her lower lip to fight back the tears. She'd promised herself she wouldn't give in to emotion. She wouldn't give these people the satisfaction. Yet despite her best efforts her eyes grew moist. Seeing her father's hands reminded her of how, when she was little, he would caress her cheek with the backs of his fingers; and how those same hands would reach out and snag her unexpectedly, lifting her onto his lap where she would be smothered by his embrace.

Priscilla remembered the way she used to sneak up on her father while he sat reading in a chair. She would duck under his book and climb into his lap, emerging only inches from his face. Then the fun would begin. At first he would act shocked, no matter that he saw her coming and she'd done this hundreds of times before. Then, with exaggerated slowness—to heighten the anticipation of what was about to come—he would mark his place in the book, set it aside, and remove his glasses. No sooner would his glasses touch the table then he would suddenly and with playful ferociousness attack her, growling like a bear. She, of course, would giggle and scream and try to get away. He'd pull her close until they were cheek to cheek. Even now she could remember his scratchy, whiskery cheeks against her own and the smell of coffee on his breath as he rocked her lovingly back and forth.

Coarse male laughter burst through the open door. It was an unwelcome sound that broke the spell of Priscilla's remembrances. The rude intrusion made her angry; and Priscilla was never one to waste good anger.

She used her anger to keep her mind from wandering back to emotional memories. The unnatural weight on her right hand provided her a ready excuse. The burden was her mourning ring.

A stupid custom, and an unnecessary cost, she thought as she twirled the ring around her finger. The gold ring was decorated with black enamel. It bore a representation of a coffin with a full-length skeleton laying in it. Next to the coffin were her father's initials—BTM—and the date of his death—June 20, 1727. Everyone in the family wore one identical to hers.

When her mother mentioned that the rings needed to be ordered, Priscilla argued against them. It was a ridiculous expense. A pound apiece! Outrageous! But did anyone listen to her? Did her family *ever* listen to her? Of course not! Break with tradition? they cried. Never! Her mother was horrified Priscilla had even mentioned it!

Rings weren't the only funeral tradition Priscilla thought should be loaded up and sent back to England on the next departing ship. Gloves were another. Priscilla shook her head in disgust as she remembered how her mother agonized over the glove list. For the governor, the magistrates, and the college staff, Constance Morgan insisted on gloves worth twelve shillings a pair; anything less would be scandalous! Indeed! And five shillings a pair for friends and family. Of course, cheap gloves of two shillings and sixpence would do for casual acquaintances. Priscilla couldn't understand why casual acquaintances needed gloves at all.

The stupidity of the glove custom was most evident when it came to ministers. If gloves were money, ministers would be rich. They not only received gloves for funerals, but also for weddings and christenings. What could one man do with all those gloves? He had only two hands! Priscilla imagined what a minister's closet must look like. It would get so full of gloves that one day he'd open the door and be buried under an avalanche of them. There was one consolation in having so many gloves, she thought. At least when ministers die, their wives don't have to buy gloves. The widow simply returns all the gloves her husband has collected over the years.

Priscilla shook her head disgustedly. For her, funeral traditions were activities designed to keep weak minds busy so they didn't have to face the reality of death.

She glanced at the clock on the mantle. Wasn't it time to start the procession? Priscilla searched the premises for the most-gloved man in Cambridge, her pastor, the Reverend Horace Russell. She spied him on the far side of the room. He was holding his unoccupied pair of gloves in one hand, slapping the open palm of his free hand with them. The person in conversation with him was her older brother, Philip, and his socialite fiancée, Penelope Chauncy.

Standing next to the short, plump minister, Philip Morgan looked even taller and thinner than he normally did. His dark brown hair fell forward and bounced back and forth in front of his eyes when he talked. Philip's head was always bobbing back and forth. It was an annoying habit. Priscilla remembered how one day following dinner her father predicted that Philip's flopping head would someday fall to the ground and he'd kick it with his big feet and never be able to find it again. Priscilla smiled as she remembered how her father pretended to be Philip searching his shoulders for the missing head.

She caught herself just as the emotions began to well up inside her. *Enough!* she scolded.

The sound of her brother's laughter provided the anger she needed to win the battle against her emotions. She envied him with a jealousy that bordered on hate. Why was he born a

male and not she? She was just as smart as he, a better orga-
nizer, better with figures. Had the funeral been left solely to
him, nothing would have gotten done! In spite of her feelings, she was the one who ordered the rings and the gloves; it
was she who had arranged for the tolling of the bell, orga-
nized the order of procession to the grave, gathered the
underbearers and pallbearers, purchased the headstone and
had the inscription carved on it, and arranged for the digging
and filling of the grave. What had he done? He shut himself
away in Father's office. Said he was going over the family's
ledgers, investments, college and personal papers. What did
he know about any of those things? He got to do it because
he was the oldest male — not because he was smarter, not
because he knew what he was doing, not even because he
wanted to do it. It was his job because he was a male and he
was older, two factors over which he had no direct control.
Just as she had no control over being born second and female.
It wasn't fair. It just wasn't fair!

Priscilla had always had trouble sharing her father's attention. Truth was, Benjamin Morgan had spent a great deal of
time with all three of his children, more than most fathers.
Philip was following his academic lead at Harvard College;
father and son spoke Latin to each other even when they
were at home, much to the chagrin of the other family members, especially Priscilla. She wished she had a secret language
known only to her and her father. Instead, she was forced to
attend Mr. Brownell's School for Young Women where she
was instructed in the housewifely arts of cooking, spinning,
weaving, and knitting. Priscilla hated the school and despised
the girls who dutifully attended. She would have given almost
anything for the chance to study Latin, mathematics, and
theology at grammar school like her brothers.

She never knew if her father gave in because he understood
her anguish, or if he did it to shut her up. But did it matter?

Benjamin Morgan made a deal with his daughter. If she attended Brownell's school, he would teach her whatever she wanted to learn at night.

Suddenly, a new world opened up to Priscilla. For hours on end she escaped from the humdrum life of women and explored the worlds described in ancient texts; she wrestled with slippery philosophical concepts; but the study that excited her most was the strict beauty of mathematics.

But those days were gone. It was Philip's study now, not Father's. He had always been the golden child, the Puritan's promise of the next generation, the epitome of everything they held most dear. Everyone expected great things of Philip. They predicted he would be president of Harvard someday, maybe even governor of the colony. He was the darling of stuffy conservatives, molded in their image. Philip wouldn't understand her anguish like Father; he would never let her into the study again.

Priscilla had considered appealing to him for study time, but she rejected the idea. Why should he let her? She was confident he hated her as much as she hated him. Priscilla would just have to admit it. With the death of her father, the door to her world of learning had just slammed shut.

The somber tones of the church bell rippled through the house. True to their cultural conditioning, everyone cocked an ear to the traditional signal and stopped what they were doing. The pastor closed the lid of the coffin as the young underbearers gathered around it, preparing to bear Benjamin Morgan's body on its last journey. However, there was an empty space beside the coffin. One of the underbearers was missing. There should be six, but only five were in place.

Jared Morgan burst into the room hopping on one foot while trying to jam a dripping foot into his shoe. *Typical Jared,* Priscilla thought. *Irresponsible. He doesn't think about anybody but himself.* He'd been out at river's edge playing in the water again. The shoe halfway on, he began to lose his balance. Instinctively his half-covered foot slammed against the wooden floor. As it hit, the shoe made greater progress on his foot. Seeing that this worked, Jared stomped his foot several times until the shoe was in place. He straightened himself, ran both hands in comblike fashion through his light brown hair, and skidded into place next to the coffin.

As the church bell continued its melancholy summons, the underbearers lifted the coffin to their shoulders. The pall, a heavy black broadcloth owned by the town, was draped over the coffin and the underbearers. The pallbearers, men of age and community standing, held the corners of the pall to keep it from slipping. The procession was ready to begin.

The minister and town magistrates led the procession. The coffin-bearers followed, then family members and close friends, finally church members and acquaintances. Priscilla looked around for her mother. She frowned. Constance Morgan had an arm linked with Philip. Daniel Cole, a bulky Boston merchant, occupied her other side while Penelope trailed behind.

Daniel Cole and Constance Mayhew had been friends since childhood, close friends. So close that most people had expected them to marry. As Priscilla heard it, everyone was surprised when Constance chose Benjamin Morgan over the promising Cole.

Constance was dwarfed by the merchant's size. He was a huge bear of a man with a massive head of white hair. One of his big paws was stretched around Priscilla's mother, resting on her shoulder. Priscilla didn't like it. Not one bit. She'd never been impressed with the man, and the thought of him touching her mother was revolting.

Priscilla Morgan joined her father's funeral procession, maintaining a good distance between herself and the rest of her family. *So this is how it is to be,* she thought. *Alone. So be it. Life's easier this way. Just look out for yourself. Don't get close to anyone. They'll only hurt you.*

"I know I shouldn't be up here," a soft voice came from behind her. "But do you think they'll put me in the pillory if I violate the order of the procession by walking with you?"

Priscilla turned to see who was addressing her. It was Anne Pierpont, a slender young lady with innocent round eyes and a quick smile. Although she was a few years younger than Priscilla, she was taller. But then most people were taller than Priscilla, who had always been petite. Anne was one of the few women Priscilla admired. She was intelligent and a gifted poet.

Priscilla thought it odd that she liked Anne so much, considering their differences. For instance, Priscilla was no stranger to anger, yet she had never seen Anne even mildly miffed; in fact, she'd never seen Anne exhibit any negative emotion at all. Remarkable. How could anyone live like that? But their personalities weren't their greatest difference. That had to be Jared. Anne was sweet on him. And he—in his own miserable, awkward way—had demonstrated some form of affection for her in return. Priscilla couldn't understand what it was about her brother that would attract an intelligent person like Anne. It just didn't make sense.

"If you'd rather be alone, I'll return to my place in the procession," Anne offered.

Priscilla hesitated. She thought of her stony resolve and dismissed it. "No," she said, "I'd like it if you would join me."

Anne Pierpont smiled. It was an affectionate smile that swept over Priscilla like a warm tonic.

The procession wound its way up the path leading from the Morgan house along the banks of the Charles River to the little church graveyard, barely a mile distant, situated on the top of a hill. Priscilla could hear Philip's wheezing cough ahead of her. He'd had the condition as a child. A coughing attack could be set off by dust, exertion, or anxiety. Priscilla always found his attacks too convenient; although she didn't believe he faked his condition, it seemed odd to her that Philip always seemed to have an attack when there was something he didn't want to do.

The mourners gathered around the open grave. It was a lonely, barren spot on the hillside. Briars and weeds grew in tangled thickets; birch trees and barberry bushes sprang up unchecked. The graves were clustered together in irregular groups showing no thought of planning, no sense of order.

The grieving family and friends of Benjamin Morgan mulled around the gravesite. There was no sermon and no religious service of any kind. The Puritans did not wish to confirm the popish error that prayer is to be used for the dead or over the dead, so they said nothing at all. They watched in silence as the coffin was lowered into the grave. The only testimony to the dead man's life, other than the human legacy he left behind, was the printed words on the headstone. They were written by Anne Pierpont.

When Priscilla purchased the headstone—a hard, dark, flinty piece of slate from North Wales, she was asked what she wanted inscribed on it. She hadn't given it much thought up until then and she asked for some examples. The standard inscription, she was told, was:

> *As I am now, so you shall be,*
> *Prepare for Death & follow me.*

Other suggestions were no better, so she asked Anne Pierpont to compose something appropriate. The inscription on Benjamin Morgan's tombstone read:

I came in the morning—it was Spring
And I smiled.
I walked out at noon—it was Summer
And I was glad.
I sat me down at even—it was Autumn
And I was sad.
I laid me down at night—it was Winter
And I slept.

"It's beautiful," Priscilla leaned over and whispered to Anne. The gentle poet blushed. "Thank you," she said.

The funeral over, those least acquainted with the deceased man headed down the hill first. Jared was with them. Philip stood close beside the open grave; Penelope stood beside him. He was head of the Morgan family now. It was still hard for Priscilla to accept. It wasn't supposed to be like this. Benjamin Morgan had lived only half a lifetime. He was such a good man, such a kind man.

Why hadn't Philip been killed instead?

It was a question that had been rumbling in her mind ever since she heard the news of her father's death. As much as she hated her brother and loved her father, still she knew the question was unfair. She tried to put it out of her mind. But the question kept coming back. Why hadn't Philip been killed instead?

Her father and Philip had gone on a journey, but only Philip returned alive. Her father was pierced by two arrows and a bullet, yet her brother received not a scratch. It didn't make sense. Surely Philip could have done something to save him! Did he try? He said he did. But did he really do all he could do, or did he save himself?

"Priscilla."

The sound of her name spoken by an unfamiliar voice caused her to start.

"Did I scare you?" It wasn't an apology. It almost sounded like a boast. Towering over her was the huge merchant, Daniel Cole. His eyes were a hard, unfriendly gray. "I want you to know that if there is anything I can do for your family . . . I mean, anything at all . . . you see . . . your mother and I have been friends for a long time."

"Thank you, sir. The gesture is appreciated," she said with a flat tone.

The merchant took offense at the coolness of her response. He whirled away, then back again. "Death is not the end, only the beginning," he said. "Why, the two days in which I buried my wife and son were the best days I ever had in the world! If you weren't so self-centered, you'd realize that this is best for your father."

He turned and stalked away. "He means well," Anne offered, laying a comforting hand on Priscilla's shoulder.

She was right. Daniel Cole was merely offering a well-known, often-expressed Puritan hope—that when a believer dies, he or she is transported immediately into God's heavenly kingdom. It was a belief Priscilla shared. Still it did little to ease her overwhelming sense of loss.

"I'll bet the day his wife and son died was the best day for them too," Priscilla said sarcastically.

Priscilla and Anne were the last to leave the hillside graveyard. Anne kept her distance, allowing Priscilla time to be alone with her thoughts, a gesture Priscilla appreciated. With the breeze whipping her dress, Priscilla stood overlooking Cambridge. The Back Bay and Boston lay in the distance. She could see the winding course of the Charles River and the roof of her house situated among the trees. The sight of home hit her hard.

Her father wouldn't be coming home tonight. She would leave him buried in the cold earth of this hill. Like lightning striking a dam, her brave resolve to control her emotions splintered and collapsed.

The tender embrace of Anne Pierpont steadied her shaking shoulders. Anne meant well, but her embrace only served to remind Priscilla of the vow she'd made to herself.

"Thank you," Priscilla said sternly. "But I'm fine now."

With renewed anger Priscilla Morgan repaired the emotional dam. On that hillside overlooking Cambridge she resolved never to love anyone again. Never to let anyone get close enough to hurt her. She would live alone. She would show them all. She would not fit their mold. She would study, she would learn, and she would become wealthy. People respect wealth, maybe even respect enough to balance the fact that she was a woman.

THE click of the front door latch startled him awake. Tired, scratchy eyes pried open, searching for a scrap of light to focus on. There was none. The room was totally dark.

The front door creaked—a low, agonizing creak, the kind of creak doors make when someone is attempting to pass through unnoticed. Then, all was silent.

Fully awake now, Philip Morgan bolted upright. There was a moment of disorientation. Where was he? He wasn't in his bedroom. Philip rubbed his eyes, hoping to hasten their usefulness. Slowly, dark forms began to take shape. That's right, he was in his father's office. He'd fallen asleep while working at the desk. His back and arms complained, aching in the places where they'd rested against the wooden chair.

The front door creaked again. Philip searched the room for some kind of weapon. For the second time the door latch clicked. Ordinarily, the click of the latch would go by unnoticed, but in a dark house, in the still of the night, the sound echoed with frightening clarity.

Philip held his breath, listening for footsteps. Nothing. *A weapon, I need a weapon!* His eyes darted around the room looking for something to use as a club. Just then he heard a voice from outside the house.

"Hurry up!" it cried.

Philip crossed noiselessly to the window, stood to one side

to avoid being seen, and peered out. A full moon splashed its silvery light on the walkway, the sloping front yard, and the random scattering of trees. A sudden movement caught his eye. Someone running from the house. The human figure ran with an easy, loping gate; a musket was clutched in his right hand while a powder horn swung rhythmically at his side.

Jared!

Philip easily recognized his brother's athletic stride. It was something he'd envied about his brother most of his life. While Philip excelled intellectually, it was Jared who had always been stronger and faster, even when they were young boys.

Why was Jared sneaking out of the house late at night? Philip made a mental note to tell his father about it in the morning. Then, like a hot poker, the unwelcome memory of his father's death burned in Philip's bosom. He couldn't tell his father . . . he had no father. That's why he was in the office. He was head of the household now. His brother was now his responsibility. Philip stared after his Jared, who was headed for a tuft of trees near the river's edge. *I should go after him and bring him back,* he thought.

In the distance two dark forms stepped from the trees' shadows. One was tall, the other shorter and chunky. When Philip saw them, his memory flashed to another time, another place when two men stepped out from among the trees.

Suddenly Philip's windpipe constricted. He wheezed and coughed, struggling to clear a passageway in which to breathe, fighting for any scrap of air. Instinctively, he steadied himself with one hand on the windowsill as violent spasms of coughing and wheezing doubled him over. Although he'd had similar attacks for as long as he could remember, they had never been this violent. Since his asthma attack on the day Father died, each succeeding attack had gotten worse, and with each attack Philip thought for sure he was going to die. And, although he didn't want to admit it, even to himself, there was a part of him that had conceded that death would be a welcome relief.

The strength of the coughing spasms began to diminish and Philip groped his way from the windowsill to the book-case to the desk to the chair. He collapsed into it. The spasms mustered for one last attack, and Philip coughed so hard his feet lifted off the floor. A few agonizing moments later it was over. Philip Morgan fell limp in the chair, his arms dangling over the sides as sweat poured down his face.

He lay still for a long time, exhausted. He thought of Jared. *Should go after him. Bring him back.* But he didn't have the strength. He'd just have to wait and confront his younger brother in the morning.

Two dark images appeared in Philip's mind again. He tried to blot them from his memory, but he could no more do that than he could stop his asthma attacks. Tears merged into the streams of sweat that coursed down his cheeks as Philip remembered the day his father died.

It was supposed to be a simple trip to Boston to check on an investment. Although Philip was the oldest of the Morgan children, he knew little about the family's financial investments. Up until now his father had taken care of these things, in a rather untimely manner as Philip was beginning to find out. Benjamin Morgan was a scholar, not a businessman. He handled financial matters only when he had to, never because he wanted to. Father and son were much alike in that manner, each preferring the classics to the ledger. But an urgent matter of business had arisen, calling the elder Morgan to Boston. Wanting someone to talk to during the journey, and thinking it was high time his eldest son learned about the family's business matters, he had asked Philip to accompany him.

Benjamin Morgan and son took the longer land route to Boston rather than using the ferry that crossed over from

Charlestown. The elder Morgan had never liked the water. He'd drink it, bathe in it, but would never ride on it. The source of his father's unabashed phobia remained a mystery to Philip. In some ways Philip respected his father more for having it. Maybe because it made his father seem more human.

So father and son left Cambridge early in the morning on horseback. They'd crossed the bridge over the Charles River on the road heading south and had just passed through Muddy River Village on the way to Roxbury. Benjamin Morgan had just turned to his son to say something when the first arrow struck him.

It came from a small patch of forest on Benjamin Morgan's side of the road. Because he'd just turned toward Philip, the arrow hit him in the back. The elder Morgan's eyes flashed wide with pain and surprise. Then a musket fired and Benjamin's body jerked with the impact. The pupils of his eyes rolled upward and he fell from his horse making the most awful thud as he hit the dirt road.

Philip jumped down from his horse. Every instinct screamed at him to attend to his father, but first he had to deal with the attackers. He had to get the musket. There was only one weapon and it was strapped to his father's saddle. Luckily, his father's horse had stopped. It stood there stupidly, staring down at its fallen master, oblivious to any danger. Philip used the horse to shield himself from the direction of the attack. He heard his father's moans as he reached over the horse and grabbed the butt of the musket. That's when he saw them emerging from the trees.

What a strange pair, Philip remembered thinking. The two attackers halted a short distance from their cover and stood there as bold as anything studying their victims. One was an Indian—Mohegan, Pequot, Narragansett—Philip didn't know which; he couldn't tell one Indian from another. The thing that was so strange about it was that the Indian's partner was a sailor! What was a sailor doing in the woods attacking his father? The sailor wore wide, baggy breeches cut a few inches above the ankle, a checkered shirt of blue and white linen, and a Monmouth cap. He was short and wiry with scraggly gray hair falling from the edges of his cap. He had a huge, bulbous nose that looked like it covered more than half of his face. Philip had never seen either of them before. He stood there, dumbfounded at the thought that these two strangers would want to hurt him or his father.

Benjamin Morgan had grabbed his horse by the front leg and was pulling himself up. The sailor saw him and said something to the Indian. The Indian drew another arrow.

Philip tried to shout a warning to his father, but before he could utter a word, a violent spasm gripped his throat. There was no warning cry, only wheezing and coughing and rattling sounds.

The Indian loaded his weapon and pulled the bow. Philip could only watch, helplessly clutching his throat and gasping for breath. The arrow whizzed through the air and hit its mark with a thump. Benjamin Morgan slumped to the ground.

By this time the coughing attack had such a grip on Philip, he could no longer stand. He fell to the ground, doubled over, racked by the spasms. He expected to be hit by an arrow at any moment, or see his attackers standing over him, ready to slit his throat or take his scalp. But no arrows came. No musket fired. No one stood over him.

Eventually the coughing subsided. Philip struggled to his hands and knees and looked around for his attackers. They were gone! Benjamin Morgan lay face down on the road. Two arrows protruded grotesquely from his back, waving back and forth ever so slightly from his father's shallow breathing. A third wound in the small of his back—from the musket ball—was splattered with powder black and wet with blood.

Philip remembered the raspy sound of his father's voice,

calling to him. He felt helpless as he kneeled over his father. Should he pull the arrows out or would that only aggravate the wound?

Benjamin Morgan lifted his head and turned toward Philip. "Come here, Son. Down here."

Philip lay beside his father, his head resting in the dirt.

"Are you all right?"

"Yes, Father."

"Do you know who it was?" Benjamin Morgan's voice was barely more than a whisper.

"No, Father. I never saw them before. It was a sailor and an Indian. Why would a sailor and an Indian want to hurt you?"

A look of confusion crossed the elder Morgan's face. "A sailor and an Indian?"

Philip nodded, the side of his head rubbing in the dirt.

Benjamin Morgan half-chuckled, then winced in pain. "Imagine that," he said, "a sailor and an Indian."

"Father, let me help you to your horse and I'll get you to a doctor."

"Too late for that," his father wheezed. Then he said, "I'm sorry to leave you like this, Son."

"Nobody's leaving anybody!" Philip shouted. "Everything will be all right! I'll get a doctor and bring him here!"

"Tell your mother I love her," said the elder Morgan. His eyes closed momentarily. "Should have told her myself more often."

"I'll tell her, Father. I promise."

"Priscilla and Jared too. Tell them I love them."

"Yes, Father."

"I know you and your brother and sister don't get along, but promise me you'll look after them. Promise me. Family is important, Son, probably the most important thing on earth. Never forget that."

Tears spilled from Philip's eyes, forming miniature craters in the dust.

"One more thing."

"Whatever you want, Father."

The elder Morgan coughed a chest-rattling cough. His eyes closed in pain. When they opened again they were unfocused to the things of this world. "I want you to complete a bit of unfinished business," he said. "In the cabinet. In my study. A diary. Read it. It belonged to one of our ancestors." Another spasm interrupted him. "It tells of a Bible. Family Bible. Ours. Lost for," more coughs, "lost for more than fifty years. Philip, I want you to find it. Bring it home. Promise me."

"I'll find it, Father. I promise . . . I promise . . . I promise."

In the darkness of his father's study, Philip's tears flowed freely. "I should have been able to save him! If only I'd acted more quickly, Father would be alive today. Why, God? Why did I have an asthma attack when Father needed me most?"

Philip wheezed and coughed.

"You chose the wrong son to accompany you!" Philip cried to the empty room. "Jared's the cool-headed one. You should have taken him. He would have acted more quickly. If Jared was with you, you'd be alive today. He could have saved you. O Father, I'm sorry. I'm so sorry. You're dead because I failed you. I wasn't fast enough, strong enough. Why didn't you ask Jared to accompany you instead of me?"

Philip buried his head in his arms on top of the desk laden with books and papers. He wept until sleep overcame him.

He didn't sleep long, maybe an hour or so. He hadn't slept through the night since his father died. And each time he awoke, he awoke to the same words swirling in his head — bring back the Bible . . . bring back the Bible . . . bring back the Bible.

Philip stood, wiped his eyes, and stretched. Reaching for the tinder box, he lit a candle and the contents of the table came to view. One stack of papers were funeral-related bills —

charges for the headstone, rings, gloves, liquor table, and a variety of other miscellaneous items. Funerals were costly; one-fifth of the deceased person's entire estate was the norm. Philip took this stack of papers, crammed them into a box, and set them aside. He didn't want to think about such things now. The remaining papers came from the cabinet his father had spoken about. In the cabinet Philip had found loose papers, books, and a journal, all related to the Morgan family history.

For almost a year his father had spent several hours a week pursuing a special course of study. Two, sometimes three nights a week, he would shut himself away in his study and work. He wouldn't tell anyone what he was working on, only that he was excited about it and hoped to share it with them soon.

The collection of loose papers scattered across the desk was a hodgepodge of research and personal notes. One paper featured a treelike structure bearing the family genealogy. Philip knew that one of his ancestors, Drew Morgan, had come over from England aboard the *Arbella* with Governor John Winthrop, but that's about all he knew of his ancestry. According to the family tree, he and his brother and sister were the fifth generation of Morgans to live in Massachusetts.

Philip held the paper up to the light and traced his lineage. The information was sketchy in spots, but adequate. Drew Morgan was born in 1611 (the month and day were not recorded) and died September 24, 1682. Drew and Nell (Matthews) had three children: Christopher, born in 1634 (no date of death was indicated); Lucy was born in 1635, died 1704; and Roger, born 1638, died 1701(?), possibly 1702. Philip's family line came through Roger, the youngest of Drew and Nell's children. Roger married Mary Shepard (no date recorded) and they had three children: Thomas, Timothy, and Tyler. Thomas, the eldest, was Philip's grandfather. Philip remembered him being a strange sort of man. He was a proud Englishman who always talked about going back home—

meaning England—where he belonged. This attachment to England was rather strange since Thomas had lived in the colonies all his life and had never been to England. His wife Ann (Grandma Ann to Philip) died of smallpox the same year their only son, Benjamin, entered Harvard at age 15. Thomas blamed the miserable conditions of the colonies for her death and within a month of her funeral sailed to England and civilization, leaving his only son to fend for himself. Philip remembered noticing a letter (buried somewhere beneath all the piles of papers on the desk) from a Master Higgenbothem in Exeter, England, informing Benjamin Morgan of his father's death in 1725, a mere two years ago.

On the family tree limb beside Thomas Morgan and Ann Weston, Benjamin had written his name and that of his wife, Constance. Beneath the names were their birth dates, his 1682 and hers 1690. He had left a space for a date of death, to match the branches of the family tree above them. With an uncertain hand, Philip Morgan took a quill and scratched in the date of his father's death—June 20, 1727. Beside the names Benjamin and Constance, a branch with three limbs was drawn, bearing the names Philip, Priscilla, and Jared.

A fistful of papers were stuffed between the pages of an old journal. The writing on the pages was in his father's hand, barely legible. The hastily scribbled letters and the preponderance of exclamation points scattered across the pages revealed Benjamin Morgan's excitement over the journal's contents. According to the papers, the journal had just recently been discovered in the attic of an old building on the Boston wharf. The owner of the building, a business acquaintance of Benjamin Morgan, upon reading the surname of the journal's author, had delivered the journal to Philip's father. The journal was the personal account of one Drew Morgan. It told of the early days of Massachusetts Bay Colony and had a few sketchy references to a little village called Edenford in Devonshire, England, but mostly the writing was about Drew's spiritual growth and his passion to train his children in the ways of God. Benjamin's loose pages marked a passage that revealed the existence of a family Bible. It read:

August 26, 1682

(Philip made a mental note. The date of the entry was just a few weeks before Drew's death. Drew was seventy-one years old.)

It has been seven years to date since we've heard from Christopher. We hold little hope he is alive. The last word we received, and that secondhand, was that he was ministering to the praying Indians of the Wampanoag tribe shortly before the outbreak of hostilities. Although his location and health are uncertain, of this we are sure — his life is in God's hands. Christopher did not fear those who could harm his body, knowing full well they could not harm his soul. My only regret is that, as far as we know, he died without issue, without fathering a son to whom he could pass the family Bible in keeping with the charge I gave to him at the ceremony. Maybe it is wrong of me to place so much emphasis on a physical symbol. God needs not a written record to know those who are His. My one last hope for this world is that the Morgan family will never know a generation that does not worship the Lord.

Nell has not been well these past few weeks. Having lost her beloved father and sister to the acts of evil men, she finds it hard to accept she may have lost her firstborn son in similar manner. Lord, grant her comfort.

We've recently received word that Lucy is with child again. If God grants this new little one life, it will be her twelfth child — three others having died in childbirth. She has done much to raise a godly lineage for the Sinclair line.

Finally, I pray that the Lord will grant me patience with Roger. There is very little regarding this life or the next in which we have agreed. Open his eyes, Lord. Teach him not to put his trust in the things of this world.

The scholar inside Philip was stirred by this original document. Drew Morgan's journal was not just a piece of Massachusetts history, it was a piece of *his* history. The man who penned these words forty-five years previous was his blood ancestor!

The balance of the papers stuffed into this section of the journal was a summary of Benjamin Morgan's research regarding the lost Bible. The notes referred to correspondence with his cousins—the children of Timothy and Tyler Morgan. The actual letters were probably crammed into one of the many little boxlike filing spaces in the desk. Benjamin had written his cousins to see if they knew anything about a family Bible. They responded that they'd heard their grandfather Roger mention it when he was drunk and angry. One cousin also remembered his grandfather cursing his brother, calling him "Jesus of the Narragansetts," and "the reservation Apostle." Benjamin's excited script followed:

I believe the Morgan family Bible still exists! Hypothesis: Christopher Morgan taught the Indians to revere God and honor His Word. Upon his death would not his disciples treasure the Bible of their teacher? To test my hypothesis, I will travel to the Narragansett reservation to see if I can recover the symbol of my family's spiritual heritage.

Philip pulled in a deep, wheezing breath of air. His father's mission was now his mission. He'd given his word. Only now, the more he thought about it, the tighter his chest became, and his forehead glistened with sweat in the candlelight.

Chapter 3

HE got the musket!" Will shouted in a half-whisper. Will Hopkins and "Chuckers" Thomas stepped from the shadows of the tree into the silvery moonlight and greeted their late-night fellow adventurer enthusiastically.

"See ya got the powder," Chuckers said, spying the horn dangling at Jared's side. "Did ya bring shot?"

" 'Course I did, loggerhead!" Jared exclaimed. "What good would a musket be without shot?"

"Let me see the musket." Chuckers held out his hand. Without hesitation Jared handed the musket over to him. That's the way it had always been. Although the boys were close enough friends to call each other names, Chuckers was the leader because he was almost a full year older than Will and Jared. The younger boys followed their leader without question.

Will was tall and lanky, almost as tall as Jared's older brother Philip even though he was three years younger. He had a huge mouth that was bent upward in a perpetual grin and ears that stuck out like mainsails in a strong wind. He was a good-natured and friendly sort of fellow, even though it seemed like God had given him a miserly share of brains.

Chuckers was shorter, wider, and much wiser than Will. A natural leader, Charles Thomas—"Chuckers" to peers and adults alike (a nickname he gained as an infant while attempting to pronounce his own name)—had a stocky frame, beefy arms, and huge hands. At age sixteen, nearly every inch of him was covered with thick black hair, an envied characteristic to his peers who interpreted it as a mark of manhood.

Of the three friends, Jared Morgan was the brightest, strongest, and fastest—which in most cases would single him out as the leader of the group. But Jared didn't want to be a leader. He was content to follow. Whenever his superior skills put him at an advantage over his friends, he would back off until the odds were even.

Over the years the three boys had their share of spats as their roles in the group developed to an unspoken level of comfort. Chuckers took the lead. Will kept them laughing. Jared loyally tagged along and was usually the one chosen to carry out their pranks.

For example, on one Sabbath Chuckers brought a bird feather with him to the church service. Will, Chuckers, and Jared sat together on the boys' pew which butted up against the side of the Tomlin's enclosed family pew. Mr. Tomlin, a beekeeper, had a notorious reputation for falling asleep during the sermon even before the hourglass had been turned once. The boys usually contented themselves with the amusement that inevitably followed when the tithingman reached into the pew with his long stick and brushed Mr. Tomlin's face with a fox tail. If the fox tail wasn't sufficient to rouse the heavy sleeper, the tithingman would prick the slumbering church member on the hand with a thorn.

On this particular Sabbath, Mr. Tomlin fell asleep as usual, his balding head leaning against the wooden wall separating him from the boys' pew. While the tithingman was busy on the opposite side of the church, at Chucker's suggestion, Jared leaned close to the slumbering beekeeper and made a soft buzzing sound and tickled the top of Mr. Tomlin's head with the feather. The sleeping beekeeper would stir and, without waking, shoo away the nonexistent insect, much to the delight of all the boys in the pew next to him. This went on for several minutes as Jared made a variety of beelike sounds—to the delight of his audience—and explored various parts of Mr. Tomlin's head with the feather.

A sharp elbow in his side warned Jared of approaching danger. He snapped his head toward the preacher while simultaneously slipping the feather under his leg. With heads forward, the entire row of boys watched with sideways glances as the tithingman approached Mr. Tomlin's pew. The church officer dangled the fox tail against Mr. Tomlin's cheek. The beekeeper brushed it away. A second time yielded the same results. Changing tactics, the tithingman reached for his stick with the thorn on it. Will Hopkins started to giggle. Chuckers had to pinch him to get him to stop.

With all the solemnity of a king bestowing knighthood, the tithingman reached over the side of Mr. Tomlin's pew and pricked his hand. With alarming suddenness beekeeper Tomlin sprang to his feet, eyes wide and hands waving furiously, as he cursed profanely and swung furiously at an invisible swarm of bees.

It was a long time before Mr. Tomlin fell asleep in church again.

On another occasion Jared and Chuckers got into mischief when they sat in the bell tower together. Because of his father's high status in the church, Jared was appointed temporary bell ringer for a Sunday while the regular bell ringer visited relatives in Providence. Jared asked his father if Chuckers could sit in the tower with him during the service. Benjamin good-naturedly, if unwisely, agreed.

That Sabbath morning, their duty completed, the two sat at the bottom of the bell tower steps. Like sparrows in the rafters, they sat high above the rest of the congregation where they could see everything that went on below them.

When Chuckers got bored, as he always did during the worship service, he began picking away at some plaster that was used to seal cracks between the wooden boards. A tiny piece broke free and fell, rolled over the edge of a step, then plummeted downward to the congregation directly below them, just missing an elderly worshipper who was oblivious to the near hit. The near accident gave Chuckers and Jared an enticingly wicked idea.

The two boys chipped away at the plaster with their fingernails, arming themselves with a handful of plaster pebbles which they intended to use as ammunition. At first they were cautious. They only tossed their projectiles during times of prayer while people's heads were bowed. Whenever one of them would score a hit, the two artillery gunners had to stifle their gleeful giggles as the startled worshiper would rub his or her head and look directly overhead at the roof, never guessing that the offending pebble had been fired at them from behind. But prayer time didn't last forever—it only seemed that way when the boys were less engaged—and it wasn't long before Chuckers and Jared grew bored with the sermon. And in spite of the heightened risk of getting caught the boys resumed their assault. Their target was the boys' pew.

One plaster pebble, thrown by Jared, hit Will's older brother who happened to be seated next to Will. The older boy punched his brother in the ribs, thinking it was Will who had plunked him on the back of the head. In vain Will pleaded his innocence, much to the delight of the bell tower battery.

The merriment ended abruptly when Harry Stanford, the fidgety ten-year-old son of the beadle, the town crier, turned in his seat and looked back just as Jared released a projectile. The pebble hit the boy in the eye. A blood-curdling scream split the air, loud enough to startle even Mr. Tomlin awake. The injured boy covered his bleeding eye with one hand and pointed to his attacker with the other.

That was the last time Jared Morgan rang the church bell. He found it difficult to sit with any comfort for several days afterward, having received a just and memorable punishment administered by his father.

But now the administrator of punishment was dead. And, although Jared wasn't so callous as to rejoice in his father's death, part of him knew that the night's adventure was less risky than it would have been if his father were still alive.

"Is that the meat?" Jared asked Will, pointing to a paper bundle the wide-eared boy carried under his arm.

"Yep. Two pieces. Also got the hammer." He lifted his shirt to reveal a hammer head, the handle stuck in his waistband. "And nails." He pulled three rusty nails from a pocket.

"What kind of meat is it?"

"Venison."

"Won't your mom miss it?" Jared asked. Will gave a dopey grin and shrugged his shoulders. Apparently he hadn't given any thought to the fact his mother might realize some meat was missing from her larder.

"Not much of a gun," Chuckers said, examining the piece. He placed the butt against his shoulder and aimed the musket over the river.

"Only one we got," Jared said. "My father isn't . . . wasn't much for guns."

The intrusion of Benjamin Morgan's death on the clandestine gathering created an awkward silence. Chuckers dealt with it effectively by urging his troops into action.

"Let's go," he said. Carrying the weapon, he led them into the woods.

Will Hopkins slapped the unwrapped venison against the tree and held it in place with his left hand while Chuckers and Jared watched. Will's right hand fished in his pocket for a nail, then the hammer. The sound of pounding echoed through the woods as the meat was nailed to the tree about chest high.

"There," he said. "But how will the wolves know it's here?"

"They'll smell it, stupid!" Chuckers cried.

"Just askin'. And don't call me stupid."

Chuckers ignored the warning. "What should I call you then? Half-wit?"

Will looked genuinely hurt. Normally this kind of name-calling went back and forth all the time without anyone taking offense. *Must be the effects of being up so late,* Jared mused. *I'm feeling a little vexed myself.*

"You put the meat too low!" Chuckers groused. "They can reach it there!"

"They're supposed to reach it! It's bait!" Will yelled.

"You really are a loggerhead, aren't you? If the wolves reach it, they'll tear it down and run away with it and we'll be lucky if we get a shot! But if it's up high, they'll dance around the base of the tree and we can pick our shot. We drag the carcass away, wait a little longer, and another one comes by because the bait's still there! We get ten shillings for each wolf—minus my brother's fee for turning them in for us. So tell me, Will, which way is better, yours or mine?"

Will didn't answer directly. With a look of chagrin he nailed the second piece of meat to a nearby tree as high as he could reach.

Shoulder to shoulder and prostrate on the ground, the boys huddled together behind a bush as they waited for their prey. A lone musket barrel protruded from the bush, cradled in the arms of Jared Morgan. It took another altercation for the musket's marksman to be determined. Chuckers assumed he would shoot the gun, but Jared claimed right of ownership. Normally, whatever Chuckers wanted to do was fine with Jared. But Jared didn't like the way Chuckers had ripped into

Will and this was his way of evening the score. There was some pushing and shoving as both boys laid hands on the musket. And it was bystander Will who resolved the issue. He suggested Jared get the first shot since it was his musket, and since they would get more than one wolf tonight, Chuckers could take the second shot. It was hard for Chuckers to argue with the suggestion since he had made such a big deal about getting more than one wolf, so the issue was resolved and the boys settled into their hiding place.

Time dragged by slowly as the anxious hunters awaited their prey as quietly as three active boys can, alone in a forest in the middle of the night. His eyes widely alert, Jared scanned the range of forest that lay before him, looking for any sign of movement. It was darker here than it was in front of the house, since the thick clustering of branches overhead filtered out most of the moonlight. Here and there spots of silver could be seen on tree trunks where the moon's silvery light had broken through. The forest was quiet with no breeze to rustle the leaves. Jared could hear the breathing of his companions, one on each side of him. The field of vision between him and the trees bearing the sagging venison was clear of obstructions. Like all colonial boys his age, he was taught how to load and shoot a musket at an early age. However, unlike the others, he wasn't nearly as practiced, his father putting a greater emphasis on trusting God for their safety. Still, Jared was confident that should any wolf appear he would be able to hit it.

"Let's go home!" Will complained. "There aren't any wolves out here tonight."

"Some hunter you are," said Chuckers.

Jared moved his head from side to side to stretch his aching neck muscles. His elbows and shoulder joints were stiff.

"I suppose you want to go home too," Chuckers said to Jared.

Jared shook his head. "I want to get a wolf."

"But what if no wolves come?" There was a whine in Will's voice as he spoke.

"Then we don't get one," Jared said.

Will sighed heavily. They lay in silence for several more minutes, then Will sighed heavily again.

Chuckers spoke up. "Jared, you stay here. Will and me will scout around to see if we can spot anything—tracks or somethin'. If we don't see anything, we'll go home."

"I don't think that's a good idea," Will said. "I'd rather stay here with Jared."

"What's the matter, Will? Scared?" Chuckers stood up and brushed off his breeches. "Afraid the Black Man will jump out from behind a tree and drag you down to his house of fire?"

"Leave Will alone," Jared said.

"I'm not afraid!"

"Then let's go!" Chuckers said.

Will got up and dusted himself off and the two boys wandered slowly into the forest. It wasn't long before Jared lost sight of them; then he no longer heard them and all was quiet. He stretched his neck again and repositioned himself. A cool sensation soaked through his shirt as he lay on fresh ground that hadn't been warmed by his body. He shook off his encroaching drowsiness and waited for a wolf to appear.

After a wait that seemed longer than a Sunday sermon, he heard a twig snap followed by a rustling sound. It came from somewhere in front of him beyond the baited trees. He raised the musket into position. More rustling of leaves. Jared's heart pounded with excitement as he stared down the long barrel searching for something to shoot at. Suddenly, he lowered his musket.

Not funny, he thought. *Will and Chuckers are pulling a prank on me. Not a very smart idea. Probably Will's. I could have killed one of them.*

Just then a large gray wolf broke through the bushes, his nose to the ground. He sniffed the ground around the base of the trees then, lifting his head, he searched the air and found the scent that led him to the meat on the trees. Prancing out of the bushes behind him were three wolf pups, jumping all over each other. Behind them came two more wolves, another male and a female. The male was black with green eyes and tiny black pupils while the female—identified by her smaller head—had the same coloring as the larger male, gray and white.

The largest of the wolves, the one first to appear, leaped at the chest-high meat and easily tore it down just as Chuckers said he would do. The wolf tossed the meat to the ground and the three pups attacked it, snipping and snarling at one another as each one vied for position.

Jared looked excitedly from side to side, hoping that Chuckers and Will were nearby so they could see him shoot a wolf. He was disappointed when they were nowhere to be seen. He'd just have to do it without an audience. Jared raised the sight to his eye and leveled the musket barrel at the chest of the largest wolf.

Just then the smaller male tried to make a grab for the meat. The large wolf bared his teeth and lunged at him, biting the smaller wolf's neck and rolling him over onto his back. Pinned to the ground, the dark wolf struggled momentarily, then lay still in resignation to the larger wolf's domination. When he was released, he cowed before the gray wolf, playfully nipping at the leader's chin. The female stood apart, watching the pups eat.

Jared waited, telling himself he wanted to get a clean shot at the leader.

The large gray wolf then jumped into the middle of the pups, snarling and growling. Startled, they backed away from what was left of the meat. The gray wolf swallowed it with a single gulp as the dark wolf, the female, and the three pups watched, all of them licking their lips.

Jared repositioned his arm to steady himself for the shot. As he did, the musket barrel brushed against a branch. The wolves froze and stared in his direction. Jared held his breath, the musket barrel centered squarely on the chest of the large gray wolf. His finger tightened against the trigger. An easy shot. His first wolf. Ten shillings. He'd be a hero. All he had to do was pull the trigger. But he couldn't.

The wolves didn't sense his presence. They turned their attention to the other piece of meat that Will had nailed higher up. Jared lowered the gun.

He watched as the three adults jumped at the meat while the pups yipped and tumbled and rolled nearby. Of the three wolves, the dark one had the greatest spring in his legs. While the two gray wolves came up inches short, he nipped the edge of the meat. Jared could have had any one of the three. Their backs were to him, stretched out, easy targets. But Jared was content to watch. He couldn't help but see similar traits between this pack of wolves and his family. The three pups were him and his brother and sister — always snapping and barking and biting each other, yet at the same time knowing they were part of the same family, that they belonged to one another. He would never admit it to them, but he liked his brother and sister. He hated being the youngest in the family; he hated when they picked on him and made him feel dumb— he was different from them, he admitted that, but he wasn't dumb; and he hated that they were more like Father than he was—interested in theology and Latin and books and school and all that stuff. Still, they were family.

It was Father who'd kept them together until now. He was the large gray wolf. The one who maintained order, saw that each child felt a part, even Jared, the different one. Mother, like the female wolf, seemed content to stand quietly at his side while he exercised dominion over the family.

Jared wasn't one to meditate on things; he could never sit still long enough to manufacture any serious thought. And it wasn't until tonight, alone in the forest watching a pack of wolves, that he realized the significance of his father's death. Their leader was dead. What would happen to them now? Who would keep them from ripping into each other? Who would hold the family together?

The dark wolf succeeded in reaching the venison and tearing it from the nail. Once again asserting his authority, the gray wolf lunged at the meat and grabbed it away from the dark wolf. He ate some of it, then stepped aside to let the dark wolf and the female eat while he played with the pups.

Just like Father, Jared thought. *One minute he's snarling, the next minute he's playing.*

"Shoot!"

Jared barely heard the hoarse cry from behind him. He turned to see the faces of Will and Chuckers poking out from behind trees.

"Why haven't you shot?" Chuckers whispered. "Shoot! Shoot!"

Jared shook his head no.

Chuckers rolled his eyes heavenward. Crouching, Chuckers moved from bush to bush until he reached Jared. The wolves were too busy playing and eating to notice. Chuckers grabbed the musket. Jared let him have the gun. He couldn't bring himself to shoot, so it seemed natural that it was Chucker's turn. After all, that's why they'd sneaked out of their houses in the middle of the night—to shoot a wolf.

The large gray wolf was now on his back, mouth open, paws dangling in the air as three playful pups jumped all over him.

Chuckers pressed his cheek against the musket and took aim.

The pups yipped with delight, oblivious to the fact that in the time it took for a musket ball to leave the musket and reach its target, their world would change forever. Their father would be dead.

"No!" Jared shouted.

The sound of his voice startled the pack. Instantly, the large gray wolf rolled to his feet, snarling in their direction as the three pups huddled beneath him. Now that he was on his feet, he was a better target.

Chuckers pulled at the trigger.

"I said no!" With a sweeping lunge of his arm, Jared knocked the musket barrel aside. It discharged. The bark of a tree splintered where the musket ball found its mark. A puff of smoke rose from the bushes where the hunters were concealed. The wolves were gone, disappearing into the woods.

"What did you do that for?" Chuckers yelled.

Now that it was over, Jared felt foolish. He'd just ruined their chance to get a wolf, which was the whole purpose of the risky outing. How could he explain to his friends that the large gray wolf reminded him of his father?

In response to Chuckers, Jared shrugged his shoulders. "I just couldn't let you do it."

Chuckers cursed and shoved the musket at him. It clattered to the ground. "You're crazy!" he shouted. "You're a bigger loggerhead than Will!"

Jared got up and brushed himself off. "Let's go home," he said. Will had joined them.

Chuckers stood, blocking Jared's path. "We're not going anywhere until you tell me why you ruined my shot! I coulda gotten ten shillings for that wolf! Ten shillings! The way I see it, you owe me ten shillings!"

"I don't owe you nothin'," Jared said, pushing his way past Chuckers.

Chuckers spun him around. "Oh yes you do!"

Jared and Chuckers stood face-to-face, toe-to-toe, their hands drawn into fists.

"Let's just go home," Will said. He pulled at Chuckers' arm. Chuckers shrugged him off.

Just then a low growling noise came from nearby. Will saw them first. "Wolves!" he shouted.

Instantly, the dispute between Chuckers and Jared was dropped, taking second place to their immediate danger. From the time they were infants they'd heard stories of wolves attacking people. Whenever they walked to school an armed adult always accompanied them to protect them from wolves. Each family carried a musket with them to the meeting house on Sabbath as protection against unfriendly Indians and wolves. They heard story after story at the dinner table of some inattentive child in Roxbury or Dorchester who'd been killed by wolves. That's what made tonight's adventure so risky, so exciting. But they had it all figured out; they would control the situation. This, however, wasn't part of the plan.

The three adult wolves surrounded them. Jared, Chuckers, and Will moved back to back. Will began to weep.

"What are we gonna do?" he cried. "What are we gonna do? I don't wanna die!"

Jared took quick glances around them, never taking his eyes off the large gray wolf opposite him for more than an instant.

"Will! Do you still have the hammer?" Jared asked.

Will sobbed.

"Do you have it?" Jared shouted.

Sniffing and sniveling, Will said, "Yeah. I have it."

"Give it to Chuckers."

A moment passed. "He won't take it!" Will whined.

"Chuckers!" Jared cried.

No answer. Jared knew Chuckers was there; he could feel two bodies pressed against him.

"CHUCKERS!" Jared shouted. "TAKE THE HAMMER!"

"He took it," Will said.

The wolves, teeth bared and snarling, moved closer.

"Circle to the right and inch your way to the tree closest to Will," Jared ordered.

"What are you gonna do?" Will cried. "Don't leave me!"

"Just do as I say!" Jared shouted. "Chuckers, if the dark wolf attacks, hit him with the hammer."

"What do I do if my wolf attacks?" Will cried.

"Pray," Jared answered.

Jared was directing them toward the tree closest to the female wolf. She was the least aggressive and the poorest jumper. The boys remained back to back as they inched toward the tree. The female wolf gave ground and the male wolves closed the distance. As they moved, Jared reached down ever so slowly and retrieved his father's musket.

"Will, position the tree between you and female wolf," Jared said. "We'll follow your lead. Tell me when you're close to it."

"I'm close," Will yelled moments later.

"Is the female on the other side?"

"Yeah, but she's moving around so she can still see me."

"Hurry! Climb the tree!"

Will scampered up the tree and perched on a limb. "I'm in the tree!" he shouted, his voice a mixture of victory and relief.

"You're next, Chuckers," Jared said.

The female wolf, seeing that Will was out of reach, centered her attention on Chuckers, along with the dark wolf. Now that it was two to one against Chuckers, the wolves grew bolder.

"They're coming after me!" Chuckers shouted.

"Chuckers! On three, throw the hammer at the dark wolf, then get up the tree as fast as you can! Got it?"

No answer.

"Chuckers! I need you now! Do you hear me?"

"On three," Chuckers said.

"And please, don't miss!" Jared cried. "Ready? One, two, THREE!"

Chuckers threw the hammer at the dark wolf. A yelp told Jared the hammer hit its mark.

"Get up the tree!" Jared shouted. He lunged at the large gray wolf, swinging the musket with all his might. The butt of the musket slammed against the wolf, knocking him down. Jared dropped the musket and ran like lightning toward the first tree he saw, knowing that the wolves were right behind him. One sturdy branch reached out to the side, but could he reach it? It was awfully high. He *had* to reach it. And he only had one chance.

Jared could hear the sound of snarling behind him. He spotted a rock about two feet high not far from the tree. He leaped to the rock, then jumped for the limb, arms outstretched. He grabbed the limb just as the large gray wolf reach the rock. It too jumped from the rock, but Jared's momentum swung him forward and the wolf flew under him. Jaws snapped viciously as he flew by.

If Jared had listened more in school, he would have known better than to feel relieved. For, just like a pendulum, his momentum stopped and reversed itself, just as the dark wolf, the best jumper of the three, caught up with him.

The dark wolf managed to grab his right ankle. Jared cried out in pain as the jaws of the wolf clamped onto him. He gripped the limb tighter, supporting not only his weight but that of the wolf as well. The female wolf was beneath him, jumping up at him, and the large gray wolf had recovered and was coming back. Jared felt like a piece of venison nailed to a tree. He tried to shake the dark wolf free. His effort was rewarded by tearing flesh and greater pain. Desperately, he kicked at the wolf with his left foot, once, twice. The dark wolf released its grip and fell to the ground. Jared pulled himself up into the tree, out of reach of the wolves.

"Jared! Are you all right?" It was Chuckers yelling from the other tree.

"I've been bit on the ankle, but I'm all right!" he yelled back.

"What do we do now?" Will cried.

"Wait for them to go away!"

"Oh."

What had begun as a glorious, late-night test of courage and manhood ended as the three adventurers sat in their trees and watched the sun come up.

THE Morgans' house lay nested among a small grove of trees less than a hundred yards from the bank of the Charles River. Those who traveled the river's winding course from its source near Hopkinton to Boston's Back Bay found their eastward journey abruptly interrupted as the river turned north just before Watertown. Then, once past the town, the river corrected itself southward until it paralleled its original point of departure (less than a half-mile due west) where it turned east again and flowed past Cambridge. The house that Benjamin Morgan bought for his fifteen-year-old bride was situated on the east side of this loop.

Those who admired the stately house from their gently rocking shallops on the river would have guessed it to be the home of a governor, a merchant, or possibly the president of Harvard College. They would have thought the house beyond the financial reach of a mere member of Harvard's teaching staff; and under normal circumstances they would have been correct. But the circumstances that led to Benjamin Morgan's acquisition of such a fine home were far from normal.

Benjamin Morgan and Constance Mayhew wed while he was still a poor teaching fellow at Harvard, one of the "Fellows of the House" as they were called. At the time he lived on campus in the great hall with the students. And since his father had returned to England, leaving him no house or land to inherit,

Benjamin was reduced to rather meager resources with which to find a suitable house for his bride. Of course he also had to consider the possibility of children who would surely be arriving within the next year or two. His pitiful savings were hardly adequate for the situation, and had he been wise, he would have waited until he could afford a house before he married. But love's decisions are seldom wise, and he found himself with a wife and without a house. He turned to his mentor and closest friend, Dr. Grove Hirst, to seek help with his dilemma.

Dr. Hirst was an esteemed tutor of Hebrew and Greek at Harvard. Benjamin was his prized pupil, intently following in his mentor's footsteps. The aged Dr. Hirst asked his student how much money he'd saved for a house. Upon hearing the sum, the scholar rubbed his chin and said, "I think I know just the house for you, and at a price you can afford."

The two men rode the short distance to the stately home on the river Charles. Upon seeing the house, Benjamin protested that it was surely worth more than he had. No, Hirst replied, he was confident the price of the home matched the amount of Benjamin's savings. To which Benjamin commented that the owner must be daft to sell such a gorgeous home for a paltry sum. Dr. Hirst laughed. "I'm the owner of the house," he said.

He explained that the house had belonged to his widowed uncle who had recently died without issue. His uncle had willed the house to him. Dr. Hirst added that he was an aged bachelor who had no use for a house this size. Besides, he preferred spending the remainder of his days at the college with his students and his studies. The house had become quite a concern for him—a distraction really—and he had no idea what to do with it until now. Although deeply moved by his mentor's generosity, Benjamin protested that the house was worth far more than he could pay. He'd feel as though he was taking advantage of a friend.

The old scholar took hold of his student by the shoulders and said, "You're the closest thing I have to a son, Benjamin. Please don't deprive me of the joy of doing this for you. I want you and Constance to have this house." And so Benjamin and his bride took possession of the house by the river. They fixed up one room for Dr. Hirst to use as a retreat from the college. The aged tutor enjoyed occasional weekends and holidays with the Morgans until he died five years later.

Six steps led to the entryway of the Morgan house, a two-storied white structure featuring four white Corinthian columns which supported a peaked gable covering. On both sides of the entryway floor-to-ceiling square-paned windows provided panoramic views of the river from the study and the sitting room. The upstairs floor featured two pairs of shuttered windows on opposite sides of the columns. The matching windows on both floors provided a symmetrical balance to the front facade. A scattering of oak, elm, and birch trees dotted the sides of the house and a grassy expanse stretched between it and the river. A small pier jutted into the water. Behind the house a spacious stable sat a comfortable distance away.

It was this house in which all three Morgan children were born and raised. They took their first steps on the hardwood floor of the family room, spent careless summer afternoons jumping from the pier and splashing in the river. In the winter the boys trudged through the snow to a one-room grammar school less than a mile away, while Priscilla practiced her housewifely arts in the kitchen and secretly studied at her father's desk. And it was in the sitting room of Dr. Hirst's inheritance where Benjamin Morgan's pierced body lay in state until it was buried.

A bleary-eyed Philip Morgan pushed open the door of the study. The smells of oatmeal porridge greeted him. He could hear kitchen utensils clanking and the voices of his sister and mother performing their morning tasks. It was what he *hadn't* heard earlier that disturbed him. He hadn't heard Jared return home from his late-night escapade.

Retrieving some water for his bedroom basin from the well, Philip made his way upstairs through the side door, washed, and put on a clean shirt. The cold water on his face temporarily revived him but couldn't wash away the aftereffects of a restless and, for the most part, sleepless night. His thoughts were clouded, and his head and eyes ached. He brushed back his hair, revealing traces of a receding hairline, pulled himself up straight, and walked to Jared's room. He knocked softly. Then, upon receiving no answer, he pushed open the door. Jared's bed was unmade, but no one was in the room. Walking down the hallway he poked his head inside his mother's room and shot a quick glance toward the fireplace. The nail upon which his father kept the family's only musket was empty, and the powder horn was gone too. Just as he'd suspected. Taking a deep breath, Philip headed downstairs to assume his newfound responsibilities as head of the Morgan household.

"Good morning, Mother, Priscilla."

"Good morning, Philip." Constance Morgan greeted her eldest son without turning from her task. With a long pole she reached toward the back of the seven-foot-wide brick fireplace, retrieving a loaf of bread from the oven. A large iron kettle of oatmeal porridge bubbled over the fire near her elbow.

Priscilla was at the table scooping butter out of a circular wooden container. She glanced up at her brother, acknowledging his presence.

"Philip, call your brother. Breakfast is ready," said Constance Morgan.

"He's not in his room," Philip said. "I already checked. In fact, I'm quite sure he's not in the house. He sneaked out late last night."

Constance Morgan placed the hot loaf of bread on a wooden cutting board. A look of concern crossed her face. Philip had seen the look before, often associated with one of his younger brother's antics—her thin lips pursed and her brow furrowed, accentuating a vertical cleft between her eyebrows. It was startling to see how much his mother had aged in the short time since his father's death. Traces of gray streaked her light-brown hair that was tightly pulled back and partially hidden under a white mobcap. There was a puffiness around her eyes that revealed more wrinkles than most women her age. She wiped her hands on her muslin apron and turned to the task of slicing the bread.

"Do you know where he went?" she asked.

"No," said Philip. "But he took the musket."

Constance paused a moment; her hand gripped and regripped the bread knife before she resumed cutting. A moment later the clatter of the knife on the breadboard announced she was finished. She placed the bread in the center of the table and said, "Let's pray so I can serve breakfast."

The table seated six people. Normally Father sat at one end and Mother at the other while the children occupied the sides—Priscilla on one side in the chair closest to her father and the boys next to each other on the other. As would be expected, since the death of Benjamin Morgan, the seat at the head of the table remained unoccupied, a painful reminder of his absence. However on this morning, the day following the funeral, Philip instinctively reached for his own chair, thought a moment, then sat in his father's place at the head of the table.

"What do you think you're doing?" Priscilla demanded.

Philip sat tall in the chair. His mother, sitting face-to-face with him at the other end of the table, looked at him quizzically at first, then with a resigned expression. It was one more reminder that her husband was dead. Philip immediately regretted his action. He could have waited; maybe if he had, it would have been easier on his mother. But there was nothing he could do about it now.

Priscilla was edging into her chair when Philip sat at the head of the table. She instantly reversed herself as if her chair were on fire. "What do you think you're doing? Get out of Father's chair!" she shouted.

"I'm the head of the household now," Philip responded coolly. "And this is where the head of the household sits at mealtime."

Priscilla's jaw was set and her hands clenched when she spoke. "I don't care who you think you are! Get out of Father's chair!"

"Priscilla!" Mother's voice cut in. "Philip's right. Please sit down."

Priscilla gaped at her mother in astonishment.

"Philip *is* the head of this household. He should sit at the head of the table." Her voice quivered as she spoke and a single tear made a track down her cheek, but there was a tone of resolve in her voice that indicated she meant what she said.

Priscilla stared pleadingly at her mother. When it became clear that she wasn't going to change her mind, Priscilla shoved her chair under the table and pulled out the chair closer to her mother and sat down.

"Thank you, Mother," Philip said. "Let's pray for our meal."

Priscilla cast one more hateful glance at Philip as they bowed their heads and folded their hands.

"Our gracious and almighty Heavenly Father," Philip Morgan began. "You alone are the only wise and true God, the maker of the heavens and the earth, the giver and sustainer of all life. It is only fitting that we should come to You at this time and thank You for food of which we are about to partake; for we recognize that You and You alone . . ."

The back door leading into the kitchen opened and closed.

"Jared Morgan! What on earth happened to you?" his mother screamed.

All eyes turned to Jared. His clothes were filthy, as were his hands and face and hair. He leaned against the musket, using it as a crutch. His right foot was bloodied and hung limply a few inches from the ground.

"Had a little trouble with some wolves," he said. "Sorry I'm late for breakfast."

He hobbled over to his place next to his mother and sat down, laying the musket on the floor. "What's Philip doing in Father's chair?" he asked. "And what's she doing over there?" he pointed to Priscilla opposite him.

"I was praying!" Philip said, imitating his father's stern tone. "And if you don't mind, I'd like to continue."

Jared looked at his mother. "Fold your hands, Son," she said. He did and Philip finished blessing the meal.

Breakfast was eaten in silence. Constance Morgan spooned her porridge slowly with downcast eyes. To Philip, it was evident his mother still bore the weight of her husband's death, but there was more. She had a different look about her, one that Philip had rarely seen. His mother looked frightened. And now that he thought about it, her fear was understandable.

Constance Morgan was a quiet, caring woman. There was no one kinder or gentler in Cambridge, or Boston for that matter. She wasn't a strong woman; rarely did she express an opinion in public or at home, preferring her husband to do the thinking and talking for the family. It was her husband who handled the finances, earned the family's income, and attended to all matters of business. She saw it as her husband's responsibility to educate and discipline their offspring. Her role was to love them, care for them, nurse them, see that they had clean clothes, a clean house, and that the food was warm and tasty and served on time. Children never had such a tender mother; a husband never had such a devoted wife. But Constance Morgan was no longer a wife. She was a widow. And Philip realized that as much as she supported her husband, to the same degree she needed his support. And now that her support was no longer there, she wasn't the same woman.

The scraping sound of a spoon against a wooden bowl drew Philip's attention to Jared. He was ravenously scraping the last of his oatmeal from the bottom of the bowl and shoveling it into his mouth. Priscilla looked at him with disgust.

Philip had always envied his little brother. Of the three children, he was the best looking—ruggedly handsome with a full head of light-brown hair that looked good even after a night in a forest. Jared's skin was tanned while Priscilla and Philip shared a pale white complexion. Jared was the quickest to make friends; he was confident of his abilities; he was strong and athletic; he was a natural leader, although he rarely assumed any leadership role. In Philip's mind the only thing lacking in his younger brother was discipline—both mental and physical. Jared Morgan had yet to discover the full measure of his abilities, and he showed no interest in doing so. He never had been able to sit still long enough to test his academic abilities and he never fully tested his physical ones—whenever he played games of strength or speed, he would toy with his opponents, letting them win. Victory was not his concern; fun and friends were. He was a carefree spirit, the exact opposite of his sister.

Priscilla Morgan was known throughout Cambridge as a red-haired ball of fire. Intense was the word that best described her. Unlike her younger brother, Priscilla had few friends, female or male, and even fewer prospects for marriage. One suitor surrendered his intended romantic pursuit after a single ill-fated afternoon. The wounded paramour fled the house muttering, "That one's kin to Beelzebub! She's got a vicious mind, a sharp wit, and an even sharper tongue! I doubt a lion tamer would have any luck with her!"

There was no doubting her strong mind and will, which she readily used to her advantage. It seemed her greatest delight in life was publicly humiliating men. Her second love was theology, an unseemly interest for a woman who should be concentrating her efforts on finding a husband and improving her housewifely skills. Instead, Priscilla preferred to critique the pastor's preaching, second-guess the elders, and entice other young women to become Bible scholars. Her most notorious victory to date was the time she petitioned the selectmen for a separate pew for young ladies. Ordinarily, the young men sat together in rows on the ground floor while the young women sat in corresponding seats on the opposite side of the meeting house. This changed when the selectmen gave Priscilla and a few other young women permission to build their own pew in the back of the gallery. To do so, Priscilla convinced them that such a pew would provide a holier atmosphere during services by eliminating the flirtatious gestures and lustful looks that so commonly passed from one side of the meeting house to the other.

The anger of the young men over the ladies' pew rose to such a fever pitch that they broke a window in the meeting house, invaded it, and broke the new pew to pieces. For their sacrilegious act they were each fined ten pounds and sentenced to be whipped or pilloried. And, at Priscilla's insistence, the young men also had to reconstruct the ladies' pew. It couldn't have worked out better for her.

Priscilla thrived on competition with males, especially at home. The only male with whom Philip was aware that Priscilla didn't compete was her father. Theirs had always been a tender, loving relationship. She never raised her voice to her father; she listened to him when he spoke, sought his advice (though she didn't always heed it), and would spend hours with him in his study. If Priscilla Morgan had a best friend, it was her father. And now he was dead and Philip occupied his chair.

Priscilla, his mother, and Jared sat at the opposite end of the table from him, which only served to increase Philip's discomfort. He would have preferred to be on the Harvard campus engaged in morning readings and translations with his fellow scholars. But for some reason, God had chosen to call his father to heavenly duties, leaving Philip in charge of earthly ones. And in God's name, he would give his new responsibilities his best effort.

The scraping of Jared's chair on the hardwood floor indicated he was done eating. To his mother he said, "I'm going upstairs to clean up."

Philip stopped him. "Jared, please sit down. We have family business to discuss."

"Let me know how things turn out," Jared replied, picking up the musket from the floor.

"Jared! Sit down!" Philip said sternly. "This involves all of us!"

A wry smile crossed Jared's face. He hadn't obeyed his brother's orders since they were both in grammar school.

Constance Morgan reached for her younger son's hand. "Please, Jared. Sit down," she said softly.

The musket clattered to the floor as Jared resumed his seat. Priscilla sat opposite him, her arms folded across her chest, her jaw set firmly as she stared at her older brother sitting in her father's chair.

"Thank you, Mother," Philip said. The room was uncomfortably still as Philip searched for a way to begin while three pairs of eyes focused on him. "Father's death has not been easy for any of us." As he paused to clear his throat, a constricting feeling grew in his chest. "But for some reason God has chosen to take him from us, and now we are left to fend for ourselves."

"I doubt God had anything to do with Father's death," Jared said, his voice heavy with sarcasm.

"In His wisdom God allowed it." Priscilla sneered across the table, "If you studied your Bible more, you'd know that!"

"If God allowed it," Jared's voice rose, "then He's no better than the men who killed Father!"

"JARED!" cried Constance. "I'll not have that kind of talk in my house!"

Everyone was stunned by Mother's outburst. None of them could remember a time when their mother had raised her voice. It was so unlike her, but then these were not ordinary times.

"I'm sorry, Mother," Jared said. "But right now, that's the way I feel."

"Be that as it may," Philip attempted to regain control of the conversation, "we have business to transact."

"What sort of business, Son?"

"The business of getting on with our lives," came the reply. "I've been going over Father's records—his ledgers, journal, papers, that sort of thing. As you know, Father acted alone in most matters of family business and though it will take a while for me to understand our situation completely, once I do we will continue in the course he had already set. As for duties and responsibilities, Jared . . ."

Philip paused until Jared made eye contact with him.

". . . Jared, it was Father's desire that you matriculate at Harvard in August. I'll arrange for your interview with the president. I suggest you spend a good deal of time practicing your Latin and Greek. Beginning today all of our personal conversations will be conducted in conversational Latin to prepare you for campus life."

"I'm not going to Harvard," Jared said.

"Say it in Latin," Philip prompted.

Jared slammed his fist on the table. "I'M NOT GOING TO HARVARD!" he shouted in English. "I was going to tell Father, so now I'll tell you instead. I'm finished with school!"

"It was Father's will that you attend Harvard!" Philip insisted.

"What will you do, Jared?" his mother asked.

"I don't know," he replied. "But Harvard is for people like Father and Philip, not me."

"You could always chase wolves in the middle of the night for a living," Priscilla snickered. "You seem to be good at that!"

Jared stood so quickly his chair flew backward, crashing to the floor. "I'll plan my own life, thank you," he bellowed. Grabbing the musket again from the floor he hobbled out of the room.

"This isn't resolved yet!" Philip yelled after him. "And we still need to talk about your sneaking out of the house last night!" Jared turned a corner and disappeared from sight.

"And what plans do you have for me?" Priscilla asked. Her eyes flashed as she bit her lower lip and lowered her head, preparing herself for a fight.

"Well," Philip swallowed hard. "I want for you what Father wanted for you."

"And what is that?"

"You're twenty years old now. It's time you found a husband, someone to take care of you."

If Philip had held a match to a keg of powder the explosion wouldn't have been nearly as great. "Someone to take care of me!" Priscilla's face was redder than her hair. With clenched teeth she said, "I'll have you know, dear brother, I don't need anyone to take care of me! And if I ever hear you say that again, you're going to need someone to take care of *you!*" Shaking with rage, she stomped from the room.

Philip sat opposite his mother, separated by a table of dirty dishes. "We're all still hurting from your father's death," she offered weakly. Philip's shoulders were slumped forward. A shallow cough rattled his chest.

"What are *you* going to do?" she asked.

Philip sighed, feeling the defeat of his first attempt to lead the family. "Return to Harvard in August, though I won't be living on campus. You'll need me here. So I'll ride back and forth like Father did. In the meantime, I'll continue to study Father's ledgers and try to understand his investments."

"You know, Priscilla is awfully good with numbers and that sort of thing," his mother said. "She might be of help to you."

Not wanting to chase away the only remaining friendly face in the house, Philip didn't disagree. Mentally, however, he discarded the idea outright.

"One other thing Father wanted me to do," he said, omitting the word he usually associated with the thought — *it was his dying request* — "he wanted me to look into this matter of a family Bible."

As soon as he said the words, his throat constricted and he coughed convulsively, an attack which lasted only briefly.

Constance said softly, "I remember how excited he was when he discovered the existence of that Bible. His personal Holy Grail, he called it, almost as if whoever possessed it had miraculous powers." She smiled as she relived her husband's excitement.

Philip started to speak, coughed, then said, "He thought it might be at the Narragansett reservation in Rhode Island. I'll leave tomorrow to see if it's there or if anyone there might know where it is." He paused as he weighed his father's desire to find the Bible with his own desire to return to Harvard. "The search for the Bible was important to Father," he concluded aloud. "If it still exists, I want to find it before classes begin in August."

Constance studied her son. Concern filled her eyes. "Maybe you ought to send Jared to search for the Bible," she suggested. "I'm concerned for your health."

Philip shook his head. "No, Father asked me to find the Bible. It's my responsibility."

Constance smiled warmly at her eldest son. She sighed the kind of sigh mothers make when their children refuse to take their advice. "I'd better see to your brother's foot," she said, excusing herself from the table.

Philip Morgan sat alone at the breakfast table. He thought about his impending journey into Indian country and, as he did, the chilling sight of two figures emerging from the forest came to mind. A cold sweat wet his forehead.

Chapter 5

"MASTER Cole! What a wonderful surprise!"
Constance Morgan opened wide the door as the wealthy merchant Daniel Cole strutted up the steps. He removed his tricorne hat made of fine Holland linen. Thick unruly hair spilled out. He entered the Morgan house with an air of familiarity, as if he owned it.

"And what brings you across the bay?" the obviously pleased hostess asked, taking her guest's hat and greatcoat.

"My name's Daniel, my dear Constance, call me Daniel." His eyes grew wide with amusement as he glanced around. "That is, unless there are some old gossips nearby that might take offense at our familiarity!"

Constance blushed like a young maid. She took his hat and helped him remove his greatcoat.

"And to answer your question," he said, turning toward her while still trying to free one arm from a sleeve, "you do, my dear! I've come to see how you are doing."

"How thoughtful."

"Not at all!" Cole insisted. "It's the least I can do for my childhood sweetheart!" He took advantage of her closeness, giving her a peck on the cheek.

Philip witnessed the entire exchange and he didn't like it. It revolted him to see another man kiss his mother, especially since his father's funeral was only yesterday. But there was more to it than that. He disliked Cole and men like him. Daniel Cole was part of a rising merchant class of Bostonians who were growing powerful, replacing Puritan ministers as the leaders of the people. As a result, secular attitudes began to eclipse biblical teachings as colonists desired wealth more than they desired to know God. Philip remembered one evening when he and his father were reading in the study. Benjamin Morgan interrupted his son's Greek studies.

"Listen to this," he said. "I'm reading John Higginson's book." He held his place with his thumb and turned the spine to read the title, *The Cause of God and His People in New England.*

"Higginson?"

"Salem minister. 1660s."

"That's right," Philip nodded, remembering now.

"This was his election day sermon, 1663," the elder Morgan continued. "Listen to what he says." Benjamin quoted: *"My fathers and brethren, this is never to be forgotten, that New England is originally a plantation of religion, not a plantation of trade. Let merchants and such as are increasing cent per cent remember this. Let others that have come over since at several times understand this, that worldly gain was not the end and design of the people of New England, but religion."* Benjamin Morgan lowered the book, rubbed tired eyes and added, "Too many people have forgotten that."

From that night on, Philip hadn't forgotten it and, to his dismay, he watched as colonists drifted further and further away from the original Puritan objectives. And from this trend he drew his own conclusion—Puritanism was dying.

From his studies he saw that the Puritan movement grew sickly beginning with the second generation of colonists. The children of the founding fathers did not share their parents' spiritual passion. Church attendance declined dramatically. When it was clear that the third generation was in jeopardy of falling to heathenism, ministers sought a way to address the problem. They met as a synod in 1662 and proposed a plan whereby church members could present their children for baptism, effectively placing them under the covenant authority of the church. These children became half-members of the church, until they were able to show proof of conversion. As half-members they were subject to the church but not able to enjoy all the privileges of membership, such as participating in the Lord's Supper. In short, it was a compromise designed to maintain the authority of the church over the colonists, and at the same time maintain some semblance of purity.

For Philip there were no halfway members. In his opinion it was a subterfuge irreligious people used to claim the grace of God yet live however they pleased—people like Daniel Cole, a fourth-generation colonist who cloaked his avaricious desires in holy piety.

"Philip! I didn't see you standing there!" the overly enthusiastic Cole boomed. The merchant extended a pink overstuffed hand toward Philip. "Truth is," he said, pumping the young man's hand, "your mother was only part of the reason I made the trip across the bay. Thought you might like a little friendly help with your father's financial affairs since they got dumped on you rather unexpectedly."

Philip looked at him suspiciously.

Constance saw the concerned look on her son's face and said, "I mentioned to Daniel . . . Master Cole . . . that your father wasn't one to talk much about the family investments; that it was all new to you. At the funeral, yesterday. Master Cole graciously offered his assistance."

His mother and Cole stood shoulder to shoulder, smiling and nodding. For some reason it reminded Philip of two children who had been naughty and had concocted a story to cover their misdeed.

"Why don't you two men go into the study, and I'll get

you something to drink," Constance suggested.

The awkward moment ended when Philip motioned toward the study. Cole bowed slightly to Constance, then joined her son.

Philip had never been this close to the man before—never had any occasion to be. From a distance Daniel Cole gave the appearance of a man of position and wealth by the way he dressed, and today was no exception. A white long-sleeved shirt with ruffled cuffs was covered by a black silk waistcoat with matching breeches. White silk stockings and black cowhide shoes with silver buckles completed his outfit—typical dress for a well-to-do merchant. What was untypical, and what Philip didn't know about the man until now, had nothing to do with the way the man looked, but how he smelled. Trailing a few steps behind his guest, Philip waded through a sea of odors. Most prominent among them was the smell of dirty laundry. Although the tops of the man's stockings were white, Philip was sure if the man removed his shoes the toes would be crusty yellow. He probably hadn't changed stockings in over two weeks. The waistcoat was no better; the smell of stale sweat hung heavily in the air. And fish. He had the odor of fish about him, not fresh though, definitely from a couple days previous. Then there was the pomatum. His hair was well-loaded with the perfumed ointment. Cole had raked his hand through his unruly hair just before shaking hands. Philip's fingers felt oily.

It all struck Philip as odd. The man was wealthy. His skin was clean. But he must, after bathing, dress in his dirty clothes. And from the odors, he must have done it several days in a row.

Philip offered a seat to the merchant, strategically maneuvering himself near a window. Before they began talking, Philip opened the window to ventilate the room. Cole seemed to take no special notice of Philip's actions.

"Philip, you're how old now? Twenty? Twenty-one?"

"I'll be twenty-one in September."

"Good. Old enough to talk to you man-to-man." He cleared his throat. "As you undoubtedly know, I'm a businessman. Quite good at it, if I do say so myself. I've made myself a tidy sum over the years."

Philip merely nodded, content to let Cole wallow in his own self-importance. He was also content to let the merchant chart the course of the conversation. He wanted to know what Cole was up to.

"And, to put it frankly," Cole continued, "your father, although a good man and wise in many things—Greek, Hebrew, Latin, that kind of thing—wasn't much of a businessman." Cole chuckled and pushed back several locks of rogue hairs that had fallen into his eyes. "That's understandable. We can't be good in everything. For example, I'm not what you would consider a scholar."

He paused to let Philip politely correct him, to assure him that he was probably just being modest. Philip didn't say anything.

"Be that as it may," Cole continued, "I'd like to help you in any way I can with the knowledge I've collected over the years." Cole didn't wait for Philip to accept or reject his offer; he just plunged ahead. "Tell me," he said, "how much do you know about the state of your family's finances? Are they solid? Shaky?"

Philip remained guarded. "I've looked over my father's ledgers and we're doing all right. Of course, it's nothing compared to your holdings, but we're comfortable. And I'm confident that when I complete my studies this semester, I'll be offered a position at Harvard. Maybe even my father's position."

"And what will you do until then? Do you have any other sources of income?"

"We have some money saved that we can use, and some investments. In fact, we have some shares in your company which provide us with a steady flow of cash."

"Yes, I know," Cole said. He edged forward in his chair. "That is one area in which I know I can help you." He paused, ran a finger under his nose and sniffed. "What did your father tell you about those shares?"

Philip sat back, inhaled deeply, and rolled his eyes toward the ceiling as he searched his memory. "I can't recall him telling me anything about them."

Daniel Cole looked pleased with his response. It gave Philip an unsettled feeling.

"I hate to be the one to tell you this," Cole said, "because in an indirect way, I feel partially responsible for your father's death."

That got Philip's attention.

"You see, the day he was killed, he was coming to see me." Daniel Cole studied Philip for a reaction.

"He was coming to Boston to sell me his shares in my company."

"I find that hard to believe." The interrupting female voice came from the doorway. Philip looked up as Cole spun around in his chair. Priscilla stood in the doorway, her hands daintily clasped in front of her. There was nothing dainty about the hostile look in her eyes or the tone of her voice.

"Priscilla, dear, how well you look!" Planting his pudgy hands on the arms of the chair, Daniel Cole launched himself upward. Although his words expressed pleasure to see her, there was no real feeling in his voice.

The merchant closed the distance between them as Priscilla offered her hand. Taking it gallantly, he bowed a slight bow. "You'll have to excuse us, dear," he said, "we're talking business."

"I know exactly what you are talking about," she retorted.

"I couldn't help overhearing as I passed by." Priscilla brushed past Cole and glided toward a round table in the center of the room as if to inspect an arrangement of lilacs. Philip saw her inspection for the ruse that it was. Priscilla cared little for flowers; it was his mother who had arranged the flowers and placed them on the table. "It seems odd to me that Father would be selling shares that have performed as well as these, shares that produce more than a quarter of our family income."

Of the two men, Philip was the most shocked at Priscilla's knowledge of the Morgan family finances. He tried not to show it, but in truth, Priscilla's revelation was news to him.

"And how is it that you know so much about your father's business dealings, my dear?" Cole was sizing her up.

Priscilla stuck her finger in the flower vase as if to check for water. Her nose wrinkled when she struck water close to the surface. Acting nonchalantly, she produced a handkerchief and wiped her finger dry. "With all respect, Master Cole," she said, "I hardly think that's any of your concern."

"And, dear lady, I hardly think it is appropriate for you to be dealing in matters you could not possibly understand. These are complicated matters best left to men. Now, if you will excuse us." With his arm the merchant made a sweeping motioned toward the door.

Priscilla appealed to Philip with her eyes. He got the message; she wanted him to insist she be allowed to stay. And Philip wanted her to stay. Another Morgan in the room would give him a measure of confidence he lacked alone. But how would it look to Cole if he depended on his sister for business advice?

"Master Cole is correct," Philip said. "This is my concern now, Priscilla. I'll handle it."

Priscilla Morgan's demur look transformed into one of fury. Her lips pursed and her eyes filled with angry tears. Cole smiled in condescending superiority.

Just then a bubbly Constance appeared at the door carrying a tray with two flip-mugs of beverage, a summer drink of water flavored with molasses and ginger. The flip-mugs were made of Spanish glass from Barbados, used by Constance only on special occasions. "Your drinks, gentlemen," she said. Then seeing her daughter, "Priscilla, dear, what are you doing in here? These men have important work to do."

Outnumbered, Priscilla fled the room. Cole turned to Constance as if Priscilla had never been there. "You always were a gracious hostess," he gushed, taking one of the flip-mugs from the tray. Constance smiled sweetly and politely excused herself so that the men could return to their business.

Cole wasted no more time. "As I was saying, your father was about to liquidate his shares in my company. At the time I was prepared to pay a fair price for them. Now, considering recent circumstances and out of fondness for your mother, I'm prepared to increase my offer by fifty percent."

Cole sat back in his chair and sipped his beverage. Philip got the impression the merchant was waiting to be thanked. There was little doubt in his mind that the offer was a generous one and, had not Priscilla planted a seed of doubt in his mind, he probably would have accepted the offer readily. Now he wasn't sure.

"A gracious offer, indeed," he said.

Cole nodded his agreement.

"However, if you don't mind, I'd like some time to think it over. With the funeral and all, I haven't had the time to study my father's ledgers in detail."

A frown crossed Cole's face, like a thundercloud blotting out the sun. "How much time do you need?"

Philip's eyes rolled upward in thought again. When they came back down he said, "Not more than a month."

"A MONTH!" The merchant bolted upright in his chair. The thundercloud flashed lightning.

Philip recoiled at the outburst. "Well . . . yes, sir . . . you see . . . well, I'm leaving on a trip soon and will be gone for a while."

"Trip? What trip?"

"A personal trip. Something I promised my father I'd do."

Cole shook his head. "Son, always put business first; personal concerns come later."

This time it was Philip's turn to shake his head. "Can't. I have to get this done before classes start at Harvard."

"Philip, let me speak frankly with you." Cole leaned forward, his cup in both hands and his elbows resting on his knees. "Your father was a dear friend . . ."

Cole's pronounced friendship with his father didn't sit well with Philip. He'd never known there to be any kind of relationship between the two men. As far as Philip knew, the only connection between them was that they both courted his mother and they both owned shares in Cole's company. For now, he let the overstatement pass.

" . . . but he had a funny way of looking at things. His priorities were all wrong. He never gave business matters the attention they deserve. And look where it got him. You have a fine house, but that's only because of an old man's generosity. You can't live life waiting for people to take pity on you and give you things. Truth is, you can't afford to pass up my offer. Your father didn't give you that luxury. Because of his mismanagement, you desperately need the money."

Philip turned away from him.

"I'm sorry if I hurt you by saying these things," Cole continued, "but for your own good you need to hear them." He paused, his bottom lip appearing and disappearing as he thought. "I'll tell you what. Forget this personal business for a week. Study your father's ledgers. You'll see I'm right. My offer to buy your family's shares is good for seven days. Be a man, Philip. Do what's right."

This was Philip's first important financial decision as head of the Morgan family and he didn't want to make a mistake. Cole's offer sounded too good to pass up. But there was something about it—more correctly, something about the man making the offer—that wasn't right. Maybe Philip had too much of his father in him, but he had never been interested in making money. He preferred scholastic pursuits. Let the money take care of itself. Just like his father, even to the end. Benjamin Morgan's dying words to his son were not about shares and finances, even though that was their primary task that day. When he realized he was dying, his father's thoughts were of the family Bible. There was something about that Bible that pushed aside all other concerns. Then there was college. Philip wasn't about to do anything that would jeopardize the completion of his degree. The sooner he took the trip, the better.

"I'm sorry, Master Cole," Philip said. "But I have to stick with my original time estimate. The trip can't be postponed. I guess we'll just have to hold on to the shares for now."

Daniel Cole lowered his head and shook it in disgust. "Just like your father," he lamented.

Philip Morgan took Cole's commentary as a compliment.

Chapter 6

PHILIP arched his back, fighting to inhale. A wheezing sound from his throat indicated at least some air was passing through. He adjusted himself in the saddle as his horse plodded dully along. It was his second day of journey, having made the forty-mile trek from Cambridge to Providence the day before. That night he'd refreshed himself at the Red Lion tavern. After receiving directions to the Narragansett reservation, he continued his journey south through Pawtucket, Warwick, and Wickford. It was just outside Wickford that he suffered the asthma attack—probably the result of two days of road dust—and now he took long, steady breaths and tried to get comfortable again. Though he couldn't see it presently, he could feel the breeze from the ocean. It was a momentary distraction, as was his recent attack, from the relentless feelings of regret that had dogged him ever since he left Cambridge.

He wished he hadn't come. He wished his father had never made such a ridiculous request. He could be home now instead of alone in the wilderness; he could be preparing for fall classes instead of chasing after a long-lost Bible that probably didn't exist anymore; he could be on Brattle Street with his fiancée's arms around him instead of remembering her angry sobs as he left.

Just when the accumulated force of these thoughts would

convince him to turn around and go back home, he'd see his father laying on the road, his face in the dirt, pleading with him to do this one thing. It was a powerful, horrifying memory. And Philip would shake off the hounds of regret and urge his horse forward. This was something he had to do. If he didn't, he'd rue the decision for all his life. If his asthma kicked up during the journey, so be it; if he was a few days late for classes, so be it; and if Penelope couldn't understand why he had to do this for his father, well then, so be it.

Philip thought of his intended and promised himself that he'd do something to make it up to her when he returned. He thought how fortunate he was to be engaged to Penelope Chauncy. Their relationship was a natural, perfect match. He was at the head of his class at Harvard, the epitome of everything the colonial institution stood for, the hope of the next generation. Some people, men of respect, talked openly of Philip someday becoming president of the college. Philip accepted these predictions with humility and all sincerity. And he was not reluctant to assume the full weight of their expectations and the responsibility that came with it, including the importance of marrying well.

That's why Penelope was perfect for him. If Philip was the epitome of a Harvard scholar, Penelope was the epitome of a scholar's wife. Raised in the shadow of the institution, her great-grandfather, Charles Chauncy, was Harvard's second president in the previous century. Her father was a Harvard alumnus and prominent Cambridge physician. The girl was raised among the Harvard elite with the expressed intention that she would someday continue the high social traditions with which she'd been bred. It was a role she took quite seriously; too seriously at times for Philip's taste.

But Philip liked Penelope. Together their future seemed promising. He realized how fortunate he was to have her. She was a refined, elegant lady, who was dutifully submissive in public. Though not a beauty, she was not unattractive. The word that most often leaped into people's minds when they first saw Penelope was that she was long. Her face was long; her nose was thin and long; her arms extended like long tree limbs and her fingers like delicate twigs; her unusual height — she was taller than Philip — could be attributed to her long legs; and she had the longest feet Philip had ever seen, which he first saw bared in a rare moment of capriciousness when she dangled them in the river one hot summer afternoon.

Their plans were to marry as soon as Philip completed his course work and secured a position on the Harvard teaching staff. He was one semester away from his goal, so naturally wedding plans had dominated their lives through the winter and spring in anticipation of his graduation. Of course the planning had been interrupted by Benjamin Morgan's untimely death and now Philip's unscheduled trip south.

When Philip told Penelope of his father's dying request and his intentions to travel to the reservation, she was upset. This was hardly the time to chase after family ghosts, she'd cried. What if he was delayed? What would become of his studies? Their wedding plans? No, the potential of delay was enough to nix the trip. When Philip insisted he would not allow himself to be delayed, Penelope appealed to her father. Dr. Chauncy dutifully sided with his distressed daughter. Surely Philip's father would not have wanted him to endanger his career at this stage. The search for the Bible could be postponed for a year or two. But Philip remained unconvinced. He was confident that if he didn't go now, he would never find time to go. When Philip left her, Penelope was furious with him. She refused to be consoled. Somehow he'd have to make it up to her when he returned.

Philip Morgan entered the Narragansett Indian reservation from the north by way of the South County Trail. Narragansett men, women, and children stopped whatever they were doing and stared at him as he passed them by. They were a big people, skin dark as bronze, though some of them inclined toward pale complexions. Their hair was black and straight, and their eyes were as black as their hair. Their coarse clothing identified them as a class of laboring poor, hewers of wood and drawers of water.

Philip stopped at the longhouse to inquire after the location of the reservation's praying Indians or their leader if they had one. He reasoned that if the Morgan family Bible still existed, one of the praying Indians would know about it.

Since early colonial days the Indians converted under John Eliot's missionary work were called praying Indians. At one time there were thirteen praying towns where these converted Indians could live in a Christian environment and they numbered more than a thousand souls. That was before King Philip's War.

In 1675 the powerful Wampanoag sachem Metacom, known to the colonists as King Philip, led a loose confederation of tribes in a series of raids on frontier settlements. Theirs was a desperate attempt to halt the rising tide of colonists encroaching on Indian lands. From the outset, the praying Indians found themselves caught in the middle of the conflict. The warring Indians accused them of being colonial sympathizers and spies; and, although used by the colonists to their advantage, neither did the colonists trust them, fearing they were Indian sympathizers and spies. Killed by their kinsman *and* the colonists, the Christian Indians were nearly wiped out; only a few isolated pockets of believers survived. One such remnant resided on the Narragansett reservation.

At the longhouse Philip was told that the leader of the Narragansett praying Indians was called Nanouwetea. Following the directions given him, he continued south down Schoolhouse Pond Road. The road veered west as he passed an English-style church building. Still further he saw a small schoolhouse that was badly in need of repairs on the south side of the road. A good-sized lake stretched behind it. Then he saw what he was looking for. On the same side of the road as the schoolhouse he spied a wigwam standing alone next to a field of corn. It was here he was told he could find Nanouwetea.

As he looped his horse's reins over a tree limb Philip tried to shake off a feeling of uneasiness. He told himself it was just the unfamiliar surroundings. This was a totally different world from what he was accustomed to. It went without saying that an Indian from this reservation would feel equally uneasy coming to his house or visiting the Harvard campus. He reasoned that there was no reason for him to feel uneasy. He would make his inquiries, negotiate for the Bible if it was here, and take his leave. It would be as simple as that.

Just then some children caught his eye. They were standing a few hundred yards off, watching him. Three of them. Boys. Clothed in a peculiar combination of colonial and Indian garb. He estimated their ages to be about nine or ten. He looked to each side and behind him. There were no other people around. He wished he had someone to watch his things and guard his horse while he went inside. Oh well, he'd just have to hurry his business along.

The wigwam was about fourteen feet in diameter. It had a pole frame and was covered with various tree barks. The opening was square and about four feet high. In front of the wigwam wisps of smoke rose from the remnants of a small fire where meals were undoubtedly cooked. A portion of a tree trunk stood upright nearby, its top hollowed out forming a shallow bowl. Bits of crushed corn scattered about suggested it was used as a mortar. In the distance a wooden tower, about twelve to fifteen feet high, stood tall next to a cornfield. Philip had no idea what the structure was used for.

"Holloa?" Philip remained a distance from the wigwam opening as he called. "HOLLOA?" he called a little louder. Still no answer. He approached the door and ducked down to enter. At that same instant, a young Indian male emerged. The two almost bumped heads.

"Excuse me!" Philip cried and backed off. "I wasn't sure anyone heard me."

The Narragansett male stood before him, unsmiling. He was a little shorter than Philip but much huskier, a fact that was easily established since the young man was bare-chested. His torso was dark bronze and muscular. A thin sheen of sweat coated his skin. Besides a leather covering tied around his waist, the only thing he wore was a white shell dangling at the end of a leather string tied around his neck. Dark black hair fell to his shoulders. Thick lips and hard black eyes showed absolutely no emotion.

"What cheer, English?" he said.

"Um . . . I'm looking for Nanouwetea. Are you he?"

The Indian studied Philip beginning with the wide-brimmed hat on his head and traveling downward to his waistcoat, breeches, shoes, then back to his face. The hard black eyes of the Narragansett bore into Philip's own. It was as if he thought that by staring into Philip's eyes long enough they would reveal some hidden purpose. A sneer formed on the Indian's lips. He said, "You're not too smart, are you? Do I look old enough to be an overseer?"

It amused Philip that this backwoods Indian concluded so quickly that Harvard's best student was ignorant. He chose to ignore the slight on his intelligence. "Where may I find Nanouwetea?" he asked.

The Indian didn't move.

"I've traveled for two days to see him," Philip insisted.

The Indian grunted. He was not impressed. "Wait here," he said. As he ducked into the wigwam he looked back.

"Don't touch anything," he said.

Philip chuckled softly. *Don't touch anything? As if there were anything around here I'd want*, he thought.

Philip waited several minutes. The Indian didn't return. He turned and studied his surroundings. To the east was the lake; land stretched southward, dotted by several wigwams; the cornfield and tower lay to the west; to the north was School-house Pond Road running east and west, beyond it further to the north there was a large swamp. Philip shifted impatiently from one foot to the other and wondered if his messenger was ever coming back. He thought of the boys who had been watching him and glanced in their direction. They were still there and they were still watching him. But they hadn't moved any closer to his horse. Good.

"Enter!" The Indian male poked his head out of the wigwam only long enough to utter the single word command, then withdrew inside.

Philip bent low and entered the wigwam. His first impression was the heat. The air inside was stifling! Now he understood why the young Indian male was coated with sweat—a huge fire was roaring in the center of the wigwam. A hole in the roof allowed the fire's smoke to escape. In spite of the size of the fire, it was dark inside, especially around the edges of the wigwam, and it took a moment for Philip's eyes to adjust.

"Over here!" The Indian motioned for Philip to follow him to the far side of the wigwam. Sitting near the fire was an old man, the oldest man Philip had ever seen in his life. The man's skin draped over his frail frame like thick leather, falling in folds over his cheeks and dangling from his jowls. His skin was lighter than his younger companion—the man's grandson? great-grandson?—more of a reddish color. A few wisps of pure white hair hovered over his head like clouds. Oblivious to the intense heat from the fire, the old man wore a heavy mantle made of feathers draped over his shoulders. His face was without expression as he watched Philip approach. His eyes—brown, clear, and sharp—revealed an active mind.

Standing next to the old Indian was a young Narragansett woman. Philip's first impression of her was that she was strikingly beautiful for an Indian. She had all the familiar characteristics of her people—the dark skin, black hair and eyes. She was clothed in deerskin and her dark hair fell modestly over her eyes. Philip felt drawn to those eyes that peered at him from behind a veil of hair; they were hypnotically beautiful, large and innocent, highlighted by thick lashes. But even more than her eyes, the thing that most attracted him to her was the way she stood there, the way she carried herself—tall and upright, but not stiff; confident, almost like royalty.

The old Indian addressed him. *"Tocketussaweitch?"* His voice was little more than a dry whisper.

Philip had never heard the Algonquin language spoken before. He looked to the younger Indians for help, first to the male, then to the young woman. They merely returned his stare. Drops of sweat trickled down the sides of his face.

"Um . . . I'm sorry," Philip said to the old Indian. "I speak English, Latin, Hebrew, and Greek, but I'm afraid I don't speak Algonquin."

"Not many people speak Latin or Greek on this reservation," the younger male said, his voice heavy with sarcasm.

The old Indian looked to the female and motioned for her to translate.

"Nanouwetea asked you your name," she said. Her voice was low and smooth as honey. Philip was mesmerized by it. He could spend all day listening to that voice.

"My name . . . my name! Um . . . yes, my name is Philip Morgan."

"Philip Morgan," the Indian girl said. Philip loved the way she said it.

"Tawhitch kuppeeyaumen?"

"What do you come for?" the maid translated.

With the Indian girl serving as interpreter Philip explained his mission—he came seeking an old family Bible that had been brought over from England by his ancestor Drew Morgan and he suspected the Bible might still be among the Narragansett Indians. According to family records the Bible disappeared during King Philip's War. The last person known to have it was Drew Morgan's son, Christopher, who was a missionary to the Indians.

The old Indian commented that King Philip's War was over fifty years ago. Why were the Morgans searching for the Bible only now? Philip answered that his father had just recently learned of the Bible's existence through Drew Morgan's journal which had been discovered in a Boston attic. It was his father's dying wish that he find the Bible and bring it back to Cambridge.

The old Indian nodded a few times, then inquired into Benjamin Morgan's death. He remained motionless as Philip described his father's murder.

At this point the old Indian grew noticeably tired. Through his interpreter he requested that Philip come back tomorrow when they would discuss the matter further.

"No!" Philip cried, a little more sternly than he'd intended. His outburst brought frowns from all three Indians. "Please understand," he said much more softly, "I'm in a hurry." He explained his circumstances—the school schedule, pressing financial decisions at home, an impatient fiancée. But his explanation only served to deepen the frown on the old Indian's face. Without responding further, he lay down and turned his back to his guest.

When Philip returned to his horse, everything was just as he left it. The boys who had watched him so intently were gone and he felt foolish for having suspected them. He spent the night under a tree next to the lake. No one offered him lodging and no one complained about the site he chose. The next morning he was summoned into the old Indian's presence. This time it was just him, the old Indian, and the maid. The younger male wasn't present.

"He says that a Bible is a personal treasure. Just as he would not give you a horse that did not belong to you, he will not lead you to the Bible unless he is sure it rightfully belongs to you," the Indian maid said, translating the old Indian's words.

"Then he knows where the Bible is?" Philip asked, his hopes rising.

The maid translated the question, listened to the old Indian's response, then said, "He refuses to say until you prove the Bible belongs to you."

"What kind of proof would he accept?" Philip asked.

"You mentioned a journal that belonged to the original owner of the Bible. Do you have that journal with you?"

Philip smiled broadly. He excused himself and returned moments later carrying Drew Morgan's journal. The pages were yellow and brittle. He turned them carefully to the page that had the reference to the Bible.

"Do you read English?" he asked the maid.

She nodded solemnly.

He moved closer to her and, with his index finger, pointed to the words. She leaned close to see. Her head came within inches of his and he could smell the fresh scent of her hair. He hoped she was a slow reader just so he could stay close to her for a while longer.

"May I show Nanouwetea?" she asked, turning toward him. With her face inches from his, Philip noticed the smoothness of her dark skin and the flecks of brown in her black eyes. Without taking his eyes off her, he nodded and released the book.

The Indian maid kneeled beside the old man, spread the book in his lap, and pointed to the words. She translated the passage that said: *It has been seven years to date since we've heard from Christopher. We hold little hope he is alive. The last word we received, and that secondhand, was that he was ministering to the praying Indians of the Wampanoag tribe shortly before the outbreak of hostilities. Although his location and health are uncertain, of this we are sure — his life is in God's hands. Christopher did not fear those who could harm his body, knowing full well they could not harm his soul. My only regret is that, as far as we know, he died without issue, without fathering a son to whom he could pass the family Bible in keeping with the charge I gave to him at the ceremony. Maybe it is wrong of me to place so much emphasis on a physical symbol. God needs not a Bible to know those who are His. My one last hope for this world is that the Morgan family will never know a generation that does not worship the Lord.*

The old Indian's face remained expressionless as she read. When she was finished, a shaking, wrinkled hand emerged from beneath the heavy mantle and rested on the open book. The Indian closed his eyes and tilted his head slightly upward.

To Philip it seemed as if he was testing the words to see if they were true by touching them. The maid waited patiently for him to finish whatever he was doing. Several moments passed, then the old Indian opened his eyes and lifted his hand and the journal was returned to Philip.

Apparently, both he and the journal passed the test, for moments later the old Indian was looking at him and speaking. Translated, this is what he said: "The Bible you are seeking exists. I have seen it. Christopher Morgan used it to teach Indians of many different tribes about the one true God."

"Did you know my ancestor Christopher Morgan?" Philip asked. The old Indian looked ancient enough; Philip thought it was worth asking.

The old Indian nodded slightly when he heard the translated

question. The scholar in Philip couldn't help but be thrilled. Here was a man who knew the brother of his great-grandfather!

"Tell him," Philip addressed the Indian maid, "that I wished I had more time to talk with him. I'd love to hear stories about Christopher Morgan."

For some reason the old Indian was displeased when he heard that. He grunted loudly and shook his head, muttering something Philip couldn't understand. The maid didn't translate the old Indian's mutterings, which was probably just as well.

"I didn't mean to offend him!" Philip apologized.

Now the old Indian spoke something he wanted translated.

"He says you hurry too much, that it will take time for you to find what you're looking for. He thinks you should go home. He says you will not find what you are looking for if you are in a hurry."

It was Philip's turn to be offended. He didn't like someone else telling him what to do and he certainly didn't like the implication that he wasn't committed to finding the Morgan family Bible. After all, he rode all the way down here, didn't he?

There was an edge in Philip's voice when next he spoke, even a hint of fire in his eyes. "Just tell Nanouwetea that if he can point me in the right direction, I will find the Bible no matter how long it takes."

The maid translated Philip's words. From the skeptical look on the old man's face, he wasn't convinced.

Finally, the old man said, "There is a group of praying Indians at the Great Swamp. Go there. You may find what you're looking for." With that, the old man lay down and turned his back to Philip the same way he did the day before.

It wasn't exactly what Philip was hoping for, but it was more than he had when he came. At least someone still living remembered seeing the Bible. He thanked the Indian maid for her assistance, then left the wigwam and the reservation and rode toward the Great Swamp.

THE Great Swamp was the site of the most famous battle of King Philip's War. From his grammar school studies, the traveling Harvard student was aware of its location—on the north side of Wordon's Pond next to the Chippuxet River—and its history. The colonies had already amassed a hundred years of history by the time Philip Morgan attended school. It was a brief amount of time considering the scope of human history, but sufficient enough for schoolmasters to form a lesson or two. One of the lessons was King Philip's War.

In the winter of 1675 a combined colonial force under the direction of Josiah Winslow defeated a fortified Narragansett village on a small island in the midst of the Great Swamp. It was a significant victory for the colonists since the village was thought to be the most secure Indian settlement in New England, and because the English were considered such poor swamp fighters. And due to its secret location, the village was virtually inaccessible to anyone who did not know the proper way to approach it.

A series of fortunate occurrences led to an English victory. A traitor, known as Indian Peter, knew the location of the stronghold and guided the colonial troops to it, revealing to them the key access route. Then the weather betrayed the Indians too. It was remarkably cold that year and the muck and water of the swamp was completely frozen. This allowed the colonials to advance across terrain that a few weeks earlier would have been impassable. The first English troops to arrive just happened to approach the camp at the one spot where the Indians' walled fortification wasn't complete. In a series of attacks the colonial troops assaulted the village through the gap in the wall. Although many of the Indian warriors escaped, hundreds of women and children were killed and their wigwams were destroyed by fire. Estimated Indian deaths were 200 warriors, 300 women and children.

Weary after several days of travel, Philip urged his horse toward the Great Swamp with hopes that the Morgan family Bible would be there so he could go home. If there was any consolation at this stage of his search, it was that the direction of the swamp was eastward, a homeward direction.

Winding his way through miles of woodland he reached a patch of rising land—the northern edge of the Great Swamp. Slowly and with great care he guided his horse along a serpentine trail until he saw a small piece of upland, five or six acres in size. Almost a dozen wigwams—similar to the ones on the reservation and each with a column of smoke emerging from the center opening—huddled together on the high ground. As if by cue Indian after Indian emerged from the wigwams until the entire village watched him as he approached.

"*What cheer, Netop?*" the village sachem greeted him. Philip smiled at the familiarity of the greeting; it was reportedly the same greeting given to Roger Williams, the founder of Providence, when he first met the Indians. The greeting was a combination of the English salutation, "What cheer?" with the Algonquin word for "friend" appended to it. The hospitality that soon followed put an anxious Philip Morgan at ease.

He became the guest of the sachem, a barrel-chested man named Quinnapin who enthusiastically invited him to dinner.

Upon entering the sachem's wigwam, Philip was taken aback by the number of people who were lounging on the skin-covered perimeter. They gathered to watch him eat and listen to the conversation between the Englishman and their sachem. Philip was served cornmeal mush, broiled venison, chestnuts, and berries. His host was gracious and cordial, though he rarely smiled, nor did anyone else. Philip soon discovered that to be a trait of the Narragansett people. They associated smiling with trickery and deception and they lived by the axiom, "Never trust a smiling man." But what they lacked in facial grins, they made up for in courtesy and friendliness.

To his disappointment, Philip quickly learned that the Bible he was seeking was not to be found among the Great Swamp Indians. However, the sachem had heard of a treasured Bible, possibly the one Philip was looking for, among the Hassanemosit people. He would give Philip directions in the morning.

"Do not lose heart," the sachem said to Philip, reading the disappointment that showed on his face. "You are here for a reason. We do not know the reason right now. But I have learned that God makes all things clear at the proper time."

It seemed strange for Philip to hear these Indians speak of God. He knew that John Eliot, Daniel Gookin, Christopher Morgan, and others had made great advances in their missionary efforts among the Indians, but to sit here and see the fruit of their work, to hear the Indians pray to God, to hear them praise God for another day or a good harvest, to hear them ask for forgiveness of their sin—these were things he'd always associated with the churches of the colonists and Harvard. Yet these people sitting on the high ground of the Great Swamp worshiped the same God as he and in much the same way. It just took a little getting used to.

"Why do you stay here?" Philip asked the sachem.

"This is our home," the sachem replied. His face was round, his cheeks plump, and they bounced as he chewed a piece of venison. "Where would you have us go?"

"It's just that you're so far removed from everything," Philip said. "If you lived closer to Wickford, or Pawtucket, or Providence, you could have more interaction with people."

"We are not removed from anything," the sachem said. "Everything is removed from us. Besides, the colonies prefer us to keep our distance and for now we prefer it too. It is easier to keep peace this way. We do not trust each other."

Thinking out loud, Philip quoted a Bible verse. *"There is neither Jew nor Greek, there is neither bond nor free, there is neither male nor female: for ye are all one in Christ Jesus —* Galatians 3:28."

Quinnapin nodded solemnly. "It is not easy to walk away from the events of the war," he said. "Most of these people here tonight have been raised with stories of injustice done to their ancestors. Many of their parents and grandparents were interned by the English on Deer Island, a bleak and barren place without adequate food or shelter. They were told they were there for their own good. The praying Indians who were fortunate enough to remain in their villages were confined to within one mile of their village. Should they venture further, they could be shot without explanation. They were hindered from hunting, looking after their livestock, and harvesting corn.

"My grandfather, Job Kattenanit, a praying Indian, left his village to rescue his three children who had been carried off by enemy Indians. Major Daniel Gookin issued him a written certificate identifying him as a trustworthy man. The note contained instructions to any Englishman who might happen to cross his path, that they not misuse or abuse him. Not long after that my grandfather was seized by scouts of Captain Henchmen. He could have hid himself when he first spied the soldiers, but because he had a pass, he chose not to. One of the scouts wanted to kill him on the spot. Instead, they took him to Captain Henchmen for questioning. My father, who spoke good English, told the Captain of his mission and showed him the note from Daniel Gookin. The Captain sent my grandfather to Boston under armed guard and he was confined to jail for three weeks. Afterwards, he was deported to Deer Island. I never saw him again. According to friends, he took sick and died."

"I'm sorry for your loss," Philip said. As he spoke, his eyes remained fixed on a twig he was twirling between his thumb and forefinger. Like an aggravated wound, his feelings over the loss of his own father burned within him.

The sachem pointed to an older Indian whose hair was short and gray and whose right eye was pinched shut. "Pessacus had a father and brother who were captured by Captain Mosely."

"Mosely," Philip said. "I've heard of him. The one with the reputation as an Indian hater?"

"The same. Mosely and his men seized Pessacus' father and brother well within the one-mile range of their village. They were bound and separated as Mosely questioned them. The father was tied to a tree. He confessed to being a praying Indian and explained that he and his son were only hunting deer. Mosely accused him of hunting colonists and wounding a Captain Hutchinson. After they questioned the old man for hours, trying to get him to confess to the deed, they fired a gun with no bullet over his head. Then Mosely questioned the son. The Captain told him that they had shot his father and would shoot him too, if he would not confess to the shooting of Captain Hutchinson. The only thing the brother confessed to was that he was a praying Indian, whereupon they brought his father and tied the two Indians together and questioned them again. When they still denied having any part of the shooting, Captain Mosely ordered them both to be shot dead."

The interior of the wigwam was still except for the crackling of the fire. Through the smoke and fire a sea of faces awaited Philip's reaction to the story. Philip could see them well, their brown features highlighted by the orange light of the fire. He wanted to assure them that not all the colonists felt as Captain Mosely. But even as the words formed in his mind, he knew them not to be true. The Christian men and women he knew were eager to send missionaries to the Indians to convert and civilize them. But they would never accept them as equals, as brothers and sisters in Christ. To most colonists, Indians—like the blacks from Africa—made tolerable household servants, but they would no more think of treating them as equals than they would the blacks.

Philip wished the colonists of Cambridge and Boston could see the praying Indians as he was seeing them tonight. If they could, surely they would change their minds about them.

"How do you convince other Indians to join you when it will mean isolation from their own people?" Philip asked.

The sachem looked puzzled. "A strange question coming from a Bible scholar. Because we are not accepted by the colonists or our own people, there are no shallow conversions among us. We consider it an honor to suffer in the same way as our Lord." Now it was the sachem's turn to quote Scripture: "*Who shall separate us from the love of Christ? Shall tribulation, or distress, or persecution, or famine, or nakedness, or peril, or sword? As it is written, For Thy sake we are killed all the day long; we are accounted as sheep for the slaughter. Nay, in all these things we are more than conquerors through Him that loved us.*"

Philip Morgan fought back a smile, not wanting to offend his host. His was a natural response, for the sachem's words warmed his heart. He was impressed with the dynamic nature of their faith. His world was one in which theology was debated; theories of man's depravity and the nature of God's atonement were discussed and memorized. Yet here were a people who chose to accept the sufferings and persecutions of this world to follow Jesus as Lord. For the first time in his life Philip Morgan felt ashamed of his scholastic standing; his theological book-learning was a pale candle compared to the roaring fire of this people's faith.

The evening concluded with the Narragansett believers teaching their guest a hymn. In true Indian fashion, they didn't smile when they sang, but their voices boomed lustily and their eyes cradled the hope that the song expressed:

I need not go abroad for joy, I have a feast at home;
My sighs are turned into songs, The Comforter is come.
   Hallelujah, Hallelujah, Hosanna, Hosanna,
   Hallelujah, Hallelujah, Hosanna, Hosanna.

Down from above the blessed Dove, Is come into my breast,
To witness God's eternal love, This is my heavenly feast.
   Hallelujah, Hallelujah, Hosanna, Hosanna,
   Hallelujah, Hallelujah, Hosanna, Hosanna.

There is a stream that issues forth from God's eternal throne,
And from the Lamb, a living stream, Clear as a crystal stone.
   Hallelujah, Hallelujah, Hosanna, Hosanna,
   Hallelujah, Hallelujah, Hosanna, Hosanna.

The next morning Quinnapin gave Philip directions to Hassanamesit. He was to follow the Pawtucket River upstream for two days. On the third day he would find a path that led across the river. He would follow that path eastward and come upon Hassanamesit within a mile of the river. Since there was only a footpath beside the river and the forest was dense with brush, Philip was advised to leave his horse behind. Quinnapin vowed to care for the creature until Philip returned.

It was with great reluctance that Philip set out on foot. It wasn't that he didn't trust Quinnapin—at least that's what he kept telling himself—it was that when he first heard about Hassanamesit, he assumed there was a road between here and there. With no road, there would be no taverns. He would be on his own, traveling alone in the forest. The idea caused him to shake nervously, and when he spoke, his voice was higher and he stammered a lot. But how could he tell these people who suffered daily for their faith that he was afraid of the forest? That if it meant traveling alone through a forest he'd rather discontinue his search for his family's Bible?

"May God guide your steps," Quinnapin pronounced in benediction as Philip started out on foot along the path that led out of the swamp. "And may you find what you are looking for."

An hour into his journey, Philip decided that walking was good for him. It was more exercise than he got when riding the horse and it seemed to calm his nerves. As he walked and reasoned, his fears began to melt away. He had no immediate concern for food. The Indians of the Great Swamp had seen to that. They had generously outfitted him with provisions. He carried parched meal, which the Indians called *nokake*, in a small pouch that was slung on his belt. He also carried a supply of dried meat and, since he was traveling next to a river for the length of his journey, there was a ready supply of drinking water.

As for clothing, the Indians had given him a pair of deer-skin moccasins which were more comfortable than his leather shoes. The moccasins were tanned and well tempered with oil, perfect for traveling through the wet terrain of the forest. His stockings were woolen, as were his trousers. He wore an open-necked shirt, with a spare should he need it. When it got chilly at night, he had a jacket rolled up in his bedroll, and a wide-brimmed hat protected his head from the cold. Since he traveled under cover of foliage almost the entire journey, he didn't need protection from the sun. By the time Philip was two hours into his journey, he was feeling bold and adventurous. It was a different feeling for someone who spent most of his time in front of an open book; it was a good feeling.

The first day passed quickly and Philip encountered no one along the way. Darkness fell rapidly in the ravine. The Harvard scholar built himself a fire, larger than what was needed for a single person, dined on his provisions, and did his best to fall asleep. The sounds of the forest kept him awake — frequent pops from the wood on the fire, the constant gurgle of the river, and an occasional rustling sound of some unseen animal which only served to remind him he wasn't completely alone in the forest. His surroundings were almost noisy with every kind of sound except the one he wished to hear — the sound of a human voice. The last voice he had heard was Quinnapin's benediction early that morning and he didn't realize until now how dependent he was on human contact.

He pulled his blanket closer to him. He would just have to satisfy himself with the memory of human conversation. Closing his eyes he conjured up Penelope in his mind and remembered past discussions — their wedding plans, intimate discussions as they talked of what it would be like to be man and wife, the sound of Penelope's shrill giggle when he playfully poked her in her side. As his conscious control of memories slipped into the uncontrollable realm of dream, his thoughts wandered from Penelope to the honey-sweet voice of an Indian maid as she spoke his name over and over again.

The second day, like the first, passed without incident, although there were a couple of times when Philip thought he was being followed. Both times his eye caught movement at the peripheral edges of his vision, but when he turned and looked, nothing was there. Probably a deer, or possibly just his imagination.

That night was long and painful. Not long after he dozed off, he had a nightmare. It began with him walking through the woods, just as he'd done all day. As he was pushing aside some tree branches, he caught a movement out of the corner of his eye. As he turned to see what it was, the huge bow of a merchant ship came crashing through the woods toward him, plowing through the trees as easily as it would through ocean waves. He tried to jump out of the way, but found his feet buried deeply in the sand. The ship bounded toward him and he pulled frantically to free himself. He managed to jump to one side just as the bow of the boat came crashing down. But he didn't jump far enough. The ship came to a crashing halt, pinning his legs under it. Strangely, there was no pain as he struggled to free himself. Seagulls with the heads of humans circled overhead, laughing at his predicament.

Just then in the dream, he heard someone calling his name. A familiar voice. His father! Searching in the direction of the voice he spied his father, the boat's bow resting squarely on his chest. Benjamin Morgan's arms reached toward Philip, his voice and eyes pleading for help. With renewed effort Philip yanked furiously, but he couldn't free himself from the weight of the ship. From above him, two heads peered over the railing. One was a sailor, the other an Indian! Somehow he had to free himself and free his father before they came down from the ship! He dug furiously in the sand around his legs to free them. The seagulls overhead began chanting his name. *Ignore them*, he thought; *dig faster, faster.* Then the sailor and the Indian appeared. He could no longer hear his father's cries. The broken body of Benjamin Morgan was lifeless. The sailor and Indian walked past his father, unconcerned. They walked toward *him*. Philip renewed his digging effort, but every time he pulled out a handful of sand from around his legs, more sand would pour in from the side and fill the hole. Now the sailor and Indian stood over him. Philip lay back in the sand looking into the faces of his executioners and resigned himself to death. The seagulls mocked him from above. The sailor lifted a heavy boot and placed it on Philip's chest. Philip found it hard to breathe. He gasped for air and tried to shove the boot aside, but couldn't. The sailor leaned on him, pressing down on his chest with a steadily increasing weight.

Philip awoke from the dream, dripping with sweat and fighting for air as his asthma clamped down on his breathing tubes. He coughed and wheezed until he nearly passed out, doubled over on the ground. For an instant he thought he saw the astonished face of an Indian peering from behind a bush, then the force of a cough closed his eyes. When he looked again, no one was there.

The attack lasted nearly a half hour. When it was over, an exhausted Philip Morgan lay face up on his bedding, drenched with sweat, his lungs and throat burning. He felt helpless and alone.

"Yes, we have a Bible," said the first Indian he encountered at Hassanamesit.

Philip reached the praying Indian town by noon of his third day of travel. As in the previous two Indian towns, his arrival prompted stares and a good number of curious bystanders. He was led to a small frame building that served as the town's meeting house where he was introduced to a short middle-aged Indian with kindly eyes who spoke broken English. Philip explained the purpose of his visit. His heart jumped when the man helping him went to retrieve the Bible.

He returned with the Bible resting on two open palms. Philip let his musket and bedroll fall to the ground as he reached toward the book. The Indian served as a book stand as Philip examined the exterior of the Bible—the cover, the spine, the thumb edge of the pages. It was an old volume, smaller than he'd expected it would be. Reverently, he opened the cover. He turned one page, then another, then another.

The disappointment that registered on his face was unmistakable. The title page read:

WUNNEETUPANATAMWE

UP-BIBLUM GOD

NANEESWE

NUKKONE TESTAMENT

KAH WONK

WUSKU TESTAMENT

JOHN ELIOT

Cambridge: 1663

This was an Algonquin language Bible, the one missionary John Eliot translated and printed. Philip explained to the man who seemed so eager to assist him that this wasn't the right Bible.

The Indian pointed to Philip and said, "Son of Eliot?"

Philip shook his head, "No. Son of Morgan."

"You help us read Bible? Teach us?"

"I don't speak or read your language," he said. The words of the young male Indian at the reservation came to him. *Not many people speak Latin or Greek around here.*

Now it was the Indian's turn to show disappointment. Philip was invited to dinner and since his provisions were running low, he readily accepted. Like the praying Indians at the Great Swamp settlement, he found this town to be small and poor in possessions, but big in spirit. During dinner he learned that the town had a lot of children, almost all of them illiterate. He sympathized with their dilemma. What good was a Bible, even if it was in your own language, if you couldn't read it? That night, with the aid of an interpreter, he taught them the parables of the three lost things—the lost sheep, the lost coin, and the lost son. In all of his years at Harvard, he had never seen a people so eager to learn the Bible.

As the Bible study broke up, a gray-haired woman took him by the hand; it took both of her prune-like hands to cover one of his. Through a companion—Philip assumed it was her daughter—the woman thanked him profusely for teaching them. Then she said she had once seen a large English Bible at the town of praying Indians not far to the east, just beyond the river. Philip thanked her, but he'd had enough chasing through the woods for the Bible. His plans now were to retrieve his horse and go home. He would begin the journey back to the Great Swamp in the morning.

Late that night, as he lay in the dark, afraid to close his eyes for fear that the nightmare that was still so fresh in his mind might return, the woman's words bothered him. She said English Bible. Not far to the east. What if it was the Bible he was seeking? He'd come so far already. It was at least two days travel back to the swamp. How far was "not far" to an elderly Indian woman? He decided to ask someone in the morning. If the town was less than a day's journey away, maybe he should make one last effort to find the Bible.

The next morning, "not far" turned out to be a half a day's journey. This time there was no river to guide him, only a footpath. He was to follow the path to a river. The town would be on the other side of the river.

The directions seemed simple enough, only Philip never

made it to the town. An hour into the day's journey the footpath was reduced to a rabbit trail and then disappeared altogether. Philip continued on, thinking that he could eventually pick up the trail again. He climbed over rocks, pushed his way through bushes, and crossed a small creek—surely not the river he was looking for; it was too small to be mistaken for a river and he'd encountered it too soon—but all of his efforts were for naught. He never picked up the footpath again.

He wandered aimlessly, through the morning and afternoon. As the sun began its downward trek, he came upon an open field with a singular tree near the center. It caught his attention because the tree had massive limbs, sparse foliage, and strange-looking stringlike things dangling from it. His feet and legs were aching, so he decided to use the tree as a resting place and examine this curious phenomenon.

Upon reaching the base of the tree, he looked up. What he saw wrenched his stomach. The dangling strings were ropes tied around the limbs; ropes used for hangings. He'd heard of this tree before. The Tree of Witness, some called it. Over thirty Indians were hanged in it in one day, their dangling bodies a testimony to all those who would rise up against the colonies. When the bodies were cut down, no one bothered to remove the rope tied to the limbs. The thought of so much violence and death in one place caused his legs to weaken. But he didn't want to sit down here. Not under this tree. As he searched for the next nearest tree, he saw them. His heart started pumping wildly. They were emerging from the forest. Three of them.

"*Awaunaguss!*" one Indian yelled, pointing at him.

Philip froze. He thought of running, but what good would it do? He doubted he could outrun them, let alone any arrows they might send his direction. So he stood there, trying to act confident, and watched as the three Indians came toward him, eyeing him suspiciously. Two of the Indians were strong and in their prime, one sporting a feather in his hair. The third was older, possibly in his fifth decade. The younger men were armed with knives, and bows and arrows. The older Indian cradled a musket in his arms. One of the younger Indians stood at a distance and kept watch as the Indian with the feather and the older Indian approached him.

"*Awaun keen?*" the older Indian asked.

Philip shrugged apologetically. "I don't speak your language," he said. "Do you speak English?"

"*Tuckowekin?*" the Indian with the feather shouted at him as if that would help him understand.

"I wish I could understand you," Philip said. "I'm looking for the praying Indian town. Can you tell me where it is?"

The older Indian shook his head and sneered. "*Mat nowaw-tau hettemina!*"

Philip shrugged his shoulders again. The third Indian, the watchman, stood with arms folded and head lowered, hateful eyes peering at the intruder.

"*Kuttokash!*" the Indian with the feather shouted, striking Philip on the shoulder.

Philip recoiled and stood his ground. "I mean you no harm," he said evenly. "Just let me go on my way."

With one quick swipe, the Indian with the feather snatched Philip's broad-rimmed hat from his head. He looked it over, removed the feather from his own head, and tried on the hat. The Indians laughed—even the angry one standing far off—as the Indian wearing Philip's hat modeled it for his companions.

Philip kept a straight face but made no attempt to retrieve his hat. *Let him have the hat*, he thought to himself. *It's hardly worth dying for.*

Then the Indian with the hat had another idea. Taking his feather, he placed it in Philip's hair. This brought a fresh round of laughter. Philip stood motionless and straight-faced. His cheeks burned with anger.

The Indian wearing his hat seemed to take offense that Philip wasn't joining in the fun. He punched Philip in the shoulder again and shouted, *"Mecauntitea!"*

As much as Philip hated the sting of humiliation when the Indians were laughing at him, now that they had returned to anger, he realized how much he preferred them laughing.

"Cowesass?"

Philip was hit with a third punch, same place. He held up both hands, palms open to his opponent.

"Niss-Nissoke!" The words came from the third Indian, the one standing far off. His words were low and guttural, dripping with hate. The Indian with the hat looked to his elder as if for some kind of confirmation. Philip had the distinct impression that this tree that once was laden with the bodies of so many dead Indians would now witness the death of an English colonist.

"Konkeeteatch Ewo," the elder Indian said evenly. Then he turned to leave. *"Nickattamutta!"* he said.

"Niss-Nissoke!" the angry Indian shouted at his elder.

"Nickattamutta!" the elder shouted back at him.

With the elder Indian leading the way, the other two followed, but not before firing parting shots of hate-filled glances at Philip. With the Indian's feather still sticking out of his hair, the Harvard scholar watched them leave. Halfway across the field the Indian who took his hat flung it as far as he could.

For nearly a half-hour Philip didn't move, afraid that if he did the Indians would reappear or shoot at him from the cover of trees. Finally, with shaky legs, he retrieved his hat, keeping his eyes on the forest at all times. He took the Indian's feather from his hair and placed it on the ground next to where his hat had been. Then, as confidently as his trembling limbs would allow him, he walked until nightfall in the opposite direction of the three Indians.

Late that night, alone in the woods, he had the dream again. The ship came crashing through the woods and landed on his legs. His father was pinned underneath its bow, crying to him for help. Seagulls laughed overhead. The sailor and the Indian appeared beside him. This time, however, they didn't step on his chest. The pirate placed his foot against Philip's side and tried to roll him over; at first gently, then more forcefully.

Philip stirred from his sleep. Something or someone was nudging his side, pushing him. He woke up face to face with a brown bear. The bear buried his nose against Philip's side and rolled him over. Philip scrambled to his feet and put some distance between him and the bear who seemed more interested in the bedroll and provisions than in Philip.

Shaking off the effects of sleep and his dream, Philip fought for control of his senses and tried to formulate a plan of action. His musket was on the ground between them, partially covered by a blanket; he'd slept with the weapon next to his side. If he moved slowly, maybe he could reach the musket without alarming the bear.

It didn't look like a big bear with all four paws on the ground as it snooped and sniffed his belongings. Finding the pouch with a little parched meal in the bottom, the bear sat and pawed at the opening. A large, pink, curly tongue unfolded from his mouth and worked its way into the pouch and the meal.

Philip eased his way toward the musket, crouching low, hoping not to startle the bear with any sudden movement. Concentrating on the meal pouch, the bear ignored him as he reached the gun. In a squatting position, Philip slowly picked up the musket which was already loaded and primed. He swung the barrel toward the bear.

He could shoot the bear and that would be that, unless of course the shot wasn't fatal, in which case he'd have more trouble than he could handle. So as long as the bear was content to ignore him, he was content to leave the bear alone. Let the bear have the pouch. He'd gather his things and slowly move away.

With the musket still leveled at the bear, Philip reached for his hat and put it on. The bear seemed unconcerned. Philip gathered in his bedding with one hand, bunching it up in a ball and stuffing it under his gun arm. The bear couldn't care less. The only thing left was his pack, which was laying at the base of a tree just out of reach. Without leaving his crouched position, Philip inched himself toward the pack, never taking his eyes off the bear. He reached for the pack but his outstretched fingers found nothing but air. A quick glance would tell him how much farther he had to go. He looked. A matter of inches. Philip stretched for the bag, grabbed it, and pulled it toward him.

The deafening roar of the bear echoed through the trees. In horror, Philip looked up just in time to see the bear towering above him on its hind feet. Instinctively he jumped backward, his heels catching a tree root. He crashed to his backside. The musket butt hit the ground.

BLAM!

The discharged musket fell to the ground, its shot hurled uselessly into the treetops. Heavy white smoke curled lazily upward. The sound frightened the bear momentarily. Now he was angry. With teeth bared, uttering another ear-splitting roar, he came after Philip.

Run! Get up and run! Philip's mind was screaming at him. But the bear was coming too fast. Philip crawled backwards on his hands and feet like a crab. When he reached a tree he clawed his way to his feet. By then the bear was on top of him.

A hot claw slammed into the side of his head, sending him sprawling to the ground. The whole world tumbled around him. He hit the ground on his back, knocking the air from his lungs. *Get up! Get up or you'll die!* But he couldn't. The world wouldn't stop spinning. The side of his head felt like it had been ripped off. It was wet and sticky. Everything around him was getting darker and darker.

As he began to lose consciousness, he remembered seeing the bear standing over him, its paws raised, ready to strike him again. Then the bear jerked suddenly. He roared and jerked again. Then again. Then everything went black.

Philip felt something move his head to the side, wounded side up. The pain was intense. It clouded his vision. Then his head was moved back to its original position. *The bear must be playing with me*, he thought. *Play dead.* It wasn't hard to do. Philip lay still, but nothing touched him. Strange. No fur. No fur on the paws. Then he lost consciousness again.

He heard leaves rustling. The bear! Philip tried to get up. He succeeded only in grabbing fistfuls of leaves and dirt. Light hit his face, then stopped, then hit him again, alternating back and forth like a signal light. It took great effort to force his eyes open just a crack. He saw the tops of trees, then a flash of light forced him to close his eyes again. On his second attempt he kept his eyes open a little longer, long enough to see that the alternating flashing was nothing more than the sun falling between the leaves in the trees as they were moved back and forth by the wind. He strained to hear any sound of the bear. The only sound was the rustle of the leaves and the occasional pop or groan of a tree limb.

Rolling to one side, he propped himself up on an arm and looked around. He groaned from the pain. There was no sign of the bear or anything else. He maneuvered himself to a sitting position. The simple effort caused him to grow faint. A white sheen covered his eyes and his head felt light. Philip hugged his knees until the feeling passed.

His head pounding with pain, he explored his left temple with his hand. His scalp stung when he touched it. Then he felt the strangest sensation. He could lift part of his scalp away from his head like a flap. Curious, really, considering it didn't hurt as much as he thought it would to lift it. The exposed raw flesh stung when the fresh air hit it, so he lowered the flap and patted it in place. That's when it hurt. He winced and stopped patting it.

Philip struggled to his feet and looked for his things. He found his wide-rimmed hat nearby and picked it up. It was shredded. He realized his hat took the brunt of the blow; it saved him from greater injury. Maybe even saved his life. He tossed it to the ground. It wasn't good for anything anymore. He found his musket, pack, and bedroll each where he'd dropped them.

He paused a moment to take stock of his situation. He was injured, but alive. He was lost. He had no food. The sun was almost directly overhead so he couldn't get his directions from it. Taking his bearings from his campsite, he continued the direction he was headed. He thought it was east.

Philip could walk for only about a half-hour at a time. By then the pain in his head would be so great he could barely see, and he was forced to stop and rest. He continued in this way for almost two hours when he heard a commotion through the trees to his right. It sounded like horses and wagons and men shouting. Altering his course, he made his way from tree to tree to investigate. He soon came to a clearing with a road not far beyond. A wagon pulled by a team of horses barreled down the road.

Stepping into the clearing, he attempted to yell after the wagon. But his voice was weak and the wagon was too far down the road. As he stood there and looked after it, a strange awareness pieced itself together . . . the road . . . the distant skyline . . . the field and forest . . . he knew this place! A sense of dread jabbed his gut. Yes, he knew this place. He knew it all too well. This was the road leading to Roxbury. The road on which his father died. An eerie sensation crept over him. He was standing on the edge of the forest from which the sailor and the Indian emerged when they shot his father.

Cold sweat formed on his upper lip as his eyes darted back and forth through the woods. There was no reason for him to think his father's murderers would still be here, but he had to look. He walked toward the road. He had to get out of here. With each stride he felt better. He wasn't far from home. He could get help. He would be safe.

"ENGLISH!"

The voice came from behind him. Philip whirled around, expecting to see a sailor and an Indian. But there was no sailor and he recognized the Indian. It was the young male Narragansett from the reservation.

"Go home, English! Go home where you're safe!"

Maybe it was the head wound, but Philip's disorientation was incredible. "What are you doing here?" Philip yelled. Even as he asked the question, things began to make sense. He answered it himself. "You've been following me, haven't you?"

"You've found what you're looking for," the Indian said. "Go home."

"But I haven't found the Bible!" Philip cried.

"That's not what you're looking for; it's over there!" The Indian pointed toward the horizon leading to Cambridge. "What you want is there—honor, prestige, high society, security. That's what you're looking for."

Philip had been through too much in the last week to allow

this uneducated Indian to taunt him. He threw his equipment on the ground and stalked toward the Indian, his face red, his hands clenched. "Don't tell me what I want out of life! Why have you been following me?"

The young Narragansett was not threatened by Philip's advance. "Nanouwetea told me to look after you. He didn't want any harm to come to you."

Flashes of memory came to Philip. It was this young Indian he'd seen out of the corner of his eye; the one with astonished eyes the night he had the asthma attack. "If you were sent to protect me, where were you when the bear attacked me?"

"Nearby."

"Then why didn't you help me?" Philip shouted.

"I did."

The bear jerked! Philip remembered now. The bear was standing over him, ready to finish him off. He was helpless. Then the bear stopped! He jerked and roared and jerked again! "You killed the bear!" he said.

The Indian nodded.

Philip's hands relaxed, the fists fell apart. "You saved my life. Thank you."

The young Indian just stood there, stone-like.

Philip looked over his shoulder toward home, then back at the Indian. "I still don't understand why Nanouwetea had you follow me. Why does he care what happens to me?"

"He cares."

"But why?"

"It's over, English. Go home."

"It's not over," Philip said. "Do you see that road?" He pointed behind him. "My father was murdered on that road. His last request to me was that I find the Morgan family Bible. I intend to do just that."

The Indian stared at him as if he were weighing Philip's

words, trying to see how much was gold and how much was dross. "What if it costs too much?"

Philip felt his anger rising again. "Cost? My father is dead! I've stumbled through a forest even though I don't know the first thing about surviving in one; I've traveled from village to village following dead-end leads; three Indians nearly attacked me; and a bear almost killed me! What more can I do?"

"Come back to the reservation with me."

"Why would I want to do that?"

"Because your Bible is there."

Philip was dumbstruck. It took him several angry moments to form his next words. "It's been there all along?"

The Indian nodded.

"Nanouwetea sent me chasing after wild geese?"

Another nod.

"Why? Can you tell me why?"

"You'll have to ask him."

Philip was nearly blind with rage. He stomped into the forest heading south.

"You'd better take your musket with you!" the Indian called after him.

It took them three days to reach the reservation. During the trip, Philip learned that his protector and guide's name was John Wampas. He had been led to the Lord by Nanouwetea. The Indian maid's name was Mary Weetamoo. Their last names were their original Indian names; their English first names were given to them at baptism. On the third day when they reached Schoolhouse Pond Road, Philip left his guide behind and ran to the wigwam beside the cornfield. Not waiting to be introduced, he ducked through the entrance and marched into the presence of Nanouwetea. Mary Weetamoo was seated next to him. They were eating dried meat.

"*What cheer, Netop?*" the old Indian greeted him.

"You're hurt!" Mary Weetamoo cried, seeing the dried ridge of blood on the side of Philip's head.

"Never mind the pleasantries and never mind this," Philip cried, pointing to his wound. "Ask him why he sent me all over God's creation looking for a Bible that he has right here!"

"Ask me yourself," the old Indian spoke in English.

"Oh, that's great!" Philip cried. "Another trick! All right, I'll ask you myself ... why?"

"It was a test."

"A test. Fine! And what gives you the right to test me?" Philip yelled.

"I have the Bible." The old Indian was calm and serious as he spoke.

"A Bible that belongs to *my* family!"

"And mine."

Philip was stymied. "How can it belong to your family? It's the Morgan family Bible."

"I *am* a Morgan," said the old man. "Christopher Morgan."

Chapter 8

RELUCTANTLY Constance Morgan concluded that Philip was dead.

When he didn't return in July she was concerned. When Harvard College began classes in August and he still wasn't home, she was alarmed. By October all hope had vanished. Jared wanted to ride south in search of his brother. But Constance wouldn't hear of it. The boy was only eighteen, maybe a man by the world's standards, but still her youngest child. Besides, he was the only remaining male Morgan in the family.

Life had been cruel to Constance. In a matter of months she had lost her husband and her eldest son. She was determined not to lose Jared too. Still, no matter how many times she forbid him to go, he talked of running off at night to find his brother. The matter wasn't resolved until Daniel Cole offered a solution.

Cole volunteered to send some of his men to the Narragansett reservation to inquire after Philip. Constance was grateful and Jared was appeased, though he was disappointed at not being able to talk the merchant into letting him go with the men. Two weeks later Daniel Cole returned to the Morgan house with the unsettling news. His men had just returned from the reservation. No one there had seen or heard of Philip Morgan. Cole could only conclude that Philip never reached the reservation.

By the end of November, six months after Philip set out on his journey, Constance Morgan put the matter to rest in her mind. Philip was dead. The president, staff, and several students at Harvard College paraded in informal procession to the house expressing their condolences. Penelope, Philip's fiancée, stretched out on a sofa in the Morgans' sitting room and sobbed convulsively.

Late at night on the last day of the calendar year Constance sat alone in a chair facing the bedroom fireplace. Although she was bundled heavily with a comforter and the logs in the fire crackled with life, she couldn't help but shiver when she thought how the cold hand of death had touched her twice in one year. She sipped her hot drink. She wept, not only for her loss but also from the gnawing ache of loneliness she felt. As 1727 ran out of time, Constance Morgan cursed the year that had caused her so much pain.

On the first day of 1728 Priscilla decided the time of waiting was over. She'd been patient long enough. It was time she do something.

Her decision was a long time in coming; the morning's personal Bible study was merely the catalyst. Benjamin Morgan's library did not go unused in Philip's absence. Priscilla took advantage of the empty room to continue her studies. She had a working knowledge of Latin and Hebrew and Greek. Her first effort targeted the Old Testament. She translated the fourth and fifth chapters of the Book of Judges, the story of Deborah.

Translating was difficult work for her. She was still learning the basics of Hebrew. Painstakingly she parsed each word and looked up its root in a lexicon. Word by word, phrase by phrase, the lines that had once been foreign gibberish crystallized into truths that revealed a depth of meaning that surpassed her English translation. Rarely did she translate a passage without finding some new gem of truth previously hidden to her. This morning, her study was especially rewarding. The seventh verse of the fifth chapter seemed to her to be prophetic. On the left side of her paper she printed her translation:

The hamlets in Israel ceased, they ceased,
Until I, Deborah, arose.

Then she numbered key words and with a corresponding number on the left side of her page, she wrote commentary:

1. Hamlet — the word refers to villages in the open regions, in contrast to walled cities.
2. To cease — from a primitive root meaning to be flabby, to fail.
3. Arose — from the verb to stand, to rise, to stir up, or to strengthen.
   As I understand this verse, the situation throughout the land was chaos. Israel was failing and on the verge of complete collapse. And the nation would have failed had not Deborah arose to bring order out of chaos, victory out of defeat. Such is the state of the Morgan household. Since the death of my father and the disappearance of Philip, we have been in utter disarray. Mother, God bless her, does not have the abilities to manage the affairs of our estate. Jared shows no interest and procrastinates at even the simplest matters. Unless something is done, we will fail. It is time for I, Priscilla, to arise and strengthen our family holdings. May God give me wisdom and strength.

Priscilla cleared the desk of study materials and pulled out her father's ledger and the wooden box in which he kept miscellaneous bills, receipts, and important papers. She set out to create order out of the chaos. When her mother saw what she was doing, she started to object, then quietly closed the door to the study so that Priscilla could work uninterrupted. Breaking only for meals, by evening Priscilla had a firm grasp on the family's failing financial status and had formulated a preliminary course of action.

Over the next several months Priscilla Morgan paid outstanding bills, arranged for credit or extensions of payments when needed, interviewed and hired servants—an Indian maid for inside work and an African for outside work; later when finances increased another Negro male, named Joseph, was added as a house servant. Priscilla contracted with necessary workers to complete much-needed maintenance repairs on the house. At first, her greatest problem was not having enough cash to work with and no current income. Although Jared talked of finding work, no job ever appealed to him. So Priscilla began to look for ways to increase their income. Two ready opportunities presented themselves. She liked neither of them.

The first income opportunity was to sell Daniel Cole the stocks he'd been after for so long. Priscilla didn't want to do this because the stock was their most reliable source of income. It didn't bring in a lot, but it was steady. To her, selling the stock would be like selling an apple tree. You might get a tidy sum from the sale of the tree, but then there wouldn't be any more apples. She decided she would sell the stocks only if absolutely necessary.

The second opportunity for income came from an unusual source. His name was Nathan Stearns and he wanted Priscilla to marry him. Nathan was short, homely, and mealy-mouthed, but he loved Priscilla and he was rich. Orphaned since he was fourteen years old, Nathan, now twenty-one, was desperate for a wife. He'd inherited his father's shipbuilding empire which made him independently wealthy, and lived with his aunt and uncle on Boston's North End, near Clark's Square. They were mean-spirited and cruel to him, and he longed for the day he could kick them out. But since single men were not allowed to live alone, the provisions of his inheritance named them as his guardians until he married. For Nathan Stearns, marriage meant freedom.

Normally, a man of wealth had little trouble finding a wife. Not Nathan. If his aunt and uncle didn't scare off the prospect, Nathan's personality—or lack of it—did. He was painfully self-conscious in public and possessed no self-image. In fact, it was worse than that. Nathan Stearns' lack of self-image was like a sponge. It absorbed all conversation, laughter, and festivity in a room. Nathan bred awkward self-consciousness with those he conversed with; women felt pity for him, men derided him. Neither element is conducive to a successful party.

As Nathan saw it, Priscilla Morgan was the answer to his problems. She was strong enough for both of them. Priscilla would not be intimidated by his aunt and uncle. As for social gatherings, she was such a dominant personality no one would even notice him. A perfect match.

So Nathan Stearns worked up his courage and asked Constance if he could call on Priscilla. His courting efforts were a painful experience for everyone. He would arrive punctually with present in hand—sometimes he'd bring sugared almonds, other times a printed sermon or tract. Then he and Priscilla would spend silent hours on opposite sides of the sitting room and stare at each other. Constance would inevitably offer refreshments. Priscilla was amused when she realized Nathan spoke more words in his refusal of the refreshments than he usually spoke all evening—"No, thank you. Thank you, no . . . thank you."

Priscilla used all the usual signals to show him she wasn't

interested. She always saw to it that some piece of furniture separated them. As a hint to indicate he should leave, she would never attend the fire. It would fall to ashes and, oblivious to the hint, the two would find themselves sitting in the dark. When he left, she would not help him on with his coat—one of the unkindest cuts of all. And she did not send a servant with a lamp to light his way to his coach, but let him stumble toward it in the dark. Although she spared no effort in thinking up new hints to indicate her disinterest, she couldn't bring herself to be rude and tell him outright never to call on her again. For even though she despised his feeble courting efforts, she felt sorry for him. And though she hated herself for thinking it, she felt an element of attraction—not to him, but to his money.

"What are you going to do when he asks you to marry him?" her mother asked one evening.

The two of them sat in the study; Constance was embroidering while Priscilla sat at the desk and scratched entries in the ledger.

"I don't think he will," Priscilla replied.

"He will."

"What makes you so sure?"

The embroidery needle paused mid-air. "Isn't that the purpose of courting?"

Priscilla snickered. "Oh, is that what he's doing?"

"Priscilla!" Constance fought back a snicker of her own. "That's unkind."

Priscilla lay down her quill. Turning toward her mother, she hunched her shoulders and pressed folded hands in her lap. "The way I see it," she said with the sound of a yawn in her voice, "love is a disease with which I have never been afflicted."

"Your time will come. And it's a wonderful affliction! One that I would not have missed for anything." Her eyes grew moist with tears.

"Momma, I miss Poppa too, but there aren't any other men like him."

"Each man is different, special in his own way. Which leads me to another topic, a question I've been meaning to ask you." Constance lay down her work on her lap. "How would you feel if I married again?"

A horrified look crossed Priscilla's face. To her knowledge, since the funeral Mother had only had close contact with one man. "Momma! You don't mean Master Cole, do you?"

Constance smiled in reply.

"Oh no, Momma!"

Constance Morgan shot a warning glance at her daughter. "I wasn't asking your permission!" she said.

"If you did, I wouldn't give it!"

"Priscilla Morgan! Is that any way to talk to your mother?" Her eyebrows bunched together in a frown, forming that prominent vertical cleft that had always been the sign to the Morgan children that Mother was angry.

"Mother, please don't marry Master Cole!" Priscilla pleaded. "Do you think Poppa would approve?"

Constance worked a stitch or two until tears so blurred her sight that she couldn't continue. "I'm lonely, Priscilla," she said. "Terribly lonely. Daniel has been a friend for years. He's not your Poppa; I know that. But I can't continue like this. I wish I could make you understand how it feels. Every morning I wake up feeling that a part of me is missing. Almost like waking up and discovering that you were blind, or that you had no arms or no legs. Only it's more than that, much more. Priscilla, it's like I'm missing part of my soul. I can't adapt. I've tried, Priscilla. I've prayed that God would heal the ache that's inside me. But it's still there. God help me, it's still there!" Constance was weeping openly now. Priscilla knelt in front of her, placing her head in her mother's lap.

"I'm here for you, Momma," she said.

"I know, dear," Constance replied, stroking her daughter's head.

"Through all of our hardships, you have been our rock. I'll always love you for that."

The two sat in silence—Priscilla holding her mother's hand to her cheek; Constance caressing Priscilla's hair.

Then Constance said, "Earlier you likened love to a disease. Unlike you, I've been afflicted with it. It's in my blood. I can't imagine living without it."

Priscilla yielded to her mother's vulnerability and said nothing. However, she had not spoken her last against Daniel Cole.

For the first quarter of the new year Priscilla was a whirlwind of activity representing the Morgan family's interests. And though Constance disliked the unladylike appearance of her daughter performing tasks normally reserved for men, secretly she was pleased with Priscilla's success and the timely manner in which things were being accomplished. The house had never been in better repair. Priscilla managed the servants firmly but fairly. Creditors no longer came to the door apologetically asking for money from a woman who had lost a husband and son within six months of each other. And Priscilla was happier than Constance had ever seen her. The young woman seemed to thrive on each day's accomplishments.

Priscilla Morgan had just entered The Good Woman Tavern on Boston's King Street near Cornhill. She was looking for an elusive blacksmith by the name of Jake Sutcliffe. After several unsatisfactory attempts to conclude her business with him through letters and by visits from Joseph, the family servant, Priscilla had no other choice than to travel to Boston herself. Trying to make the best of it, she talked her mother into accompanying her on the trip, thinking it would be good for her mother to get out of the house. Priscilla was pleased when her mother agreed. Then, to her chagrin, her mother arranged to visit Daniel Cole while Priscilla conducted the business at hand. The turn of events put Priscilla in a sour mood as they arrived in the city.

The two women journeyed by carriage. Joseph drove them, taking the water route and entering Boston's north end by way of the ferry from Charlestown. After depositing her mother at Cole's three-story house on Beacon Street, Priscilla proceeded down the hill toward Cornhill Street and Sutcliffe's blacksmith shop.

Since the time they left the house early in the morning, Priscilla's anger had grown steadily and by this time she was furious. She resented wasting a whole day because a Boston blacksmith was at best, inept or at worst, a crook. But what really made her angry was the giddy way her mother acted all the way to Boston. She giggled at everything, was overly concerned about her appearance and, the closer they got to Master Cole's house, she kept placing a dainty hand against her chest, sipping deep breaths of air to calm herself. Priscilla thought such behavior repulsive when girls her age acted this way; to see her own mother playing the lovesick maid was infuriating.

Her mood took a turn for the worse when Sutcliffe wasn't at his shop when she arrived. His apprentice explained the blacksmith had stepped out for a moment. Priscilla took him at his word and waited for an hour. Meanwhile, she watched as the apprentice matched wits with a mare over a matter of whether or not the apprentice would be allowed to remove the horse's shoe. Priscilla concluded that in that particular battle of wits, the apprentice was woefully overmatched. After an hour, when the proprietor still hadn't returned, Priscilla took her turn at the apprentice and bullied him into revealing that Jake Sutcliffe had gone to one of the taverns on King Street, but he wasn't sure which one. Setting off to find him, she inquired at The Rose and Crown and The Royal Exchange before coming to The Good Woman Tavern.

The stage had arrived moments before her and she followed the dusty driver through the door beneath the tavern's sign, which portrayed the figure of a headless woman. No one else from the stage disembarked. The tavernkeeper and "Camp" (the name by which the stage-driver was called) exchanged banal male witticisms as the driver dropped a bundle of letters on the counter. The tavernkeeper had snipped the string binding the bundle and was sorting through the letters when he spotted Priscilla.

"May I help you Mistress . . . "

"Morgan," Priscilla said in a businesslike tone. "I'm in a bit of a hurry to return home to Cambridge and I need your assistance."

"Ma'am," the stage-driver said, tipping his wide-brimmed hat to Priscilla. "Your timing couldn't have been better." Then to the tavernkeeper, "Next week I'll collect on that ale you owe me, Gibbs."

Priscilla looked at the stage-driver oddly, unsure as to the meaning of his remark.

"Morgan?" the tavernkeeper repeated the name with a smile. He took two letters from the bundle and tossed them beneath the counter. "And how may I help you, Mistress Morgan?"

The tavernkeeper was a tall, young man with a ready smile. His hair was brown and rather curly, but showed traces of Irish red. He came across as self-confident and friendly, attractive traits for his profession.

"I'm looking for a blacksmith by the name of Master Sutcliffe," Priscilla replied. "Might I find him here?"

The tavernkeeper leaned forward on the bar, speaking in

low tones. "Important business?" he asked.

"I fail to see where that is any of your business, sir!"

"Gibbs. Peter Gibbs." A toothy smile punctuated with dimples accompanied the introduction. He held out his hand to her.

Priscilla looked at his hand, then back at him. "Surely the question is not too difficult for you," she said, ignoring his hand. "So I'll ask it again. Is Master Sutcliffe here?"

Conceding that she wanted to keep things formal, the tavernkeeper withdrew his hand. "Mistress Morgan, I don't want to pry into your business. I'm only trying to help you. Your Master Sutcliffe is here. He's had too much to drink. And when he drinks too much he gets ugly." The tavernkeeper thought a moment, then added, "Uglier than usual. It would be best if you conducted your business with him tomorrow."

"If you would be so kind as to point him out to me," Priscilla said.

There was a pause as the tavernkeeper seemed to calculate the young lady's chances against the blacksmith. "You'll find him in front of the fire."

What Priscilla found was a big-bellied, dirty blacksmith reclined in his chair, his right hand gripping the handle of his tankard on the table beside him, his left hand dangling with knuckles brushing the floor, his shoeless feet stretched toward the fire, and his head drooping over the back of the chair, his eyes closed, and his mouth open.

Priscilla mustered up what little stature she had and stood over the snoring blacksmith. "MASTER SUTCLIFFE!" Her voice was clear and cutting. The blacksmith's extended legs recoiled as he snapped up in his chair. Pressing her advantage, Priscilla stood in the space vacated by his legs. She closed in on the blacksmith so he couldn't stand up.

"You have double billed me," Priscilla shouted, producing

two papers and slapping them down on the table. "Not only that, you have failed to perform the work. I want an explanation!"

The blacksmith was clearly disoriented. He fought to gather what little wits he had. A half-dozen patrons were scattered throughout the tap room. The red-haired complainant and groggy blacksmith had everyone's attention. Peter Gibbs, the tavernkeeper, looked on with unconcealed amusement.

"No sooner had I paid this bill . . . " she rattled one sheet, " . . . than I received this one," she rattled the other.

The blacksmith's head began to clear. He looked at Priscilla, not the papers. "Little lady, this involves business accountin' procedures. It's complicated, far too complicated for a woman."

Sutcliffe made an attempt to get out of his chair, but Priscilla refused to give him room. "Maybe you can help me understand, Master Sutcliffe," Priscilla said. She pointed at the two papers. "Tell me if I'm wrong. The date of the two transactions is identical, the work description is identical, and the price is identical."

"Look, lady . . ."

"Mistress Morgan!" she corrected him.

The flush of anger began to rise in the blacksmith's smudged cheeks. "Look, Mistress Morgan. You tell your Poppa . . ."

"My father is dead. My older brother is dead. I have no husband. I'm handling the family affairs and I want some answers. Not only are you trying to cheat me, you haven't even done the work!"

Sutcliffe's chair scraped angrily across the floor as he made room to stand. Now he was towering over her. Peter Gibbs jumped from behind the counter and stood between them.

"Stay out of this, Gibbs!" Sutcliffe warned. "Lady or no, this filly is calling me a liar!"

The tavernkeeper picked up the two invoices and studied

them. "Looks like she has a case, Jake," he said. "These two invoices are identical and this one here is marked paid. That's your signature, isn't it?"

The blacksmith looked around him. Everyone in the room was watching them. Reluctantly, he looked at the bills.

"See there?" the tavernkeeper pointed to the signature.

"Yeah, I guess so," he groused. "My apprentice must have messed up and sent another bill," he said loud enough for everyone in the room to hear.

"Did your apprentice forget to put shoes on the horse too?" Priscilla asked.

"Now I remember that! I shoed that horse myself! And nobody's gonna tell me different!"

Priscilla stared into the faces of the two men looking down at her. She hated being a woman. The blacksmith thought that just because he was a man he was right and the tavern-keeper was amused at her accusations. What would a man do in this situation? Probably hit somebody. Which, of course, wouldn't solve anything. That's why she chose not to do what a man would do. She grabbed the signed invoice from the tavernkeeper and stalked out of the room in a huff.

Even before she was out the door Jake Sutcliffe was bad-mouthing her. A woman like her needed some man to tame her. Put her in her place. And he knew just who could do it too.

A moment later the front door of the tavern swung open and in walked Priscilla Morgan. With reins in hand she led her horse into the tavern. Patrons of The Good Woman Tavern gawked and laughed, and some even had to get up to make room for the horse. Following its master, it obediently clomped over to an equally dumbfounded blacksmith and tavernkeeper. Priscilla reached down and pulled up the horse's left front leg. "Look at this, Master Sutcliffe," she said point-ing to an old, cracked shoe. "Do you still insist you put new shoes on this horse?"

Tavernkeeper Peter Gibbs amused his customers with the story of the woman, the horse, and the shame-faced black-smith for days afterward. With so many witnesses on hand, the blacksmith had no choice but to offer to put new shoes on the horse, which he promptly did.

When things finally settled down, the tavernkeeper got back to his regular routine, picking up where he'd left off — sorting the mail that had been delivered by the stagemaster. Then he remembered the letters he'd tossed beneath the counter. He retrieved them. One was addressed to Constance Morgan, Cambridge; the other to Penelope Chauncy, also Cambridge. Both letters were from the same person, Philip Morgan. He again thought of the red-headed woman. She said her name was Morgan, Priscilla Morgan.

The tavernkeeper finished sorting the mail so that each piece would reach its intended destination. He did this for all the letters except the two from Philip Morgan. Those he placed in his pocket.

PRISCILLA relished her victory as her carriage, pulled by a freshly-shoed horse, rounded the corner of Treamount and School streets. She sat back and watched the scenery go by.

King's Chapel—the first Anglican church in Boston—stood on the corner as a reminder to the colony of controlling powers that lie across the sea. It had been built several decades earlier by the much-despised Governor Andros, who had been dispatched by the mother country to stem growing colonial independence. His was a turbulent administration that still left a bad taste in the colonials' mouths.

Opposite the King's Chapel on the hillside and set well back from the street was a house so magnificent, Priscilla ordered Joseph to halt the carriage so she could get a better look at it. The house belonged to the Faneuils, a wealthy merchant family, and loomed among scattered trees like a large medieval castle, minus turrets and moat. Until today, Priscilla had only heard about it. Now that she saw it for herself, it was bigger than she'd imagined. If the stories she heard were true, fabulous gardens extended up the hill behind it. She wondered what it must be like to live in such extravagance. God willing, someday she would no longer have to wonder.

Beyond the Faneuil property, the coach turned onto Beacon Street. They passed a handful of country houses with beautiful gardens, but none that could compare with the Faneuil mansion. One of these houses belonged to Daniel Cole. A black iron fence stretched between white brick pillars, separating the grounds from the street. The iron gate opened to an expansive stone stairway leading up to the three-storied mansion. The climb was a good one, situating the house high enough on the hill to give it a considerable view of the city and the bay. Behind the house was a succession of terraces filled with flowers and fruit trees.

For the most part, the exterior of Daniel Cole's house reflected the richness of its neighborhood. However, there was one touch of garishness that, to Priscilla, epitomized Daniel Cole. Hanging on a protruding rod over the doorway was a huge pewter kettle, to indicate his trade and the means by which he'd acquired his wealth. It was the kind of blatant detail one would expect to find on a shop on Boston's south side; certainly out of place on Beacon Street. But then, that was Daniel Cole. He shared the money of Boston's wealthier residents, but not their tastes and certainly not their manners. Priscilla's good mood vanished as her carriage pulled to a halt in front of his house.

"Master Cole will see you in the parlor."

Priscilla was ushered into the house by a large, hulking, African servant. She didn't want to come in at all. She'd sent Joseph up the steps to inform her mother that they'd arrived to take her home. He returned alone moments later bearing a message from Cole. He insisted she come in.

The parlor was an expansive room with an enormous multipaned window overlooking Boston Bay.

"Master Cole will be with you shortly," said the servant, excusing himself.

Priscilla found herself alone in the parlor. There was no sign of Cole or her mother, and the servant disappeared before she could inquire about them. Everything in the room spoke of the man's wealth; from the chandelier overhead, to the oil paintings on the walls, to the shelves filled with books, to the delicate French tables and the Chinese vases sitting on them. Priscilla had never seen so much evidence of wealth displayed in one place. Frankly, she was impressed and she hated herself for it. She'd always despised Daniel Cole and the more she knew him, the less she liked him. But this room was magnificent; it was a side of Daniel Cole she'd never seen before. The furnishings spoke of a man of taste, of culture.

She meandered to the far side of the room, admiring every artifact, every polished surface along the way. The view overlooking the bay took her breath away. Arranged in an intimate semicircle in front of the window was a sofa and two chairs. She absentmindedly lowered herself onto the sofa as she tried to take in the panorama that lay before her.

"Priscilla, my dear!" Cole clomped across the wooden floor and plopped into a chair beside the sofa. His white hair scattered every which way as he slumped down in the seat, his legs stretched out and his arms draped over the sides. His present posture dictated that any conversation would have to be held over his enormous protruding belly. The odor of unwashed stockings and two-day-old sweat accompanied him, quickly putting the room's extravagance back into proper perspective.

"Stay for dinner!" he said.

Priscilla noticed it wasn't a request. Daniel Cole always told people what to do, he never asked them.

"Your offer is kind," Priscilla said as she stood. "But we must be on our way. I'd prefer to complete our journey before it gets dark."

"Then stay the night!" Cole boomed.

"We really couldn't. Jared is expecting us to come home. He'd worry."

"He's old enough to take care of himself. He'll be fine."

Priscilla laughed. "You don't know Jared very well," she said. She straightened her skirt to emphasize her intention to leave. "Now if you'll tell Mother I'm here . . ."

"Sit down, Priscilla."

"Master Cole, I must insist . . ."

"Sit down, Priscilla!" His tone was hard, demanding. When she didn't respond, he softened it. "Please, I want to talk to you."

Priscilla sat on the edge of the seat, her hands folded neatly in her lap. At this lower level, Cole's belly rose up between them again. From the far side, a pair of unblinking pewter-gray eyes bore down on her.

"You're a stubborn young woman," Cole said. "Too stubborn for your own good. It's unbecoming a lady."

"Is that what you wanted to tell me, Master Cole?"

The merchant ignored her remark. He pulled himself up in the chair and leaned toward her. "I'm stubborn too," he said. "I'm not sure which of us is more stubborn and, to tell you the truth, I hope we never have to test it."

Priscilla sat rigidly, her lips tightly pursed, wishing he'd get to the topic.

"I'm a man who gets what he wants," Cole said matter-of-factly. "Always have. Look around you. There's more wealth in this house than I could spend in a lifetime."

Priscilla kept her eyes fixed on Cole.

"I used to enjoy building my business, making money, and accumulating expensive things. Not any more. It's lost its attraction. So where's the joy in living?"

No response was forthcoming from Priscilla. She didn't think he wanted one anyway.

"I'm like a little boy," Cole said with an impish smile. "I've discovered that the greatest joy in life is getting what you want. The greatest disappointment is not getting what you want. All that is left is deciding what I want. Once I decide that, I go after it. I get it. No matter what it costs . . . no matter where I have to go to get it. . . ." He leaned toward Priscilla to emphasize this last point. As he did, white clusters of hair fell forward and bounced against his forehead. ". . . no matter who currently possesses it."

Cole smiled confidently, straightened himself, then turned toward the panorama of Boston harbor. "You see, my dear, I don't need your family's shares in my company. I already have a controlling interest. But I'm going to get them simply because one morning I woke up and decided I wanted them. I want to own all the stock. And so I will."

"So that's what this is all about!" Priscilla cried. She stood. "Well, I'm afraid you're just going to have to be disappointed then, Master Cole. Keeping the stock is in my family's best interests. Now if that's all . . ."

Daniel Cole smiled at her with a cold, wicked smile that nearly took her breath away. "You weren't listening, my dear. I care nothing for your family's interests. I'll have those shares."

"You are correct in one thing," Priscilla said. "I *am* stubborn. And as long as I have anything to say about it, you'll not buy the shares."

Cole laughed. It was a long laugh, a cruel laugh. "That's the beauty of it!" he cried. "I never said anything about buying them!"

Priscilla wore a puzzled expression.

"The stocks will be mine," he said, "when I marry your mother!"

Priscilla was too dumbfounded to speak.

"Don't you see how wonderful this works out for me?" Cole gloated. "I get the stocks by marriage, don't have to pay anything for them, and as a bonus I get the woman who should have been mine years ago!"

"Mother won't marry you when I tell her about this conversation!"

"She won't believe you. She's a very lonely woman. And she's convinced I love her."

Priscilla felt her face growing flushed and hot. Her breathing was becoming labored. "You would marry her just to get our shares?"

Cole was cool, almost cold—totally devoid of feeling. He was playing a game and Priscilla and her family were merely pieces. "I told you. I decide what I want and I get it—no matter the cost."

Her mind raced for alternatives. Cole was right about one thing—her mother probably wouldn't believe her if she reported this conversation. She wouldn't believe that Cole would bargain with human lives just to pick up some shares of stock. Priscilla wouldn't have believed it before now herself. Then she had an idea.

"All right, Master Cole, you win. I'll sell you our family's shares if you promise to leave my mother alone."

"Priscilla, my dear, you have a sharp mind for a woman. Unfortunately, your offer comes too late. Why should I pay for something when I can get it for nothing? Besides, along with the stocks I now also get someone to warm my bed on cold winter nights."

Priscilla could no longer control herself. "You unfeeling, lecherous. . . ."

"Ah, there she is!" Daniel Cole beamed, his arms outstretched toward Constance who had just entered the room.

In horror, Priscilla watched as her mother allowed Cole to kiss her on the cheek. Both of them were all smiles. She bolted from the room, flew down the hillside stairs, and flung herself into the back seat of the carriage.

While Daniel Cole and Constance Morgan leisurely took their leave of each other, Priscilla fumed in the carriage, frantically searching for a way to stop the merchant from getting his way.

Constance Morgan was aglow the entire ride back to Cambridge. If she wasn't staring absently at the passing scenery, she was telling Priscilla what a wonderful time she had and what a wonderful man Master Cole was. Priscilla wanted to scream, to shake her mother, to reveal everything Cole had said to her. But she knew in her mother's present state of mind it would do no good. Better to wait a few days. Let the aura of the trip fade. Then, at the right time, she would tell her mother everything that had happened. Somehow she would have to make her mother understand.

While Priscilla agonized over a way to open her mother's eyes to the present danger, she began to conclude that the problem with her mother was a symptom of a much greater problem. People were forsaking God for personal desires. They were religiously active, but spiritually insensitive. The more Priscilla thought about this, the more she was convinced she was right. The church was still authoritative in the lives of the people, but the men of the church were more concerned with the seating arrangement, and building a new meeting house, and acquiring a personal fortune, than they were about promoting spiritual things. They maintained the form of their faith, but lacked the conviction. Wasn't that in the Bible someplace? Where had she read that?

When the Morgan carriage reached its destination, Priscilla ran into the study to get a Bible. She wanted to confirm her thoughts with Scripture. After several abortive attempts, she found what she was looking for—2 Timothy 3:1-5:

This know also, that in the last days perilous times shall come. For men shall be lovers of their own selves, covetous, boasters, proud, blasphemers, disobedient to parents, unthankful, unholy, without natural affection, trucebreakers, false accusers, inconti-

nent, fierce, despisers of those that are good, traitors, heady, highminded, lovers of pleasures more than lovers of God; having a form of godliness, but denying the power thereof: from such turn away.

"Having the form of godliness, but denying the power." She said it aloud several times over. In her mind she reviewed the Sabbath procedure. It was the same every week. All work ceased on Saturday afternoon. The reason? To prepare for the Sabbath. It was supposed to be a time of Bible reading and family devotion, but in reality most families used it as a time of leisure. Come Sunday morning, when the bell sounded for services, fewer and fewer families were following the minister and his wife up the hill to the meetinghouse. Those that went did so woodenly. There was no sense of anxious anticipation, of preparing for a spiritual encounter with God. They were fulfilling an obligation, participating in a public spectacle that announced they were good people.

Inside the meetinghouse there was more passion over the annual seating arrangement than there was over the proclamation of God. Hardly had there been a more passionate oration in the church than when the committee failed to promote Mrs. Alexander and her husband to the second pew from the front following his election as a magistrate. The remembered event validated Priscilla's theory: people were more passionate over self-advancement than they were the advancement of the Gospel.

Master Hale could pray for over an hour, and did so regularly, but he didn't have five minutes to spend with his daughter. And when he finally finished, the thundering crash of pew seats being lowered into place indicated that the people were more grateful that they could sit down than they were that God heard their prayers. And Reverend Russell knew how to begin a sermon, but couldn't find a way to end one. Several times the hourglass had turned three times before he finished, when in reality he'd run out of things to say before the glass had turned once.

What was the result of all of this? What change did it make in people's lives? How could godly people follow this routine every week and still be blind to the wickedness of men like Daniel Cole?

Like Israel of old, the American colony needed a spiritual leader. They needed a Deborah. But where to begin? Priscilla smiled as the answer came to her. She would begin in her own pew and work outward.

Priscilla Morgan grabbed a piece of paper and a quill. She wrote invitations to each of the ladies who shared her pew. Invitations to a weekly Bible study. Those attending would be called "Deborah's Daughters."

"I don't think my father would like it if he knew what we were doing." The spokesperson was Tabitha Hale. Her admission was shared by others in the room, as indicated by nodding heads.

"We're not doing anything wrong!" Priscilla insisted.

She looked around at those in attendance at the first meeting of Deborah's Daughters. Seated next to her was Anne Pierpont, the poet who had eyes for Priscilla's brother Jared. Like Priscilla, Anne did not share Tabitha's fear. Also at the meeting was Penelope Chauncy, Philip's former fiancée. Priscilla had just gotten to know her since the crisis of Philip's disappearance. She had invited Penelope to join her and the other ladies in the woman's pew and Penelope had done so ever since. Next to her was Emma Alexander, the extremely shy daughter of the town conveyancer who drew up documents transferring property from one person to another. Next to Emma was Tabitha. And lastly, next to Tabitha was Ruth Cooper, daughter of a prominent shoe merchant with shops in Boston, Roxbury, and Cambridge.

"Our purpose is to pray for the spiritual revival of our colony," Priscilla said. "What's wrong with that?"

"Isn't that a job for men?" Penelope asked.

"It's the job of every Christian," Priscilla answered, "regardless of gender."

The looks on the faces of the other ladies told Priscilla her argument was falling on skeptical ears.

"The way I see it," Priscilla said, "when God raises a concern in a person's mind, it's God's way of saying to that person that he or she should do something about it. In the same way, if God gives someone a gift, that person should use it to the glory of God."

"A gift?" Penelope asked.

"A spiritual gift or talent," Priscilla explained. "For example, most of you know that God has gifted Anne with the ability to write poetry. Why would God give her that ability to write poetry if He didn't want her to use it?"

No one raised any objections to this line of argument, so Priscilla continued.

"The Bible says that God has given every one of us gifts. I just thought it might be helpful if we met together to encourage and support one another in using our gifts. Then, maybe our example will inspire others to join us. Our purpose in all this is that we might be a testimony to others that spiritual things are important."

"I don't think I have any gift," Emma said.

"We'll find it together," Priscilla replied.

"Then we're not doing anything wrong?" asked Tabitha.

"Not unless prayer and encouragement are wrong," said Priscilla.

Deborah's Daughters met faithfully every week. For the first two months everyone was content to let Priscilla do all the talking. She read Scripture to them, encouraged them to discover God's gift, and prayed for them individually. After two months of meetings, Priscilla asked Anne to read some of her poetry to the group.

"Poppa says writing is a man's work," Tabitha said. "Women don't need to waste their time learning to read and write."

Anne smiled. "My father thinks that way too," she said. "He doesn't like me writing poetry. Says it'll scare off prospective husbands."

"And you still write, knowing your Poppa doesn't want you to?" The very thought was incredulous to Emma.

"I tried to stop," said Anne. "But the words keep coming. I believe they come from God. How can I not write them down?"

Shocked faces stared back at her.

"It really bothered me, until I found out I wasn't alone. My favorite poet felt the same way."

"Who's your favorite poet?" Ruth asked.

"Anne Bradstreet."

The blank look from the girls seemed to shock Anne. "You've never heard of Anne Bradstreet?" she asked.

Several shook their heads.

"She's one of us," Anne explained. "A colonist. She came to America in 1630 with her family. They settled right here in Cambridge, only then it was called Newetown. She was a wife, a mother of eight children, and a gifted poet, though she was always made to feel defensive about her poetry. Not everyone appreciated a woman poet. This is what she wrote in the heat of frustration." Anne produced a piece of paper and began to read:

I am obnoxious to each carping tongue
Who says my hand a needle better fits,
A poet's pen all scorn I should thus wrong,
For such despite they cast on female wits:

If what I do prove well, it won't advance;
They'll say it's stol'n, or else it was by chance.

Anne Pierpont folded the piece of paper reverently. "Her poetry dramatizes the very problem we face now: how to live in the world without becoming worldly. In 1650 a volume of her poems was published in London and I, for one, am glad that she chose not to be intimidated into being silent."

The poetry of Anne Bradstreet was just what the ladies needed. Beginning with that meeting, there was a spark of excitement each time they met as one by one they discovered their special gifts and talents. About that time, Priscilla told them how her father allowed her to study his textbooks and how she secretly learned several foreign languages. As the days progressed, they grew stronger and bolder in their faith. Priscilla couldn't have been more pleased with their progress.

They soon learned that Penelope was not only a wonderful hostess, but that she had an unusual ability to sense people's feelings, especially when they were troubled. She became the group's comforter. Ruth exhibited exceptional needlework skills. At first she felt disappointment that she had a gift associated with housewives, until Priscilla read to her from Acts 9 which described the sewing ministry of Dorcas. With the help of her friends, Ruth began to use her gifts to provide clothing for the poor. Tabitha Hale discovered she had an exceptional mind. She'd never learned to read, but knew hundreds of Scripture passages just from hearing them read, sometimes only once. Encouraged by her friends, she stayed after the others left and Priscilla began teaching her to read. Emma Alexander was the real surprise. Rarely had anyone heard more than two or three words from her at a time, and then they were spoken softly and toward the ground. To everyone's amazement, Emma Alexander was a gifted vocalist. She loved to sing and knew almost every song in *The Bay*

Psalm-Book. She was the last one to shed her inhibitions with the group. When she finally did, her singing became a required feature of every meeting. Following the Bible study and prayer time, Emma would sing a song appropriate to the Scripture lesson. The message of the psalmists never had a truer interpreter than when it was borne on the lyrical wings of Emma's voice. More than once the ladies were so moved, the meeting closed in tears.

BAM! BAM! BAM!

The sound coming from the front door was not the gentle knock of an afternoon guest; it was the insistent pounding of an angry fist.

Priscilla emerged from the study at the same time Constance came from the sitting room. They looked at one another quizzically.

BAM! BAM! BAM!

Priscilla opened the door. Constance stood behind her.

Three gentlemen, all in black, stood stiffly on the porch. Priscilla instantly recognized them—Reverend Horace Russell, the pastor of the church; Edward Chauncy, Penelope's father and member of Harvard's Board of Overseers; and Andrew Hale, Tabitha's father and deacon of the church.

They were invited into the house, declined refreshments, and got right down to business. Priscilla Morgan was charged with encouraging erroneous opinions, conducting unauthorized meetings, and insulting the leadership of the church. She was summoned to appear before the church to answer these charges.

Chapter 10

I LOVE you," Jared whispered.

He spoke the words into the mouthpiece of a courting stick and awaited Anne's reaction at the other end of the tube. The courting stick was a device that had been developed precisely for the situation in which Jared and Anne found themselves. It was a hollow stick about an inch in diameter and six feet long. Fitted with ear- and mouthpieces, it allowed a courting couple to whisper endearments back and forth to one another in the presence of the entire family.

The young couple sat on opposite ends of a settle, a long wooden bench with arms and a high back, the seat of which also served as a lid for a storage chest. The courting stick stretched across the distance between them. Anne's mother sat in a rocker on one side of the great fireplace intently sewing. Her father was on the opposite side of the fireplace intently snoring; a copy of *The Boston News Letter* rose up and down as it lay across his stomach. The remainder of the room bustled with the activity of an anthill as Anne Pierpont's eleven brothers and sisters occupied themselves in a variety of distractions. Some played with wooden toys; some read quietly; some read aloud; little William sat in the middle of the room holding a psalm book upside down singing as loud as he could while Mary and Margaret hushed their rag doll babies to sleep behind him.

There were fourteen Pierpont children in all, Anne being the oldest girl and fourth oldest child. Charles and Benjamin, her older brothers, had families of their own now. Those still at home ranged in ages from sixteen (George, her remaining older brother) to six months (Sarah, who slept peacefully in a cradle beside her mother, oblivious to the din in the room).

A puzzled expression formed on Anne's face in response to Jared's attempt to express his love. "What?" she mouthed the words without the use of the stick. Pointing to the earpiece she said, "I couldn't hear you!"

Jared signaled her to lift the earpiece to the side of her head. He looked around him. A four-year-old girl — Maggie he thought — stared at them, more interested in the stick than anything else. Jared ignored her and sent his message again, this time a little louder. Anne's downcast eyes and sweet smile indicated she received the message.

At fifteen years old, Anne Pierpont was all at the same time a little girl and a woman. She was old enough to wed and have children of her own; yet place a rag doll in her arms and she still had the innocence of a little girl. Her complexion was fair and smooth. Her light-gray eyes and slightly wide nose were framed with dark-red hair that swept across her forehead and fell loosely over her shoulders. At the moment her cheeks were flushed as she glanced coyly at Jared out of the corners of her eyes.

Jared pointed to the mouthpiece at her end of the courting stick. He wanted her to reply to his pronouncement of love. Anne lifted the hollow tube to her lips and said, "I know."

"You know?"

"I know you love me."

"You're supposed to tell me you love me too!" Jared protested.

She shook her head no. She was teasing him.

Jared pointed again to her end of the stick. "Tell me!" he insisted.

Anne lifted the mouthpiece and spoke into it. "Why should I tell you something you already know?"

Jared grinned. "I like to hear you say it."

"Anne!" her mother called out across the room. "Take Sarah to bed for me, please." Her mother nodded toward the tiny human figure curled up in a ball in the cradle.

"Yes, Momma," Anne said. She scooped up the sleeping child and carried her out of the room.

Jared looked at Anne's mother who was staring at him. They exchanged smiles and Mrs. Pierpont returned to her sewing. Jared glanced from one active child to another as he waited for his favorite Pierpont to return.

Moments later Anne expertly navigated her way around the hazards on the floor and returned to her seat. Jared indicated for her to pick up her end of the courting stick.

"Do you think we'll ever be alone?" he asked.

Anne shrugged sheepishly.

"Maybe you could talk to your mother about us bundling."

"Jared!" Anne reacted loud enough to get her mother's attention. Mrs. Pierpont looked at them suspiciously, chuckled, shook her head, and returned to her sewing.

"Why did you do that?" Jared said. "I didn't say anything wrong!"

It wasn't unusual for New England courting couples to spend the night together in bed as long as they remained fully clothed. Sometimes a "bundling board" was placed between them; at other times in addition to their clothing the couples were individually wrapped in sheets. Bundling was done with parental approval under the supervision of the mother and sisters. It offered the couple privacy and warmth. Parents and youth shared the expectation that sexual intercourse would not take place, but if it did and pregnancy resulted, the couple would certainly marry.

"Chuckers and Millie bundled last night!" Jared said.

"They didn't!"

"Yes they did!"

Anne's faced reddened as she envisioned the possibilities.

"Ask your mother!" Jared insisted.

"We couldn't do it here!" Anne said.

"Why not?"

Anne's eyes grew wide. "I sleep with three sisters!" She held up three fingers to emphasize the number.

"So?"

"Jared!"

They both laughed. It was the most intimate conversation they'd ever had. A milestone for their relationship. An unspoken commitment that they would some day be man and wife.

"Will you ask her?"

Anne lowered her eyes in thought. Then she said, "I'll think about it."

A duel cry intruded on their intimacy as two Pierpont children fought over a wooden toy horse.

"I've got to go," Jared said. He jumped to his feet.

"It's still early!" Anne protested. Her lower lip protruded in a slight pout. It was a playful pout. She'd used it before. Jared loved it.

As Jared was leaving, Thomas Pierpont awoke and the newspaper that was balanced on his belly fell to the floor. He walked Jared to the door, made inquiries into Jared's plans for the future, and seemed disappointed that the boy had none.

"I could use an apprentice at the bakery," he said, slapping Jared on the back. "You're young and strong. It's good, honest work. People will always have to eat. You could do worse."

"Thank you for the offer, Master Pierpont. I'll give it some thought."

Both of them knew it was a polite response. Jared had no

intention of becoming a baker. He was young and reckless and wanted more of a challenge than kneading dough afforded.

After Jared was gone, Anne dutifully helped her mother get the younger children ready for bed. When the last one was tucked in, she changed into her bedclothes and sat by the window in her upstairs bedroom, brushing her hair while the wiggling bodies under the covers of her bed finally succumbed to the stillness of sleep.

She thought of Jared. And of bundling. She wanted to be alone with him, but the thought intimidated her. As for asking her parents . . . she couldn't begin to predict their response. It had never been discussed in her hearing before. It was a common practice. She was sure she and Jared would never do anything her parents would be ashamed of. Still, she didn't know if she could bring herself to ask her mother.

Anne giggled girlishly as she thought of laying side by side in bed with Jared Morgan. She opened the window a crack to let some fresh air in. The last of the winter snow had melted weeks ago and the nights were growing warmer.

The cool air from outside refreshed her as the bristles of the brush brought a shine to her long, full hair. Anne began humming a tune from the church hymnal. Emma Alexander was the one who first showed it to her. Shy, introverted Emma. The lyrics were inspired by the Song of Solomon. At first Anne was shocked at some of the descriptive phrases. But then she reasoned there was nothing wrong with it. It was a love song. A beautiful one. And it was in *The Bay Psalm-Book.* Would the ministers of the church allow a song that was unholy to be sung in church? Most assuredly not! Besides, the poet in her loved the imagery and rhythm of the song. And it made her think of Jared. It put to words her love for him.

Softly, as Anne stroked her hair, she sang the hymn:

Let him with kisses of his mouth
　　be pleased me to kiss,
Because much better than the wine
　　thy loving-kindness is.
To troops of horse in Pharaoh's coach,
　　my love, I thee compare,
Thy neck with chains, with jewels new,
　　thy cheeks full comely are.
Borders of gold with silver studs
　　for thee make up we will,
Whilst that the king at's table sits
　　my spikenard yields her smell.

Like as of myrrh a bundle is
　　my well-belov'd to be,
Through all the night betwixt my breasts
　　his lodging-place shall be;
My love as in Engedi's vines
　　like camphire-bunch to me,
So fair, my love, how fair thou art
　　thine eyes as doves eyes be.

A clapping sound outside her window startled her.

Her brush clattered to the floor as she jumped from her seat and pulled her bedclothes tightly around her neck. She peered outside the window to see what was making the sound.

On the other side of the half-open shutters, just a matter of feet from her was the grinning face of Jared Morgan. He was laying full-length on a sturdy tree limb, perfectly balanced, freeing his hands to clap.

"Jared Morgan!" she whispered while opening the shutters, "you scared me half to death! What are you doing out there?"

"Being romantic!" he replied. "It was you who gave me the

idea." When it was clear Anne wasn't following him, he added: "Remember? A couple of months ago. You read to me from that poet fellow you like so much. The story about the boy and girl who kill themselves."

"You mean Romeo and Juliet!"

"That's it! Don't you remember now? Romeo sneaked up on Juliet at night while she was in her bed chamber. You said it was romantic. So I figured if you thought it was romantic, I'd do it for you!"

"But that was months ago!"

"Well, pardon me, Juliet, but this is the first time it's been warm enough to climb a tree at night!"

"I'm sorry. I didn't mean to belittle your romantic gesture. I think it's sweet."

"Really?"

"Yes, really."

"Your hair sure is pretty at night."

Anne ran her fingers through her hair like a comb. "I just brushed it."

"I know."

"Oh, really? And how long have you been watching me?"

"Long enough to hear you sing that song."

Anne blushed, more at the song's imagery than in getting caught singing.

"I didn't mean to embarrass you," Jared added quickly. "I really liked the song. And it was just that, well, I was here and you were singing and there wasn't much I could do about it."

"I'm glad you heard it," Anne said.

There was a moment of silence between them.

"This is nice," Jared said. "It's quiet and we're alone."

Anne nodded. "It *is* nice," she agreed.

"Well," Jared began pushing himself up into a standing position on the limb, "I guess that's enough romance for the night."

"Jared Morgan!" The pouting lower lip appeared.

"I'm just joking!" He grinned his boyish grin. "I like being alone with you. I wish we could do it more often."

"All right! I'll ask my mother about bundling!" Anne said.

"You will?" Jared fell back down onto the limb, prompting a frightened squeal from Anne. He inched his way closer to the window. "Really? You'll ask your mother?"

Anne opened the window wider and sat on the sill. Jared scooted as far out on the limb as he dare.

"Yes, I promise to ask mother," said Anne.

"Tell me tomorrow what she says?"

Anne lowered her head and nodded.

"Oh wait! Not tomorrow. I'm going to Boston tomorrow," Jared remembered aloud.

"Oh?"

"Yes, I meant to tell you earlier and forgot. My mother arranged for me to meet with Master Cole. She said he wants to talk to me about something."

"What?"

Jared shrugged his shoulders. "I don't know. But Mother thought it was pretty important, so I told her I'd go. So you'll just have to tell me about the bundling in two days."

"I'll miss you. Will you be gone all day?"

"Probably. I'll come back as soon as I can."

Ever so slowly the two of them leaned closer to each other. It wasn't something either of them had planned; it was just happening like an invisible force drawing them together.

"I love you, Jared."

"I know," he said with a smile.

"Aren't you going to tell me you love me?"

"Why should I tell you something you already know?" he teased.

Now they were inches from each other. Jared had gone as far as he dare on the limb. Even now the slightest movement caused the limb to bounce. Still, he leaned a little farther. He could feel the warmth of her skin, her breath. He leaned just a bit more. Their lips brushed with the movement of the tree limb.

"I love you, Anne," he said. "Never forget that."

"I never will," she whispered as their lips touched again.

Early afternoon the next day Jared found himself sitting opposite a scarred wooden desk in a warehouse near Clark's wharf on Boston Bay. On the opposite side of the desk sat Daniel Cole, puffing on a cigar and signing papers. Jared had found the warehouse easily enough and arrived on time for his meeting with the merchant. And although Jared had been there for nearly half an hour, at best the two of them had talked maybe five minutes. As soon as Cole would begin to say something, someone would interrupt and Cole would sign some papers, or bark orders, or ask a series of questions then make a decision. Jared still didn't know why he was here.

When Priscilla heard that Cole wanted Jared to come to Boston, she informed her brother of everything that had happened between her and the merchant during her previous Boston visit. She told Jared not to agree to sell any shares unless Cole agreed to leave their mother alone. And above all, Priscilla threatened Jared lest he speak any of this to their mother.

Jared was taken back by his sister's story and the intensity of her feelings when telling it. He was also taken back by the fact that she was telling him anything at all. Up until now, Priscilla had as little to do with him as possible. To say they weren't very close would be an understatement.

Jared decided he would form his own conclusions. He would wait to see what Cole was after and then act accordingly.

"Well, son." Cole slapped the quill he'd been signing papers with to the table. "That's done. Hopefully we won't have any more interruptions like that one."

Jared straightened himself in his chair.

"Do you know why I've asked you here?" Cole asked. He interlaced his fingers, resting them on his paunch. His chin showed several folds as it rested on his chest.

"No, sir. I don't." Jared said.

"Your mother or sister said nothing to you?"

"Mother said you wanted to talk with me about something special. She didn't get any more specific than that, although she seemed quite excited about us meeting. As for my sister. . . ." Jared searched for the words to describe her advice to him. He didn't want to say too much or too little. "Well, she told me about your meeting with her and warned me to be careful."

"She was disturbed by her visit to my house?" Cole sat up, a surprised look on his face.

"Um, well . . . yes. She was disturbed by the meeting."

Daniel Cole shook his head in bewildered fashion. "Frankly, I'm shocked," he said. "I thought our meeting was very pleasant and cordial. I did confess my love for your mother to her. That was probably unwise of me this soon after your father's death. I wouldn't have said anything if I'd known it would disturb her. I was simply trying to assure her that when it came to your mother, I have only the best of intentions. I'm sorry she misunderstood me. Did she mention anything else?"

"Priscilla said something about stocks."

Cole waved his cigar in the air, dismissing the topic entirely. "I'm not interested in your family's stocks. I tried to explain that to her. When I was out at your house, I did offer to buy them from Philip if your family needed the money, but that was all. I was only thinking of your family's welfare.

But these matters can get complicated and women have a difficult time understanding them. And Priscilla can get excited at times." The merchant let out a huge guffaw. "Ha! But I don't have to tell you about your sister, do I? You know far better than me how unreasonable she can be! Once she gets something in that head of hers, a team of horses couldn't break it loose!"

Several deep puffs on the cigar clouded the area with suffocating smoke.

"Heard anything new about your brother?" Cole asked. Jared shook his head no.

"Pity. Such a promising lad." Cole slapped the table. "As are you!" he said. "Which brings me to the reason why I asked you here." Cole puffed a few more puffs before getting down to business. "Jared, we're a lot alike. I think I understand you. I know your father wanted you to attend Harvard College—your mother has told me a lot about you—but you don't have an interest in book learning. In that way we're alike. I hated school. Never went to college. Life was too short to spend it reading something some dead man wrote centuries earlier that has nothing to do with life today." Daniel Cole raised his arms over his head motioning to the warehouse. "This has been my school. And it's been a good one too. It taught me that if I worked hard I could have anything I wanted out of life. I learned my lesson and graduated from this school and now, just as promised, there isn't anything I can't have. There isn't a house in Boston I couldn't buy. There isn't a business in Boston I couldn't own. If I took a fancy to sail to China, I could go tomorrow! There's nothing I can't do!"

Jared hung on every word, yet still he wondered what this had to do with him.

"As a favor to your mother," Cole said, "I want to offer you a chance to enroll in the same school that made me rich.

You see, part of my job is to hire bright young men like you. I don't want any of that Harvard crowd here. No sir. Give me someone with a sharp mind and strong back. Son, I'm prepared to offer you a position in my warehouse. It comes with a handsome salary, more than any of those Harvard professors make. If you enroll in my school, I'll teach you how to become a merchant and in ten years—ten years, guaranteed—you will have enough money to be able to do anything you want with your life."

Cole stood to his feet. Jared stood with him.

"I'd like you to meet someone," Cole said. The merchant stepped around some boxes, hollered to a man named Frank, and told him to get Magee. A few moments later, Jared shook hands with a good-looking young man, about his age, named James Magee.

"James is one of my apprentices," Cole said. "I gave him the same offer a month ago. He took me up on it." Turning to Magee, he said, "Any regrets?"

"No sir," Magee answered.

"Why don't you show Jared Morgan around the warehouse, describe your duties, and bring him back to me in about a half hour?"

"With pleasure," the apprentice said.

Jared was impressed, not only with the offer but with James Magee. The two of them took an immediate liking to each other. In fact, they looked so much alike, they could be mistaken for brothers. Both were of good height, slightly taller than the average man, solidly built without being stocky, and sported a thick head of unruly hair, although this is where they differed most. While Jared's hair was light brown with blond highlights, James Magee's was black as a bat. Within the hour Jared had seen the warehouse and had agreed to work for Daniel Cole. The merchant was ecstatic over Jared's acceptance of the position. He told Magee to take the rest of the day off and take Jared to a nearby tavern where they could celebrate the transaction. Although Cole would not be joining them, he volunteered to pick up the tab.

The Good Woman Tavern was alive with shouts and raucous male laughter when James Magee and Jared Morgan arrived. Magee spoke to the tavernkeeper, a man by the name of Gibbs, and arranged for their drinks to be charged to Daniel Cole. The tavernkeeper nodded in understanding. His readiness to grant Cole credit impressed both Magee and Jared.

Magee turned from the counter and yelled across the room to Jared who had spotted an empty table. "Morgan! What'll you have?"

"Ale, I guess," Jared shouted back. Although the colonists were a beer-drinking and ale-drinking race, Jared had never acquired much of a taste for it. He preferred sweet drinks like chocolate and his mother's molasses and ginger beverage. But considering where he was, he thought it safest to order the standard drink.

While Jared waited for Magee, he casually looked around the tap room and listened in on some of the louder conversations. There were several small parties—two, three, or four persons; mostly adults, some children—scattered around the room. They were dressed in traveling clothes. Most had a fresh layer of road dust on them. The bulk of the patrons, and certainly the loudest among them, were sailors. From their conversations Jared learned they were crew members of the merchant ship, *The Golden Princess*, recently returned from Barbados. They'd been at sea for three months.

Jared was lost in the glamour of world travel when Magee arrived with two tankards of ale.

"It's one of our ships," Magee explained. He meant *The Golden Princess* belonged to Daniel Cole's merchant empire of which they were employees. "Just got in from Barbados this morning. We unloaded cask after cask of rum. There's big money in the triangular trade."

"Triangular trade?"

Magee nodded as he sipped his ale. A rim of foam lined his upper lip as he explained. "Cole imports sugar, molasses, rum, and cotton from Barbados, and dry goods and hardware from England. Then he sells them wholesale to shopkeepers in the colonies."

"I thought Master Cole made his fortune from importing pewter," Jared said.

"That's how he began. Then his operation got bigger and bigger until now he's one of the richest men in Boston. That's why I signed on with him."

"Because he's rich?"

"Mostly because he has one of the largest merchant lines going. He has ships going to London, Glasgow, Bristol, Liverpool, the West Indies, and even India! And there's talk on the wharf that Cole's considering starting a run to China!"

Jared liked James Magee. There was a light in his eye and a yearning in his voice as he spoke of these faraway places. Jared hadn't met too many young men his age who shared his hunger for world travel. Most of the families his parents associated with were attached to Harvard College in one way or another. For them the college was the center of the universe. All aspirations, hopes, and dreams centered around it. Nothing else seemed to matter. But never once did James Magee mention Harvard, or school, or book learning of any kind. The thoughts that stirred Magee's blood were identical to the thoughts that excited Jared.

"You know," Magee said, hurriedly gulping down a swallow of ale so he could get out what he wanted to say, "if we do well on the wharf, show ourselves to be hard workers and learn the warehouse business, Cole could transfer us to Barbados for a year or two."

"Really?"

Magee grinned widely and nodded his head. "The guy who trained me was sent there two weeks ago. He said he'd recommend me to Cole first chance he got."

"If you get sent there, will you recommend me?"

Magee burst out laughing. "That's some request for someone who hasn't worked on the wharf a single day!"

Magee was right. Jared was embarrassed. He felt like a dumb kid, caught in a moment of boyish immaturity.

"Don't let it bother you." Magee shrugged off Jared's naive request. "I like you, Morgan. You and me are gonna be good friends."

"Did I hear you gents say ye was workin' for Master Cole?" A weathered, unshaved face poked its way between Magee and Jared; it swiveled on a wrinkled, brown, leathery neck, glancing from one boy to the other.

"We do, sir," Magee responded coldly, "if that's any of your business."

"Lower your defenses, lad! 'Tis a friendly visit I intend to pay ye. Me name's Zeke and I was one what just returned from Barbados! We work for the same man, you and me!"

"So we do," Magee responded. "Welcome home. Now if you'll excuse me and my friend here."

"A point of order I would have with ye." The uninvited guest rested both elbows on the table. " 'Twas a dangerous voyage we took. Yessir, downright stormy, waves twice the size of the mainmast, winds that ripped our best sheets to shreds. Three men didn't make it home. They sleep with the clams now." A couple at a time, other sailors in the tavern began to gravitate toward Jared and Magee's table.

"I'm sorry about your shipmates," Magee said. "Now if you'll excuse. . . ."

"And I asked myself, 'For what did they die? Indeed, sir, for what?' Well, I'll tell you lads. For this!" The grizzled sailor reached behind him and grabbed a drink. He slapped it down none too gently, spilling almost half of its contents on the table. "Rum!" he bellowed. "Poseidon's nectar. The drink of sailors the world over!"

By now, Jared and Magee were completely encircled by sailors, listening to their spokesman with amusement.

Magee began to speak, but the orating sailor was waiting for him and cut him off before a single word was uttered.

"Now it seems to me, considerin' all the sufferin' and pain it took for us to deliver this rum to Boston, the least our fellow employees could do would be to drink it in honor of those what brung it here."

"Here, here!" the company of sailors cheered.

"We already have drinks," Magee said.

"Those aren't drinks, lad. That stuff's weaker than your mother's milk. Why me own mother weaned me from herself with ale and I cried 'cause her milk had more kick to it!"

The bystanding sailors laughed and guffawed.

Magee looked all around him, then at Jared. "Gentlemen!" he cried loud enough for all to hear. "I want to thank you for pointing out our bad manners. And in the spirit of our adventurous company, my good friend and I would like to toast your crew members who went to their graves!"

Cheers erupted all around them.

Two mugs of rum were produced and Jared followed Magee's lead in standing for the toast. The only hard liquor Jared had to this point in his life was some hard apple cider Chuckers had stolen from his uncle's shed. He remembered the liquor stinging his throat and clouding his head so that it felt like it was floating.

"Just before you make your toast," the orating sailor broke in, "let me inform ye of one other bit of sailor etiquette lest ye unintentionally offend us again."

"And what might that be?" Magee asked.

"When sailors drink to somethin' or someone, they don't do it in a genteel way with tiny sips. I ask ye, what kind of tribute is a sip to a sailor?"

A chorus of cuss words was the general response from his shipmates.

"When we drink to a mate, we always empties the glass. Once for each mate we drink to!"

"How many did you say died?" Jared asked.

"Three, me lad."

Jared looked up at Magee. He was smiling confidently, not intimidated in the least by the sailors or their drink preference.

Magee raised his mug. "Gentlemen!" he cried. "A toast! To . . ." He turned to the orator. "What were the sailors' names?" The orator didn't seem to remember their names. Neither did any of the other sailors in the room. A fact which made Magee's grin grow even wider. He began again, "Gentlemen! A toast! To our dear friend sailor number one! May he rest forever in Poseidon's arms, may all his sailing be free from storms, and may the fortune of Atlantis be forever his!"

A chorus of cheers followed along with a sea of upturned mugs. Jared looked at Magee. His mug was emptying as fast as all the others. Jared closed his eyes, took a deep breath, and gulped the brown liquid as fast as he could. After two gulps it felt like he was drinking fire, but he continued. After four gulps his stomach threatened to send the liquid back from whence it came; still he gulped. Jared gulped until he hit air. With a gasp he collapsed into his chair, the mug slamming to the table at the end of his limp arm.

All around him sailors pounded his back in congratulations.

"Gentlemen!" Magee cried out in strong voice, the rum not seeming to have the same effect on him that it had on Jared. "I propose a second toast!"

James Magee toasted the nameless dead sailors numbers

two and three. Jared joined in. The second mug was just as nasty as the first. But by the time the third mug was lifted, Jared's head and throat were numb. He imagined he knew what it must feel like to sail because it seemed as if the ocean was sloshing back and forth in his head. The sailors, satisfied with the three toasts to their friends, had returned to their tables and Jared and Magee were once again left alone.

Jared didn't know if he was imagining things but the third mug had tasted different from the first two. It left a rancid taste in his mouth. At first that's all it was, an annoying taste that wouldn't go away; then the rancid taste was accompanied by sharp stomach cramps. Jared doubled over. He was really beginning to hurt. Lifting his head, he looked across that table at his new friend. Magee looked as bad as Jared felt.

"I don't feel so good," Jared groaned.

"Let's get outta here," Magee replied.

Jared pushed himself away from the table and tried to stand. His legs didn't want to cooperate. They buckled beneath him. His arms slapped the table as he caught himself; his cheek rested against the tabletop.

"Need a hand, lad?" It was the sailor orator. "Looks like we shoulda left you alone with your mother's milk. Well, what kind of friends would we be if we didn't help ye home?"

His head swimming in a nauseous sea, Jared felt himself being lifted to his feet. It took a great deal of effort, but he managed to shuffle one foot in front of the other. "Magee," he said weakly. "My friend, Magee . . ."

"We're helpin' your friend too," said the orator sailor. "We'll take you the back way. Wouldn't want ye gettin' caught in this condition. 'Twould be a pity if ye wound up in the stocks with a red D hangin' from yer neck."

Although the colonists were an ale-drinking people, they wouldn't abide drunkenness. Those caught drunk were subject to fine and imprisonment in the stocks. Habitual drunkards were punished by having a great D made of red cloth hung around their necks or sewn into their clothing.

The cool air of the alley was pungent with rotten trash and waste. It triggered a violent series of retches in Jared. His companions waited until he was finished before they continued. They hadn't gone much farther when he was dropped in a heap in the middle of the alley. Jared felt a cool, wet, and gritty cobblestone against his cheek, and for the time being was content to lie there. He heard voices a short distance away, but was unable to make out what they were saying. Summoning his last remaining strength, he lifted his head. Four sailors stood at a distance, huddled together in casual conversation. Not far from him lay James Magee, unconscious; his face and clothes were soiled by the refuse in the alley.

"Mathers!" a voice came from above and behind him. He couldn't see who it belonged to. One of the four conversing sailors turned toward the voice. "Not this one," the voice said. "This one's off limits." Now the voice was coming from directly overhead. The person speaking was right above him! As much as he tried to see who was speaking, his body finally ran out of energy. His cheek banged against the wet cobblestones.

Jared heard footsteps. Then another voice, presumably Mathers. "What's your interest?" he asked.

"Personal," said the voice.

"You can have any of the others," Mathers said, "except that one. He's special."

"I'll pay you for him. How much will you get for him? I'll match it."

"You couldn't pay me enough," Mathers said. "The guys that want this one are real mean. They don't fool around. I give him to you and I'm dead by sunset."

"Look, just turn your back for a minute and I'll. . . ."

Suddenly the voice stopped mid-sentence. There was an ugly-sounding thump. Jared groaned as the weight of a full-grown man dropped on him. The limp body rolled to one side. Jared forced one eye open and strained to focus his vision. Inches from his nose was another nose. It took several moments, but he eventually recognized it. It was the face of the tavernkeeper.

"What did you do that for?" Mathers yelled.

"He was showing too much interest in my cargo." From the silence, it seemed Mathers chose not to plead the tavernkeeper's case any further. "Is this all you have for me?"

"I'll have more for you tomorrow," said Mathers.

"Fine. As long as you got Morgan. Get the tavernkeeper outta here. Dump him in the field."

Jared felt the limp body being lifted off of him. Then, someone used his foot to turn Jared over so that he was face up. The light of the sky burned his eyes. Everything was unfocused. He could barely make out the forms standing over him. He blinked and the focus sharpened, but only slightly. Just as he lost consciousness, Jared Morgan saw who was standing over him. His mind screamed danger, but no other part of his body was paying attention. A black veil crept over him and soon everything was black. The last thing he remembered thinking was: *A back alley in Boston. What a strange place to see the sailor and the Indian.*

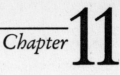

Chapter 11

HIS head rocked, then banged against the wooden wall behind him. Jared winced in pain. A violent movement threw it forward, then back against the wall again. More pain. The pain felt like liquid and his head was the container. Each time the container rocked from one side to the other, the pain sloshed inside. His head rocked forward and slammed back again. He wished his head would fall off and have done with it.

Jared groaned and raised his hands to hold his head in place and keep it from rocking. All the while he was still barely aware of what he was doing. His eyes were closed. As his senses rallied, he braced himself against a new assault, this one coming on waves of foul odors. The stench was thick and suffocating; so strong that he had to fight back the bile that rose from deep within him.

What is this place?

Through the slits of half-opened eyes Jared saw James Magee propped against a curved wooden wall. His whole body was being rocked back and forth; he was making moaning sounds. Next to Magee was another fellow. He was crumpled in a heap on the wooden floor with his face buried. A mop of black hair laying beside a pile of body parts. There wasn't enough of him for Jared to make any attempt at identification. One thing was clear though, he was no better off than Jared or Magee.

"ON DECK! ON DECK!" The shout came from above them. "Move it, gents! Everybody on deck!"

A crack of light in the planks above them split wide open. It was some kind of door. The light that tumbled in illuminated a wooden ladder upon which a pair of legs in baggy breeches descended. "Sleepy time is over, gents!" Jared saw a man about ten years older than himself. His cheeks were hollow and covered with a black stubble of two or three days' growth. Thin black hair was pulled back and tied behind his head. The man's forearms were thick, dark with hair, and strong. He carried a long, curved sailor's cutlass in his right hand. "On deck!" he shouted again. His voice hurt Jared's head. "The mate's waitin' for ye. It's time to evaluate the merchandise."

Jared sent a command to his legs to get up, which they ignored. He groped for something to brace himself against. The wall behind him was wood and curved outward, just like the one behind Magee. Leaning against the wooden wall, Jared managed to maneuver his feet under him and rose uncertainly. Just then the floor dipped to one side and he crashed to the planks in a heap.

The bellowing man in baggy breeches cursed. "What a lot we got this time!" he said sarcastically. "Ah well, we can always use 'em for fish food."

Jared's second attempt to stand was more successful. He looked around. Magee was on his feet. So was the other fellow, a skinny, frightened-looking young man. All of them had to steady themselves against the wall to keep from falling.

"Praise be!" the bellowing man smirked, lifting his face heavenward. "It's a miracle! They can walk! They can walk!" Then, glaring at the three unsteady young men, he said, "Now let's see if ye can climb that ladder yonder."

Jared glanced at Magee and the other fellow. They both had blank looks on their faces. He imagined he looked no different. Magee led the way, Jared followed, and the other fellow fell in behind Jared. Just as Jared raised a foot and aimed it toward the first rung, it moved on him. He fell forward and caught himself just inches from the heel of Magee's boot. He steadied himself again and proceeded slowly up the ladder.

The ladder led into the open. A huge blue sky spanned the heavens like a giant dome. As Jared's line of sight cleared the top of the landing he saw a wooden deck, wooden siding with rope webbing tied to it, and beyond the siding—an endless blue sea!

"Come on, gents, let's move it!" the bellowing sailor yelled from below.

Jared joined James Magee on the deck of the ship and stared in wonder at the sights around him. He was aboard a two-masted ship; not many sails were up at the moment so Jared could clearly see the skeletal structure of mast and booms and rigging. Six to eight sailors could be seen at various points of the ship, all of them staring at the three fellows emerging from the hold. Jared looked past them in all directions. There was nothing but sea all around them. No land in sight!

"Over here, gents." Jared looked in the direction of the voice. He saw a sailor wearing a white shirt with puffed sleeves and traditional baggy breeches tied at the ankles. The man was barefooted. His face was weathered, his hairline red and receding, but what hair he lacked on the top of his head, he made up for with a full, bushy, red beard. In his hand was a coiled whip. He motioned for Jared and his two groggy compatriots to come toward him.

"Allow me to do the pleasantries, gents," the bellowing man said from behind them. "This here's Patrick Tracy, first mate. If you know what's good for you—and I doubt you do, otherwise you wouldn't be here in the first place—you'll do whatever he says."

The bearded first mate approached Magee and stood toe-to-toe with him. Tapping him on the chest with the coiled whip he said, "What's your name, son?" The man's voice had an unmistakable Irish accent to it. From the look in Magee's eye it was evident he was debating whether or not to answer the question. The first mate inched closer. "There's no reason to make this unpleasant," he said. "All I asked you for was your name."

"Magee. James Magee."

The first mate smiled. Calmly, slowly, he said, "Pleased to meet you, James Magee."

The first mate stepped in front of Jared, then the third fellow. Both gave their names readily and Jared learned that the other fellow's name was Benjamin Wier.

The first mate moved back a few steps. "Behind you is bos'n—that's boatswain for you landsmen—Whitmore. Most of the crew call him bos'n Witless, but I suggest you get to know him before you use such familiar terms. Gentlemen—and you'll notice I call you gentlemen, because that is what you are; you have to earn the right to be called seaman or tar on this ship—I want to thank you for volunteering for this duty."

The bearded Irishman grinned exuberantly at them.

"Forgive my sense of humor, gentlemen but I wouldn't think of starting a day without it. You might wonder why you are here. I'll tell you. As of this moment you are crew members aboard the *Dove*, the best pirate ship to sail the Atlantic."

"Pirate?" The word exploded from Ben Wier's mouth.

The red-headed first mate's bushy red eyebrows shot upward as he grinned and nodded. With the coiled whip he motioned for them to look upward. Atop the tallest mast waved a black flag featuring a skull and crossbones, the infamous Jolly Roger.

Jared was stunned.

"Master Morgan," said the first mate. "Didn't your mother ever teach you it was bad manners to leave your mouth hanging open like that?"

Jared's mouth snapped shut. *What was going on here?* A wild thought crossed his mind that he was still drugged and lying in the alley behind the tavern having a weird dream. This was too strange to be real.

"Some of you," the first mate continued, "may feel you have volunteered for duty prematurely, and upon deeper reflection, you would like to reverse that decision. For those of you who feel this way, you are free to disembark now."

Jared, Magee, and Wier looked stupidly all around them at the endless stretch of sea. The Irishman guffawed at their bewildered expressions. "So you all choose to stay aboard! Good! Now that that's settled, let's get down to business."

"Not so fast!" Magee yelled. From the fire in his eyes, it was evident his head was beginning to clear. "Why were we brought here against our will?"

"Against your will?" the first mate said. Then to the bos'n who was still standing behind them with cutlass in hand: "Bos'n Witless, were these men brought on board against their will?"

"No, sir," Whitmore replied. "I didn't hear a single one of them complain when we carried them on board."

"You drugged us!" Magee shouted.

"Drugs? Ah, that would explain it!" cried the first officer. "I thought you were just heavy sleepers! To be truthful, gents, we were running low on new recruits and the three of you were the best looking prospects we saw sprawled in the alley. But if you're looking for someone to blame for your aching heads, you must blame the crimps. They were the ones that drugged you. We merely bought you from them."

"You bought us from crimps?" Jared's tone and posture

matched that of Magee. The question was important to him.

"Would it make a difference, lad? You would be here re-gardless." The first mate wasn't smiling. His shoulders were squared and his right hand gripped the butt of the whip.

"It makes a difference," Jared said. "The men who drugged us killed my father."

The first mate didn't laugh and Magee looked at Jared in surprise. This was new to him.

"I see your concern," said the first mate, rubbing his beard. "To answer your question, lad, no, we didn't drug you. We're pirates, not crimps. If you have a grudge with the crimps, you'll have to take it up with them next time you see them."

"When do we get back to Boston?" It was Wier, his voice high-pitched and nervous. He was scared.

The question prompted the return of the first mate's smile. "Well, that's hard to say. You see, we aren't exactly welcome in most ports," said the first mate. The bos'n chuckled be-hind them. "You see, lad, we're pirates. And the good up-standing people of Boston—and London and Bristol and most other ports—have this nasty habit of hanging pirates. One of the minor inconveniences of this job, I'm afraid."

"That's what caused the recent opening positions among the crew," Whitmore added.

"On the other hand, the benefits aboard ship are numer-ous. There is no finer pirate ship afloat. You see, gents, we are unique. Most pirate ships our size have more than twice the crew. They rely on superior numbers to ply their trade." He shook his head in disdain. "A crude tactic. We, on the other hand, attack ships with even numbers. When we fight, we're fighting one-to-one. So I hope you gents are good with a sword. You are, aren't you?"

"Never fought with one," Magee said.

"Me neither."

"Me neither."

"Pity," said the first mate. "I hope you are fast learners. Now what was I talking about?"

"Our tactics," Whitmore prompted.

"Ah, yes! You see, gents, we survive by being better than other ships. Which isn't hard considering the sad state of the crews on most merchant ships. In actuality, you are fortunate, gents. It could be worse for you. You could have been sold to a merchant vessel." The Irishman made a nasty face and shuddered. "An ugly thought, to be sure. Life's much better on a pirate ship. The pay's better too. On a pirate ship you can have a good time without getting in trouble for it. Of course, we all pull our share of the load. And we all have a healthy fear of the sea's moods. But for the most part, there's no better life than that of a pirate! As for authority, we operate as a democracy—within reason, of course. We even choose our own captain. You'll meet him later. His name's Jack Devereaux. There's no finer man alive. A word of warning, though. You move against him and he'll crush you. But if you fit in with the rest of the crew, he'll treat you like sons. The way I see it, gents, the best thing you can do is to look at today as the first day of a promising new career!"

Jared looked at the other two standing with him. Magee was tense, angry. Wier looked like he was going to cry.

"Now then, any of you have sailing experience?"

All three shook their heads.

"Pity." To the boatswain: "Bos'n Whitless, enroll these men in pirate school."

As much as he tried, Jared Morgan couldn't sustain his hatred for his captors. He didn't want to admit it to Magee and Wier because they still hated the idea of being on board a pirate ship, but if the truth were known, Jared was having the time of his life. It was everything he'd ever dreamed he'd wanted—well, almost everything. His present circumstances had no place for Anne. But for the moment Jared was so excited about being on a sailing ship he temporarily shoved aside several unpleasant realities, among them the fact that Anne didn't know where he was, that he had no idea when he'd see her again, or that if he was caught with these pirates he'd most certainly hang.

Jared's thoughts were of the opportunity before him. The wooden world called *Dove* fascinated him. The ship was a self-contained universe, completely separated from Cambridge and Boston and Harvard—the world that belonged to Philip and Priscilla, never to him. This was a sovereign kingdom afloat on the high seas. His kingdom. One that knew nothing of Philip's exalted academic standing. One that knew nothing of Priscilla's condescending theology and superior intellect. In this world, Jared didn't live in the shadow of Harvard and the memory of his father's constant disappointment in him. Aboard the *Dove* Jared Morgan was a recent emigrant with no past, no history to haunt him. He was determined to learn all he could about his new world.

Like other nations, this floating world had a dialect and vocabulary unique to its history and environment. Learning the language was more than necessary for communication purposes; it was often a matter of life and death. The basis of the language was brevity and lack of ambiguity, the purpose being to eliminate as much unnecessary time between command and action as possible. The crew's precision was impressive. An order would be given, the appropriate men sprang to action, and within moments the ship surged in obedient response to the command.

At first, nothing made sense. As far as Jared was concerned, the crew could be speaking Chinese. But soon Jared was able to associate new terms with their appropriate ship parts. He learned the difference between stem and stern, port and starboard. He was taught to distinguish between backing, reefing, balancing, furling, and loosing the sails. As for the lines, he learned to tell a splice from a hitch from a knot. He had to learn the difference between cat-harpins and nippers, belaying pins and can-hooks. He had to master the terms for rigging, masts, and sails and understand basic maneuvers such as beating against the wind, tacking, and box-hauling.

Not only did he have to learn the vocabulary of the ship, but of the elements as well. There were tradewinds and their patterns, variable breezes, slatches, "cats' paws," gales, and fresh gales. "Fair winds" favored a ship's movement on course, while "foul winds" hindered it. As an apprentice seaman he had to master the terms associated with the oceans and seas, their currents, calms, swells, and breakers. He studied types of storms, squalls, and tempests. He had to be able to identify types of clouds and their formations and to identify heavenly bodies and constellations by which the vessel was steered.

The society onboard ship defined authority from the captain to the common tar. Every sailor was expected to know every aspect of sailing a ship. Each took his turn at the helm as well as his turn keeping lookout or making soundings. He needed to know the difference between standard rigging and running rigging and when each was to be used. On the tedious end of the work scale, every sailor developed strong, nimble fingers working the ropes. He needed superior knowledge in tying and connecting ropes, whether by hitches or knots, using lanyards or lashings, or splicing one piece of hemp to another. He needed to be able to arrange a cat's paw, a Flemish Eye, a sheepshank, a timber-hitch, or a diamond knot on a moonless night.

And there was plenty of manual labor, smaller but crucial chores such as hauling the rigging, coiling the ropes, repairing and oiling gear, changing and mending sail canvas, tarring ropes, cleaning the guns, painting, swabbing the deck, and checking the cargo.

It was the kind of work in which Jared excelled. No books. No recitations. No standing in front of professors and students alike making a fool of yourself. In sailing, either the work was done or it wasn't. The knot was tied correctly or it wasn't. And much more was at stake than a grade, scholastic award, or class standing. Failure to do your work well could mean someone's death. At sea the chances of catastrophe were high. Sloppy work could result in a fall from the rigging or someone being fatally struck by falling gear. Lack of caution could result in being washed overboard. It was a life of hard work and high risk. It made Jared giddy with excitement.

Sundays allowed time for social events among the crew. Drinking occupied a central place in seafaring culture. For many sailors, drink provided an escape from the harsh, unrelenting conditions of a punishing life. One sailor described it poetically to Jared as he passed the newcomer a bottle:

So that when Sailors get good wine
  They think themselves in Heav'n for the time;
It hunger, cold, all maladies expels,
  With cares o' th' world, do trouble not ourselves.

Some sailors escaped more than others, drinking to the point of deadening excess, though this rarely occurred aboard the *Dove.* The captain made it clear to his crew that because their complement was smaller and their reward greater, he expected a greater level of responsibility from his men. He didn't want his ship and other men's lives dependent upon a drunken sailor. If any sailor preferred liquor over his crewmates, he was welcome to find work aboard another ship. As for mistakes in judgment, the captain would forgive a crewman once. After the second offense, the crewman was immediately dispatched in whatever manner was most convenient.

Sometimes that meant he was left behind at port, sometimes it meant he was set adrift at sea. Either way, he no longer had a place aboard ship.

Sometimes the crew members danced themselves dizzy to pass the time. For most of them, dancing was not a sequence of steps; rather it was a matter of hopping about. Some, however, were nimble-footed dancers, having learned to dance at the music houses around Wapping, the sailors' district in East London. Occasionally they used the main mast as a maypole around which they would dance to a variety of forecastle songs, most of them ridiculous in nature.

More often, though, they would spend the time on deck or below spending endless hours telling tales. Some tales chronicled the adventurous, or the dangerous, or the miraculous. Some were even set to rhyme, sailors loving a good poem, which was rarely what they wrote. More often the poems were "roaring bad verses," as Jared heard one sailor describe them. The sailors aboard the *Dove* loved tales of heroism, glory, and courage. Portions of the tales were even true. Although some sailors read, it was hard to keep books on board due to the dampness and mildew.

Jared had been aboard the *Dove* for more than a fortnight. He'd gotten to know most of the crew by now and they him as they took turns in turning the three gents into tars. Besides Patrick Tracy, the Irish first mate, and Henry Whitmore, the bos'n, there was Thomas Bardin, a Welshman, the ship's carpenter. He was a specialist in the wooden world. He repaired masts, yards, boats, and machinery. He checked the hull regularly for leaks. Generally, he was responsible for the soundness of the ship. Rudy Shaw was the gunner. It was his job to tend the artillery and ammunition. His expertise was to avert potential disaster should a cannon burst, overheat, or recoil out of control. The quartermaster, John Wendell, was an experienced sailor who could read and write. He kept the ship's log, separate from the captain's log. The cook, Nathaniel Ropes, in the tradition of most ship's cooks, had no experience at all in cooking. He acquired the position when his leg was accidentally broken by a falling tackle. The leg hadn't set correctly, and it healed straight and stiff. He couldn't bend it at the knee and always walked with a limp. The other veteran seamen without specific titles were called able seamen. There were three able seamen aboard the *Dove*—Michael Dalton, Jeremiah Lee, and George Cabot. Jared Morgan, James Magee, Benjamin Wier, and a fourth sailor who had run away from a merchant ship a week before Jared came on board, Richard Derby, rounded out the ship's roster.

"What's with them? They still sore about bein' here?" Dalton sat with his back against the main mast on a late Sunday evening.

He'd pointed at Magee and Wier who were seated apart from the others, still reluctant to accept their presence aboard ship. Jared sat in the midst of the lounging crew members as they gossiped and gabbed. The sea was calm with only a slight breeze ruffling the sails. Slack rigging beat against the wooden masts. Overhead the stars were brilliant.

"They're still homesick for their mommies," gunner Shaw sneered.

Jared choked back a smile, not wanting to offend his friend.

"Life don't get better than this," Derby said to Magee and Wier. "That's the truth. I deserted the *Loyal George* when I heard Devereaux was sitting off Boston. I would have done anything to get on board this ship."

"Where was the *Loyal George?*" Shaw asked.

"Philadelphia," Derby replied. "Sneaked aboard a shallop to get from there to Boston. Even then it took me two weeks to finally make contact with Devereaux. Almost got caught in the process. Barlow had men looking for me."

"Edmund Barlow?" Dalton sat upright at the sound of the merchant captain's name.

"The same."

"I've heard stories about him," said Dalton.

"They're true," Derby replied. "Every one of them."

Dalton screwed up his face, and with a tone of mock authority said, "There is no justice or injustice on board my ship, lad. There are only two things: duty and mutiny—mind that. All that you are ordered to do is duty. All that you refuse to do is mutiny."

Derby laughed at the impression of his former captain. "That's Barlow, all right. Do you know him?"

Dalton shook his head. "Heard of him from many a maimed sailor in taverns from Boston to Bristol."

"I once saw Barlow beat a man with a stone mug. Broke four teeth out of his head," said Derby. "Another time he broke a large broomstick into splinters over a man's back. Then he thrust his thumb into the man's eye and put it out."

"Why didn't someone stop him?" Jared asked. "Or inform the authorities?"

"You have to understand one thing, son," Dalton said to Jared, "the captain of the ship is god. He can do whatever he wants. The merchants he works for and land officials don't care what he does onboard his ship as long as he sails on time and makes them a profit. The only way to get rid of a man like Barlow is to mutiny."

"A dangerous business," added Derby.

"That it is," Dalton agreed. "There were a couple of round robins started."

"Round robins?" Jared asked.

"A sheet of paper with two circles, one small circle in the middle encompassed by a larger circle. In the small circle the organizers write what they have in mind to do. One of the round robins was to throw the captain overboard. Another was to steal the ship when it was in port. Then, between the two circles those who will join the mutiny write their names beginning at the four compass points and then in between. That way if the paper is discovered, no name is at the top or bottom of the list. All share the guilt equally," Derby explained.

"What came of 'em?" Dalton asked.

"Barlow never laid his hands on either paper, but he heard about them. The first time the whole crew went without food for three days. Second time he did the same thing, only this time he learned the identity of the sailor who wrote out the round robin. That night Barlow came below and attacked the man in his sleep, punching him repeatedly all the way up to the deck. On deck the captain gave him ten to twelve more blows with a marlinespike. The man was so bloodied, he began to have convulsions. Barlow fully intended to kill him, but wanted to make it appear like an accident. So he ordered the man to go aloft in a hard, cold rain to loose the foresail. The man was in no condition to climb aloft and Barlow knew it. He fully intended that his victim would fall overboard. The man was bloodied and wore nothing but his shirt and breeches as he started climbing. Halfway he began having another fit of convulsions. I started to climb the rigging to help him when Barlow aimed a pistol at me. He said he'd shoot anyone who attempted to help the man."

"What happened?" Jared asked.

"The man held on for a while, but he was too weak. He was blown from the rigging and fell overboard. The sea was rough. It swallowed him up immediately." Derby lowered his head. "His name was Richard Wherry. He was my best friend."

The sailors were silent out of respect for Derby's loss.

"It was then I knew I had to get off the *Loyal George*," Derby said. "If I stayed I would have killed Barlow. I would have killed him. I know I would."

Again there was silence. Dalton pulled out a knife and stick and set to whittling. The night grew even more still. The soft sounds of conversation could be heard coming from the captain's cabin. First mate Tracy's unmistakable laugh echoed around the deck.

"Has there ever been a mutiny aboard the *Dove?*" Jared asked.

"You don't ask questions like that," Dalton said.

Jared lowered his head.

Dalton seemed amused at Jared's reaction. "But the answer is no. Not with this captain." He smiled. "You know, that's the first time the lad's stop smiling since he came aboard."

Jared looked up. He smiled.

"Yeah!" Shaw said. "What is it with you, gent? Why aren't you like your mates over there?" Shaw pointed to Magee and Wier who were still huddled together sullenly.

"I can't speak for them," Jared said. "But I like it here."

"Good for you, lad!" Derby said. "Like I said, life don't get better than this."

"Well, I like it too," Shaw said. "But I don't go around grinnin' like a lovesick female."

Jared grinned even wider.

One by one the other sailors testified to Jared's ever-present grin. He grinned when he was taught the rigging, when he was taught knots, when he hauled rope, when he swabbed the deck, even when Quartermaster Wendell taught him the basics of swordplay.

"I showed him how to skewer a man's chest," said Wendell, "and the lad's grinnin' at me from ear to ear. Never seen anyone like him."

"I don't like a man who smiles too much. Can't trust 'em," Shaw said.

"Morgan's all right," Wendell replied.

"Smilin' Jack Tar, that's him," Dalton said as he whittled.

It was the first time anyone had called him tar instead of gent or lad. It meant he was accepted by the crew. Jared grinned even wider.

The presence of the new recruits prompted a series of new recruit remembrances. First captains, first battles, first storms, and the first encounter with unexplained phenomenon.

"When I was on the *Abington*," Dalton said, a pile of shavings between his feet, "we were two days off the coast of Africa when we were struck by a thunderstorm, worst I've ever been in. We were lashing down everything in sight while waves taller than the mainmast crashed down on us. I had just finished securing a hatch when a wave nearly struck me senseless. If I hadn't been lashed down myself, it would have washed me overboard. I remember it bouncing me against the deck a couple of times. Then, after it passed over me, I found myself clutching the rope and looking up. I couldn't believe my eyes! At the top of the mainmast was the corposant!"

"Corposant?" Jared asked.

"A ball of fire," said Dalton, "like a star affixed to the mast. Everything on deck was lit up by it. I thought for sure it was the angel of death comin' for me. Just then another wave hit, but I couldn't take my eyes off that fire. I could still see it through the water."

"I met a brother tar in Glasgow who says he saw two of 'em on the mast!" Shaw said.

"If they're on the mast, they're a good omen," Wendell said. "It's when they're laying on the deck like a great glowworm that it's bad."

"All I know is that I don't care if I ever see one again," said Dalton.

"The strangest thing I ever saw was aboard the *William Galley*," said Wendell, the quartermaster. "I was working my watch around nine at night when I spotted a boat off the starboard side. It was a tiny craft with oars. At first, it was difficult to see, but as it came nearer to us, it became quite plain. We were somewhat surprised, not expecting a craft of that size to be on the high seas. I sent a seaman to fetch the captain, which he did. The captain was no less perplexed than the rest of us since land was nowhere near. We hailed it several times. There was no answer. At times we saw men rowing very plainly. Then at other times they just sat there and stared at us. This went on for nearly a half hour as it came near to us, then drifted away. When it continued to ignore our hails, the captain ordered me to fire a shot at it, which I did. The shot had no effect on it. It stayed near us for another quarter of an hour, then it was gone. Mr. Pugh, our chief mate, said it was Charon's boat and that the old man had come to ferry Mr. Nesbitt, who was very ill, over the river of death. And sure enough, Mr. Nesbitt died about the same time the boat disappeared."

"Do you think it was Charon's boat?" Jared asked.

"Don't rightly know," Wendell replied. "Never have been one to believe in apparitions, but then I can't explain what I saw."

"Hey, Smilin' Jack Tar!" Dalton cried.

It took Jared a moment before he remembered that was him.

"Don't you have watch now?"

Jared grinned. He should have spent the last four hours sleeping, but he didn't want to miss anything. It was going to be a long night. But he didn't care. He loved being on deck at night.

The other sailors rose and stretched and made their way below deck.

"Don't fall asleep now or you'll ruin your brief but brilliant career as an old salt," Wendell said.

"Don't worry about me," Jared said with a smile. "I'll do fine."

"I'll bet you will," Wendell replied.

That night as Jared Morgan stood watch, he studied the stars, testing himself on the constellations quartermaster John Wendell had taught him. The ship bobbed contentedly on the waves, matching his mood. "Life don't get much better than this," he said, echoing Derby's sentiment. However, as soon as he said it, he thought of one way in which it could be better. It could be better if Anne were here to share the stars with him.

Chapter 12

THE meetinghouse was alive with sound—boards clapped as pew seats were raised and lowered; whispers rippled through the crowd like wind through a grain field; an occasional cough or louder-than-usual parental warning rose above the din as Priscilla Morgan's trial was about to get underway.

"This meeting will come to order." The Reverend Horace Russell put on his preaching voice. Even so, he had to repeat his call-to-order several times before finally gaining control over the assembled people. The church pastor stood behind a long table in the front of the meetinghouse. Seated at the table were: Edward Chauncy, Deacon Andrew Hale, and town magistrate Thomas Alexander. Behind them in a row of chairs sat the assembled deacons of the church. Priscilla sat opposite her accusers on the front pew. She sat alone. Her mother sat in the family pew, accompanied at her request by Daniel Cole. Priscilla turned in her seat and looked into the balcony at the young ladies' pew. It was empty. No one else from her Bible study group was at the hearing.

Priscilla turned forward and straightened the folds on her skirt. She tried not to let her friends' absence bother her. In the Bible, Deborah stood alone. Now, Priscilla stood alone. Priscilla consoled her wounded pride by reasoning that it was better this way. She didn't need any help defending herself.

Pastor Russell spoke: "We have gathered in the sight of God and this assembled congregation to address a serious concern that has been brought to our attention. At present, by decree of the local magistrates, this is only a matter of church discipline since the contamination seems to be limited to our church alone. Should this hearing prove otherwise, the accused will be surrendered to the civil magistrates for further prosecution. That decision, should it have to be made, will be at the sole discretion of Thomas Alexander," the pastor said, gesturing toward a small, bespectacled man seated at the table, "whom you all know is one of the town magistrates and also a member of this church."

The magistrate moved his spectacles to the end of his nose and gazed grimly at Priscilla. His balding head, face, and arms were covered with brown splotches, common in a man of his advanced age. Priscilla met his gaze, which seemed to unsettle him. She smiled inwardly. If they expected her to cower before them in abject contrition, they were going to be surprised.

Pastor Russell introduced the remaining two men at the table and the deacons behind them before addressing Priscilla. Looking at her, he said, "The accused will stand as the charges are read."

Priscilla stood, very much aware that everyone in the room had given her their full attention, for the only sound was the rustle of her skirt as she rose.

"Priscilla Morgan, you are charged with encouraging erroneous opinions, conducting unauthorized meetings, and insulting the leadership of the church. Are these charges true?"

"As God is my witness," Priscilla said, "I have done nothing contrary to His teachings."

"Please respond directly to the accusations," said the pastor.

"I just did."

Pastor Russell uttered a perturbed sigh. "Obstinacy is not only unbecoming a lady, it is unchristian and counterproductive."

"Forgive me if I appear obstinate, Pastor Russell, for that is not my intention. My intention is to make it clear that before God I have done nothing wrong; and that since this body's authority rests upon God's Holy Word, you can reach only one conclusion—that I have done nothing to warrant trial or punishment."

"We'll draw our own conclusions, young woman," Alexander barked.

Pastor Russell still wasn't satisfied. "Since you still refuse to answer the charges in a direct manner, I will ask them bluntly. Did you encourage erroneous opinions?"

"No."

"Did you conduct unauthorized meetings?"

"No."

"Did you insult the leadership of this church?"

"No."

Pastor Russell smiled a sarcastic smile. "Thank you for answering directly."

"You're welcome. I'm glad you're finally able to understand."

"IMPERTINENCE!" the aged Alexander shouted, slapping the table. By the outburst of gasps and whispers, the congregation agreed with him. "You will show proper respect for the clergy or I will have you jailed!"

Priscilla knew she'd gone too far. She also knew that if she didn't control her tongue, everything she was fighting for would unravel.

"My apologies, Pastor Russell," she said.

Without acknowledging her apology, the pastor said, "Tell us about Deborah's Daughters."

"Deborah's Daughters is a group of women who meet at

my house for Bible study, prayer, and encouragement."

"Bible study, prayer, and encouragement," the pastor repeated.

"Yes, sir."

"Are my sermons and the weekly Lecture Day messages inadequate to meet the needs of the ladies of this community?" he asked.

"Our studies are supplementary to those messages."

"Mistress Morgan, supplement implies inadequacy. A supplement is something that makes complete something that is incomplete. So it is your contention that this church—and community—is inadequate in its scriptural teachings to its members?"

Priscilla struggled to find an appropriate response. Not that she was at a loss for one. She wanted to say that the level of spirituality in the community was evidence enough that something was lacking in the church's teaching, but she knew that would only anger her accusers further, something she didn't want to do. So she said, "I am of the opinion that one can never study the Bible too much."

"I see," said the pastor. "And who was the teacher of this Bible study for women?"

"I was."

"And what qualifications do you have to teach the Bible?"

Again Priscilla hesitated.

"Do you have a degree from Harvard?"

"No."

"Of course not. Have you studied theology? Do you know the ancient languages? Are you acquainted with the rules of hermeneutics? Have you . . ."

"Yes." She said it softly, but she said it.

"Yes? What do you mean, yes?"

"I know the ancient languages. I've studied theology and hermeneutics."

The congregation exploded with noise. It was several minutes before order was restored. During this time, Priscilla turned toward the family pew. Constance Morgan's face was buried in the shoulder of Daniel Cole. Her shoulders shook with sobs. Cole sat there, stone-faced.

"Mistress Morgan," Pastor Russell continued, "you say you are a student of these disciplines. Kindly tell us where you studied them."

"In my father's study."

"So then, in your father's absence, you read his books?"

"No, that's not what I'm saying."

"Then what are you saying, Mistress Morgan?"

"I did not sneak into my father's study and I did not study alone. My teacher was the best faculty member on Harvard's staff—my father."

Again the room burst with noise.

"Now Priscilla, your father was a godly man, respected and revered by all. And you want us to believe that he taught you secretly at night?"

"Whether you believe it or not, it's the truth."

Pastor Russell looked for confirmation at the Morgan family pew. "Constance," he said softly, "is this true? Did your husband teach Priscilla ministerial disciplines at home?"

Constance Morgan wiped tear-stained cheeks and nodded affirmatively.

"For what purpose?" the pastor asked her. "Surely it's wasted knowledge. Can she teach at Harvard? Become a minister or even a deacon? Is there any good reason he would do such a thing?"

"I can answer all those questions," Priscilla said. "He did it because he loved knowledge and he loved me."

"An unwise love, I daresay," said the pastor, "for look at the unfortunate predicament in which such knowledge has placed you."

The pastor produced a handkerchief and slumped into his chair. After wiping his brow, he huddled momentarily with the other men seated behind the desk.

"To continue then," the pastor said as he stood, "since you had a degree of unauthorized learning, you felt equipped to supplement the teaching of the church. Yet you did not come to the church seeking permission to hold these Bible studies. Why?"

So this is their real concern! Priscilla realized. *It's a matter of control!* "To be frank, I didn't think of it. My intentions were to encourage the spiritual growth of my friends. I was unaware such actions might be offensive to anyone."

"But certainly, with all your biblical knowledge, you are aware that God has provided for overseers to see that His teachings and precepts are proclaimed without error!"

"I'll say it again. Our intentions were not to undermine any authority, but to build the Christian character of those who attended the meetings."

"LIAR!" Andrew Hale jumped to his feet and leveled an angry, shaking finger at Priscilla. "Those meetings at your house were a malicious attempt to undermine the authority of both church and family. You poisoned my daughter's mind and all the other women who listened to you!"

Priscilla was shaken by the force of the man's anger. His face was scarlet and his eyes bloodshot; veins bulged on his forehead and his voice quivered to the point of uncontrol when he spoke.

"Do the Ten Commandments mean nothing to you?" he shouted.

"I don't see how . . . exactly to what are you . . ." Priscilla stammered.

"Particularly the one that says, 'Honor thy father and thy mother'!"

"I still don't understand what you . . ."

Pastor Russell intervened: "What are you getting at, Andrew?"

"I'll tell you what I'm getting at! My Tabitha was a sweet, obedient daughter until she came under Mistress Morgan's evil influence. Since then she's been argumentative, disobedient, and has been caught telling lies!"

Priscilla replied stiffly: "On one thing we agree, Master Hale. Tabitha is an exceptional young woman, with a remarkable mind. However, I never taught her to be disobedient to you or to tell lies."

"Now it's time for the serpent to be caught in her own lies," Andrew Hale sneered. "Have you or have you not been teaching my daughter to read?"

Priscilla held her head high as she replied. "I have."

"On what day of the week?"

"Wednesdays."

"At two o'clock in the afternoon?"

"We begin at two o'clock."

"And end at three thirty?"

"Actually, we conclude at three. Tabitha stays after to learn to read."

"Do you know where Tabitha told me she was at that time each week?"

Priscilla thought it was a rhetorical question, so she didn't answer.

"Well, do you?" Andrew Hale screamed.

"No, Master Hale, I don't know where Tabitha told you she was going on those days."

"She told me she was learning to embroider at Widow Underhill's. Only one day I needed her and I sent John to get her. And guess what I discovered? Widow Underhill isn't teaching anybody to embroider. Widow Underhill doesn't even know how to embroider! So where is my Tabitha? She's at your house learning to read! Says she lied to me because she knew I wouldn't like it! In that she was right! Why do women need to read anyway? Reading spoils their minds. Fills their heads with thoughts they shouldn't have. Makes them argumentative and unhappy with life. Wasn't it just two years ago that Josh Hoskins' woman learned to read? Not long afterwards she called Josh an ignorant pig and ran away with another man! It's poison, I tell you. And I'll not have it in my house!"

"Master Hale," Priscilla said, "I just wanted to . . ."

"Shut your mouth, woman! I don't want your apology! You've done enough damage already! First you lure my daughter to your house, then you teach her to read, and now when I tell her she can't learn anymore, she yells that she hates me and she's gonna learn to read whether I want her to or not! You're an evil one, you are!"

"Master Hale! I wasn't *going* to apologize. I was going to say that Tabitha shouldn't have lied to you, but that she wouldn't have had to lie to you if you had wanted what was best for her in the first place."

Hale was growing redder by the moment. "So now you're saying all this is my fault? That I'm not a good father? What you need is a good thrashing, young lady, and in the absence of your daddy, I'd sure be more than happy to give you one!"

Once again Pastor Russell intervened: "Andrew, calm yourself! Sit down and calm yourself!"

Andrew Hale took his seat, but he was far from calm.

"Have we heard enough, or will there be further testimony?" The pastor directed his question to those seated behind the table. It was conceded that they had heard enough testimony and were prepared to deliberate Priscilla Morgan's fate. The congregation remained in their places as Pastor Russell and Masters Chauncy, Alexander, and Hale filed out of the meetinghouse.

Priscilla took her seat. For the hour the four men deliberated, no one talked to her. But she could hear plenty of people's not-so-quiet conversations about her. Terms like self-righteous, arrogant, prideful, and rebellious were spoken often, along with hundreds of phrases like, "If she were my daughter, I'd. . . ." The deacons glared at her. Without exception, they sat with arms folded across their chests, indicating they'd already passed judgment. Priscilla tried to convince herself that the things people were saying about her didn't matter; that their words didn't hurt. The longer she sat there alone, she wondered why her mother hadn't come forward to comfort her or even just to ask if she was all right. Priscilla couldn't bring herself to turn around and look for her mother. If she hadn't come forward by now, she wasn't going to come forward. Apparently her mother didn't want to share her shame. Priscilla guessed she couldn't blame her. But a hand to hold would mean an awful lot right now.

The four deliberating men filed back into the meetinghouse and Priscilla was asked to rise again. It was Edward Chauncy, Penelope's father, who summarized their findings: "It was nearly one hundred years ago that another colonial woman stood trial in Boston. Her name was Anne Hutchinson. Although the controversy surrounding that trial had a stronger element of theology, and the damage to the colony was more widespread, nevertheless, there are some direct parallels between that trial and this. Madame Hutchinson held illegal meetings in her home which she used to spread her seditious doctrine. She had a low opinion of the magistrates and often criticized the clergy. Her outspokenness and pride were her downfall. Standing before us today is a young woman in the same mold as Anne Hutchinson. Without formal training and without church approval, she took it upon herself to educate the young women of Cambridge. Her erroneous teachings led to the destruction of order in several families, the case of Tabitha Hale serving as but one example. There were other cases unspoken, my own family being one of them. To the best of our knowledge, only five young women were contaminated by Mistress Morgan's harmful teachings. For that, we thank God. It could have been worse had it not been caught in its early stages. In conclusion, this board has heard sufficient evidence to conclude that Mistress Priscilla Morgan is guilty of encouraging erroneous opinions, conducting unauthorized meetings, and insulting the leadership of this church. Brother Alexander will pass sentence."

The aged magistrate rose while a din of reaction to the verdict rippled through the meetinghouse. He adjusted his spectacles several times waiting for the noise to die down. When it did, he read: "Having been found guilty of these offenses, it is our judgment that Mistress Priscilla Morgan will be placed in the stocks on Lecture Day next with a cleft stick on her tongue as an indication of the nature of her offense. We find it regrettable that she has no father or husband to exercise future control over her. Therefore, upon her release from the stocks, Priscilla Morgan will be banished from the Massachusetts colonies. In this way we will rid ourselves of her poisonous influence on our children."

Priscilla didn't see the reaction of the people behind her, but she heard it. In the midst of the uproar was one clear sound, that of her mother. Constance Morgan gasped, then cried out: "O Benjamin! Our baby . . . our baby!" For the first time since the trial began, Priscilla's knees grew weak. She collapsed onto the front pew, managing to prop herself up with one arm.

"May I address this sacred assembly?" The voice was familiar. At the moment Priscilla's mind was too confused to identify it. She looked at the speaker. Cole! What did he want? Wasn't exile enough? What more did he want? Her death?

"Please identify yourself," Pastor Russell said.

"My name is Daniel Cole. I'm a resident of Boston where I ply the trade of merchant."

"Yes, Master Cole! Your successful reputation precedes you!" Pastor Russell was more than visibly impressed, almost giddy. "It is an honor that you should choose to honor us with your presence! Do you have any comments that might have a direct bearing on this trial?"

"I believe I do, sir."

"Then, please come forward so that all may hear."

Daniel Cole moved unhurriedly, enjoying the attention the entire congregation was giving him. As he approached the front of the meetinghouse, he walked directly to Priscilla and placed his hand on her shoulder. He brought with him the aroma of unwashed stockings.

"I'm here to help you, my dear," he said in a near-whisper.

Daniel Cole straightened himself and addressed the four men behind the table. "Although I am not a member of this sacred congregation, I am a full member of the North Church in Boston where I have been privileged to sit on the board of elders. I would like to speak on behalf of the accused, specifically in regards to her sentencing. The Morgan household has been visited by more than its share of tragedy. It was almost a year ago that Benjamin Morgan died. Since then, both of his sons have mysteriously disappeared. I fear that the exile of Constance Morgan's remaining child will be more than this good woman is able to bear and was wondering if I might suggest an alternative that would be in keeping with the verdict and intent of the sentence?"

It was the magistrate, Thomas Alexander, who answered him. "In punishing the daughter, it is not our intention to injure her godly mother," he said. "If you have a suitable alternative, we are willing to hear it now."

"Correct me if I heard you incorrectly, but didn't you say that your sentence was based on your regret that Priscilla has no father or husband to exercise future control over her?"

"You heard correctly, sir."

"And if I were in a position to assure you that she would have someone to exercise control over her until such time as she marry, could I persuade you to amend the portion of her sentence pertaining to exile?"

Alexander removed his spectacles and cradled them in his hands. "And are you in such a position?" he asked.

"I believe I am, sir," Cole said, glancing toward Constance. "Though this is not the most opportune place in which to make such an announcement, let it be known that Constance Morgan and I are soon to be wed."

This time the gasp that was heard came from Priscilla.

"That would make me Priscilla's stepfather," Cole continued. "And as such, I could assure this most sacred assembly that there would be no further secret meetings of women. Furthermore, what I am sure will be welcome news to Master Hale, Priscilla will no longer live in Cambridge. She will live with her mother and me in Boston until such time as she is married."

The four heads huddled together and discussed Daniel Cole's proposal.

"One more thing," Cole added, interrupting their whispers, "I believe with all my heart that the fault for this unfortunate circumstance does not lie solely with this dear girl, but with her father, Benjamin Morgan. It was he who secretly encouraged her in these questionable activities. However, as her stepfather, all that will change. Under my parental influence, I'm confident Priscilla can yet assume her rightful role in society as an obedient daughter and, some day, God willing, a submissive wife."

Once again there was a huddle. A short time later, the conferring men came to an uneasy decision in which it was evident Master Hale was in disgruntled agreement.

Magistrate Alexander spoke: "It is our considered opinion that you are a godly and good man who desires mercy as well as justice in this matter. We are impressed with your willingness to assume responsibility for Mistress Morgan in the matter of her rehabilitation. It is our prayer that you will be successful. We have agreed to accept your generous offer. Therefore, when Priscilla Morgan is released from the stocks on Lecture Day, she will be turned over to your custody." To Priscilla he said: "Mistress Morgan, do you understand what Master Cole has done for you?"

Priscilla sat on the pew, still propped up on one arm, her head lowered. She was seething at the injustice of the meeting. These so-called men of God convicted her of the crime of teaching the Bible and promoting spiritual growth among women; then, to compound their blind error, they remand her into the custody of an unethical, unscrupulous mercenary whom they consider a saint! It was more than she could stand! But what could she do? One word, a single negative word at this point, could send her into exile. Where would she go? Rhode Island? She didn't know anyone there. How would she live?

"Mistress Morgan! We're waiting for an answer!"

Priscilla sat upright and looked the magistrate in the eye. "I understand fully what is being done," she said.

"Priscilla," Pastor Russell said, "considering Master Cole's gracious defense, don't you think a token of appreciation would be in order?"

O Lord! Is there no end to this injustice? Not only do they swallow Cole's hypocrisy, now they want me to thank him!

"Priscilla?"

Priscilla stood and faced Daniel Cole. His eyes glimmered with amusement. He was enjoying every second of this! "Master Cole, I wish to thank you for coming to my defense," she said.

"And may we offer our congratulations on your impending marriage!" the pastor beamed.

"Thank you," Cole said. "I know we all will be very happy together."

The trial concluded with a prayer offered by Pastor Russell. He thanked God for giving them the wisdom to settle this matter in a way that preserved the sanctity of God's Word and the church. And he thanked God for sending Daniel Cole to serve as Priscilla's kinsman-redeemer.

Priscilla, however, did not join in the prayer. She and God were no longer on speaking terms.

Lecture Day dawned clear and warm the first Thursday in May. The breakfast hour had passed and the inhabitants of Cambridge, instead of going to their workshops and places of employment, wandered the streets casually. Lectures wouldn't begin until one o'clock so that the lecture-goers might first eat their noon dinners at home. Those who didn't attend the lectures would find recreation in cruder diversions such as wolf-routing, where men would drive the beasts from the forests to be killed outright for sport; or wolf-baiting, where the wolf would be tied to a stake and dogs set on it; or sometimes wolves would be dragged alive at the end of a horse's tail. Other amusements consisted of hunting bears and foxes, shooting at a mark, or "pitch the bar," a trial of strength rather than skill.

The punishment of transgressors through public shame was the typical morning amusement for these days of leisure. On this particular day, the featured wrongdoer was Priscilla Morgan.

She was escorted to the pillory scaffold by the town beadle, carrying the staff which indicated his position, and the four men who deliberated and rendered her verdict in this order: Pastor Russell, Magistrate Alexander, Edward Chauncy, and Andrew Hale. The beadle, or town crier as he was sometimes called, cleared the way for the procession.

"Make way! Make way for Mistress Morgan! Shortly you will see God's justice done! Make way! Make way!"

Like Moses parting the sea, so the beadle parted the crowd while the four judges and the judged followed in his wake. Priscilla had thought she'd prepared herself to be the town spectacle. She'd even managed to find some levity in it this morning when she dressed herself. *What does one wear to a pillory?* she mused. Something simple. Plain. It wasn't the time to be ostentatious. She chose a blue dress with a fitted bodice and full skirt. Also a plain white fichu for her shoulders and her wide-brimmed straw hat, the one she normally wore in the sun. Now, as she was paraded through the crowd, her dilemma over what to wear seemed even more ridiculous in a fearful way. These people were not concerned in the least about her dress. They were too busy hating her. When she had imagined what it would be like, she hadn't expected sympathy, but neither had she expected this level of animosity. They loathed her, despised her with the same intensity they would show to a murderer or pirate. For them sin was sin. Iniquity knew no shades of gray. This woman had steeped herself in black sin and it was their task to exorcise it out of her with their taunts and jeers.

Their anger served a double purpose that day. Not only did it work to cleanse the sinner, but it also acted as a protective shield, guarding them against the infectious nature of sin. Their anger was a public demonstration of how they felt about sin. They were against it. They arrayed themselves on the side of God and against evil in all its hideous forms. On this May morning, the hideousness of sin took the form of a red-headed woman in a blue dress.

People Priscilla had known all her life joined forces with strangers as they hurled insults, condemnations, and (some of the meaner sort) spittle at her. Their faces were hard; their eyes squinted; their lips arched in vicious sneers, showing uneven yellow teeth. Some of the braver ones shoved or punched her, careful not to let their hands linger, fearful that prolonged contact would prove injurious to them.

Presently they reached the scaffold upon which the pillory perched. The accused followed her entourage up the wooden steps and faced the gathering crowd. As the three charges and verdict were read, she set her jaw and raised her gaze past the crowd. The words that were spoken meant nothing to her. It was the meaningless babble of self-important men who thought her evil because she loved to read, and learn, and think; because she formed opinions and expressed them. If these were the charges being read, she would plead guilty and willingly submit to their punishments. But their words were different: unlawful meetings ... erroneous opinions ... insulting the leadership. In their eyes she stood as the symbol of Benjamin Morgan's secret sin, giving knowledge to a woman. If she had to do it over, she would do it all again. Every minute with her father was worth an hour in the stockade. *O Poppa*, she thought, *how glad I am you're not here. I will survive the puny fury of their little minds. But how hard it would be for me to see them hurt you.* As the beadle concluded his reading, Priscilla realized how much she loved her father for teaching her; and how much she hated these men for condemning him; and how much she resented God for allowing petty men to triumph.

"You must remove your hat, Mistress Morgan."

"My hat?"

The beadle pointed to the open stocks.

"Oh, of course, my hat." If she'd thought about it, she wouldn't have worn the hat. Funny how the mind works at times like this. She figured she'd be out in the sun all day so, naturally, she'd need her hat. How silly, wearing a hat in the stocks.

She untied the ribbon under her chin and removed her hat

and handed it to Pastor Russell who was uncertain what to do with it. "Could you see my mother gets it?" Priscilla asked.

The pastor nodded.

"Head here, arms there," the beadle instructed.

The pillory stood open before her like the mouth of a gaping alligator and this strange little man was telling her to put her head in it. It was made of rough lumber with three half-circles notched on the lower board with matching half-circles on the upper board so that when they came together they formed enclosed circles. The center circle was large enough for a man's neck, while the two smaller side circles fit his wrists. The lower board was fixed in place to a post on the scaffold. The upper board was attached to one end with a rusty hinge.

Priscilla stepped up to the pillory.

"Pull your hair forward, miss," the beadle said. He made a bunching motion with his hands around his ears to show her what he meant. "So that it won't get snagged in the wood."

Reaching behind her head with both hands, Priscilla grabbed equal parts of blazing red hair and pulled them around her ears. She laid her neck down in the center half-circle. From behind her, the beadle gently took her right hand. Her hair fell naturally to the side of her face.

"Here," he placed one wrist, "and here," he placed the other wrist.

The hinge squealed briefly as the upper board swung over her wrists and neck and thudded into place. Priscilla heard the padlock click as the open end was secured. The crowd cheered. Some called out to her to look at them. She ignored them.

"One more thing, Mistress Morgan."

Priscilla rotated her head toward the beadle.

"Open your mouth and stick out your tongue," he said. She did.

The beadle produced a cleft stick and proceeded to fasten it to her tongue. There was the earthy taste of wood as her tongue touched the stick. "Push!" the beadle ordered.

"Oww! 'aa hurth!"

"It's supposed to hurt, Mistress Morgan. It's punishment."

It felt ridiculous to have a stick clamped to her tongue and dangling out of her mouth. It was impossible to talk, and nearly impossible to swallow. The times she was unable to swallow, the spittle ran out the side of her mouth and there was no way she could wipe it away. As the day progressed she found this to be true with tears and a runny nose. It was humiliating.

Satisfied that Priscilla was secure in the pillory, the beadle and four judges departed from the scaffold, leaving her to the crowd which dissipated rather quickly since there wasn't much more to see. From that point on, through the rest of the day, a variety of people stopped by for a variety of reasons. Parents would pass, holding their children's hands, stop and kneel down so that they were at eye-level with their children. They'd point to Priscilla and say, "See that lady up there? She's a bad lady. She did things she wasn't supposed to do. Now she's being punished. That's what happens to bad people. They get punished. You would never do anything bad like that lady, would you? Of course not. You're a good girl. But remember, if you ever do anything bad, that's what will happen to you."

If the child asked what Priscilla did that was so bad, the parent would say: "She disobeyed her pastor," or "She taught other ladies bad things, that's why she has that stick on her tongue."

Every time the child would stare at her in wide-eyed horror and promise never to be bad like that lady up there.

Andrew Hale dragged his tearful daughter Tabitha to the scaffold and lectured her in front of Priscilla. "Take a good look at her, Tabitha, because that could well be you up there on that scaffold with the whole town ridiculing you! And that's exactly what will happen unless you give up this nonsense of learning to read." He slapped her face. "Are you listening to me?" He slapped her again. "Is any of this getting through to you? Sometimes I swear you're dumber than a mule! I never want to see you reading anything again, do you hear me?" Another slap.

"Yes, Papa," Tabitha cried weakly.

"Did you say something?" Andrew Hale slapped his daughter again.

"Yes, Papa!" she cried louder.

He turned to Priscilla. "And you stay away from her or I'll beat you too!" His finger shook uncontrollably at her. He was so red with anger and so wild-eyed, Priscilla thought he would go into convulsions. "Stay away! Stay away! Stay away!" he shouted. He then dragged Tabitha away by the arm. She was sobbing so uncontrollably her father had to hold her up to keep her from falling to the ground.

Priscilla had been in the pillory for a little over an hour, and she was beginning to experience physical discomfort. Her neck and wrists were beginning to chafe against the wood and pick up splinters. And her back was hurting. She would shift her weight from one foot to another to relieve the stress on it, but after a while that did little good. There was pain between her shoulder blades and her lower back was starting to cramp. No matter what she tried for relief, the pain grew stronger.

"Well, look who's here!"

Priscilla instinctively tried to raise her head. She succeeded only in thumping the back of her head against the board. Her forward sight extended no more than a few feet in front of the scaffold. Moments later three faces appeared, bending down so they could get a good look at her. Three young men. Priscilla didn't recognize them.

"I told you it was Philip's sister!" one said.

"Are you sure?"

"Sure I'm sure! I saw her on campus last year."

By now the three of them were squatting near the base of the scaffold looking up at her. They were alike in that they all wore silly grins, obviously enjoying her dilemma.

"What'd she do?" one asked.

The other two didn't know.

"She's kinda pretty. Look at all that red hair!"

"Forget the red hair, look at that figure!"

"I've seen better."

"Sure! In your dreams!"

"Gah away!" Priscilla said.

One of the three rose on one knee and held folded hands against his chest. "Ah! She speaks! Speak again, fair Juliet! That we might hear thy dulcet tones and be stirred!"

"Gah away!" she said more persistently.

The boy on one knee looked behind them and all around. Then he spoke to his pal who was between the other two: "Nobody's around," he whispered. "I'll bet you a pound you won't climb up there and kiss her!"

"No!" Priscilla cried.

"Kiss her how?" the one in the middle said. "She's got that stick sticking out of her mouth!"

"On the cheek, dunce!" the first boy said.

"Two pounds if you . . . " The boy on the other end whispered something that made his companions laugh.

"No!" Priscilla cried louder. She rotated her head to one side, then the other. As far as she could see there was no one else in sight.

The boy being challenged looked all around him. "One pound for a kiss, right?"

"Right!" said the first boy.

"Right, and hurry!" said the second.

The boy in the middle jumped onto the scaffold and approached the pillory.

"Noooo!" Priscilla yelled as loud as she could. "Heeelllp!" She did her best to maneuver her legs to one side of the pillory post so she could kick at the boy coming toward her. Her efforts were useless. By standing directly in front of her he could stay well out of her reach and still reach her by bending at the waist. Looking out of the tops of her eyes, she saw an unshaved grinning face coming toward her. She jerked her head to one side in a futile attempt to pull away.

"This won't hurt a bit," he said, bending closer.

Priscilla shook her head back and forth violently. Her hands pushed as far forward through the pillory holes as they could, clutching furiously, but they grabbed nothing but air.

"Hold still!" he said, grabbing her head.

As he leaned closer to her, Priscilla could smell the odor of stale beer on his breath. It made her want to wretch.

"HOLD! WHAT ARE YOU BOYS DOING THERE? GET AWAY FROM HER!"

Like animals in the forest picking up the hunter's scent, the three boys started, froze for an instant, then scampered away as fast as their legs would carry them.

"GO ON, GET OUTTA HERE!" the voice cried after them.

Priscilla craned her neck in every direction to see who it was who saved her from the unknown pranksters. Whoever did it was not in her restricted field of vision. By turning her head left and right, she was able to see off in the distance on both sides. However, it was a different story entirely with her vision straight ahead which was limited to only a few feet. Whoever had frightened the boys away was standing somewhere directly in front of her because she couldn't see him.

"Thank ouuu!" she said.

"You're welcome," said the voice. It was male and kind.

"Who ahh ouu?" Priscilla asked.

There was no answer. Priscilla strained to look in front of her, but succeeded only in hitting her head against the board. However, as she rotated her head to the right and looked into the distance, she saw someone between two trees which were planted within a foot of each other. He was leaning against one of them. Tall. Unless she was mistaken, brown hair. And familiar. She'd seen him somewhere before, but where?

"Priscilla?" the voice was soft, but it startled Priscilla nonetheless.

Looking toward the steps of the scaffold, Priscilla saw Anne Pierpont walking up them. Her hands were folded timidly in front of her and her head was bowed.

"You probably don't want to see me," she said softly. But she was wrong. Anne's was the first friendly face Priscilla had seen all day.

"I'm sorry I let you down during the trial," the younger girl said. "Does it help if I told you I wanted to come?"

Anne walked softly toward the pillory.

"My father wouldn't let me. He locked me in my room. In fact, he didn't want me to come here today either. But I had to. I climbed down the tree outside my bedroom window."

"O, Ahnnn!" Priscilla began to weep when she saw the pain and concern in Anne's eyes.

"Here, let me help you." Anne hurriedly reached for a handkerchief and dabbed Priscilla's eyes. Then, seeing the need for further assistance, she gently cleaned the rest of Priscilla's face.

"Thank ouu," Priscilla said.

"What an awful position to have to be in!" Anne cried. She moved behind Priscilla, out of the range of her vision. Moments later, Priscilla felt small, kind hands rubbing the small of her back.

It felt so good that an involuntary sigh escaped from her

mouth. Tender hands worked their way up her back, knead-ing Priscilla's shoulders. The feeling of relief went beyond words.

"Thank ouu, Ahnnn," she said. "Wi ou geth in thouble?"

"Will I get in trouble?"

Priscilla nodded.

"Probably," she said. "Actually, yes. Father will beat me. But I just had to come. I'm as guilty as you." Then she added quickly, "But we didn't do anything wrong, did we Priscilla?"

Priscilla shook her head no.

As the shadows grew long across the green expanse in front of the pillory scaffold, Anne Pierpont attended to Pris-cilla Morgan, reading poems to her, rubbing her back, and doing whatever else she could to ease Priscilla's ordeal.

At sundown, the beadle came alone and unlocked the pillo-ry. Priscilla had to lean upon Anne the first time she tried to stand up straight. Anne rubbed her back vigorously to get the blood flowing again.

With a final verbal warning about hoping she learned her lesson, the beadle sent Priscilla on her way. Anne accompa-nied her on the walk to the Morgans' house.

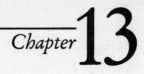
A MAN stepped from the shadows, frightening Priscilla Morgan and Anne Pierpont as they walked at dusk, arm in arm down a tree-lined road that led to the Morgan house.

"What do you want, sir?" Anne cried, shielding Priscilla by stepping between her and the unidentified man.

"I mean you no harm," said the man, holding up empty hands.

"Then why do you leap from shadows?" Anne asked.

"Let's just say it wouldn't be good for me if certain people knew I was here. Please, I merely wish to speak for a moment with Mistress Morgan."

Priscilla looked him over. The figure in the tricorne hat and knee-length coat prompted a recollection; a distant recollection, not in time but in proximity. The man leaning against the trees. The one who frightened away the college boys when they tried to take advantage of her vulnerability on the scaffold.

"It's all right, Anne. I recognize him," Priscilla said.

"You do?" the man said hopefully. He removed his hat to reveal nearly shoulder-length, brown, wavy hair, an eager smile, and a young, handsome face.

"Indeed I do, sir," said Priscilla. "And I wish to thank you for coming to my rescue." Priscilla explained to Anne what the stranger had done. Anne added her gratitude to Priscilla's.

"Oh, that. I didn't think you could see me," the young man said. He looked disappointed. "I thought you recognized me from before."

"Before?" Priscilla asked.

"In Boston."

Priscilla showed no hint of recognition.

"The Good Woman Tavern?"

Still no positive response. Which really discouraged the young man.

"I'm Peter Gibbs, the owner of the tavern."

The light of recognition highlighted Priscilla's face. Finally.

"I guess I was being foolish to think you'd remember me," Gibbs said. He chuckled and looked in the direction of the scaffold. "You, on the other hand, seem to have no problem making an impression on people, whether in Boston or Cambridge."

All hints of friendliness drained from Priscilla's face. The pain in her neck and back was too fresh for her to share his humor. With Anne at her side again, she pushed past the grinning tavern owner, resuming her journey home.

"No!" Gibbs cried. "Please forgive me. When it comes to beautiful ladies I can be an insensitive clod. Please stop. I didn't intend to offend you."

Priscilla kept walking. Over her shoulder she said, "And just what *did* you intend?"

"To be forthright with you, I really don't know." He followed behind the ladies as he spoke. "It's just that there has been a lot of Morgan activity in my tavern and, knowing the source behind some of the activity, I can't help but think something is wrong, that's all."

Priscilla stopped. Hesitantly, she turned around. "Morgan activity?"

Gibbs nodded. "More than coincidence, I'm afraid."

"Would you care to elaborate?"

Gibbs stared down at his hat, self-consciously rotating it along the headband as he spoke. "Of course, you know about the day you came in. . . ." His grin grew wide. He addressed Anne: "Did she tell you about that? There's this really obnoxious blacksmith in Boston with whom Mistress Morgan had unfinished business. When he wasn't at his shop—he rarely is, by the way—Mistress Morgan learned he was at my tavern and . . ."

"Master Gibbs," Priscilla interrupted, "if you don't mind, I'll tell my friend that story later. It's been a trying day for me. Is there anything you can tell me that I don't know?"

"I'm being insensitive again," Gibbs apologized. The hat in his hands turned faster. "Of course it's been a trying day for you. It's just that when I came to Cambridge looking for you, little did I know I'd find you in the . . ."

"You came here just to see me?" Priscilla asked.

Gibbs nodded. "Like I said, all this Morgan activity is both puzzling and disturbing."

Priscilla waited a moment. Gibbs just stared at her. "Morgan activity. . . ." She raised her eyebrows and hands simultaneously to indicate she was expecting more.

"Oh, yes," Gibbs stammered, "the Morgan activity. Well, like I said, you know of your appearance at the tavern. On that day, do you recall that the stage had arrived just before you?" Priscilla nodded. She remembered. "Well, the driver of that stage delivers the mail from Providence and regions south. From my place it's distributed to Roxbury, Watertown, Cambridge, etc. On the day you were there, he delivered a letter from another Morgan—Philip Morgan . . ."

"Philip?" Priscilla cried out.

"You know him?"

"Yes! He's my brother! We thought he was dead!"

Gibbs winced and nodded his head. "Just as I thought. Something bad is going on here. The letters are addressed to a

Constance Morgan."

"My mother."

"And a Penelope Chauncy."

"Philip's fiancée!"

Gibbs pinched his lower lip between a thumb and forefinger as he took this information in.

"Did you bring the letters?" Priscilla cried.

The tavernkeeper shook his head. "I don't have them," he said.

"Where are they? We haven't received them."

"I know. You haven't received them because they've been delivered to someone else." Priscilla was sure she knew the answer to her next question, but she asked anyway. "And how do you know that?"

"I'd rather not say."

"You'd rather not say because you are the one who has been misdirecting the letters."

Gibbs smiled slowly. It was almost a smile of admiration. "And how do you know that?" he asked.

"When I came into your establishment, you asked my name. When the stage driver heard it, he made some comment about me being there at just the right time. At that time I didn't understand what he meant. Now it makes sense. He'd just delivered a letter from a Morgan and figured a Morgan was there to pick it up."

"You're remarkable!" Gibbs said.

"And you're an insect!" Priscilla shouted. Her face was red, her eyes wet with anger. "Why have you rerouted my brother's letters?"

The tricorne hat stopped twirling. Priscilla's words had stung. "I can't tell you that," he said. "But I have my reasons. They're personal ones, having nothing to do with your family."

Putting an arm around Priscilla, Anne Pierpont said softly, "On the contrary, Master Gibbs, your actions have a great deal to do with the Morgan family. Whether willingly or not, you have led them to believe Philip is dead. You should be ashamed of yourself for causing a family needless grief."

"I didn't know that's what I was doing!" Gibbs defended himself. He too was getting angry. The hat fell to his side, held in his left hand, while he used his right index finger as a lecturing stick.

"You were a party to it, nonetheless!" Priscilla cried. "Now if you will excuse us." She whirled around to leave. Anne joined her.

"There's more." Gibbs said, his tone low and no longer friendly.

Priscilla stopped, but she didn't turn around.

"Look, I want you to know I never set out to hurt you, only to protect my tavern. Everything I own is tied up in that tavern. If I lose it, I lose everything!"

Once more, Priscilla turned around. Her eyes were a blue fire, her mouth a thin, determined line. "You said there was more."

"There might be more. I don't know for sure."

"Tell me anyway."

Their eyes locked. What Priscilla saw led her to believe she might have been mistaken about him. Her first impression of him had been that he was a mindless dispenser of ale who had never grown up, preferring to spend his days spinning verbal yarns with lazy men whose sole creativity was in their ability to find ways of avoiding work. Now she saw a spark of intellect in his sharp brown eyes. These weren't the shifting eyes of a dishonest man at all. There was earnestness and compassion in them. At the moment, there was none of the dancing humor she'd seen before.

"There was another Morgan in my tavern," Gibbs said. "A young man. Light-brown hair, thin but of good build. The man he was with called him . . ."

"Jared!" Anne cried.

Gibbs looked at her in astonishment. "That's right! Jared!"

"Sir, do you know where he is?" Anne ran to Gibbs, grabbed his arm, and looked up at him with pleading eyes. Even Priscilla took a step forward in anticipation.

"Jared and Anne have been courting," Priscilla explained.

"We're to be married!" Anne said.

"And he's my brother," said Priscilla.

"I'm sorry," the tavernkeeper said.

"He's dead?" Anne cried.

"I don't know," Gibbs replied. Sensing an angry retort from Priscilla was imminent, he explained: "Jared and another man were in the tavern. They became the targets of a crimp gang. As far as I know, he's on board some ship right now, but I don't know that for sure. The men who took him don't play games. He may be on a ship; he may be dead. I have no way of knowing."

"He's alive! I know he's alive!" Anne cried. "Thank you for coming to Cambridge, Master Gibbs. You've given me hope!"

"I wouldn't get my hopes too high," Gibbs said to Anne. "Like I said, he may be dead."

Priscilla's tone was caustic as she said, "Thank you for that wonderful bit of consoling news. I'm sure Anne feels better now."

"Look, Mistress Morgan, I didn't have to come here at all," Gibbs said, freeing his arm from Anne. "I just wanted to help."

"If you really wanted to help, you should have stopped those thugs from taking my brother!" Priscilla shouted.

"I tried to stop them!" Gibbs shouted back. "And for my effort I was rewarded with a huge lump on the back of my head! Which is more thanks than I'll ever get from you!"

"Thanks?" Priscilla shouted. "Thanks? You expect me to

thank you for diverting our mail so that I think one brother is dead while you let crimps use your tavern to abduct my other brother? Well, I'm sorry, but I'm just not feeling very grateful!"

"I knew it was a mistake coming here!" Gibbs said. "I knew better than to get mixed up with a family like this! What kind of people are you anyway? What have you done to get someone so mad at you that he'd . . . forget it! I don't even want to know. Forget I was here, because that's exactly what I'm going to try to do!"

Gibbs backed away.

"Oh no you don't!" Priscilla ran and caught him by the arm. "What have we done to get *who* mad at us? Who? I want to know!"

The smile returned to Gibbs' face as he looked at Priscilla's grip on his arm, then up at her. "Or what, Mistress Morgan? Are you going to hurt me if I refuse to tell you?"

Priscilla didn't move. Nor did she say a word. But her gripped tightened on his arm. "If he finds out I told you, everything I have is gone. And, knowing the kind of man he is, he might even kill me. So there's nothing you can do to me that he couldn't do better with more permanent results."

"Then why did you come here if you weren't going to tell me?" Priscilla asked.

Gibbs hesitated.

Anne said, "It's because when you were in his tavern he saw something in you he likes. He came here because he's attracted to you."

Gibbs laughed. "Your friend couldn't be more wrong," he said. "I came because of the mystery. I wanted to see if there was some central tie to all these Morgans who kept coming through my tavern."

"And there was, wasn't there?" Priscilla asked. She released Gibbs' arm. "And you know what—or more correctly who—

that central tie is, don't you?"

Gibbs remained silent.

"Can't you see that such knowledge may mean life or death for my family?" Priscilla said. "If you know, Master Gibbs, please tell me."

Gibbs looked at the ground, fighting a battle between his own needs and the needs of the woman standing before him. When he spoke, it was almost a whisper. "The man to whom I've given your brother's letters, the man for whom the crimp gang works is Daniel Cole."

Anne appeared shocked. Priscilla didn't. She wasn't surprised at the revelation. In fact, if there was any emotion, it was pleasure. At last she had an objective source with which to indict Daniel Cole! Something concrete to use to convince her mother!

"I don't know why Cole has it in for you," Gibbs said, "but my suggestion is to stay away from him and, definitely, stay out of his way!"

"Thank you, Master Gibbs," Priscilla said. "Unfortunately, that's not an option."

"Why not?"

"It's personal."

"Oh no you don't!" It was Gibbs' turn to grab Priscilla's arm.

"Let go of me!" Priscilla cried.

"Look, I've risked my livelihood and possibly my life telling you about Cole! I've been whacked on the head trying to keep your brother from being impressed onboard a ship. The least you can do is tell me what your family has done to make Cole so angry!"

"All right. It's as simple as this: we got in his way," Priscilla said. "And now, if you'll let me go, I've got to try to stop him."

"You're crazy if you think you can stop him!" Gibbs cried.

"She has to try," Anne said.

"Why? Why does she have to try?"

Anne looked at Priscilla. There was no sign warning her to stop, so she said, "Because earlier today on the meeting-house door Daniel Cole posted his intentions to marry Priscilla's mother."

Constance was livid. Nothing Priscilla said could convince her that Daniel Cole had a hand in Philip and Jared's disappearances. After her encounter with Peter Gibbs on the day of her public humiliation, Priscilla confronted her mother with the tavernkeeper's testimony, without naming him directly to protect him from any retribution Cole might enact. If Priscilla had given it more thought, she would have realized that Constance would give little weight to the word of an absent, unknown tavernkeeper. Even if she'd weighed the evidence beforehand, she still would have presented it. She would do anything, say anything, to keep her mother from marrying Daniel Cole.

And that's exactly what Constance accused her of. Whether Priscilla fabricated the tavernkeeper was not the issue. If he was real, he was a wicked man who had a grudge against poor Daniel, and this vindictive attempt to tarnish a good man's reputation wouldn't work. And Priscilla wouldn't succeed, no matter what she said or did. Even Anne was ineffective, as much as Constance liked Anne Pierpont. Her expressed disappointment in Anne left both women in tears. But nothing was changed and nothing would change. Constance Morgan let her daughter know that she was going to become Mrs. Daniel Cole. As for her sons' disappearances, Cole himself had assured her that he would do everything humanly possible to discover the truth about their fate. And as far as Constance was concerned, the subject was closed.

For two months Priscilla took every opportunity to discredit Cole. Her efforts only served to alienate her mother further. The more Priscilla argued, the more Constance defended him—until even Priscilla had to admit that there was nothing she could do to stop the marriage.

Reluctantly she had to admit Peter Gibbs was right. Cole was too powerful. The image of an honest, caring merchant that he had created in Constance's mind was too strong for her to combat. But even though Priscilla failed to stop the wedding, there was one thing in which she was determined not to fail—she was not going to spend a single day, not an hour, not a single minute in that man's house with him as her guardian. The specter of banishment hung over her head as her only alternative until she remembered a key phrase in the verdict. The bargain Cole made had placed her in his custody until she married. Here was her escape. So Priscilla moved quickly to bring to pass her only alternative other than banishment.

Nathan Stearns was surprised when Priscilla called on him at his north Boston home. And even as desperate as he was to get married, Priscilla's recent appearance in the pillory was not something to be taken lightly. Nathan's aunt and uncle certainly didn't. But then they had a personal interest in discouraging any relationship Nathan might have with the opposite sex. Once he married, their guardianship over him would end and they would no longer live off of Nathan's inherited wealth.

Priscilla saw it as a saving solution for both of them. Nathan would finally escape from his aunt and uncle, and she would thwart the devious scheme of Daniel Cole. In fact, that's how she worded it to Nathan—as a solution to their problems. He said he favored the arrangement and didn't seem offended at the lack of romance in the wedding plans. For his part, he was willing to overlook Priscilla's recent public embarrassment. And so the marriage contract was arranged.

Even after the marriage Priscilla was never sure what had ultimately convinced Nathan to overlook the pillory incident—whether his desire for freedom from his aunt and uncle's guardianship outweighed it, or whether his love for Priscilla overcame any moral concerns. But then it really didn't matter to Priscilla why he agreed to marry her, just as long as he did it. After all, the result was the same.

Within two weeks of Priscilla's initial call on Nathan, the two were wed and Nathan's aunt and uncle were dismissed from their responsibilities and the house. The wedding took place a full week before Daniel Cole and Constance Morgan were wed. In this way Priscilla succeeded in her pledge to herself not to spend a moment in Cole's house under his guardianship.

Thus on a sunny day in July, 1729, two desperate people became man and wife. On their wedding night, Priscilla Morgan Stearns lay awake as her husband snored softly beside her. He was curled up contentedly in a fetal position with his back to her. She had endured his awkward attempt at love-making, and in the darkness of their bedroom in their three-storied house, Priscilla thought of her father. She curled up her legs and hugged them when she thought of how much she missed him. A year ago, everything was peaceful. About this time of the evening Father would be in his study, Mother in her room, Philip would be in his room at school, Jared would be doing who knows what. In that previous world there was order and security. And love. Priscilla always knew her mother loved her, but it was her father's love she felt most deeply.

Now, a nightmarish year later, she was in bed with a man she didn't love, and she felt ashamed and empty. She had known loneliness before. But nothing like this. There was a bottomless pit inside her into which all emotion and feeling and sentiment had fallen. She had nothing to live for. There was no one she truly loved.

Priscilla took stock of her situation. Her father was dead. Her mother wasn't speaking to her. God alone knew where Philip and Jared were at this moment, if they were alive or dead. The only person who was better off in all this was Cole—he'd gotten his shares, just like he said he would, along with the Morgan house on the Charles as a bonus. And where was God in all this? Silent! While the wicked triumphed, God looked the other way! Now Priscilla had nothing. Her life consisted of an empty marriage—which was less than a day old—and an empty house. She had no family. She had no God. She had no hope.

Priscilla Morgan Stearns ached so badly she wanted to die.

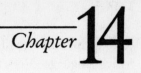

P HILIP wiped the sweat from his forehead with the back of a hand, dipped his quill in the ink, and finished the sentence he was writing. He didn't consciously think of the heat in Christopher Morgan's wigwam anymore; it had become a way of life for him. Nanouwetea—the Indian name by which Christopher Morgan was known—was old. His circulation was poor. The fire raged furiously year-round for his sake.

Setting down the quill, Philip rubbed his eyes. The smoke and soot from the fire stung with each rub. Arching his back, he stretched, careful not to knock over the shallow ink container that balanced precariously on the board across his legs. He sat cross-legged on the dirt floor of the wigwam, the board serving as a desk. From the long stretch of light streaming through the open door he could tell it was late afternoon. Nanouwetea sat a few feet from him, a blanket draped over his shoulders, intently reading a copy of John Eliot's Algonquin version of the Bible. With hands so wrinkled they looked two centuries old, Nanouwetea cradled the Bible in one hand while using the index finger of his other hand as a pointer. He held the Bible less than an inch from the end of his nose, an indication of his failing sight.

On the other side of the old Indian missionary sat Mary Weetamoo, studiously reviewing a page of Philip's work—

testing the sentences for correct grammar and spelling in her native language. Stretching his back was a common ruse Philip used to steal glances at Weetamoo. (He preferred calling her by her Indian name since her Christian name was so common. To Philip, there was nothing common about this striking Indian maid.) Her coal-black hair was streaked with yellow and orange highlights from the fire. For the moment her expression was serious, her dark-brown lips pressed together in thought, concealing white, even teeth that sparkled when she smiled, something she didn't do often enough in Philip's opinion. But when she did, it made Philip absolutely giddy, though he did his best to hide it from her.

"Enough for today." The open Bible lay in his lap while the missionary's tired eyes focused on Philip. "If I have learned anything this past year working with Philip, it is that we will get little work out of him once he has allowed Weetamoo's beauty to distract him."

Philip blushed and fumbled for the quill on his desk. "Um . . . I was just stretching," he mumbled. "I'm good for at least one more page." He cast a quick glance at Weetamoo and what he saw wasn't good. One corner of her mouth was pulled back in annoyance; slumped shoulders showed her displeasure.

Finally managing to get a grip on his writing instrument, Philip hastily dipped it in the ink. "Really," he insisted, "one more page . . . at least."

With a note of exasperation in her voice, Weetamoo rose. "I'll grind the grain for supper," she said. Without even so much as a glance toward Philip, she walked around the far side of the fire and ducked out the door.

Philip was left alone in the wigwam with a grinning missionary and the sound of a crackling fire. Reaching for a piece of cloth he wiped the tip of the quill. A disgusted sigh escaped from his lips. He set aside the board that served as his desk.

"You have feelings for her," the missionary said.

"I'm being that obvious?"

The missionary's grin was answer enough.

Philip sighed again. "I really shouldn't," he said. "I keep reminding myself I have a fiancée in Cambridge — or at least I think I still do. But when it comes to Weetamoo, I have very little control over my thoughts or emotions."

"Never be ashamed of your passions," said the missionary. "While thoughts are the voice of the mind, passion is the voice of the heart. We must listen to both voices to know what is right."

"But it doesn't make sense to be in love with two women!" Philip said.

"That is your mind speaking."

Philip's eyes grew wide. "Are you suggesting I marry both of them?"

The missionary smiled. "It is not an uncommon practice among the Narragansetts," he said. "But I don't recommend it. It is not a wise thing to do."

"But you implied . . ."

"We were talking of love, not marriage."

"So you're saying it's all right to be in love with two women at the same time?" Philip asked.

"I'm saying it's possible to be in love with two women at the same time."

"But how am I supposed to know which woman is the right one for me?"

The old missionary chuckled. "The answer to that question requires great wisdom," he said, his eyes turning heavenward as a wrinkled finger pointed upward, "and all wisdom comes from God."

"I can sure use some wisdom right now," Philip groused.

The missionary set his Indian Bible aside and reached for a larger volume. The book he reached for was also a Bible, an

English translation. It was the Morgan family Bible, the one Philip had come in search of almost a year previous. "There was a time when my father was loved by two women," he said. "They were sisters."

Philip leaned forward in anticipation of what was about to come. Over the past year Christopher Morgan had told him stories of his father, Drew Morgan, and about how Drew had fled England to escape the wrath of the notorious Bishop Laud.

"Nell and Jenny Matthews were the daughters of an English curate in Edenford, England," the missionary continued. "My father was sent to spy on their father, Christopher Matthews, who happens to be my namesake. Unfortunately for my father, he fell in love with the daughters of the man he was spying on and they with him."

"From what you've already told me, I know that Drew married Nell. If both women loved him and he loved both of them, how did he know which one to marry?"

The old man shook his head. "I don't know how he knew; I only know that at some point God made it clear to him."

"Wasn't Jenny hurt when her sister married the man she loved?"

The missionary lowered his eyes and moved a gentle hand across the cover of the Bible on his lap. "She didn't live long enough to see them married. But when my father told her that he loved Nell, Jenny was hurt. Deeply. Her pain made her vulnerable to the schemes of one of Laud's operatives in the colonies—I can't remember his name right now. Anyway, the operative convinced Jenny that he was a convert to Christianity and the Puritan way just like my father. Jenny believed his lie. They married."

"What happened to them?"

"The operative beat Jenny and used her to get to Drew. He would have succeeded too, if it wasn't for Jenny. She shot her husband just as he was about to kill my father. Both she and her husband died in the fight. Jenny's last words were of her love for my father."

Philip could hear Weetamoo humming outside the wig-wam. The soft thud of mortar against grain beat the rhythm. "Nanouwetea," he said, "you know how much I enjoy hearing stories about my ancestors, but the story you just told me doesn't make my decision any easier. In fact, it makes it more difficult. You've taught me that whatever choice I make is going to cause someone pain."

"I never said your decision would be an easy one," the missionary replied. "I said it would require great wisdom."

The year had passed quickly for Philip since he returned to the Narragansett Indian reservation following his wilderness pursuit of the Morgan family Bible. At first he was incensed that Nanouwetea tested him in this way. However, he calmed himself quickly when he learned the identity of the Indian overseer and his reasons for the test.

The tradition of the Morgan family Bible began with Drew Morgan. It was the Bible version translated by order of King James of England, given to Drew by the powerful Bishop of London when Drew was in his service as an undercover operative. Originally the Bible was used as part of a secret code by which Bishop Laud and Drew passed messages to each other. However, it was during his spy mission to Edenford that Drew discovered the real value of the Bible. Christopher Matthews, the curate of the village, taught Drew that the Bible was the divinely inspired Word of God, useful for all matters of life and faith. The combination of the curate's personal witness and the Bible's powerful message led to Drew's conversion.

No longer able to be a part of Bishop Laud's crusade of hate and persecution, Drew helped the people of Edenford escape to the New World. He came over with them and brought his Bible.

If there were two things that Drew valued above all else on earth it was his family and his Bible. It was this realization that prompted him to establish a family tradition designed to perpetuate both things he held most dear. He designated his Bible as the symbol of the Morgan family faith. The person in possession of the Bible was responsible for seeing that Christian beliefs were perpetuated in the present Morgan generation and into the next. At the time of his choosing, he was to select from among the next generation of Morgans the candidate most likely to continue this family tradition of the propagation of faith. At a family ceremony, the person chosen would have his name added to the list of Morgans in the front of the Bible.

So it was that Philip learned the history and significance of the Morgan family, and that his quest was more than just a matter of finding the Bible and taking it home with him.

Christopher Morgan, Drew and Nell Morgan's eldest son and missionary to the Narragansett Indians, had kept the Bible all these years seeking God's will regarding its future. For years it troubled him that he never married and produced an heir. Like the Apostle Paul, he felt that a marriage and family would serve as a distraction to his ministry. So how was he to pass on the family Bible to the next generation of Morgans? He had no family of his own and had lost contact with his brother and sister and their heirs. His troubled heart was calmed, he told Philip, one night when God gave him a dream. The old missionary called it his "Simeon dream." Like God's assurance to Simeon that he would not die until he saw the Lord's Christ, so Christopher Morgan was assured that he would not die until he saw the heir to the Morgan family faith.

It seemed that the old missionary's dream was fulfilled the day Philip entered his wigwam. However, being a Morgan was not enough to satisfy the tradition's criteria. In the front of the Bible Drew Morgan had penned the qualifications that each candidate for the honor must meet.

On the day of Philip's return to the Indian reservation, Christopher Morgan showed him the family Bible. Together they viewed Drew Morgan's criteria written in his own hand:

1) The candidate must give demonstrable proof of salvation and devotion to Jesus Christ as Lord and Savior;

2) The candidate must confess that the Bible is the supreme authority for life and faith;

3) The candidate must willingly accept the responsibility to teach the next generation of Morgans the fundamentals of our faith and the heritage of our family.

Opposite the list, printed on the back of the Bible's cover, were the names of those Morgans who had borne this responsibility. There were only two to date. Beside each name was a Scripture reference.

Drew Morgan, 1630, Zechariah 4:6
Christopher Morgan, 1654, Matthew 28:19

When Philip said he wasn't familiar with the Zechariah reference, the old missionary quoted it to him without looking it up. *Not by might, nor by power, but by My spirit, saith the LORD of hosts.* Christopher explained that his father had been a man of action and adventure. His greatest struggle in life was learning to trust the power of God's Spirit more than his own strength. He learned this lesson the hard way when his actions led to the death of the man he most admired. It was this same man who, even on the day of his death, urged Drew to learn the wisdom of this verse.

Drew Morgan picked the verse that accompanied his son's

name. *Go ye therefore, and teach all nations, baptizing them in the name of the Father, and of the Son, and of the Holy Ghost.* He chose this great evangelistic Scripture for his son because already Christopher had been helping John Eliot in the Roxbury pastor's early work among the Indians. Drew was proud of his eldest son's humble personality and willingness to forsake personal interests for such a noble ministry.

Christopher was twenty years old when his father presented the family Bible to him in a family ceremony held under the tree in Boston at which the earliest colonists met on the Sabbath to worship. For seventy-six years, the eldest son of Nell and Drew Morgan had been true to his missionary calling.

Evangelizing the Indians had been one of the early goals of the Puritans as expressed in the charter of the Massachusetts Bay Colony. Its seal bore the image of an Indian and the words of the Macedonian in Acts 16, "Come Over and Help Us." Yet, the task of establishing a foothold in the New World proved to be so all-consuming that it was years before any missionary work was started.

It wasn't until 1646 that the minister of Roxbury, John Eliot, preached successfully to an Indian audience in their own language. Previous attempts had been thwarted by an inability to understand the Indian's culture and early conflicts with the Pequot tribe in Connecticut. Two years later, Wauban, chief of the Nipmucks, became the first Indian chief to profess Christianity. By 1651, there were enough Indian converts to Christianity to establish the first "praying town" at Natick. This community of Christian Indians was laid out in imitation of the Puritans' own settlements. The general belief of the colonists was that the Indians had to be civilized before they could be Christianized. Praying towns provided a place where Indians could escape the corruption of their former way of living and embrace not only Christianity, but Christian culture as exemplified by the Puritans. Eliot wrote a constitution for the town, relying on the Old Testament as a model. Under the supervision of colonial officials, Indians elected leaders of ten, fifty, and one hundred, this according to the pattern of Exodus 18.

Christopher Morgan heard John Eliot preach for the first time in 1652 in a sermon describing his work among the Indians. From that moment Christopher knew what he wanted to do with his life. It was as if God spoke to him directly, saying, "This is the work to which I have called you. You are to become My missionary to the Indians. Teach them about Me. Through you My glory will shine in their towns among their people." Immediately following the service, Christopher pleaded with his father to invite the missionary to their home for the afternoon meal. The invitation was given and the missionary accepted.

There was little eating at the meal as Christopher bombarded the missionary with questions. It was then that Christopher learned that most of Eliot's time was spent among his own congregation in Roxbury, and that he was only able to give one day every other week to his missionary efforts. Therefore, he relied heavily on helpers and assistants—both Indians and Englishmen. As John Eliot told him later, at that moment the look on Christopher's face was an unmistakable plea of one wanting to help. The missionary asked Drew Morgan for permission to enlist his son in the cause of Christ among the Indian nations. At age eighteen, Christopher accompanied John Eliot to Roxbury that same day.

Christopher assisted Eliot in the translation of the Bible into the Algonquin dialect. The New Testament was complete in 1661, the Old Testament two years later. With a translation of the Bible in their own tongue, the work of the Gospel progressed rapidly. By 1675, nearly twenty percent of the Indian population of New England had become at least nominally Christian. There were thirteen thriving "praying towns."

But the uprising of Metacom, the Wampanoag sachem known as King Philip, brought a halt to all evangelistic efforts. Christopher was with Eliot when the missionary tried to engage Metacom's attention in religion. The sachem took hold of a button on Eliot's coat and said he cared no more for his religion than he did for that button. Metacom's antagonistic attitude was reflected by other chiefs. When Ninigret, chief of the Narragansetts, was asked to give liberty to missionaries to preach to his people, the chief told the missionaries to go and make the English good first. He added that as long as the English could not agree among themselves what religion was, it ill became them to teach others.

The spark that ignited the war was the murder of the Indian John Sassamon. Highly skilled in the English language, Sassamon was well-known for his Christian influence among the Indian praying towns. He was raised under the influence of Puritanism and educated at Harvard. In a moment of weakness, he fled from his Christian upbringing and returned to his native people, where he became an aide to Metacom. Sassamon's English skills were invaluable to the uneducated sachem. In time, however, the prodigal regretted his decision to run from his faith. He returned to Natick where he was readmitted to the Christian community. From that time, he was a model Christian. When a native preacher was needed by the Indians, he was chosen for the position, a position he served with distinction, honored by English and Indians alike.

Not many days before his death Sassamon warned the government of Plymouth Colony that the Wampanoags, under the leadership of Metacom, were organizing a general conspiracy against the English. His warning was taken lightly by Governor Josiah Winslow. However, when Sassamon's body was discovered at Assawompsett Pond a short time later, the Plymouth authorities became alarmed.

A group of local Indians happening by noticed Sassamon's

hat and gun lying on the surface of the frozen pond. Beneath the ice they found his body. The dead man's head was badly bruised and his neck was broken, as if by a violent twisting motion. It was determined he had died before being put in the water. John Sassamon didn't die from drowning. He was murdered.

In the investigation that followed, an eyewitness was discovered and three Indians, all Wampanoags, were brought to trial for their lives. The eyewitness was an Indian who claimed to have seen the murder from atop a nearby hill. Based largely on his testimony, a jury of twelve Englishmen along with a smaller auxiliary jury of Indians found the three men guilty of murder. Trial evidence also indicated the three Indians were acting under direct orders from their sachem, Metacom.

It seems the sachem was convinced English settlements were strangling Indian life. For him, John Sassamon's adoption of the Englishmen's faith and his alliance with their evangelistic efforts among the Indians was an example of everything that was wrong in New England. So he ordered Sassamon's death as an example to other Indians who would follow him. Thus, John Sassamon became the first Christian martyr of the New England tribes.

The hanging of the three convicted murderers only heightened tensions between the English colonists and the Indians. In an all-out attack by the Wampanoags, the tiny frontier village of Swansea was the first to suffer. Other attacks followed, taking many lives and destroying much property.

Immediately, the praying Indians and their teachers and leaders—including John Eliot and Christopher Morgan—became suspect. Colonists assaulted the praying Indians, rounding them up and shipping them to desolate Deer Island in Boston Harbor where they lived for the duration of the conflict with meager provisions and inadequate shelter.

During one colonial expedition against the marauding Indians, Job Nesutan, one of Eliot's assistants, was killed. Like Christopher Morgan, he had lived with the Eliot family and had helped translate the Bible into the Algonquin language. The three men were working on other translation and writing projects when Job was killed.

The death of such a trusted assistant and godly friend shook Eliot. More than ever before he realized that no one was safe who stood in the breech of this conflict. As pastor of the church at Roxbury, he felt he had no choice but to stay with his church and family. However, he feared for his assistant and friend Christopher Morgan. So he formulated a plan by which he might protect the life of this dear brother in Christ.

John Eliot sent Christopher Morgan to Deer Island, explaining to his assistant that the Indians on the island needed spiritual guidance lest they fall from the faith during this time of testing and hardship. The elder missionary argued that with the loss of John Sassamon and Job Nesutan, no one knew the Indians' needs better than Morgan. He knew their language, had lived with them, taught them, led them; Morgan was the ideal candidate to minister to them in their time of crisis.

Eliot's attempt to insure the safety of his coworker, although transparent, was successful. Christopher Morgan was reluctant to leave his mentor, but he could not bring himself to disobey Eliot. So for the duration of the hostilities, Christopher lived in the squalor of Deer Island. He suffered the hatred and abuse many of the imprisoned Indians on the island now felt for all English colonists. And though he was free to leave the island at any time, he remained with them. Daily he taught them; he prayed with them and for them; he preached the Word of God to them; he ministered to their sick and dying; he suffered cold and illness with them. Some, blinded by their hate, never returned to the faith; others, seeing the selfless sacrifice of Christopher, were encouraged and strengthened by his example.

Following the hostilities, the Narragansetts were one of the most devastated of all the New England tribes. All the buildings of the Narragansetts, from Providence to Stonington, a tract of about fifty miles, were burned or otherwise destroyed. It was here Christopher Morgan felt God was calling him to minister. He knew his ministry would be a difficult one, quite possibly deadly. Yet he was determined to fan the small kindling of Christian flame among the Indians of this tribe, lest the fire go out completely. His experience among the Indians on Deer Island taught him that there was no substitute for shared suffering. He determined that if he would ever gain a hearing among the Narragansett people he would have to live with them as one of them. It was the only way he could convince them that the God of the Bible was not just an English God, but a God of the Narragansetts and the Nipmucks and the Wampanoags.

Christopher Morgan believed in his missionary methods though other English ministers and missionaries spoke against them. He ignored his critics and decade after decade he lived with the Narragansetts, earning their trust and teaching them the message of Christ. When Philip arrived, the now aged missionary used an incident in the history of the Narragansetts to explain the success of his missionary method.

"In 1643, the Narragansetts and Mohegans were involved in a series of quarrels. Uncas, the Mohegan sachem, accused the Narragansett sachem, Miantonomi, of trying to kill him. The accusation led to a series of skirmishes between the two tribes. Miantonomi prepared to lead a war party of about 1,000 men into Mohegan territory. Samuel Gorton, an English friend of Miantonomi, loaned the Narragansett sachem a heavy suit of English armor to protect him in battle. Although the Narragansett outnumbered the Mohegan two to one, Uncas gained the advantage over his foe by pretending to negotiate. He then led a surprise attack. The Narragansett warriors retreated. Miantonomi, slowed by the heavy armor, was unable to keep up with his men. He was captured and killed. For many years the Narragansetts mourned their leader's death. Whenever a Narragansett passes by the site of his burial near Norwich, he drops a stone as a gesture of mourning and respect. Even today, the stone pile can be seen," Christopher said. "Every September a party of Narragansetts travels to the stone pile. They break forth in loud lamentations and add more stones to the heap in memory of their once-great sachem."

Christopher explained the parallel between this story and his missionary work by comparing English weaponry with English methodology. "There is little doubt that in Europe, the suit of armor is invaluable in warfare. But then continental armies use different methods to fight each other. However, just because the English armor is useful on the continent doesn't mean it will be useful here. In this instance, not only was it not useful, but it was the instrument of Miantonomi's death. In the same way, English methods and culture—although useful in England and among the colonists—often times prove to be stumbling blocks or unnecessary weight to the conversion of the Narragansetts. My testimony to the Indians has been that Jesus Christ wants to be Lord of their wigwams, their villages, their towns. They don't have to dress like Englishmen, eat English food, and wear English clothes to be Christians. All they need do is call upon the name of the Lord and they will be saved."

Upon hearing the story and explanation, Philip nodded his head in understanding and said, "Like David facing Goliath. You have chosen to ignore the advice and armor of Saul and do battle with the weapons with which you are most familiar, trusting in the Lord to give you victory."

It was the first time Philip saw the aged Christopher Morgan smile.

Chapter 15

"ANY letters from home yet, English?"

John Wampas peered over the edge of his bowl of samp as he asked the question. The question hit Philip like an arrow. And from the mischievous glint in the young Indian's eyes, Wampas knew he'd scored a direct hit.

It was mid-September, 1729. Philip had been gone from home for over a year. Every month he'd written to his mother and Penelope. Every month he hoped for a response to his latest letter. Every month he was disappointed. It was maddening. No matter how hard Philip tried, he couldn't think of a good reason why no one answered his letters. If they were angry with him for not returning home immediately, the least they could do is express their anger in a letter. After a year of silence Philip would welcome even an angry letter. It just didn't make sense. He'd considered the possibility the letters weren't reaching them. But if that were the case, surely by now they would have sent someone to look for him!

The more Philip thought about it, the angrier he got. Each month for the last four months he told himself he wasn't going to write another letter until he heard from them. But before the month was out, his resolve would waver and he'd write, only to be disappointed one more time. It was a sensitive topic for him and Wampas knew it. It was the Indian's favorite method of goading him.

Philip swallowed the bite in his mouth then mumbled, "No. No letters yet." He set aside his bowl. As much as he liked the hot cornmeal mush samp, he couldn't finish it. He'd lost his appetite.

The old missionary, however, had cleaned his bowl and plopped it triumphantly on the ground. It was his public declaration that he'd eaten it all. Weetamoo was pleased. For several weeks the old missionary had hardly eaten anything. The amount of time he was able to put into his primer project grew shorter each day while his periods of sleep grew longer. It wasn't unusual for the old missionary to sleep an entire day. At times he would grow so still that his breathing would be barely noticeable. On one occasion, out of concern, Weetamoo tried to rouse him. He wouldn't wake. Only by placing her ear next to his chest could she determine he was still alive. This return of his appetite was the first healthy sign he'd shown.

"Weetamoo," the missionary said cheerfully, "wouldn't tonight be a good night for some chestnuts?"

The Indian maid looked surprised. "You are feeling that well?"

"I am," he replied. "Besides, we need a little merriment in our wigwam. Your chestnuts will get us started."

Weetamoo laid aside her bowl of samp. She rose and walked to a row of baskets and sacks. Having no shelves, the Indians used these for their household and food stuffs. Digging to the bottom of a hemp sack, she retrieved a small basket holding the chestnuts. The Indians had an art of drying their chestnuts and preserving them in such a way that they were eaten year-round as special treat. Philip was especially fond of them.

The old missionary was correct in his assessment of the mood in the wigwam. Tensions among Philip, Wampas, and Weetamoo were strained, enough that Philip was seriously considering returning home. The only thing that kept him there was Christopher Morgan's frailty. It was the old man's age that prompted him to stay in the first place and that's what kept him here now. Philip feared that if he went home, by the time he returned, Christopher would be dead. There was something about his ancestor that attracted him. Philip couldn't put it into words. Maybe it was the depth of the man's spirituality, or the fact that he was a living link to Philip's past. Maybe it was the way Philip felt around him. It was the same kind of feeling he had when he was with his father. Maybe God was allowing him this time with an elder Morgan to make up for the premature departure of his father. Philip didn't know for sure. But one thing he knew. The opportunity to enjoy this feeling was a short one and nothing was going to cause him to miss it.

Actually, the opportunity was lengthier than Philip had originally anticipated. His initial estimation over a year ago was that the old missionary wouldn't last the winter. As much as he wanted to complete his course work at Harvard, he wanted to get to know Christopher Morgan more. Harvard could wait. Penelope, poor Penelope, would have to understand. And so Philip chose to stay at the reservation until his aged ancestor died.

In exchange for his board and meals, Philip agreed to use his linguistic skills, the skills that so impressed his colleagues at Harvard, to help Christopher Morgan complete an Algonquin primer. It was the missionary's express desire to finish the primer before he died. He claimed he could have no greater legacy than to leave behind a book that would equip the New England tribes to read the Bible for themselves. Of course, Philip would have to learn Algonquin, something he was eager to do if he was going to spend any more time on the reservation. Although he never considered himself a fearful man, there were times when he'd catch people looking at him while they carried on a conversation he couldn't under-stand. He knew that just because their eyes rested on him didn't mean they were talking about him. Still, it would ease his mind if he understood what they were saying.

Now here it was over a year later. He understood enough Algonquin to get by in most any conversation, the primer still was not finished, and Christopher Morgan was looking healthier than Philip had ever seen him. A month ago Philip agonized as another matriculation at Harvard began without him. Still, the old missionary was ninety-five years old. How much longer could he live? In spite of the growing tension between him and Wampas and Weetamoo, Philip knew he would stay at the reservation until either the primer was com-plete or Christopher Morgan died.

Weetamoo held the container of chestnuts in front of the old missionary. He leaned forward with the expression of a child picking out a piece of candy. Wrinkled fingers pushed the chestnuts around until he found one that obviously pleased him. Next, the bowl was offered to Wampas who flashed a triumphant grin at Philip. Apparently he took the order of serving as something of a victory. Finally, the bowl was offered to Philip. The hostess extended it to him without looking at him, her eyes focused on the chestnuts.

"No thank you," Philip said, hoping to catch her eye. Weetamoo didn't look up. Her eyes rested on the small bas-ket of chestnuts as she withdrew it.

"Take some!" The old missionary flicked the back of his hand toward Philip, encouraging him to take a chestnut. Crushed chestnuts coated his tongue as he spoke. "They're your favorite! Take some!"

Weetamoo offered the bowl again. Never once did she look at him. Philip couldn't help but notice her delicate brown fingers curved around the bowl. He followed them to her dainty wrist, up a slender arm, past her covered shoulder, to the curve of her neck and the smoothness of her cheek. Then he caught himself and glanced quickly at Wampas. The Indian's jaw was set, his eyes angry. Philip reached into the basket, withdrew a couple of chestnuts, and uttered a curt thank-you.

Without any kind of acknowledgment, Weetamoo returned to her place, set the basket of chestnuts beside her, and resumed eating.

"Let's sing!" the old missionary cried. Without waiting for a response, he began.

Glory to God the Father be, Glory to the Son,
Glory to God, the Holy Ghost, Glory to God alone.

He sang with his eyes closed and a smiling face turned heavenward. His voice was raspy but his enthusiasm was robust. By the second stanza he was not singing alone.

Hallelujah, Hallelujah, Hosanna, Hosanna,
Hallelujah, Hallelujah, Hosanna, Hosanna.

As soon as one song was finished, the missionary launched into another. And in spite of himself, Philip found that his spirits began to lift. As the four voices joined in singing praises to God, the mood inside the wigwam rose to a loftier plane. It didn't dissolve the tension. It was still there. But it felt good to set it aside for a while.

When Philip was sure Wampas wasn't looking, he stole a couple of glances at him. John Wampas was strong, handsome, and self-assured. Philip couldn't help thinking how much the Indian was like his athletic brother Jared. The comparison between the two extended to his relationship with them. He didn't get along with either Jared or Wampas. He tried to get along; at least he thought he did. Philip's mind wandered back to their first days together.

When Philip and Wampas returned following Philip's excursion into the forest, Philip had strong feelings of fondness for the Indian who had saved him from the bear. And Wampas seemed to warm to him during their three-day return journey. However, once they reached the reservation, Wampas changed. He grew cold and distant, and at every opportunity he played the antagonist. Philip had no idea what had prompted the change.

Since Philip was on unfamiliar ground, he chose to ignore the Indian's slights and try to find out about him. He learned through Christopher Morgan that both Weetamoo and Wampas were orphans. The old missionary took Wampas into his wigwam when his parents were killed by a white renegade from Providence colony and no relatives were left to care for him. A year later Weetamoo's parents died of fever. Now the missionary had two children. He saw them as gifts from God and raised them as his own.

Christopher Morgan took his family obligations very seriously. And since the two orphans were little children when their parents died, he was the only family they knew. Philip was impressed with the closeness of the family, the way they cared for each other. This patchwork family cared more for each other than his family ever did. At least, that's what he saw initially. The longer Philip stayed with them, the more disharmony he saw among them. And he couldn't help feeling that it was his presence that was upsetting the balance.

So Philip set out on a private crusade to win the friendship of John Wampas. He looked for ways to commend the Indian; he volunteered to perform his chores; he even asked Wampas if he could tag along on some of the reservation entertainment activities. Wampas was not receptive to his efforts.

When Philip learned that Wampas and some friends were going to the hothouse, he decided to join them. He thought that if he could get Wampas' friends to accept him, it would make it easier for Wampas to accept him. When Wampas left for the hothouse Philip waited a few minutes, then followed him.

The hothouse was located on the far side of the reservation. It was a cavern about six to eight feet deep and eight feet high carved into the side of a hill. Inside, in the middle of the cave, a fire was built over a heap of stones. When the stones were red-hot, the Indians removed the fire and the hothouse was ready. Ten to twelve men entered at a time, leaving their clothing outside the cave's entrance. For an hour or more they would talk and smoke tobacco and sweat together in the belief that the sweating cleansed their skin and purged their bodies of disease. Then they would run from the cave and jump into Pasquiset Pond.

The Indians were already inside when Philip arrived. Their breeches and other coverings lay piled outside the cave. Philip put his clothes with theirs and entered.

The air inside the cave was heavy with the smell of tobacco and human sweat. It was so thick and oppressively hot Philip struggled to swallow his first gulp of hothouse air. All talking ceased the moment the Indians saw him. There were eleven Indians lounging in various positions of comfort around the cave's perimeter. Philip nodded at Wampas, who did not look pleased to see him, and searched the cave's edges for a place to sit, hoping that his awkwardness would ease once he was settled. He encouraged them to continue their conversations which, after several more uneasy moments, they did.

Back then Philip knew just a little of their language, so he was only able to pick out scraps of their conversation. His contribution was limited to a few short phrases or one-word responses. But over all, his plan seemed to be going well. At least it was with everyone but Wampas. While the rest of the Indians seemed to adjust to the presence of a white man in their hothouse, Wampas never did. The orphan Indian sat glumly against the wall and stared at the hot rocks in the center of the cave.

Philip didn't see any signal, yet almost simultaneously all the men in the cave jumped to their feet and crowded through the cave opening. Yelling and whooping, they scurried down a small hill and plunged into the pond. Philip followed them down the slope and into the water. There was an initial shock as cold water hit hot skin, but once the shock passed, it was the most refreshing feeling Philip had ever experienced. He whooped and splashed with the rest of them. It was a wonderful feeling. And he wasn't just thinking of the physical sensation. It was wonderful to be a part of a male activity again. Not since Harvard had he done something like this with a group of fellows. Not until now did he realize how much he missed it.

His good feeling ended abruptly soon afterward. The last one to get out of the water, he trudged up the hill to the cave well behind the others. When he reached the entrance to the cave, the ground around the entrance was as bare as he was. His clothes were missing! Frantically, he searched everywhere—inside the cave, in the bushes, in the trees, back down by the edge of the pond. No clothes! Someone had stolen his clothes!

Not only were there no clothes in sight, there were no other people around either. All the other Indians had left him. If that wasn't bad enough, an entire reservation of men, women, and children lay between him and Christopher Morgan's wigwam.

Philip gritted his teeth. "Wampas! It had to be Wampas!"

He pulled two branches from a bush, the fullest branches he could find. *Well, if it was good enough for Adam and Eve...* he thought. Covering himself in the front with one branch and in the back with the other, Philip Morgan set out down the dusty road that led across the Narragansett reservation. He winced at every step that landed on a rock and cringed when he had to leave the tree and bush covering of the hill and walk into the wide open plain upon which the sparsely spaced wigwams and buildings of the reservation set.

By nature, the Narragansett Indians are a sober people. This day was an exception. Bellies were held. Tears were shed. The sounds of laughter were so loud it pulled people from their wigwams. By the time Philip was midway down Schoolhouse Pond Road he'd attracted a parade of children. They were so captivated at the whiteness of his skin, some ran up and took swipes at his legs and chest to see if he was painted.

Philip ran past the church building and the northern edge of Adam's Pond. He bolted into Christopher Morgan's wigwam. A startled missionary and his young female assistant gawked at his sudden appearance and lack of attire.

Weetamoo covered a snickering mouth. She rose and excused herself.

Christopher Morgan was sympathetic. "Wampas?" he asked.

"Wampas," Philip answered.

The ending of the song jolted Philip's mind back to the present. "Shall I read from the English Bible or the Algonquin Bible tonight?" the missionary asked.

Wampas was quick with his preference. "Algonquin," he said.

Since there were no objections, he reached for the Indian Bible. Turning to the Book of Acts, he began to read where he'd left off the night before—the passage about the disagreement between Paul and Barnabas over taking John Mark with them on their second missionary journey. *So, I'm not the only one who has trouble getting along with other people*, Philip thought. While the missionary continued reading, Philip continued his mental review of his relationship with Wampas.

After the hothouse incident, Philip charted a different course with Wampas. It was clear to him Wampas didn't want to be friends, and for the sake of harmony in the wigwam Philip did not want to make him an enemy. So he decided to stay out of Wampas' way and hoped that Wampas stayed out of his.

At meals Philip was civil but distant with the Indian, only answering questions put to him directly, never initiating conversation. Most days were free of conflict since Wampas was usually away hunting, or searching for and preparing poles or stakes when the wigwam needed repair. Philip was left alone with the missionary and Weetamoo writing the Algonquin primer. It was work and company he enjoyed.

Philip thought that the lack of contact between them would help ease the strain of their relationship. It didn't. It seemed like every day Wampas grew more surly. He went out of his way to take a verbal, and sometimes physical, jab at Philip. Philip responded by increasing the distance between them.

One day Wampas entered the hut holding two replacement poles in his hand during the middle of the day. The elderly missionary was napping. Philip and Weetamoo were going over some of the pages he'd printed earlier that day. The grammar was all wrong and while he held the page Weetamoo kneeled behind him, reading it over his shoulder, and pointing to mistakes he'd made. At first they didn't know Wampas had entered the wigwam. He didn't say anything. He got their attention by throwing the poles to the ground, then fleeing the wigwam. He didn't return for supper.

Christopher Morgan wasn't feeling well at the time, and went to sleep early that night. Weetamoo went outside for a walk by the lake. Philip stayed with the sleeping missionary and read from Drew Morgan's journal about a time earlier in the settler's life when he was in Edenford, England. He described a humorous event when Nell and Jenny Matthews tricked him into reading aloud a graphic passage of Scripture from the Song of Solomon.

Just then a noise caught his attention. He cocked his ear first one direction, then another. Did the sound come from outside or inside? He looked over at the sleeping missionary. The sound he heard was a moan. Christopher Morgan seemed to be sleeping peacefully.

There it was again! It came from outside. He focused his attention beyond the walls of the wigwam. It wasn't a moan he heard—more like a muffled cry! The cries grew louder and more intense. Philip set his book aside to investigate. It was dark outside. A bare sliver of a moon reflected in the pond. While it took his eyes a few moments to adjust, his ears directed him toward the pond. The clear night air carried the sound well. Philip headed toward the lake, squinting into the darkness to see what or who was making the noise.

Just as the ground began to descend toward the lake, he saw two figures beneath a lone tree. It looked like they were wrestling, and that one was gaining the advantage. Now the sound was clearer. Philip began to understand words and phrases. "No . . . no. Wampas, don't do this! No . . . "

It was Weetamoo's voice!

Philip raced toward them. Wampas was clumsily pulling at Weetamoo's clothing while at the same time trying to keep her hands and arms pinned against the ground. He was bare-chested, wearing nothing but a pair of leather breeches. Philip leaped at him, knocking him backward. The two men tumbled over tree roots toward the lake's edge.

Wampas was the first to regain his feet. Normally this wouldn't have surprised Philip, Wampas being the better athlete, but as the two rolled on the ground Philip smelled the strong odor of liquor. Wampas was drunk, very drunk. And even though he was on his feet, he was having a hard time staying there. He wove back and forth unsteadily, rubbing his eyes with the backs of his hands, trying to clear them, to see who had attacked him. For Philip, the moment of recognition was unmistakable. The Indian's expression mutated from one of confusion to one of rage.

As Philip struggled to get up, Wampas screamed hysterically and kicked him furiously in the side. The blow sent Philip rolling into the edge of the lake, knocking the wind from him. He doubled over and, laying on his side, gasped for air. The blow also sent the unsteady attacker falling to the ground beside him. Again Wampas was up before Philip. This time he produced a knife from his leather breeches. He waved it menacingly over the floundering Philip.

"No!" Weetamoo screamed. "Wampas, don't do it! Please . . . for me . . . don't do it!"

The Indian hesitated. The diversion was long enough for Philip to get to his feet. The pain in his side kept him from standing up straight. With one hand he clutched his ribs; with the other he prepared to defend himself.

Wampas yelled something at Philip he didn't understand, words he hadn't heard before. But the sneer and hate on the Indian's face communicated their meaning.

The three of them stood there for a long moment, as if time were frozen—Philip was hunched over, eyeing Wampas. Weetamoo stared at Wampas. Wampas glared at Philip. His face was dripping wet and his chest heaved furiously.

"Wampas! Look at me!" Weetamoo screamed.

Wampas refused. It was as if he knew that once he looked at her it would be all over.

"Wampas . . ."

Suddenly Wampas turned and ran before she could complete her sentence. The effects of the alcohol caused him to slip and fall a couple of times as he ascended the slope, and when he was on his feet he staggered from side to side.

Though slowed by his condition, a moment later he was gone. The night was still and peaceful once again.

"Are you hurt?" Philip asked.

Weetamoo adjusted the top of her dress around her neck. "I'm fine," she said. Reaching behind her she brushed the grass from the back of her hair. "And you?"

"I'll live," Philip said.

"Good." Weetamoo turned and walked up to the slope toward the wigwam.

Philip stared at her in disbelief. "Good?" he yelled after her. "That's all? Just 'good' and walk away?"

Weetamoo wheeled around, her hands on her hips. She was furious and Philip didn't know why. "What do you want? My undying gratitude?"

"No! Of course not! It's just that ... well, what was Wampas doing?"

A look of exasperation crossed her face. "What did it look like he was doing?"

Philip had no idea why she was treating him like this, but he knew one thing—he didn't like it. "Look, I don't understand why you're treating me this way. It was clear what he was trying to do. What I want to know is, why? Why was he doing it?"

Weetamoo rolled her eyes heavenward and threw her hands up. "I can't believe how ignorant you can be at times!" she shouted.

"All right!" With exaggerated motions Philip nodded his head. "So I'm ignorant! I'll admit it. Now will you tell me why Wampas was trying to rape you?"

The word hit her hard. Until it was spoken, she could pretend Wampas' actions were something else. But no longer. Her anger turned to tears. She wrapped her arms around herself and sobbed. Philip wanted to go to her, but something warned him not to.

"It's your fault," she sobbed.

"My fault? I don't believe this! Wampas tries to . . ." he stopped himself and started again. "Wampas attacks you and it's my fault?"

"Yes, your fault!" she screamed. "His drinking, his gambling, that stinking tobacco smell all over him . . . what happened tonight. It's all because of you."

"This is incredible!" Philip yelled. He kicked the edge of the lake, sending a water spray along the bank. "Simply incredible! Would you mind explaining to me how all those things are my fault?"

Weetamoo wiped away tears with determined strokes. She was regaining her composure. "Can't you see that Wampas is crazy with jealousy when it comes to you?"

"Jealous?" It was an absurd idea. The Jareds and Wampases of the world weren't jealous of anybody; people were jealous of them.

"Yes, jealous! You threaten everything that's important to him! He can't compete with you, Philip!"

"There's nothing I have that he wants."

"Yes there is! He wants the attention Nanouwetea gives you. And he thinks you're trying to take me away from him! And there's nothing he can do to stop it. So he turns to liquor and gambling and. . . ." She clutched at her throat as the realization of what almost happened tonight struck her again. When the words came out, they came out in a whisper. "And even rape, or at least the attempt. Wampas is angry and hurt."

"Now I've heard it all!" Philip cried. "He has nothing to be jealous of!"

"No? Before you came, Wampas wanted to do the work on the primer you're doing now. Nanouwetea gave him a chance. Wampas couldn't do it. He doesn't have your skills, your education. Not only did you get the job he wanted, but every day you earn Nanouwetea's praise. The praise he so desperately craves!"

What Weetamoo was saying made sense. Philip hadn't thought about it that way before.

"And then there's us," she continued softly.

"Us?" Just hearing her mention the possibility of them being an "us" caused his heart to beat faster.

"The amount of time we spend working together," she explained. "He thinks you're taking me away from him."

"Taking you away? Are you pledged to him or something?"

Weetamoo shrugged her shoulders. "We have an understanding. There are so few Christians our age. When we were younger we talked about how we could be the Adam and Eve of a new generation of praying Indians." Instantly she regretted revealing such a personal glimpse into her life. She waved it aside angrily. "What matters is that Wampas feels you're a threat even though I've told him there is nothing to worry about."

Philip tried not to let Weetamoo see how much her last sentence disappointed him. "I understand what you're saying," he said. "But you can't make me responsible for someone else's actions!"

"All I know is that before you came, there was peace in our family!" Tears filled her eyes as she spoke. "And look at what's happening to us now!"

"Weetamoo," Philip said softly. He stepped toward her.

Weetamoo's response was to turn and run away. Then suddenly she stopped and yelled back at him. "Promise you won't tell Nanouwetea what happened tonight! Promise me, Philip Morgan!"

"I promise," he said.

That was a week ago.

Christopher Morgan lowered the Indian Bible. "May God

bless the reading of His Holy Word," he said. "Sleep well, my children."

"Sleep well," the three replied in turn.

Philip looked at the other two as they said it. Weetamoo still would not look him in the eyes and Wampas looked as angry as ever.

Chapter 16

THE Narragansett procession to church each Sunday was a visible demonstration of their deep reverence for Nanouwetea, their spiritual overseer. Following the practice of other colonies, the morning began when a signal called the faithful to worship. Some churches used bells, others used drums; still others, like the Narragansett church, assembled the people by blowing a conch shell. At the sounding of the conch, the reservation's faithful lined the short section of road that led from the missionary's wigwam to the crude meetinghouse in which they worshiped. They were a poor rural people living on the fringes of a plantation economy. Many of them worked as house servants or common laborers in Charlestown, a small village to the west which bore the same name as the town located at the mouth of the Charles River north of Boston. On the Sabbath they were free to worship, which they did with much reverence. Speaking only in hushed tones they waited in patience for their spiritual leader to pass by. When he appeared they fell in behind him. Because of the missionary's age, it was a slow procession to the church, one that he could not make without assistance.

Two church-appointed guardians flanked the aged overseer, assisting him as needed. The Christian worshipers of the reservation loved their leader and he them. He had not only taught them the teachings of Christ for over five decades, he had proved the teachings with his life, never once providing anyone with an excuse to disbelieve or fall away on account of his speech or his dealings. Early in his ministry he told them repeatedly that he had consecrated himself first to God, secondly to them. He no longer told them this. He didn't need to tell them. Although many refused to worship his God, there was no doubting the sincerity and love of God's missionary. They knew a holy man when they saw one.

Of course the missionary, in keeping with Puritan doctrine, taught the people to refrain from all popish practices. However, if there was anything in the Narragansett Sabbath that resembled ecclesiastical ritual, it was the procession that followed their sacred teacher to the place of worship. The pope himself never had such a worshipful following.

The tradition of the missionary's attendants was founded on practical necessity. Christopher Morgan's advanced frailty required someone assist him. The honor of being one of the two church-appointed escorts soon grew in importance until they were coveted positions, as much as any attendant position in Rome.

The last time an attendant vacancy occurred, the missionary himself asked for the privilege of recommending his own escort. It soon became apparent that he had someone in mind even before he asked. John Wampas had just turned sixteen and, in recognition of the boy's growth in God, the aged missionary recommended his son-in-the-Lord to fill the vacancy. The church was pleased to honor their missionary's request. They readily appointed John Wampas to be a processional attendant. With humility, the young Indian accepted. And for three years he fulfilled his responsibility with solemn dignity. Never once did he miss a Sunday procession. Until today.

When the conch sounded on this September Sunday, there was only one escort present at Christopher Morgan's wigwam. And it wasn't John Wampas.

Several frantic moments followed as the remaining attendant and several close followers buzzed around searching for an answer to this dilemma. This hadn't been anticipated; attending the missionary was such a prized duty it was unthinkable that anyone would fail to show up. No one had even thought of having substitute attendants. But that was beside the point now. What should be done today? The conch had already sounded! People would be waiting for Nanouwetea to pass by! Should the remaining attendant escort the missionary alone? What if Nanouwetea stumbled and fell? Was a single attendant sufficient to keep him from harming himself? If only one was needed, only one would have been appointed in the first place. Two were needed. But how could anyone serve who hadn't been appointed by the church?

When Christopher Morgan could take no more of this fluster that was masquerading as a crisis, he said, "Philip Morgan will fill in for John today."

"But he hasn't been appointed by the church! And there are a lot of men who have been waiting a longer time for the privilege of . . ."

The missionary raised his hand to cut off the objections. "Philip is here and we are late. Let's not keep the Lord waiting any longer."

With the help of Weetamoo, Christopher Morgan adjusted the heavy feather mantle on his shoulders. The church-appointed attendant took one arm and, handing his Bible to Weetamoo, Philip Morgan took the other. At the opening of the wigwam one attendant preceded the missionary outside. With one assistant outside and one inside, they helped the old man through the low door.

It was a bright, hazy day with a light breeze coming from the south, the kind of day that was neither summer nor autumn, but that had traces of both seasons in it. The processional began as the missionary and his two attendants made their way down the road at a turtle's pace.

They hadn't gone more than a hundred yards when John Wampas came running up to them. His face, arms, and chest were smeared with dirt. He smelled of dried sweat and alcohol. "Take your hands off of him!" he yelled at Philip. "That's my position! The church appointed me!" The Indian's speech was slurred and his eyes were bloodshot, the aftereffects of heavy drinking the night before. "I said take your hands off!" he shouted. Wampas lunged at Philip, shoving him in the chest with all his might.

Philip was caught off guard. Try as he might to release his hold on the missionary and still retain his balance, he stumbled backward with his hand caught in the crook of the missionary's arm. Philip crashed to the ground. The missionary stumbled backward. The second attendant did his best to keep Christopher Morgan from falling, but couldn't. Scores of helpless followers watched in disbelief as their ninety-five-year-old overseer fell. With the feather mantle crumpled beneath him, he looked like a fallen eagle.

"Stop! Don't touch him!" Weetamoo cried. Her frantic order was directed at the appointed attendant. Much like he would a basket or vessel that had tipped over, he was trying to right the fallen missionary as quickly as possible. The young maid rushed to Christopher Morgan's side. "Are you all right, Nanouwetea? Are you hurt?"

The old man seemed embarrassed that so many people were looking down at him. Everyone except Philip and Wampas. Philip was on his backside; Wampas stood horror-stricken a short distance away.

"Don't get up if you're hurt," Weetamoo cautioned.

A thin smile appeared on the old man's lips. Even though it stretched the skin around his mouth, it still wasn't enough to take the wrinkles away. He patted her on the hand. "I may be an ancient clay vessel," he said, "but thank God

I'm still a whole one."

The church-appointed attendant took one arm while Weetamoo took the other to help him stand.

"Please, let me." It was Wampas.

Weetamoo whirled toward him. She was about to yell at him to stay away. But when she saw Wampas' face, she swallowed her words and gently stepped aside. The Indian's cheeks that were once filthy with dirt showed streaks of clean skin, washed by streams of tears that flowed from pools in his eyes.

When the missionary was once again on his feet, he turned to his Indian son. "Go home," he said. "Wash yourself. Then join us for worship."

"But Nanouwetea, I must assist you to the meetinghouse, then I will do as you say."

The old missionary shook his head. "It is more important that you prepare yourself to come before the Lord so that He can cleanse you. Philip will assist me to the meetinghouse."

By now Philip was standing. Wampas' volatile nature kept him at a distance. The Indian didn't want to let go of the missionary's arm. Wampas shot an angry glance at Philip. The young Indian's jaw was set and his chest heaved as he battled his raging emotions.

The missionary placed a hand on his arm. "Wampas," he said. When the young Indian didn't acknowledge him, he said it again, "Wampas!" Slowly Wampas broke the lock he had on Philip and turned toward the missionary. Not until their eyes met did the missionary speak again. Then he said, "Do as I say."

It was as if he was in a trance. Wampas looked down at the old man's arm and his hands, his eyes focusing on neither. Slowly, almost a finger at a time, he released the missionary's arm. He took one half-step backward, then another.

Philip eased himself between Wampas and the missionary, gently taking the missionary by the arm. The procession began again at an even slower pace. Once, Philip glanced back. Wampas hadn't moved. He stood in the middle of the dirt road where they'd left him.

The worship service bore close resemblance to the worship services in Cambridge in the church where Philip grew up. The major exception was that the service was conducted in Algonquin. The meetinghouse was a simple one-room building. The pews were benches with no backs. There were no enclosed private pews and apparently no seating order, since Philip saw some people change seats before the service began. Christopher Morgan sat elevated beside the pulpit like a patriarch. The deacons sat below him, also facing the congregation. From his prominent position the aged minister observed every part of the service, joining in the hymns, joining with them in prayer (although he remained seated while they stood), and nodding at key points during the sermon which was preached by a middle-aged Indian by the name of Jedediah Pomham, who was serving as the reservation's minister. His was a simple sermon, not the doctrinal discourses which Philip was accustomed to, being raised in a college town. But the presence of God's Spirit was evident and His Word was proclaimed. It was a short sermon, barely an hour long, and as the service ended, everyone remained in their place until the two assistants, Philip standing in again for the absent Wampas—who did not show up for the second time that day—led the missionary from the building. The pastor and deacons followed. Finally, the congregation was dismissed.

"I'm worried about Wampas," Weetamoo said as she collected the bones from their afternoon meal of cold pigeon. No one had seen the young Indian since he had been left behind during the morning processional.

"He's in God's hands," said Nanouwetea, who was picking off the last bit of meat from the bird's carcass.

The young maid's furrowed brow indicated she wasn't fully appeased by the missionary's response.

"Should I go look for him?" Philip asked.

The question seemed to surprise both the old man and the maid. A slight smile crossed Weetamoo's lips.

"Your offer is appreciated, Philip, but Wampas is best left alone," said Nanouwetea. "Like the prodigal, he will come to himself and find his way home."

"Then if you will excuse me . . ." Weetamoo said flatly. "I think I'll make a call on Namumpum."

"She was bigger this morning than I have ever seen her," said Nanouwetea.

"The baby should have come two weeks ago. The poor woman is suffering. Says she feels as big a cow. Most of the women of the church believe she's carrying more than one baby."

"Is this her first?" Philip asked.

Both Nanouwetea and Weetamoo smiled broadly. "Fourteenth," Weetamoo said. "Maybe fifteenth too if the church women are right."

"Offer her prayers on my behalf," said Nanouwetea.

Weetamoo bundled up a few things and was gone, leaving Philip alone with his ancestor. Philip had come to treasure these private moments. They were few, given the missionary's busy schedule. What with two other people living in the wigwam, the work on the primer, and a never-ending parade of church members stopping by with grievances or seeking spiritual guidance, these personal times came too infrequently. And Christopher Morgan's time was steadily running out, like sand through an hourglass. Wasn't that life the way God intended? Unlike Philip's father, whose hourglass had been dashed before the full measure of sand had a chance to pass through. For whatever reason, God had granted Philip the privilege of sharing what little sand was left in the old missionary's hourglass, and he intended to savor every moment of it.

Philip scanned the interior of the wigwam, hoping to burn its image into his mind so that he would never forget it. The blazing fire in the center cast everything in an orange light. The hole directly over it let most of the fire's smoke out and some of the outside sunlight in. The wigwam's frame of poles arching upward and covered with bark was crude compared to the home in which he'd grown up along the Charles River. Strange though, how this shelter with its dirt floor felt so much like home to him now. Of course, everything inside smelled of smoke, a smell Philip had come to associate with feelings of home. Baskets and sacks lined the far edges of the wigwam while books, Bibles (including the Morgan family Bible), papers, and writing instruments were scattered around the area where Christopher Morgan always sat. Then there was the missionary himself. Cross-legged, hunched slightly forward, huddled under his feather mantle. A wise man if ever there was one—unselfish, truly a man of God.

"Will you be leaving us soon?"

Philip had been so caught up in his thoughts, the sound of the missionary's voice startled him.

"Leaving? Why do you ask?"

"You are looking at everything as if it will be the last time you see them."

"I fear my presence here has been disruptive."

"Wampas," the missionary said softly.

"And Weetamoo. I think she will be just as relieved when I leave."

The missionary studied Philip's face as if testing it for sincerity. "Weetamoo is double-minded when it comes to you."

"I don't understand," said Philip.

"Then may God grant you understanding. Will you leave before the primer is finished?"

Philip lowered his head. It flopped from one shoulder to the other as the whole cyclical argument played itself out in his head. "That's my dilemma," he said. "The longer I stay, the worse things get between me and Wampas. The worse they get, the more upset Weetamoo gets with me. So it seems that the best thing for me to do is to leave. But then, there's the primer and my work with you. I want to finish it. If I leave it solves one problem, but creates another."

The missionary showed no reaction to Philip's dilemma. In fact, his reaction was so neutral it seemed like to him there was no dilemma at all.

"So you can see the problem I'm facing."

"Tell me more about your sister and brother," the missionary said.

A complete change of subject. Philip thought this was the missionary's way of saying it was his decision to make and that he would have to make it alone. "Well ..." he did his best to jump to the new subject, "Priscilla, my sister, is ... well, she's an average young woman, rather short with red hair — oh, and stubborn as the day is long — she seems more interested in books than she is with young men. And Jared is ... well, I guess you could say he's good-looking, but he's undisciplined and lazy. For years, Father has had to deal with his pranks and antics. Jared has a knack for getting into trouble."

"And your mother?"

Philip smiled as the image of his mother came to mind. "She's soft-spoken. A perfect wife and mother. Never argued with Father, always supported him."

"Do you love her?"

"My mother? Of course I do!"

"How about your sister and brother?"

Philip wasn't nearly as quick to respond to this question. "As much as a brother can love his sister and brother . . . yes, I guess I do."

"Do you like your brother and sister?"

A puzzled expression formed on Philip's face. "Like them? I just told you I loved them. Why would you ask if I liked them?"

"Because I don't think you do," said the missionary. "Neither do you love them."

There was something about having his affections called into question that angered Philip. Who was Christopher Morgan to say Philip didn't love his family? Philip knew what he felt. His mind searched for ways to reinterpret the meaning of the questions so they didn't sting as much. But he couldn't. The missionary's statement was too blunt. He tried not to sound offended when he answered. "What makes you think I don't love my brother and sister?"

"From what you told me, your sister is stubborn and your brother is lazy. These are not traits we admire. Who likes people who are obstinate? Who can love someone whose chief characteristic is sloth?"

Philip laughed self-consciously. "Oh, that's just brother-talk," he said. "They'd say the same kinds of things about me if they were here."

The old missionary closed his eyes. His head tilted back slightly so that the light coming from the opening in the roof washed away the orange glow of the fire from his face. The white light of day made Christopher Morgan look older than ancient. He held this pose for so long that Philip grew concerned. The deathly pallor of his face was only part of Philip's concern. Had the old missionary fallen asleep? or was he. . . ? Philip forgot all about his anger and rose to his knees. He leaned forward looking for signs of life. The old missionary's chest didn't rise or fall. His hands lay folded in his lap, motionless. The aged man's face seemed frozen—no blinks, no twitches, nothing. Philip reached toward Nanouwetea's shoulder to give him a gentle shake when he saw it. A sparkle, in the corner of his eye. Philip watched as a single tear formed, then held on precariously to the corner of the old man's eye.

He spoke. His voice sounded as if it had been dragged up from the bottom of a well. "Our families are much alike," he said. His eyes remained closed. "My sister Lucy was a strong-willed and outspoken woman. A strong believer in the power of God's grace, her self-appointed mission was to revive the work of Anne Hutchinson in Boston. She was received in no more friendly manner than Mrs. Hutchinson and was forced to flee to Providence with her family. My brother Roger never found his calling in life. He was charismatic and strong. His weakness was drink and he died a drunk. The only thing the three of us had in common was our last name. I was no better—single-minded in my devotion to my missionary work. It consumed me."

Here the missionary paused. He took a deep, shuddering breath that shook his chest. The single tear was pushed out of its place by another . . . then another. Philip's concern grew. Christopher Morgan looked so frail, so vulnerable. No longer a living legend, or great patriarch, but like a child before his daddy.

"We were a tremendous disappointment to my father," he said.

"Not at all," Philip said softly. His chest hurt with emotion for his ancestor. "I'm sure your father would be proud of all you've accomplished."

Nanouwetea gave no indication of having heard him. "My father's one desire in life was to have a family like my mother's family in England. The closeness of the Matthews of Edenford so impressed him. It was so influential in his conversion. His hope was to re-create that spirit of family love among us. And he tried. Oh, how he tried. Every day he prayed to that end. Every day." The old missionary slowly turned toward Philip, giving a soft chuckle. "At the time I thought his prayer was intended to shame the three of us to stop our fighting. I thought he was praying selfishly, that all he wanted was a little peace and quiet in the house."

Philip shifted uneasily. He wanted to say something that would comfort his ancestor, but everything that came to mind sounded trite and inadequate. So he said nothing.

"It wasn't until you arrived that I realized how much our family meant to him."

Philip wasn't sure what he meant by that. Apparently his confusion showed on his face, for Nanouwetea explained.

"The journal. The entries in my father's journal."

Philip nodded in understanding.

"In nearly every passage my father agonizes over us." He closed his eyes again, this time to quote one of the entries from memory: *April 24, 1652 — I am in pain until the love of the Lord Jesus Christ is formed in my children. Dear God in heaven, my greatest fear is that they will never know the rich blessing of family love. It is with great fondness that I remember the close-ness of my beloved Nell and her sister Jenny — their souls were knit together. When I think of how their father willingly sacri-ficed his life for them and how Jenny died for me and Nell when she might have saved herself. And then I see the way my chil-dren claw at each other. They care for no one but themselves. O Lord, where have I failed them? I would willingly give my life if in doing so my children would come together in love.*

Tears flowed steadily now. Philip had to say something. "But you were just children when he wrote that, weren't you?"

"I was eighteen years old in 1652. Old enough to leave home with John Eliot and begin my life's work. So it wasn't a matter of age. It was a matter of self-centeredness. I loved my work more than I loved my brother and sister, mother and father. I could have written them, but I didn't. The lapse in our communication became so great it was embarrassing. What could I tell them? That my work was more important than them? I promised myself I'd make it up to them by going to see them personally. But there was never a convenient time and then the war began. In a way, I was relieved when hostilities between the colonies and the Indians broke out. I finally had a legitimate excuse for not visiting them. Then the war was over and I was preoccupied with the work here at the reservation. It was by accident that I heard that my father had died — from a casual remark by a trapper who was passing through. So his prayer for his family was never answered."

The old missionary reached for his Bible, the one that once belonged to his father, the one that had been given him at the special ceremony that passed on the family heritage to him. It was with difficulty the old man lifted the Bible; it not only contained the weight of its bulky pages and binding but also the weight of responsibility to his family line.

"It was after my father's death that I began praying for God to reveal to me His will for this Bible. In his graciousness, God granted me the reassurance that my prayers would be answered. I promised God that if He gave me this opportunity, I would do my best to correct the course of the Morgan family."

"I must be a disappointment to you," Philip said.

The old missionary cradled the Bible in his arms. It was clear he was back in the present when his eyes focused on Philip. His mannerisms and speech were that of Nanouwetea again. "Initially you were a disappointment. Your single-minded obsession with your life reminded me of myself at your age. Since then you've changed. Grown. Your concern for Wampas is one evidence of your growth. The old Philip wouldn't have cared unless Wampas was in some way standing between you and your goal."

"And the questions about my sister and brother?"

"When I was given this Bible," the missionary continued, hugging the book to his chest, "I received it in the historical Christian sense. By that I mean that the Bible had been handed down from believer to believer for generations. If that were not so, it is questionable that Christianity would still exist. What I failed to understand—much to my shame—is that it is more than a Bible. It's the Morgan *family* Bible. The emphasis for us is twofold. What kind of legacy would it be for us if the book survived but there were no Morgans to read it, to teach it, to live it? So, we're family. And there is little on this earth that is more important than family."

Like an instrument string that hums when an identical pitch is sounded, so the old missionary's words hummed with familiarity in Philip's mind. They were nearly identical to his father's dying words on the road outside Roxbury. *Family is important, son, probably the most important thing on earth. Never forget that.*

The emotional memories had depleted Nanouwetea's diminishing reserves of strength and he was soon asleep. With only the constant crackle of the fire to keep him company, Philip weighed in his mind the things Christopher Morgan had said. He thought of his mother, Priscilla, and Jared. Unlike previous times, his thoughts didn't lead to anger over their not writing him. He wondered what they were doing this very moment. If they were well. If they were happy. How they were getting along. He smiled at the thought that Priscilla probably had the study in perfect order, so that she knew exactly where every book and paper and invoice was. He had no doubt that their family records were in better shape than they'd ever been. He wondered what Jared was doing. If he'd found a job. If he and Anne were married yet. He wondered how his mother was adjusting to being a widow. If she was lonely. And for the first time since leaving Cambridge, Philip prayed for them a tearful prayer.

After his prayer, his thoughts turned to his immediate relationships. The distance between him and his family prevented him from doing anything for them at the present. He would just have to trust God and be patient until he could do something to remedy that. However, there was nothing preventing him from mending his relationships with Wampas and Weetamoo.

The sky was a soft, hazy blue. The sun was a little more than eye-level high if measured by Indian timekeeping standards. The year was far enough into autumn that the sun had lost its morning strength. Moisture still coated the leaves of the cornstalks, enough to make Philip's shoulders and sleeves wet as he brushed by them. The ground was cold on his hands. The knees of his breeches were soaked through. He crept between the rows of corn, careful not to brush the stalks so that they would signal his presence.

Halfway down the row he was having second thoughts. Maybe this wasn't such a clever idea after all. But on his hands and knees there wasn't enough room between rows for him to turn around without hitting a stalk, so he continued on until Weetamoo came into sight.

When Philip first arrived at the reservation he noticed a wooden tower, twelve to fifteen feet high, standing next to a cornfield. At the time he didn't know its function. Since then he learned that the tower was used to safeguard the cornfield from birds that would feast on the field's fruit, especially during the morning hours. It was Weetamoo's task to sit in the tower and drive away the pesky birds by throwing rocks or sticks at them from her elevated vantage point.

The field's protector had come into sight after Philip had crawled nearly three quarters of the way down a row. Careful not to knock a cornstalk, he positioned himself comfortably on his knees in a place where he could see her through the leaves of corn. She was unaware of his presence.

Philip's heart was pounding and he breathed in quick, shallow breaths. There was something wickedly exciting about watching a woman who thought she was alone. This is not what he'd come to do. His plan had been to sneak up on Weetamoo, not to spy on her. But he couldn't resist the chance to look at her for more than just the quick glances he could manage in the wigwam.

The young Indian maid sat serenely atop the platform. Rocks and sticks were piled next to her. Though her gaze extended over the cornfield, her mind was elsewhere. At times her lips would move, but no sound came forth. Was she talking to herself? Maybe she was talking to God. Weetamoo sat upright and stretched her back and neck muscles, then brushed something from her sleeve. She was elegant in the way she moved, even while doing simple, common things like brushing something from her sleeve or throwing her long black hair over her shoulder. Philip could easily watch her for hours if it weren't for the guilt that jabbed his insides. This was wrong. It was unfair to Weetamoo and the longer he watched her, the harder it would be to explain. Still he had to force himself to take his eyes off her and reach toward a cornstalk. He grasped it firmly and shook.

By doing so he lost sight of Weetamoo. Her presence was soon made known in other ways. The first rock zinged over his head. The second one gashed his cheek.

"Ouch!" He jumped up. "Stop! It's me!"

"Philip?" Weetamoo stood at the edge of the platform, a rock poised in her hand. "Philip Morgan, what are you doing in my cornfield?"

"Getting pelted by rocks!" he shouted back at her.

"How did you get in there? I didn't see you walk in!"

"I didn't exactly walk in," he said. "I snuck in."

"Then you deserve everything you got! And more!"

Philip lifted a hand to his cheek. It was bleeding.

"Are you hurt?"

He pulled his hand away and looked at the blood on his fingers. "My cheek is cut," he yelled.

"It's bleeding, isn't it?" she cried. "I can see red from here." Weetamoo dropped the rock that was in her hand and scrambled down the tower's ladder. She ran down Philip's row in the cornfield as he was headed out.

"Let me see it," she said. She lifted his hand away from the cut. Concerned black eyes examined his cheek. "It doesn't look too deep," she said. "Does it hurt?"

"No," he said. "I don't even feel it." It wasn't Philip's bravado speaking. It was true; he didn't feel it. The only thing he was feeling was the hypnotic effect the closeness of Weetamoo's presence was having on him. The warmth of her hand touching his. The powerful attraction of her tender gaze.

"You're too tall," she said. "Bend down a little so I can get a good look at it."

He bent down. He would have done anything she asked. With their faces mere inches from each other as she studied his wound, he studied her eyes. Deep black with flecks of brown in them.

"It doesn't look too deep," she said. Because they were so close she spoke in almost a whisper. If the depth of the wound was directly related to the depth of her concern, Philip would have wished for a near-fatal encounter.

She stepped back. "You still haven't told me what you were doing in my cornfield . . . and why you snuck into it!"

This was the Weetamoo he was accustomed to. Standing at

arm's length, strictly business.

All of sudden Philip's clever idea seemed stupid. Too stupid to put into words. But it was the only explanation he had.

"I know how annoying the black birds around here are to you. . . ." It was even more stupid now that he was saying it.

"And?"

"And I thought that I've been sort of like them to you . . . annoying . . . and that if you wanted to throw rocks at me, I'd let you. I thought it might make you feel better." He added quickly, "But nobody told me you had such a deadly aim!"

"You came out here so I could throw rocks at you?"

"Because I've been so annoying, like the birds . . . well, it seemed like a good idea."

"So you're saying this is your way of apologizing?"

Philip looked at the ground, looked at an ear of corn next to him, and shrugged. "Well, yeah, I guess so."

When she didn't respond, Philip glanced up to see her reaction. Weetamoo's arms were folded in front of her, her head was shaking in disbelief; brilliant white teeth formed a laughing grin. "You are unbelievable!" she said. "You couldn't just tell me you were sorry?"

Philip instinctively reached toward the cut on his cheek. It stung when he touched it. "No," he said. "No, I don't think I could have. You would never let me get close enough to apologize."

Weetamoo's grin vanished.

"It's true and I think you know it!"

It was Weetamoo's turn to gaze at the ground. "If I admit it, does that mean I can't throw any more rocks at you?" She wore an impish smile as she gazed up at him through strands of black hair that fell across her eyes.

They sat opposite each other atop the wooden tower.

"You surprise me," Weetamoo said.

"How so?"

She held a short stick in her hand, one that might at any moment go sailing through the air toward a black bird. Now, however, she scratched one end of it absentmindedly on the planks of the platform as she spoke.

"You're so different from when you first came here."

"I don't think I'm different. You've just gotten to know me."

"No, you're different. The Philip Morgan that came looking for his family's Bible was arrogant and self-centered."

"If I've changed, I hope it's for the better," Philip joked.

His attempt at humor got the desired response. Weetamoo smiled and whacked him playfully on the leg with the stick.

"I'm going to be permanently crippled if you keep hitting me with things!"

"The rocks were your fault!" she cried.

"You're right, I take full blame for the rocks," he conceded.

Weetamoo stared at his injured cheek. Then her eyes crept upward to the scar on his forehead. "Even a bear couldn't knock good sense into you." She pointed at the scar with her stick. Philip ran a finger along the scar line.

"How far back does it go?" Weetamoo asked.

Philip pulled his hair back. She leaned forward to get a closer look at it.

"It's a nasty scar," she said. "You're fortunate that most of it's covered by hair." She returned to her place. "I was shocked when you returned, especially considering your wound."

"My family's Bible was here. After all I'd been through, I wasn't going to give it up so easily."

Weetamoo nodded. "When you returned, you were still arrogant and selfish. All you wanted was your Bible. And even though I was sorry you were wounded, I hated you.

Then, just like that, you changed."

"You say it like it happened instantaneously."

"I think it did," she said.

"When?"

"When you learned that Nanouwetea was Christopher Morgan." She laughed softly. "You should have seen your face! I've never seen someone look so dumbstruck before!"

"Thank you for those kind words," Philip chuckled with her.

"You've not been the same since," she said.

"You think so?"

She nodded. "It's the way you look at him. How can I describe it? It's a mixture of love and awe."

"He's a remarkable man," said Philip.

"I think so," she agreed. "Sometimes I feel guilty."

"Why?"

"Unlike so many other families, growing up with him I've never known hunger or fear. When I was old enough to begin understanding spiritual things, it was easy for me to accept the fact that I had a loving Heavenly Father because I'd known such love from my earthly father."

"It was the same way for me and my father."

"You must miss him terribly."

Philip nodded. "Nanouwetea has helped ease my pain."

"Is that why you've stayed? To be near him?"

Again Philip nodded.

Weetamoo tossed the stick over the side of the platform. Looking at the level of the sun in the sky she said, "It's time we get back to the wigwam. Nanouwetea will be expecting us." As she spoke and made her way past Philip to the ladder, never once did she look at him.

Philip stood and followed her. "Weetamoo, wait," he said. "Did I say something wrong?"

She was already halfway down the ladder. He hurried after

her. When she reached the bottom, she turned quickly toward the wigwam. Philip jumped the last four feet down the ladder and blocked her way. The face that he confronted wasn't angry, but neither was it friendly.

"We have a lot of work to do on the primer today," she said coolly.

"Fine, I just want to know what I said to upset you."

"You didn't upset me." She retreated to the ladder and leaned against it, wrapping her arm around a wrung trying to look casual.

"I've seen you often enough to know when something is upsetting you."

A spark flashed in her eyes. "That's exactly the point, Master Morgan," she said. "Don't you think I've seen the way you've looked at me?"

Philip's first impulse was to deny her allegation, but it was difficult to deny the obvious. He'd been caught too many times.

"Don't you think I know you have feelings for me?" she said.

Even though she was angry, Philip was thrilled at the direction this conversation was taking. "I didn't think you wanted to have anything to do with me," he said.

"I don't!"

Philip was confused.

"It's wrong!" she shouted. Then softly, "It's just that I can't help myself."

Philip stepped toward her. He placed his hand on top of her hand that rested on the ladder rung. Her fingers opened as his slid between them. He moved closer. Her black eyes were moist and vulnerable to his gaze. Slowly he leaned forward and their lips touched. He pressed forward. They were soft and warm.

Weetamoo turned her head. She pulled her hand away.

"No . . . no . . . no . . ." she wept. She pushed past Philip.

"Weetamoo! Wait!" Philip called after her. "Why not? What's wrong?"

"Don't you understand?" she cried. "You're forbidden fruit!"

"Forbidden fruit? I don't understand."

"I can't have you."

"But why?"

"What can this lead to?" she asked. "Will you forsake your life at Harvard forever and stay with me here?"

"I'll take you with me when I leave!" Philip said.

She shook her head. "I can't go with you!" she cried. "My life is here! It will always be here. You are a temptation, Philip Morgan! A loving, adorable temptation. But temptation leads to wrong. And I must resist you, Philip Morgan! I must resist you!"

Mary Weetamoo turned and ran toward Nanouwetea's wigwam.

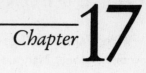

Chapter 17

PHILIP'S pen scratched dutifully against the paper. He forced himself to focus on the words. Yes, they were correct. He sighed. *Working on the primer was a lot easier when I thought she hated me.* For the past week the primer's progress had been slowed by an increased number of mistakes. Philip's mistakes. Without raising his head, he sneaked a glance at Weetamoo and caught her looking at him. The instant their eyes met, she frowned and returned to the pages she was checking. He grinned at having caught her as he loaded his pen with ink for the next phrase.

Like a pendulum, Philip's hopes swung back and forth from high to low; and the force moving the pendulum was Weetamoo. At times she was sweet and tender, almost inviting in the way she looked at him or spoke. Other times she was cold as stone and just as hard in her resolve to resist him as an evil temptation. And from day to day, even moment to moment, he never knew which Weetamoo would appear. At times his anger would rise and he would determine not to let her have that kind of control over him. His time at the reservation would end; he would return to Cambridge and Harvard and Penelope. Resist him, would she? He would resist her! Then inevitably, while handing him a manuscript page or a bowl of samp, she would intentionally brush her hand against his and Philip's resolve would fly away like blackbirds from the cornfield.

With Wampas still gone, the two of them had most of the evenings alone. Nanouwetea was still in the wigwam, but he always fell asleep early. Their conversations ranged from the primer's progress to Nanouwetea's health to Wampas to church events to the spiritual state of the Indian reservation. The events in the cornfield were never brought up. At the end of the evening Weetamoo would retire to her side of the wigwam and Philip to his. Before, when Wampas was there, she would quickly settle herself with her back to the fire and the men. Now, with Wampas gone, she sometimes faced the fire and stared at Philip. No words were ever spoken. Nor did she smile. She just looked at him until she fell asleep.

"Philip! Philip! You have to stop him!"

It was early evening. The hole in the wigwam's roof had just turned black. An occasional star could be seen through the rising smoke. Philip was telling Nanouwetea about Priscilla's late-night tutoring sessions with Father when they were interrupted. Weetamoo had gone to check on Namumpum, who had yet to deliver her baby and wasn't expected to return any time soon. Suddenly she appeared through the wigwam opening. Her eyes were wide with fear. She ran toward Philip, grabbed his arm, and tried to pull him up.

"Hurry!" she yelled, "You have to reach him before the game starts."

"Whoa!" Philip exclaimed. "Slow down. Stop who? From what?"

"Wampas!" Weetamoo cried, struggling to get her words out between breaths. "I went to visit Namumpum . . . and learned that the men are gaming tonight . . . with the Wampanoag tribe. They've chosen Wampas as our player . . . they think that Wampas will bring them good luck because he knows Nanouwetea's God."

Nanouwetea spoke first. "Has Wampas agreed to do this?"

"I don't know! But I think so. All I heard was that he was our player. Philip, you have to stop him!"

Philip spoke to Nanouwetea. "It could hurt the church," he said. "If Wampas wins, many will believe it's because God has favored them with good luck; if he loses, many will believe that God is weak and impotent."

"So you think we should stop him from harming the church's reputation?"

Something in Nanouwetea's eyes told him the question was more than just a clarification of what he'd just said. It was a teaching moment. What was he missing? What was he overlooking? Then he smiled. He smiled because he knew the answer. For the first time in his life he knew the correct answer to this question.

"No," Philip said firmly. "We shouldn't stop Wampas because he might injure the church's reputation. We should stop him for his sake, because we love him."

The pride that glimmered in the old missionary's eyes was his reward. "Go bring Wampas home, my son."

According to Weetamoo, the gaming area had been erected on the north side of the longhouse. As Philip walked there along Schoolhouse Pond Road, he came to a disturbing realization. Unlike the tests at Harvard, this one wasn't over simply by giving the correct answer; in this test, he not only had to know the right answer, he had to carry it out. Was it possible to know the right answer and still fail the test?

The road north was dark with little moonlight to illuminate it, and because it was filled with ruts, Philip had to watch every step. But he wasn't alone on the road and the closer he came to the longhouse, the heavier the traffic became with Indians. They were all on foot and headed the same direction as he. Some walked on the road, others cut through adjacent fields.

Philip had not had much experience with gambling. However, he recalled the unbridled excitement of his classmates at Harvard as they would occasionally sneak out for a night of gambling and drinking. He observed they never returned with the same level of enthusiasm; having left excited and with money, they inevitably returned drunk and broke. The Indians he saw traveling to the gaming area tonight showed none of the excitement of his former classmates. These men were stone-faced serious. They wore their shell-money on strings around their necks and various colors of paint on their cheeks, arms, legs, and chests. It was as if they were in a trance, drawn to the gaming area against their wills. One of them, a particularly tall man with a nasty scar on his left shoulder, gave Philip an appraising glance. Philip smiled at him and received an angry glare in return. Philip was straight-faced for the rest of the evening.

The sky was lit with bonfires beyond the longhouse. Whoops and hollers could be heard a good distance away. Even the sound of merriment reminded Philip he was among a people with a vastly different culture. The sounds he heard tonight were nothing like the sounds that could be heard entering Boston for Lecture Day or a designated day of thanksgiving. The colonists made merriment with barrel laughs and guffaws and a variety of shouts and curses. The Indians, on the other hand, yipped and whooped with high-pitched screams. The difference unsettled Philip, who realized how sheltered he'd been while on the reservation. Since his arrival more than a year earlier, there had been only one other time when he had entered the mainstream of reservation life—when he joined Wampas' friends in the hothouse. Hardly a pleasant memory. The rest of the time, his experiences had been confined to those who knew and respected Nanouwetea and had ties to the church. With those Indians there had been a common bond of Christianity. Not so tonight.

All of a sudden he felt like David going out single-handedly to do battle with the Philistines. At least David had stones and a sling. What did Philip have?

His chest began to tighten. And the closer he came to the roar of the gaming area the tighter it became. *No! Not now!* Philip silently cried. *I don't need this to happen to me now!* The more he fought the feeling, the stronger it came. Like giant hands reaching into his chest, his air flow restricted. He wheezed and coughed, fighting for breath. It had been months since his last attack. Months of bliss.

Philip struggled to keep on his feet. He left the road and stumbled to the longhouse. His back arched. He gasped for air, and what little air came through burned. It felt like he'd swallowed a small cup of fire. He staggered into the shadows of the longhouse, not wanting anyone to see him like this. He thought of Weetamoo and Nanouwetea. They would be disappointed. Of course they would understand once he explained to them how he was hindered by an asthma attack. They would understand and forgive him. They'd tell him he tried his best.

"No!" Philip cried. He didn't want their sympathy. He didn't want to make excuses to them. He didn't want to fail. *Please God, help me not to fail!* The response was more fire in his chest. Philip fell to his knees and doubled over, wheezing and coughing. He fought to get up but couldn't. The harder he struggled, the greater the pain. *O God, help me!* In agony, his hand clawed the dirt. He lifted his head, gasping for more air. His hand clutched a rock, which he squeezed and squeezed until his fingers hurt.

At least David had stones with which to fight.

Philip looked at the stone in his hand. The thought came again, just as mysteriously as the first time.

No, that's not right. That was the voice of fear that said that. It wasn't the stones that gave David the victory. It wasn't the stones that made David fearless in the face of the giant. It was God who gave David the victory! *And all this assembly shall know that the Lord saveth not with sword and spear: for the battle is the Lord's.* That's what David had said. Philip didn't need David's stones; he needed David's God!

In the depths of the shadows of the Narragansett longhouse, with the noise of gaming Indians in the background, Philip turned the battle over to God.

The arbor, or playhouse as it was called, was made of four long poles planted in the earth. The poles were set in a square and reached eighteen to twenty feet high. Horizontal rods spanned the poles. The game's bets were hung on these — furs of various kinds and strings of wampum and suckauhock. The wampum were beads of polished white shells made from periwinkle, an edible freshwater snail. Suckauhock were black shells with a bluish tint, made from the shellfish. As for value, a black shell was worth two white shells. The game itself was played within the square structure. Each tribe selected a player to represent them by rolling painted plumb stones like dice in a tray. Wampas would play for the Narragansetts unless Philip could convince him to come home.

As Philip approached the gaming area, bonfires blazed with such intensity he had to look up at the stars to remind himself it was night. Everywhere he looked were Indian males of every description. How was he going to find Wampas in this crowd? He wandered among them going from face to face. Most of them had painted their faces and bodies with stripes and circles, red by far being the favorite color of the Indians over yellow, green, blue, white, and black. As Philip searched for Wampas he saw short Indians carrying tobacco pouches, tall Indians with strings of wampum around their wrists or necks, Indians with feathers and plumes, Indians wearing animal skins, or leather breeches, or a combination of Indian and

English dress, or barely anything at all. He walked through tobacco smoke as it curled around the heads of those he passed by; the smell of rum was heavy on many of their breaths. The bonfire and tobacco smoke only served to make Philip's lungs burn all the more.

Everyone's attention was centered around the playhouse. The Narragansetts crowded together on one side, the Wampanoags on the other. On both sides Indians held up strings of wampum, shouting and placing bets or shoving to get a better view of the playhouse. Because Philip was taller than most of them, he was able to see over their heads.

He spied Wampas standing next to the playhouse the instant Wampas spotted him. The Indian had several strings of wampum around his neck. Red and black stripes lined his cheeks. The instant Wampas recognized Philip, his brow furrowed and his neck muscles tensed, a glaze of anger covering his eyes.

Philip took a deep breath. *The battle is the Lord's,* he reminded himself. Then he worked his way through the crowd of Indians between him and the playhouse.

"Go home, English. You're not welcome here," Wampas said. His tone and his eyes were harder than the plumb stones he held in his hands. He reeked of rum.

"I will go home," Philip replied. "If you come with me."

Wampas threw the plumb stones at Philip, hitting him in the chest. Looking at the lie of the stones on the ground Wampas said, "This is your lucky day. You win. You can leave without getting hurt if you go now."

"What is this?" Standing next to Wampas, his back to Philip, was a tall muscular Indian taking strings of wampum from several other Indians and hanging them on the betting poles. He turned to see whom Wampas was arguing with. The Indian was so tall Philip had to look up to him. Next to smaller Wampas he looked like Goliath. The tall Indian focused red glassy eyes on Philip and he flicked long bony fingers at him like he was shooing away a bug. "Leave here," he said. "This is no place for you."

"I'm not leaving without Wampas," Philip replied.

By now other Indians within hearing distance turned their attention toward the confrontation. The number of angry faces staring at Philip multiplied. Wampas closed the distance between him and Philip until less than a foot separated them.

"I hate you, English," he said. "Leave now or I'll kill you."

The tall Indian signaled two other Indians standing nearby. They responded by flanking Philip, one on each side.

"Come, Wampas," said the tall Indian, picking up the stones and placing them in Wampas' hand. "Don't concern yourself with the Englishman. I will see that he's removed from here."

The Indians beside Philip grabbed him with firm hands. Instinctively Philip struggled to free himself, but they were too strong. He doubted he could break free from one of them alone, much less two. He felt his feet being lifted from the ground as he involuntarily began moving backward.

"Wait! Stop!" he cried. "Wampas, listen to me!"

It was no good. Wampas had already turned his back on Philip to face the playhouse. All the other Indians around him did the same. Philip had been nothing more than a minor distraction.

"Wampas!" Philip cried to him. "Mecauntitea! MECAUN-TITEA!"

Wampas froze, as did all the others who heard Philip, including the tall Indian who turned and looked at Philip with a greedy grin. Philip's abductors halted but didn't release their grip.

Wampas turned to Philip. "You want to fight *me?*"

"That's what I said."

The Indian passed through the sea of bettors until he stood

face-to-face with Philip. He wore a satisfied smirk. "I'd kill you," he said.

"I've come in the name of the almighty God," Philip replied. "He will give me the victory."

In this exchange of verbal blows, Philip was the clear winner. Wampas was stunned. Philip had jabbed his Christian conscience awake. Now for Philip the question was, would it be enough? He moved to take the advantage.

"Listen to me!" Philip shouted to the Indians who encircled him and Wampas. "You have chosen Wampas to be your player because his God is powerful. Indeed, there is no other god stronger than the God Wampas worships. And if God were on your side in the games, you would most surely win. But He isn't. Because what Wampas has failed to tell you is this—his God has forsaken him!"

The Narragansett Indians burst into a frenzy. Immediately the tall Indian had Wampas by the shoulders. "Your God has left you?" he shouted.

"This man lies!" Wampas protested. "My God is still with me."

"Make him prove it!" Philip said.

Without releasing Wampas, the tall Indian turned to Philip. "In a fight?"

Philip nodded. "It will prove that what I am saying is true."

"You are a puny man," said the tall Indian. "You cannot win."

"I will win because God is with me. He will make me strong!"

"He lies!" Wampas countered. "And I'll prove it by fighting him!"

A cheer went up, accompanied by a general cry which became a chant. "Stakes! Stakes! Stakes!"

Philip held up both hands. "No stakes! No stakes!" he cried.

"There have to be stakes!" said the tall Indian.

Philip shook his head. "There can't be any stakes," he said, "because either way you win. If I win the fight, you will know that God has forsaken Wampas. You will have been saved from certain defeat against the Wampanoags. If I lose, then you will know without doubt that God is still with Wampas and I will leave. Either way you win."

The tall Indian nodded his head in agreement. He ordered the area cleared for the fight. Narragansetts and Wampanoags alike formed the arena. Everywhere Philip looked Indians haggled with one another over side bets. The arguments weren't over who would win or lose, but the odds of Philip surviving.

Philip soon found himself standing near the center of the dirt arena, surrounded by jeering Indians. He knew this was a crazy idea, but he'd run out of choices. He'd smelled the rum on Wampas' breath and saw a yellow tint in his eyes. Philip was hoping that Wampas was drunk enough to make the fight even. At the edge of the arena Wampas removed the shell necklace he always wore. He rubbed his arms and legs to warm them. Philip rubbed his chest and throat. The burning had not gone away. He looked heavenward and took as big a breath as his lungs would let him. "Thy will be done," he prayed.

Wampas and the tall Indian joined Philip in the center of the human arena. Wampas had the fierce look of a fighter. "I'm going to enjoy this!" he said.

"No weapons," said the tall Indian. "This is a test of strength. The fight is over when one man can no longer stand." He pushed the two opponents apart, then said, "Fight!"

With a savage cry Wampas hurled himself at Philip. His shoulder slammed into Philip's chest, hurling him backward. The fighters crashed to the ground. The full weight of his opponent knocked the wind from Philip's lungs. Any thought of Wampas being weak with drink was instantly dispelled. Wampas raised himself and rammed a forearm into the side of Philip's face, nearly knocking him senseless.

Philip was dazed and out of breath. He had to do something to bide a little time. Reaching up, he grabbed Wampas around the neck. With all his strength he held the Indian's head against his chest where Wampas could do little damage. The Indian tried to free himself, but Philip held on, all the time gasping for air. His throat and lungs were on fire.

Wampas tried to roll off Philip, but Philip held on to him. Together, they rolled over and over in the dirt while hundreds of Indians yelled and jeered and whooped. Finally, Wampas broke free. He scrambled to his feet.

Philip rolled to his side. Propping himself up, he tried to catch his breath. The din of shouting men all around him was deafening. He struggled to his feet. Cheers went up. The fight would continue.

Wampas crouched in the center of the arena. He taunted Philip to come at him. Philip bent over and rested his hands on his knees, hoping to trick Wampas into lowering his guard. Suddenly, he rushed at the Indian. Wampas was not surprised. Stepping to the side, he grabbed Philip's shoulders, and using Philip's own momentum, sent him flying through the air. There was a thud followed by a cloud of dust as Philip tumbled in the dirt.

Responding to the cheers, Wampas raised his arms in victory. His celebration was premature. Philip was unsteady, but he was back on his feet.

Again Wampas taunted him. Again Philip came at him, this time slowly. The fighters locked arms like wrestlers, their heads side-by-side, their feet spread apart, each trying to knock the other off balance.

"Why did you come here?" Wampas screamed. "I can kill you if I choose."

"You once saved my life. The way I see it, it's yours to take."

Wampas dipped his shoulder inside so that Philip was draped over his back. With a loud scream, the Indian sent Philip flying over his shoulder. Another thud. Another cloud of dust. Philip didn't know how much more of this he could take. But he had to try. Rolling over, he got to his knees, then to his feet. He came at Wampas again and they locked arms.

"Why don't you use holds?" Wampas cried.

"I don't know any!"

With lightning speed Wampas sidestepped Philip, placed a leg behind him, and pushed him backward. Philip plummeted to the ground. Wampas landed on top of him. Philip's eyes bulged as the full weight of the Indian landed on his chest. With the burning in his chest and lack of air, Philip felt like he was going to die. At this point he would have welcomed death if it meant that the pain would stop. Just as he thought it was hopeless, he saw Wampas' face. The Indian's eyes had softened; Philip saw a glimmer of compassion.

Wampas jumped to his feet. He raised his hands, "It's over!"

Philip raised himself up, first one foot, then the other. "It's not over!" he shouted.

Wampas whirled around. "You have no brains at all, do you, English?"

"Seems like you accused me of that once before."

The two squared off at a distance and moved sideways around an invisible circle. Slowly, Wampas closed the distance between them. Then suddenly, he lowered his head and, like a battering ram, plowed into Philip's stomach.

"Now stay down!" Wampas told him.

"I'm not leaving without you," Philip replied.

It took him a little longer, but Philip managed to get to his feet again. Wampas shook his head in disbelief. There was an anguished look on his face.

This time Philip came at Wampas. The Indian ducked, catching Philip in the midsection. With all his might he thrust upward, sending Philip over his back.

For Philip it was the strangest sensation to see the stars at his feet. However, he didn't have long to relish the view. The next moment he came crashing to the earth with a jolt that felt like lightning had struck his body. This time he didn't get up. Just before he blacked out, he saw the worried face of Wampas bending over him—and Philip knew that he had won!

It was the same nightmare he'd had in the forest. His father was running toward him. A merchant ship with the sailor and Indian at its rail was coming up fast behind him, parting the trees like water. It crashed down upon his father and continued on toward him. The bow of the ship plowed into the ground just short of his chest, but not before it hurled a giant wave which splashed down on top of him.

Philip sputtered and coughed. Water ran down his chin as he tried to sit up, then fell back again. He blinked several times to see where he was. Even though he knew the ship was his dream again, the pain and the water were real. Slowly things came into focus—tree limbs overhead; his back resting against its trunk; a lake in front of him with a faint glimmer of moonlight on its surface. Adam's Pond? He wasn't sure.

He tried to turn his head to look around. His effort was rewarded with a jolt of pain down his neck and back and arms. "Ohhh," he moaned.

"You are stubborn, English."

Philip smiled, then groaned. It hurt to smile. With great care he turned his head until Wampas came into view. The Indian was dirty, beaten, and bruised; his right eye was black and swollen shut. In his hands was a leather pouch wet with water.

"What happened to you?" Philip asked.

"You did this to me."

"Nonsense. I never landed a single blow."

"Remember the tall man who started our contest?"

"He did that to you?"

Wampas nodded. "When I refused to continue the gaming."

Even though it hurt, he couldn't help it. Philip smiled again. "I won," he said.

"You're crazy! You lost the fight!"

Philip shook his head. "I won because I got what I wanted. You're here."

"I could have killed you!" Wampas shouted. "Maybe I should have."

"I knew you wouldn't," Philip said. "I was counting on the fact that your faith in Jesus Christ was real. I knew that if it was, you couldn't kill me. He wouldn't let you."

Wampas hung his head. He touched his swollen eye and winced. "Why didn't you stay down when I told you to?" he asked.

"I promised to bring you home. I couldn't give up until I was sure you would come home with me."

"You couldn't have known!"

It took a good deal of effort, but Philip pulled himself away from the tree and sat up without support. "I saw it in your face. Before I lost consciousness, I knew I'd won."

"No." Wampas shook his head as he stood to his feet. "No, there's no way you could have known that I'd leave after beating you. That's the stupidest plan I've ever heard in my life."

Philip painfully shrugged his shoulders. "It worked."

Wampas turned his back on Philip and took a few steps toward the lake. He stopped and turned around. "Why?" he asked. "Look at you! Why did you do it?"

There it was again. The test. And Philip not only *knew* the right answer, he *did* the right answer. The way he felt right now, despite the raw feeling in his throat and pain in his limbs, was extraordinary. For the first time in his life he had done a totally selfless deed. Not some insignificant little nothing like giving someone his favorite dessert. He'd risked his safety, his very life for someone else and it felt wonderful! "I did it," he beamed, "because you're my brother in Christ and I love you."

The look on Wampas' face was the same one he had when Philip challenged him to fight—bewilderment. A look of unbelief. He turned away. "I can't go home with you," he said. "I've disappointed Nanouwetea and Weetamoo and disgraced the cause of Christ."

Placing his hands on the ground, Philip pushed himself up. The sudden rise caused him to become momentarily lightheaded. He steadied himself against the tree. Once his head cleared, he hobbled down the slope to where Wampas was standing. "Who do you think sent me to bring you home?" he asked.

Wampas weighed Philip's words. "It still wouldn't work," he said. "Nothing has changed. I wouldn't be home but a few days and it would begin all over again."

"It's me, isn't it?" Philip asked. When Wampas didn't answer, he continued, "Would it help if I left?"

"Nanouwetea and Weetamoo would only blame me if you were to leave."

Philip knew he was right. "Wampas," he said, "I never meant to take your place. When I found out Nanouwetea was my ancestor, I only wanted to help."

"When you first arrived, I had an advantage because you couldn't speak Algonquin. You learned quickly and I lost that advantage."

"Languages have always come easily for me," Philip confessed. "I remember telling you I spoke Latin, Greek, and

Hebrew. And you said, 'There aren't many Indians around here who speak Latin, Greek, or Hebrew.' "

Wampas laughed with him at the memory. Then he said, "What is it like at Harvard?"

The question took Philip by surprise. He examined Wampas with an appraising eye. There had to be some logical connection he was missing. "Why do you ask?"

"No reason. Forget the question."

"Wampas. Tell me. I'd like to know."

The Indian looked across the lake to the distant shore. "I've never told anyone this," he said. "Not Nanouwetea. Not even Weetamoo. I've hated you because you've been given the chance to attend Harvard. From the first time I heard about it from Nanouwetea, I've wanted to go."

"The Indian school?"

Wampas nodded.

"That's great!" Philip yelled. Then, more softly, "I know you have your reasons. Can you tell me why you want to go there?"

Wampas lowered his head and spoke softly. "So I can be wise like Nanouwetea."

"We have that in common. Someday I hope I'm as wise as Nanouwetea. Why haven't you told anyone you want to go to Harvard?"

"It can never come to pass," Wampas said. "I don't have the learning. They would never let me in. I've heard that the test to get in is hard."

"Not if you know the right answers," Philip said with a grin. "Wampas, my brother, I'll make a deal with you."

"A deal?"

"If you come back with me to Nanouwetea's wigwam tonight, I'll teach you Latin and everything else you need to know to pass the entrance exam to Harvard. Then, when I return to Cambridge, I'll personally introduce you to the president of the college."

Wampas' eyes brightened. He had the look of a little boy on his face. "You would teach me Latin? After all I've done to you? Why?"

Philip grinned. "To paraphrase a friend, 'Because the president of Harvard doesn't speak Algonquin.' "

Philip Morgan and Wampas walked side-by-side up the slope to the wigwam of Nanouwetea. They talked eagerly of all the subjects that would need to be covered to prepare Wampas for his interview with the president of Harvard. Weetamoo heard them coming and appeared at the opening of the hut. Although she was obviously pleased that the two of them were both home on friendly terms, she gasped when they drew close enough for her to get a good look at them.

"You've been fighting!" she yelled.

"Just using a little strategy," Philip said.

"One that almost got us both killed!" Wampas added.

"Not at all!" Philip protested. "I knew what I was doing all along!"

Weetamoo interrupted. "I'm sure you'll tell us all about it," she said. "Whether we want to hear it or not. But right now Nanouwetea is waiting for you." Both men showed surprise because the hour was late. "He stayed up praying for the two of you."

Weetamoo ushered Philip and Wampas into the missionary's presence. And there was great rejoicing because the prodigal had come home.

Chapter 18

I T was the kind of day when the earth was filled with promise and it felt good to be alive. The sun was bright and hot for late October; St. Martin's summer some people called it because it was close to the day the saint was honored. Philip stood silently waiting for the ceremony to begin. He enjoyed the feel of the tree's shade as it settled on his skin with a tingling, moist feeling. The air blew fresh and sweet. Adam's Lake sparkled happily in the distance.

"It was on a day much like today that my father handed me this Bible." The aged missionary held the Morgan family Bible against his chest as he spoke. "We were in a setting much like this one too, under a tree overlooking Boston harbor. It was one of the first meeting sites of the early colonists before they built a shelter large enough to meet in. My mother stood beside my father. I remember her being prettier than usual that day. My sister and brother were there, as was my sister's intended, William Sinclair. I was twenty years old at the time."

John Wampas and Mary Weetamoo exchanged glances. They seemed to share a similar thought—that it was hard to imagine the aged man they had grown to love ever having been twenty years old. Their attendance at the service was Philip's idea. This pleased the old missionary immensely. In the absence of Morgan family members, Wampas and Weetamoo were invited to witness the ceremony as Philip's brother and sister in faith.

"On that day my father began a tradition which he prayed would continue until the return of Jesus Christ. This tradition was based on two basic beliefs for which my father lived and died. The first belief was that the Bible is God's infallible guide in all matters of life and faith. The second belief was that family is our most precious earthly possession." Christopher Morgan's cheeks became wet with tears. "Although I was faithful in preserving the first truth, I fell woefully short in keeping the second. An omission I deeply regret. I thank God that He allowed me to live long enough to know the joys of having a family. John Wampas, Mary Weetamoo, Philip Morgan—you are my greatest treasure."

"I love you Nanouwetea," Weetamoo whispered softly.

"This Bible..." Christopher Morgan held the Bible in trembling hands, "...was brought to Boston colony by my father, Drew Morgan, when he fled England with the Puritan faithful from Edenford." He opened the Bible and pulled a cross bookmark of exquisitely crafted white lace from among its pages. "This is my mother's handiwork and her contribution. It's a fitting family heirloom in her memory." He replaced the bookmark and closed the book. "Together, this Bible and lace cross are the symbol of the Morgan family faith."

The old missionary paused and struggled to catch his breath. He was visibly tired. When asked if he wanted to rest awhile before continuing, he insisted on completing the ceremony.

"The person who possesses this Bible has a twofold obligation. First, it is his responsibility to ensure that the spiritual heritage of the Morgan family is passed to the next generation. Second, it is his responsibility to choose a person from the generation following him to succeed him. When my father gave me this responsibility it was his prayer that I would have a son to whom I could give this Bible. It was not to be.

But in God's graciousness, He has given me a blood relative through my younger brother. And I have grown to love him like my own son."

Christopher Morgan shuffled over to Philip.

"Philip, I want you to know that I am not presenting this Bible to you simply because you are my only blood relative present. If I were not convinced you were God's choice for this responsibility, I would wait until God brought the right person to me." Then with a smirk he added, "Which is exactly what I thought I'd have to do when you first entered my wigwam. Since that time you have proven yourself to be worthy of this honor. Two things convinced me. First, your perseverance. When I sent you into the forest, I deliberately led you on a path that would take you to the edge of home. You could have chosen to remain there. But you didn't. You came back. And second, I have watched as you have grown in faith and Christian maturity, most recently evidenced in the way you acted regarding your brother in Christ, John Wampas. You demonstrated courage and unselfishness. These two traits are the hallmark of Christianity and, I pray, also of the Morgan family. Philip, it is with pride that I add your name to the list of names in the front of this Bible."

Christopher Morgan opened the front cover of the Bible. A third name, added to Drew Morgan's and his own, had been printed in the book. It read:

Philip Morgan, 1729, Philippians 2:3-4

"In case you don't recognize the Scripture reference, it reads: *Let nothing be done through strife or vainglory; but in lowliness of mind let each esteem other better than themselves. Look not every man on his own things, but every man also on the things of others.* The handwriting is Weetamoo's. I asked her to write it since, as you know, my hands shake so badly. I was afraid you wouldn't be able to read it if I wrote it."

Philip looked at Weetamoo and smiled appreciatively. She returned the smile.

"My son, I entrust the future of the Morgan family to your hands. Don't make the mistake I made in neglecting your immediate family. When your work is finished here, return to Cambridge. Teach them the love of God and the power of His Word. Set an example. If you fail at everything else, don't fail in this—bring your family together in unity and love. My prayers go with you."

Christopher Morgan released the Bible. It belonged to Philip now. The symbol of the Morgan family faith had been passed to the next generation.

"May I say something?" Philip asked. Christopher Morgan nodded.

"I can't help but feel there is a name missing in this Bible, that of my father, Benjamin Morgan. It was his vision that sent me on this quest. He was the first of our family to realize the importance of this Bible. I can only hope that he is standing beside Drew and Nell Morgan at this moment observing this ceremony from on high because this is the beginning of the fulfillment of his dream. And as God is my witness, I will make every effort to complete what has begun here today, the uniting of the Morgan family."

The remainder of the afternoon was treated as a holiday among the four residents of Christopher Morgan's wigwam. They were of different blood lines, but they had come to think of each other as family. Wampas and Weetamoo heaped congratulations on Philip as they all sat in the shade of the tree overlooking Adam's Pond and enjoyed a feast of corn and venison and some of Weetamoo's special chestnuts. They listened intently as the aged Morgan patriarch told the story of the beginning of the Morgan family faith just as it had been told to him. "The story begins at Windsor Castle," he said, "the day Drew Morgan met Bishop Laud. For it was on that day his life began its downward direction. . . ."

Weetamoo had taken firm control of the time they spent alone — when, where, for how long — and this frustrated Philip greatly. There were days when he was convinced she was toying with him. It seemed that when he wanted most to be alone with her, she would be cold and distant. Then, when he would resolve to let her go, she would encourage him. Her timing was perfect torture. He considered walking away from the whole thing. Except for one thing. The few moments they spent together alone were better than his best dreams. So naturally, the evening of the ceremony, with his mind set firmly on Cambridge and the difficult task ahead of unifying his family, Weetamoo whispered that she wanted to meet him in the cornfield after Nanouwetea had fallen asleep.

Wampas remained in the wigwam and didn't ask questions when Philip slipped out of the tent. As far as Philip knew, Wampas and Weetamoo never talked about the night he almost raped her. Weetamoo seemed content to let the memory of that night remain buried in the past. Wampas still bore the guilt; Philip could see it in his eyes. The Indian couldn't forgive himself. Although Wampas and Weetamoo remained friends, Wampas would never be able to approach Weetamoo romantically again; it would only serve to remind him of his shame.

So the Indian lost himself in his studies. When Philip left the wigwam he was studying Latin grammar. Never had Philip seen anyone with such a thirst for learning and with such a determination to succeed. At times Philip found it difficult to find enough assignments to keep Wampas busy. He was a model student, even when it came to his tutor. Their relationship healed more quickly than the wounds they both received the night Wampas came home. It was a good feeling for Philip. All his life he'd never had any trouble sustaining a relationship with his elders—his father, his teachers, Christopher Morgan. But he'd never been good at relationships with his peers. Wampas was a refreshing exception.

Philip stepped into the moonlight. It was bright tonight. A perfect evening. The moon was full and large as it hung low over the cornfield. The tower and cornstalks shimmered in the silver light. Since the day Weetamoo had pelted him with stones, the cornfield had been their rendezvous site. They'd always been brief encounters. Usually just a few words. An occasional touch of the hands. But nothing more than that.

"Weetamoo!" he called softy. She wasn't on the tower and he'd reached the first row of stalks. The corn was gone, except for the unpicked ears, and the stalks were dry, brown, and brittle. She wasn't down the first row. "Weetamoo!" he called again.

"SHHH!"

He heard her, but he still didn't see her. He quickened his step, looking down each row as he passed. She wasn't in row two, three, four, five, six. . . . Just as he was about to pass the seventh row, he saw her. And what he saw made him stop dead in his tracks. Several yards into the cornfield, Weetamoo stood sweetly, innocently, her hands clasped in front of her; her head was bowed slightly; she gazed out of the tops of her eyes through strands of black hair highlighted by the moon; her smile was warm and inviting. Philip couldn't imagine anything having a more powerful effect on him than the feeling that washed over him at that moment when he saw Weetamoo.

Philip entered the seventh row of corn and the wigwam and the rest of the reservation was cut off from sight. It was as if it was their own private room—the rows of cornstalks served as walls and they had a canopy of stars for a ceiling.

"Thank you for coming," she said softly.

Philip grinned, a little too widely. He couldn't help but be amused at her greeting. It was so polite, so formal. If she only knew the kind of power she had over him.

"Are you laughing at me?"

"No, no . . ." Philip stammered. "I just . . . I mean . . . what did you want to see me about?" He mentally scolded himself. He had to control his emotions. If he didn't, he'd ruin what was turning out to be a perfect day.

She looked at him skeptically a moment, then apparently decided she was overreacting. "I wanted to congratulate you personally," she said while still keeping a distance between them. "You know, Nanouwetea is quite proud of you. And so am I."

"Thank you. It means a lot to me."

It was her turn to grin widely. "I never would have thought you had it in you," she said. "You've really surprised me. You got what you came for."

"And more!" he smiled affectionately.

Weetamoo's smile vanished, replaced by a scowl. "Philip, don't start this," she warned, "you know there can be nothing between us . . ."

Philip held up a hand to stop her. "I was referring to the chance to get to know Christopher Morgan! When I left Cambridge I never suspected that I'd actually meet one of my ancestors."

Weetamoo covered her mouth and nose with delicate fingers to hide her embarrassment. "I'm sorry," she said. "I misunderstood."

There was an awkward pause, then Philip said, "But since you mentioned us . . ."

"There is no 'us'! There can't be any 'us'!" She took a step backward as she spoke.

Philip raised two hands in surrender. He apologized.

"When will you be leaving?" Weetamoo asked.

"Winter isn't far away," he said. "I really thought I'd be

gone by now, but Nanouwetea's health has slowed the work on the primer considerably. Wampas is progressing well, but still he won't be ready for the entrance exam for several months. I don't know. I'll just have to see what happens."

Weetamoo nodded. She brushed a couple of stray strands of hair out of her eyes. "I'm so proud of Wampas," she said. "Have I ever thanked you for tutoring him?" She giggled. "A noble gesture on your part considering he once stole your clothes and you had to walk naked across the reservation!"

Philip laughed with her. "Don't remind me!"

"It will be lonely here once the two of you are gone," she said.

"Weetamoo, I've been thinking about it. . . . I have to go— I don't have a choice—but I've decided that I'm coming back."

Her reaction befuddled him. It was exactly the opposite of what he'd expected.

"Don't speak such nonsense!" she shouted. The hurt in her eyes was quickly overwhelmed by anger.

"I'm telling you the truth!" Philip protested.

"I don't believe you! What is there to come back to? Nanouwetea will be dead. Wampas will be gone." As if to illustrate her next point she took a dried cornstalk and shook it at him. "We're nothing but a poor reservation living off the scraps of Charlestown society. What are you going to do here? You're trained for academic studies at Harvard. That's your life! Not this!" She shook the cornstalk again.

"I'd come back to be with you," he said.

"For a college-educated man, you can really be dumb sometimes!"

Philip felt his face and neck flush with anger. He shook a rigid finger at her. "I'm tired of people on this reservation calling me dumb!" he shouted. "And I'm tired of you holding my education against me as if it were something I should be ashamed of! If I say I'll come back, you can count on it!"

"Don't speak to me that way!" She folded her arms and turned her back on him. "Either we change the subject or I leave. I just can't talk about this right now."

"Fine!" Philip shouted.

"Fine what?" she yelled over her shoulder. "Fine, I should leave?"

"No," Philip said with a little more control. "I meant, 'Fine, let's change the subject.'"

For a long time neither one spoke. It was easier to agree to change the subject than it was to find a new subject to talk about. The silence hung uncomfortably between them.

"Namumpum gave birth today," Weetamoo said softly.

"Did she? I thought she was supposed to give birth over a month ago!"

Weetamoo nodded. She didn't turn around. "Namumpum was never good with numbers. We think she counted the months wrong. Then again, maybe she needed extra time. She gave birth to twin boys!"

"Twins!"

Weetamoo looked over her shoulder at Philip with a smile and nodded, then slowly turned to face him. "They're both big already, and healthy. Namumpum's grateful the wait is over. It was hard on her." Then, with a grin she added, "But I think her work's only just beginning."

There was a radiance on Weetamoo's face as she spoke of birth and motherhood. Philip thought how she would make a wonderful mother someday.

"What?" Weetamoo wanted to know what he was staring at.

"Nothing. I was just thinking." He folded his arms nonchalantly.

"What were you thinking? It was like you were far away for a moment."

"I was far away. In the future."

"Tell me." She reached out and touched his arm. "Please?"

"I just noticed how your face brightens when you talk about children. And I was thinking that you will make a good mother someday." Then he added hastily, "But I didn't mean to imply anything! Honestly! Besides, you asked!"

She pulled her hand away. "Yes, I did." With her eyes lowered, she admitted, "That was a very sweet thing to say."

The damage was done. She'd touched him. Like a spark to dry tinder, it ignited a fire in his belly that wouldn't go out. He had to do something, say something—or be consumed from within.

"Weetamoo, we have to talk about us," he began. From her posture, the set of her jaw, the look in her eyes, he could tell the defenses were raised, but he had to continue. "I have deep feelings for you. Feelings that won't go away. I've tried to pretend they don't exist, but pretending doesn't alter reality. When I said I'd come back, I meant it! I'd willingly spend the rest of my life here if it meant spending it with you! Weetamoo, I love you. I love you!"

"Don't say that!" she said, backing away again.

"I can't hold it back any longer! Whether you want to hear it or not, I have to say it because that's the way I feel!"

"No it's not!" she shouted. The moonlight highlighted the wet streaks that appeared on her cheeks. "When you go back to Harvard, you'll forget all about me! You'll go back and Penelope will be there waiting for you. You'll leave and you'll never come back! I don't believe you, Philip Morgan! I don't believe you!"

Weeping, Weetamoo pushed past him and ran out of the cornfield. The instant she turned the corner at the end of the row she was out of sight. A moment later he could no longer hear her sobs.

Philip stood with shoulders slumped, his arms limp, his face toward the stars. It was a short-lived resignation over what had just happened. For Weetamoo's outburst did nothing to extinguish the fire in his bosom. The longer he thought about it, the more fuel was thrown onto the fire until his chest expanded to the point of bursting. Philip Morgan raised his fists overhead and yelled with all his might.

"Aaaahhhhhhhhh!"

He slapped a cornstalk. It felt good, so he slapped another. "Why does she do that to me?" he yelled to the stalks. "Better yet, why do I let her do that to me? She drives me crazy!"

His chest heaving, he paced up and down the row slapping cornstalks until finally his anger began to subside. His thoughts became more rational and his pacing slowed. The fire within had lasted but a short time, yet in that time it had drained him of energy. Philip Morgan slumped to his knees.

"God in heaven," he prayed, "maybe they're right. Maybe I am dumb, dumb as a cornstalk, because I don't know what to do. When it comes to Weetamoo, everything I do is wrong. Everything I say is wrong! I want so desperately to be near her, yet every time I'm near her, I say something stupid and she runs away. She doesn't want me to express my feelings for her. I've tried to suppress them, to pretend they don't exist—God, You know how hard I've tried—but I just can't stop thinking about her. I just can't stop loving her. The harder I try to stop loving her, the more I love her! Am I condemned to love someone for the rest of my life who doesn't love me in return? How can I go on living like that? Should I ask You to kill my feelings for her? No. Never. I'd rather live with my love unfulfilled than stop loving her. Lord in heaven, I'm a fool. Teach me to be wise. Show me what to do. If it is best for Weetamoo's sake that I leave and never return, then that's what I'll do. Only make it clear to me. Please, Lord, make it clear."

A slight breeze rustled the cornstalks as Philip opened his eyes. He inhaled deeply and rose, brushing the dirt from the knees of his breeches. He felt better. It was no longer his problem alone. He was confident God would guide him in this. He walked down the row and decided to walk to the lake just to be alone for a while. He didn't want to go back to the wigwam yet—it would be uncomfortable with Weetamoo still awake, and Wampas would probably want to talk Latin or go over his lessons and Philip didn't feel like answering questions tonight. He reached the end of the row and turned toward the lake. There stood Weetamoo.

"Did you mean what you just prayed?" she asked.

"You listened to my private prayer with God?"

"You pray rather loud. Did you mean it?"

Philip looked into those deep black eyes that had the sparkle of the moon in them. "Every word," he said.

"O Philip!" Weetamoo flung herself into his arms with such force he staggered backward. She kissed his lips, "Please forgive me . . ." his chin, ". . . for hurting you . . ." his cheeks, ". . . it's just that . . ." his nose, ". . . I was . . ." his lips again, ". . . so scared."

Philip pulled away. This was too good to be happening. He wanted to look at her. He saw bottomless black eyes that proclaimed her love, tender lips that were warm and inviting. He pulled her to him with such force she let out a whimper. "I'm sorry, my love," he apologized for his roughness, "I can hardly believe that this . . ."

"Stop talking and kiss me."

He did. Again and again.

Philip Morgan and Mary Weetamoo sat atop the tower. Her back was nestled against his chest, his arms were wrapped around her waist. They watched the last bit of the moon slip beneath the horizon. Philip rested his cheek on her hair. He squeezed and she responded by rubbing her cheek against his arm with a contented sigh.

"This is wonderful," she said.

"You'll get no argument from me."

She leaned her head back. They kissed.

"When did you first know that you loved me?" Weetamoo asked.

"I'm not sure I can point to a specific time," he replied. "You sort of grew on me."

"Grew on you? You mean like a fungus?"

"I mean, from the first time I saw you, I knew there was something special about you. And then I found myself looking at you more often. There were times I entertained thoughts of us getting together, then dismissed them. It wasn't until tonight that I knew how much I loved you. The thought of not being near you was more than I could stand."

"You said you dismissed thoughts of us being together. Why?"

"Because of the way you treated me. Every time something brought us together, you would do something to discourage me. I thought you hated me."

"No," Weetamoo said softly. "Just the opposite."

"Now I'm really confused."

"I'd put you off because I felt vulnerable around you. I knew that if I didn't scare you away, all you would have to do is say one word, make one gesture, or look into my eyes and I'd crumble. The only time I would let you near me was when I was feeling strong enough to resist you."

"But if you loved me, why didn't you want me to know it?"

Philip felt Weetamoo shudder. He pulled her more tightly against him. Her voice was sad when she spoke. "Because I know that when you leave here, you'll never come back."

"How can you say that after what has happened tonight?"

"Don't you think I want to believe you? I can't explain it. It's just the way I feel."

"If that's the way you feel, then why are we kissing and holding each other tonight?"

Weetamoo rubbed her cheek gently against his arm. "Because I love you," she said. "I may not have you forever, but at least I can have you for one night."

Philip leaned forward and whispered in her ear. "I love you, Weetamoo. And I promise you, nothing will stop me from coming back to you. Nothing."

"Let's talk about something else," she said.

"What will it take to convince you that I'll return?" Philip asked.

Weetamoo thought a moment before answering. "When I see you standing in this cornfield again. Then I'll be convinced."

During the winter Christopher Morgan developed a rattling in his chest which he could not shake. He died in May, not long after spring rid the earth of the last remnant of an unusually harsh winter. The night before his death Nanouwetea had commented that the primer was nearly finished and that he was pleased with the result. To celebrate he had Weetamoo pass around the chestnut basket. He said his good-nights and went to sleep as usual. He never woke up. When Weetamoo couldn't rouse him the next morning, she called Philip. He confirmed that what they had been dreading had finally come. Christopher Morgan was dead.

Nanouwetea had spoken freely of his death for years. He wanted to be buried on the reservation since he had spent most of his life there. In keeping with both cultures that comprised his life, he wanted his funeral to be a mixture of Puritan and Narragansett practices with one unique addition of his own.

It was the tradition of the Narragansetts to paint their faces black with soot to mourn the dead, much like black clothing was used by colonists. Christopher Morgan neither encouraged nor discouraged this practice, but left it up to the individual mourner. Often mourners would grieve for a year if the deceased was a great public figure. No one could mention the name of the deceased person; those who did were warned, then fined. Those who had the same name as the deceased would change their name. Although Christopher Morgan didn't approve of these practices, he realized that many of the Indians would keep them regardless of his wishes, so he left no instructions regarding them. As for the grave, the Narragansetts placed the body in a fetal position facing southwest. The fetal position was their way of associating birth and death, seeing the death of a person as a birth into a different existence. They believed that Cautantowwit, the god of the underworld, lived in the southwest and that's where the souls of the deceased went to live. A giant dog guarded the realm of the dead, protecting them from harm.

Christopher Morgan instructed that his body be buried in keeping with the traditional Narragansett practice, in a fetal position and pointed southwest. To identify himself with the English settlers, he also wanted a headstone. This was where he added his unique contribution. Neither the Puritans nor the Indians eulogized their dead at the graveside. Christopher Morgan asked Philip to say a few words at the grave site and told him what to say. He wanted them to know he was to be buried in the fetal position because he too believed that death in this life was a birth into a new life. And although he allowed himself to be pointed toward the southwest, he wanted Philip to inform everyone that his soul resided in heaven, not Cautantowwit's house.

The day of the funeral was cloudy and overcast. A somber mood permeated the reservation even among the majority of residents who did not share the old missionary's faith. They were quick to recognize his wisdom and leadership among them. They knew him to be an honest, trustworthy white man—a rare commodity in their minds. The loss was felt more deeply by the church members. They filed in and out of the wigwam consoling Weetamoo, Wampas, and Philip with the traditional greeting, *kutchimmoke,* "be of good cheer"— accompanied by stroking the cheek of the bereaved.

At the graveside Philip read from the Algonquin Bible the familiar resurrection passage from 1 Thessalonians 4. There Paul instructs believers not to be ignorant about those who have died so that they grieve like the rest of men who have no hope. Philip painted a verbal picture of what it must be like for Christopher Morgan to be reunited with his father and mother, to sip the clear waters from the stream that flows from God's throne, and to take up residence in the house which Jesus Christ had prepared for him.

Following the service, Weetamoo, Wampas, and Philip talked late into the night, telling one hundred and one different stories about Christopher Morgan. That night, as they went to sleep, the wigwam felt empty. The absence of their father, ancestor, advisor, and friend was felt by them all.

For the remainder of May and into June, Weetamoo and Philip worked closely to complete Christopher Morgan's primer. They worked carefully and deliberately, wanting to do their very best as a lasting tribute to the book's author. But there was another, unspoken reason for their slow pace. They knew that once the primer was finished, Philip would be leaving soon after.

In the meantime, Philip not only served as project coordinator for the primer, he also continued tutoring Wampas in preparation for a possible August entrance into Harvard. While Wampas studied at night, Philip and Weetamoo would take walks in the cornfield, beside the lake, or sometimes just sit atop the tower and talk. As the two of them grew closer together, Philip was concerned that Wampas might object. Instead of waiting for a confrontation to develop, Philip asked Wampas directly if he was offended at the amount of time he and Weetamoo were spending together. To Philip's relief, Wampas said he not only was fully aware of what was happening, he approved.

He described it to Philip this way: "There can only be one great love in a person's life and I have fallen in love with learning. I will always love Weetamoo as a sister, but I could not give her more than that. She would always take second place to my learning and that wouldn't be fair to her."

Weetamoo was as pleased as Philip to hear Wampas' philosophical expression of his feelings. The three of them were never closer than they were now.

There was one other activity that took a portion of Philip's time and attention, one that came as a surprise to him. Several members of the church who had come in the past to seek Nanouwetea's advice continued coming to the wigwam. In Nanouwetea's absence, they sought Philip Morgan's advice. He helped them settle arguments, work out strategies for reconciliation, and counseled young couples who were considering marriage. For Philip, it was rewarding work. He couldn't tell which he enjoyed more: the fact that they accepted him or that they saw him as a successor to his wise ancestor. Regardless, it was difficult for him to think of leaving his work on the reservation; much more difficult to think of leaving Weetamoo. But he'd run out of excuses to stay.

The primer was complete and ready to print. He would take it with him and deliver it to a printer in Boston. Wampas was ready to take his entrance examination and classes would start in just over a month. Philip had the Morgan family Bible and unfinished family business to take care of in Cambridge. He could delay no longer. It was time to leave.

They stood under the tree next to the lake. It was Philip's last night on the reservation. Come morning, he and Wampas would ride for Cambridge. He held Weetamoo in his arms.

Her body next to his felt so good, so natural; he couldn't bear to think of letting her go.

"Your horse is ready?" Philip felt her jaw move against his chest as she spoke.

"Yes. Although I don't think he remembers me. The Great Swamp tribe spoiled him."

"You and Wampas aren't both going to burden that poor animal at the same time, are you?"

Philip smiled. "We'll share. I'll ride for a couple of miles, then tie up the horse and start walking. Wampas will come upon the horse and ride him for a couple of miles, then tie him up, and so on."

"I'm going to miss you."

Philip took her by the shoulders and looked her directly in the eyes. "I'll come back!" he said. "I promise you!"

Tears filled her eyes. "I want to believe that," she said.

"Believe it!"

She responded by clinging to him so strongly it restricted his breath.

"One year? Two?" she asked.

"If I'm coming back here, I don't need to complete my course work," he said.

Weetamoo shook her head. "We've already discussed that," she said. "Since you have no idea what has happened to your family, it will take you time to get reacquainted. At least a year. You might as well complete your studies during that time."

It was old ground. They'd gone over it several times before and Weetamoo was right. So Philip nodded in agreement.

"Will you write me?" she asked.

"As you know, I've not had much success with letters," he said. She chuckled. "But I promise to write faithfully."

"I know you will."

"And I'll come back!"

As the moonlight sparkled on the surface of Adam's Lake,

Philip and Weetamoo held each other late into the night. In spite of Philip's assurances, they both knew that there were no guarantees they would ever embrace each other again.

The horse's hoofs clattered across the wooden bridge that spanned the Charles River. Philip was almost home. Wampas was a mile or so behind him on foot. It had been three years since he'd left in search of the family Bible. Three years without any family contact. He didn't know what to expect. Yet a sense of thrill stirred within him as he saw roads and bridges and houses that at one time had been so much a part of his life. The colors surprised him. There was so much more color here. On the reservation the brown earth and wigwams and blue sky dominated. Here, the houses were painted different colors, as were the signs and fences. It was a different world.

Philip rode up to the Morgan house expecting to see Jared and his friends — Chuckers and Will — swimming in the river. The river was empty of activity. Scanning every inch of the front of the house, Philip dismounted. A rush of excitement sent his heart racing as he walked up the steps and opened the front door.

"Mother? Jared? Priscilla? It's me — Philip. I'm home!"

There was no immediate response. Then Philip noticed that the entryway was different. The furniture, wall hangings. All different. He chided himself. Did he really expect everything would be unchanged after a three-year absence?

"Young man! What are you doing in my house?" A squat, round-bellied man came from the study. His glasses sat low on his nose. Angry eyes peered over the top rims at Philip. "I must ask you to leave immediately!"

A middle-aged woman, equally short and round, came down the stairs. "Arthur? Did you say something? Oh!" She started when she saw Philip standing in the entryway. "Arthur, who is this?" she asked, obviously not pleased that she hadn't been warned they had a guest.

"I don't know who it is," said Arthur.

"Then why did you let him in?"

"I didn't let him in, he just barged in!"

"Oh my!" The woman grabbed the front of her dress and pulled it higher up her neck.

"What are you people doing here?" Philip asked.

"I think that's a question you should be answering!" Arthur was getting agitated.

"This is my house!" Philip said. "I live here!"

Arthur stepped between Philip and his wife. "Young man, I am not a man who tolerates pranks! Either you leave at once or you force me to get my saber!"

"I'm not leaving until I get some answers!" Philip yelled.

"Problems, sir?" A large, black, male servant appeared behind Philip in the doorway.

"Abel, this young man is an intruder! Throw him out."

"Yessir."

"Wait!" Philip cried. But Abel already had a grip on him and Philip went sailing down the front steps. He picked himself up and considered challenging the Negro. Apparently the slave read the intentions in his eyes. He took two steps toward Philip. The closer he got, the bigger he was, so Philip mounted his horse and left.

He found Wampas and together they went to Brattle Street. Penelope wasn't home and her father, Dr. Edward Chauncy, was none too pleased to see Philip. It was a terse conversation which Dr. Chauncy terminated quickly, but in that brief amount of time Philip learned several distressing bits of information. His mother had married Daniel Cole and the Morgan house had been sold about two years previous. Dr. Chauncy offered one other piece of information and a threat—Philip had broken his daughter's heart three years ago and didn't have the decency to write; the threat was contingent upon him ever being seen on Brattle Street again.

Philip was confused. He'd been sufficiently knocked off-balance by Dr. Chauncy's news; he wasn't sure what he should do next. It was Wampas who suggested that his first course of action should be to see his mother. He offered to walk back to the forest where he would stay until Philip came for him. Philip wouldn't hear of it. He insisted Wampas stay with him. So the two friends took the ferry crossing from Charlestown to Boston.

It wasn't difficult to get directions to Daniel Cole's house. Nor was it difficult to find, being the only house on the street with a giant pewter kettle hanging over the door. A maidservant answered the door when Philip knocked. He introduced himself and asked for his mother.

Moments later, he heard voices from the other side of the door.

"My Philip?" It was his mother's voice! "My Philip? Can it be true? Philip?"

The door swung open. The anxious face of Constance Morgan Cole appeared.

"I've come home, Mother," Philip said.

Constance looked at him, then behind him at Wampas. Her eyes rolled upward into her head and she fainted. Two male servants helped Philip carry her into the parlor while the maid ran to get a wet towel in hopes of reviving her. Several anxious moments later, Constance Cole's eyes fluttered open.

"Philip, is it you? Is it really you?" she cried.

The booming voice of Daniel Cole interrupted them. "What is going on around . . . ?" He saw Philip. For an instant Philip saw a look of annoyance on his face. Quickly it was gone, followed by a jovial grin and good-natured guffaw. "Well, well, Philip!" he boomed, casting a suspicious look at Wampas, who stood quietly to one side. "What a happy surprise! Oh, it's good to see you, son! Welcome home!"

Chapter 19

J ARED found the life of a pirate to be an unvarying daily routine interrupted by adventure and the most fun he'd ever had in his life. Most sailors found the daily routine monotonous. Not Jared. He loved every part of his new life — from swabbing the decks to scraping the rust from the anchor. His love for the work perplexed him at first, since at home he often employed his considerable imaginative powers to figure out ways to avoid it. Somehow, it was different here at sea. Maybe it was because the scope of his world was smaller, more manageable. Onboard ship, his entire world had been reduced to the wooden universe called *Dove,* a two-topsail schooner. And it was *his* world, from beam to beam and bow to stern, and there wasn't anything he wouldn't do for it.

At daybreak, the morning watch would "turn to" and swab the decks, fill the scuttlebutt (a cask of drinking water) with fresh water for the day's use, and coil the rigging. These daily chores usually took two hours, filling the time until seven bells (half past seven) when all hands got breakfast, which usually consisted of cold salt beef and a biscuit. At eight bells the day's work began and lasted until sundown.

Besides the task of sailing the ship and keeping watch, the sailors were constantly at work maintaining their vessel. As Tracy, the first mate put it, "A ship is like a lady's watch, always out of repair." Upon leaving port, all the running gear was examined, and that which was not fit for use had to be replaced. Then the standard rigging was examined for chafing and wear, and it was repaired. All the small lines — marline and seizing stuff — were made onboard ship from junk line which the sailors unlaid, knotted, and rolled into balls. When the rigging was set up, one line could seldom be touched without requiring a change in another. Add to this all the tarring, greasing, oiling, varnishing, painting, scraping, and scrubbing that needed done, and it was easy to see how a sailor's day was spent. And if there ever was a time when a sailor had nothing to do, there was always oakum stuffing to be placed about in different parts of the ship. This loosely twisted hemp was impregnated with tar and stuffed into the ship's wooden seams like caulking. No matter the task, Jared Morgan enjoyed it all.

The first words Captain Jack Devereaux spoke to Jared were in the nature of a reproach. Jared had finished scrubbing the deck well before breakfast. Not knowing that it was a sin for a sailor to appear idle, he leaned against the bulwark and watched the sunrise while waiting for seven bells to sound breakfast. The captain came on deck and, spotting the unbusied sailor, reprimanded him, ordering him to slush the mainmast from the masthead down. Jared was so delighted with the assignment, the reprimand had no effect on him. He grabbed a bucket of grease, which smelled slightly better than bilge water, and climbed up the mainmast. This was his first climb to the mainmast, something he'd been wanting to do since his first week onboard, and it was glorious. The rocking motion of the vessel increased with every foot he climbed. Clinging to the masthead he felt he was floating above the world.

Jared adapted more quickly to the sailing environment than most men. While most new recruits spend the majority of their first two or three days laying over the leeward side of the ship emptying themselves, at no time did Jared suffer the effects of nausea. From on high he swung back and forth like an inverted pendulum, slushed his way down the mainmast in time for breakfast, and devoured his food as if he were an old salt, with one difference. Old salts didn't grin all day long.

Jared's ready adaptation and willing spirit proved to be a hardship for James Magee and Benjamin Wier, who lagged behind in training. The *Dove* sailed south toward the Bahamas, a haven for pirate ships with its many islands and coves. For the crew, the trip south served as a shakedown cruise. Once they reached the Bahamas they would careen the ship in a bay at low tide and remove all the barnacles and marine life from its hull to increase speed—an essential for a pirate ship. Hunting season on the shipping lanes was not far away, and Captain Devereaux wanted his ship and crew to be ready. To get the crew ready, the captain set up competitions between the larboard watch—gunner Rudy Shaw's watch in absence of a second mate, and the starboard watch—first mate Patrick Tracy's watch. But first there was the training and initiation of the new crew members, after which the first mate would appoint them to permanent watches.

Jared was the easy favorite among the two watch leaders, and Shaw had already conceded that the first mate would pick him for his own watch. Of the two remaining recruits, it seemed like he didn't want Wier more than he wanted Magee. At every turn Shaw would carp about the struggling Wier to his face or to anyone who would listen.

Storm clouds hugged the horizon as the crew, those who weren't standing watch, gathered at the fo'csle (forecastle) for an initiation exercise. First mate Tracy explained the exercise:

"See that, gents?" The mate pointed to a pole jutting out from the ship's bow. "In case you don't know yet, it's called the bowsprit. Occasionally a line will jam on the sprit sail and someone has to climb out there and free it. Can any of you gents figure out who that 'someone' might be?" A grin filled his face as his red eyebrows bounced up and down. The sailors on the fo'csle laughed at the nervousness of the trainees. Tracy continued: "It's one of the better rides on the ship. Wier, you're first! Climb out on the bowsprit, touch the head, and come back. It's simple!" He looked into the distance at the approaching foul weather. "Let's get this done before that storm hits!" he said. "Wier, you're up. Go!"

Wier stood there, frozen in place, watching the bowsprit rise and fall as the ship plowed through the water. There was the spar itself and the rigging to hold onto, nothing else. Beneath was nothing but sea and an onrushing ship. Fall from the bowsprit and you not only take a swim, you get plowed under by your own ship.

"Any time now, Wier," watch leader Shaw said, his voice heavy with disdain.

Benjamin Wier stared straight at the bowsprit and shook his head. "I don't think I can do it," he mumbled.

"Every sailor's got to do it," the first mate said.

"You can do it, Wier," Jared said.

Benjamin Wier looked at Jared, who nodded encouragingly.

Wier inched himself toward the bowsprit. Slowly he straddled the spar at its base and looked down the length of the pole as it pointed high into the sky, then fell down toward the depths of the sea before coming up again.

"You can do it, Wier!" Magee joined Jared in encouraging their fellow recruit.

Wier hugged the pole and began inching his way out over the ocean. The way his bottom rose and fell he looked like an inchworm on a tree limb. His head cleared the bow of the boat, then his torso and feet until nothing was under him but rushing water. He looked down and froze.

"To the end, Wier!" Shaw shouted. "All the way to the

end! This is no time to stop and take a snooze!"

"Don't pay any attention to him," Jared yelled, which earned him a snarling glance from the watch commander. "Don't look down! Look at the pole and work your way to the end!"

"Come on, Wier, move it!" the first mate cried.

But their words weren't reaching him. Benjamin Wier was frozen to the pole. He didn't want to go farther out and he didn't want to come back. With his head against the pole and his eyes closed, he just clung onto the bowsprit for dear life. Finally first mate Tracy climbed out after him. When he touched Wier's foot, the frightened recruit started and gripped the pole all the tighter, his eyes wide with terror. It took a while, but Tracy finally convinced him to begin working his way back to the ship a quarter of an inch at a time. At last, Benjamin Wier rolled off the pole and onto the deck where he collapsed. Tracy helped him over to the side where he sat with his back to the bulwark, hugging his knees. The frightened trainee stared at the deck, refusing to look at or acknowledge anyone.

"A fine example of manhood!" Shaw crowed.

"Shut up, Shaw!" Jared rose to the trainee's defense.

Instantly, the gunner came at Jared. The first mate warned him off with a glance, then turned to Jared. "You're out of line, Morgan!" he said. "Keep your mouth shut. Magee! You're next!"

The wind and waves had picked up with the approaching storm and the bowsprit swung as wildly from side to side as it did vertically. James Magee approached the spar cautiously, swung his leg over it and slowly worked his way out over the bow. The spray was kicking up and the bowsprit was getting wet and slippery. Magee slipped and nearly lost his balance, catching himself just before he swung around to the bottom side of the spar. A cheer went up from the crew when he touched the head of the bowsprit and began working his way back. It took him nearly twice as long to make the trip in reverse, but soon a grinning trainee touched the deck. He was rewarded with another cheer.

"Not bad for a recruit," the first mate said. "I'd hate to be headed for some rocks while we waited for you to complete the trip, but still not bad."

Just then it began to rain and hail. They'd reached the storm. The winds beat harder and the waves grew in size. Like a horse rearing, the bow of the ship would raise then crash down into a wave; the bowsprit would disappear under water completely.

First mate Tracy examined the conditions and said, "Sorry, Morgan, looks like you'll have to do this some other time."

"Let him do it now!" Shaw shouted.

"It's too rough! He can do it later."

"You're just tryin' to mother him! Either he can do it or he can't. Why not find out what he's got?"

Captain Devereaux had joined the men on the fo'csle. He was dressed in heavy weather gear. Tracy appealed to the captain for a decision. None was forthcoming.

"I can do it!" Jared said to Tracy.

The wind had really picked up now. The bow of the ship rose, then crashed into the waves.

"It's too risky for your first time. The spar is slippery, so are the lines. It's tough enough for a seasoned sailor," said Tracy.

"Quit treating him like a baby!" Shaw shouted. "Is he a sailor or isn't he?"

"It's my decision, Shaw!" Tracy shouted back.

"This is part of being a sailor, isn't it, Mister Tracy?" Jared asked.

The first mate stared hard at him.

"I can do it!" Jared said.

"All right, go!"

Jared jumped down to where the bowsprit joined the deck and lined himself up. He looked out at the spar rising and falling violently like an untamed horse.

"What are you waiting for?" Shaw shouted.

Jared leaped forward with all his might just before the spar reached its peak. He'd timed it perfectly. He hit the spar the moment it peaked and wrapped his arms and legs around it for the downward ride. The ship plowed into two waves, one right after the other, plunging Jared into the sea. It was all he could do to hold on. He found footholds on the rigging and slid to the end of the spar. He touched the head just as it crashed into a wave. Completely underwater, he lost his foothold and wasn't sure he had a hold of the spar until it jerked up and pulled him out of the water. He dangled from the end of the spar, holding on with only his hands. The spar reached its upward peak again. Jared's hands slipped down the spar. He would have lost his grip if the spar hadn't stopped in its upward direction. He regained his hold and looked down at the ocean far below. The next instant he saw it come hurtling up toward him. Somehow he was able to swing his leg over the spar just before it hit the water. When it drew out of the water, he found himself facing the boat! It took him two more rides up and down on the spar, but he managed to scoot his way back to the deck. The relative firmness of the deck beneath his feet was the best thing he'd felt in a long time.

There were no cheers for his accomplishment. The fo'csle was clear of sailors; the needs of the ship in the storm had called them all to work. The first mate alone was there to greet him.

"Well done, sailor!" he shouted over the noise of the sea. The first mate gripped his hand and shook it vigorously. From the main deck the captain looked up as the first mate and Jared scrambled to get to their positions. He took a long look at Jared and nodded.

The gale lasted two days. During that time Benjamin Wier suffered the continual verbal abuse of his watch commander, Rudy Shaw. Each attack seemed to draw the boy deeper and deeper within himself. He spoke to no one, ate little, and performed his menial tasks as if he were sleepwalking. On the other hand, James Magee was beginning to accept his fate as a sailor and was showing some of the brash characteristics Jared had seen on Cole's warehouse docks the day they met.

The third day dawned with clear blue sky accompanied by a warm, drying sun. It was one of those idyllic days at sea. There was just enough wind to drive the sails, the sea was calm and blue, the sky was clear and fresh. The daily routine began as usual. After swabbing the decks and eating breakfast, the sailors set to work at their chores when the cry, "Land ho!" was sounded. Jared looked over the leeward side because that's where all the seasoned eyes were looking. A strip of land the length of the horizon was visible, the first he'd seen since coming aboard ship.

The sighting of land caused some concern among the officers. From what Jared could hear, they weren't expecting it. The captain ordered the ship on a larboard tack while he checked his instruments. The parcel of *terra firma* grew larger and larger. While the watch was instructed to look for landmarks that might help determine their location, the captain and first mate tried to figure out which navigational instrument was giving them faulty readings, the chronometer or the sextant. The ship was well within sight of land when it was decided that the chronometer was the culprit. As word spread that they were off the coast of Florida, the captain ordered the ship to come about on a starboard tack which would take them back out to sea.

SPLASH!

"Man overboard! Man overboard!" The cry came from the starboard watch.

"What happened?" the captain bellowed.

"It's Wier, sir," said Whitmore. "He jumped overboard. Deliberate, he was."

All eyes searched for Benjamin Wier as the captain ordered the ship to come about. Wier could be seen making deliberate strokes toward land. From the way his arms splashed, Jared could tell he wasn't a very good swimmer.

"He'll never make it," Tracy said. "It's a lot farther than it looks."

The bow of the boat swung around, reversing its course. As it did, Jared lost sight of Wier. Tracy had a better view.

"He's struggling," said the first mate. "I think he's in trouble. The clothes are weighing him down. I've lost sight of him!"

Jared scanned the surface of the ocean. He couldn't see anybody.

"There!" Tracy yelled.

For just a second Jared caught sight of Wier. His face broke the surface of the water, his mouth open; he was gasping for air, his arms slapping the water frantically.

SPLASH!

"Man overboard!"

"Another one?" The captain cursed.

Jared had stripped off his checkered shirt and baggy pants and shoes and dove over the bulwark into the ocean. With strong, steady strokes he swam to the place where he'd last seen Wier. Jared was alone on the surface. Wier must have gone under. Sticking his head under water, Jared looked around. The light on the surface faded quickly into darkness below. There was no sign of Wier. Jared surfaced to the sounds of shouting from the ship.

First mate Tracy shouted and signaled for him to move to his left. Jared swam in that direction until the first mate told him to stop. Quickly he dove beneath the surface. Time was running out for Wier. Jared had to find him soon.

The area below was heavy with kelp, row after row of it like an underwater forest silently swaying from side to side. The water was murky with sand that sparkled as it caught rays of sunlight. There was very little marine life. The fish that were there darted away in fear. Jared swam deeper toward the kelp. He pushed aside column after column of the stuff, each time hoping to find Wier behind the next row, then the next, then the next.

With his lungs begging for air, Jared surfaced. The ship was within a hundred yards of him. Jared filled his lungs and went down again. Still no luck. He surfaced. No one on the ship had seen any new sign of Wier. Jared went down again. Then again.

"He's gone," shouted Shaw. "Don't waste your time."

If anyone else had said it, Jared might have agreed with them. Wier had been under for too long to survive. It was the way Shaw said it that angered him. *Was trying to save someone's life a waste of time?* Angry, Jared dove again for another look. The kelp bed was becoming familiar to him and Jared knew he was looking places he'd already looked. Still he didn't want to admit there was nothing he could do. He surfaced for air.

"Jared, you've done all you can do!" the first mate shouted.

"Face it, Morgan, he's dead!" Shaw shouted. "He took the coward's way out!"

Jared dove again. He kept thinking that if he could just find him, get him to the surface, everything would be all right. *Wier would make a good sailor. Just give him time. Sure he was scared. Everyone gets scared now and then. All he needs is a chance. Give the guy a chance!*

Jared stayed under so long he almost didn't make it back to the surface before his air-starved lungs gulped involuntarily for relief.

"Morgan! Get back on ship. That's an order!" The voice was stern; the voice of authority. It belonged to Captain Devereaux.

Jared scanned the surface of the water; with one last desperate chance he hoped to catch a glimpse of Benjamin Wier.

"I said that's an order, Morgan!" the captain shouted. "When you've dried off I want to see you in my cabin!"

On the top of his head Captain Jack Devereaux was as bald as bald can be. It was a fact that was quite unavoidable to Jared as he stood in front of the captain's table. Devereaux was bent over his log scratching away at an entry. The candle on his desk, the sole light in the cabin, reflected with near equal intensity off the captain's shiny pate.

The captain's baldness captivated Jared because until now he had no idea the captain was bald. He'd seen the man hundreds of times, mostly at a distance and always on deck. In those encounters the captain had never been without his cocked hat. Equally deceiving was the crop of black and gray hair around the sides and back of the captain's head. Although it was thin, it was long enough to curl at the ends. Jared had assumed that such lush foliage naturally extended all the way to the summit. It didn't. Like a tree line on the mountain, the man's hair went only so far up the sides of his head and stopped.

The scratching of the captain's pen ceased. Devereaux lay the quill down with a sigh. "An unpleasant task, recording the death of a sailor." The heaviness in the man's eyes matched the tone of his voice. The loss of Wier had moved him. Jared had always thought of ship's captains as being hardened men, devoid of any feeling other than anger. Even more so for pirates. They were supposed to be tough, ruthless, cold-blooded. The man seated behind the table did not fit this description.

Devereaux interwove his thick fingers and plopped his hands on top of the still-open journal. He took a hard look at Jared. Was Devereaux trying to intimidate him? If so, it was working.

Pale blue eyes peered from what looked like caves beneath bushy gray eyebrows. The eyes were sharp, but it was their color that was unsettling. So pale, they were almost gray. They had a cunning look about them. They reminded Jared of the light-blue eyes he'd seen on one of the wolves the night he and Chuckers and Will went hunting.

The captain's nose was thick at the bridge and spread wide at the nostrils. A gray mustache continued where the nose left off and spread even wider. As one would expect from an old salt, his face and neck and arms were deeply tanned, his cheeks sunburned.

"Morgan, we have procedures we follow when a man is overboard," said the captain. "Jumping in after him is not one of them."

The man spoke in even tones, almost like a father reviewing the Sabbath rules with his son. Again Jared was surprised. He was expecting yelling, cursing, possibly blows. But there was no rampage. And, in a way, Jared was disappointed. All the other sailors had horror stories to tell about their previous captains. Unless Devereaux suddenly transformed into an inhuman monster, Jared wouldn't have any horror stories with which to scare future recruits!

Thinking about it, though, Devereaux's attitude made a little more sense to him when he remembered first mate Tracy's explanation of the authority onboard a pirate ship. Jared had learned that on pirate ships the captain and officers are elected by the crew. At the time of the election, a contract was drawn up designating the line of authority, rules of the ship, the methods of discipline to be used for various offenses, and the terms for distribution of the plunder after another ship was seized. Whereas merchant ships were run by dictators, pirate ships were run by elected authorities. On most pirate ships the captain had sole authority when it came to fighting, chasing, or being chased. All other decisions were brought to the crew and decided by majority rule.

"Death is an inescapable part of a sailor's life." The captain's voice brought Jared back to the present. "Accidents, storms, battles, disease—these are just as much your shipmates as the men out there. So is death. It's part of the crew and there's little we can do about it, except to be careful and to follow orders and procedures. Do you understand?"

Jared nodded.

The captain's eyes hardened. His tone became deadly serious. "I hope so," he said, jabbing a finger at Jared. "Because men's lives depend upon it!" Then, like the sudden passing of a squall, the captain's face was friendly again. Jared saw slightly uneven teeth and a cleft in his chin that deepened when he smiled. "I'll tell you one thing, though," he said, "if the ship ever goes down, I hope you're nearby. You swim like a dolphin, Morgan. Never seen anything like it. Where'd you learn to swim so well?"

"I grew up on the Charles River. Swam a lot."

The captain nodded. He got up from his desk, retrieved a pipe, loaded it with tobacco, and lit it. He propped himself against the front edge of his table. "Been watching you." Jared had to listen more closely. With his teeth clamped onto the pipe, the captain mumbled his words. "You're a born sailor," he said. "The mate shows you how to do something one time and you do it like you've been doing it all your life. Your father a sailor?"

Jared shook his head. "A teacher at Harvard. At least, he used to be. He's dead now."

The captain drew long on his pipe. Smoke circled upward above his head. "Did you go to Harvard?"

"Never was much for book learning. I was a disappointment to my father. He wanted me to go. It wasn't for me. Two scholars in the family was enough."

"Two?"

"My father and my brother. Both of them are good at that sort of thing."

"Do you play chess?"

"I know how. Haven't played much."

"I'm always looking for a good game. How about if we play Sunday?"

"Fine with me."

"Good!" The captain slapped the table and stood. "That'll be all, Morgan."

Jared rose. "Captain?"

"Yes?"

"Wier never wanted to be a sailor. He wasn't cut out to be one."

"I know."

The reminder of the boy's death cast a dark shadow over the captain again, and Jared was sorry for that, but he had to say what he said. He wanted an explanation, maybe an admission of regret. None was forthcoming.

"What about Magee?" the captain asked. "Is he a sailor?"

"He's coming around," Jared said. "He'll make a good sailor."

The captain's head bobbed up and down. Smoke circled around him. "Good. Good," he said.

Benjamin Wier's funeral service was held at the main mast that same afternoon. Rituals of death at sea were characterized by simplicity. There were prayers for the dead, someone offered a few words in memory of the departed brother tar, and that was followed by the usual ceremony of firing the guns. Gunner Rudy Shaw argued strenuously that firing the guns for Wier was a waste of gunpowder and an insult to true sailors. He insisted the boy had not attained the status of a sailor and had no right to have a sailor's burial salute. The captain argued that Wier died while serving aboard the ship and thus earned a proper burial. Gunner Shaw insisted the captain bring it before the crew for a vote. The crew voted unanimously with the captain, and the funeral ceremony began.

Captain Devereaux offered a brief supplication on behalf of Benjamin Wier. In his prayer he said he couldn't help wonder how things might have turned out differently for Wier if he'd never been brought onboard, since the boy showed little aptitude for sailing. Then he balanced that thought with the realization that life is uncertain and we all must make the most with what we have been handed. James Magee was the only person to offer a few words in memory of the deceased. Wier didn't talk much, but he had told Magee a few things, such as the fact that he was raised in Hingham by his mother and two older sisters. He'd never known his father, who had died of smallpox while Benjamin was still young. He was good with numbers and had just moved to Boston seeking a position on the docks as an accountant when his path crossed with some crimps. In the days before his death all he could talk about was how he never should have left Hingham, and the first chance he got he was going home. Magee said it was his guess that's what Wier was trying to do when he jumped overboard. The ship's guns were fired and the ceremony was over. One other ritual usually followed the burial ceremony, sometimes a couple of days afterward, to give the sailors a chance to get a handle on their emotions. The ritual involved auctioning off the dead man's goods—his chest, bedding, clothes, and what few personal items he had onboard. Since Benjamin Wier's possessions consisted of nothing more than a hammock—a piece of canvas six feet by three feet—the captain and crew dispensed with this part of the funeral ritual altogether.

With Wier no longer around, gunner Rudy Shaw looked for someone else to be his whipping boy. He chose James Magee for this dubious honor. As expected, when the watches were set, first mate Tracy appointed Jared to his watch and Magee to Shaw's watch. Shaw then selected Magee to be gunner's-mate-in-training or, as Shaw described the position, "powder monkey." This put Magee under Shaw's authority twenty-four hours a day. And from the first day on, Shaw leveled a barrage of criticism at Magee that began with sunrise and lasted long after sunset.

Jared could hardly stand to watch as his friend labored under the abusive gunner day after day. On behalf of his friend, he went to boatswain Whitmore, then to first mate Tracy. Both of them acknowledged Shaw's surly moods and abusive methods, but refused to intervene unless the safety of the ship was affected. Jared watched helplessly as Magee's spirits and self-confidence deteriorated day after day. At every chance, which were rare since they were on opposite watches, Jared lent Magee a listening ear and offered words of support in an effort to offset the damage Shaw was doing.

Jared learned that Shaw was a lazy fellow with low moral character. His only redeeming quality was that he knew guns and ammunition. However, he never did any of the work himself. He sat idly by, ordering Magee around like a slave. Whenever anyone came down to the gun deck, Shaw would hold them up, chatting endlessly with them, much of the time criticizing the captain and first mate. On watch he would frequently fall asleep, leaving orders with Magee to wake him up should anybody come.

During one of his harangues against the captain, Magee

learned the source of Shaw's discontent. The previous summer, when the number of sailors onboard the *Dove* had swelled to the extent that a second mate was needed, Shaw was the logical choice for the position based on his years at sea. But instead of endorsing the gunner for the position, the captain merely suggested the crew hold free elections. They didn't choose Shaw. The gunner was not the type of person who lost gracefully. He needed to vent his anger. A couple of months later, three young prospects were dumped on the deck of *Dove*.

Magee warned Jared to steer clear of Shaw. Though the gunner rode him all day long, it was Jared he truly hated. "Tracy's boy," he called him. "Some day I'm gonna get Tracy's boy," he'd say.

Jared responded to Shaw's threat to get him as only a boy his age could—with practical jokes. The first practical joke Jared did alone. At dinner, when Shaw was distracted, Jared dropped a cockroach into his beer. To the delight of half the mess who witnessed the prank, the gunner took several casual sips of the beer before he found the surprise. From that point the practical jokes got more complicated, but Jared found no shortage of volunteers to help him. One night, Shaw being a sound sleeper, several of the sailors tied the gunner into his hammock. He was blindfolded and gagged before he could recognize anyone. When the gunner was late for his watch, the first mate came looking for him and found a furious Shaw thrashing around, unable to break his bonds. Another time, Shaw was waylaid in the hold by hooded attackers, stripped of his pants, and his backside was tarred. He eventually retrieved his pants, but for days afterwards they stuck to him constantly.

The culmination of the pranks came following a storm that had battered the ship for three days. The storm's delay was serious. The captain feared the premature onset of the hurricane season and wondered whether they should attempt to make it to their winter port or find another location. The men were exhausted after their brutal battle against the elements. Soaking wet, everyone except the crew on watch stumbled to the crew quarters and fell into their hammocks. All except gunner Rudy Shaw. Unknown to him, Jared had cut a slit in the bottom of his canvas hammock. Instead of falling into his hammock, Shaw fell through it.

Jared never figured out whether Shaw had actually discovered that it was he who was the mastermind behind the practical jokes, or whether Shaw attacked him because he was laughing the loudest; either way, the gunner lit into Jared and the two sailors fell to the deck, rolling this way and that, exchanging punches.

Minutes later, attracted by the commotion, first mate Tracy broke up the fight. The articles of the ship were clear on the matter. They contained a section specifically written for maintaining order. It read: "No striking one another onboard, but every man's quarrels are to be ended on shore at sword and pistol." Tracy explained: Upon reaching the Bahamas, the antagonists were to fight a duel with pistols. If both missed their first shots, they then would fight with swords. The first man to draw blood was declared the victor. The intent of the article was to settle such conflicts off the ship and so promote harmony in the crowded quarters below deck.

Jared and Shaw agreed to wait to settle the matter on shore. Open hostilities between them and the pranks ceased for the remainder of the voyage.

Chapter 20

JARED sat with his head in his hands. Devereaux faced him on the other side of the captain's table. A chessboard was spread between them. It was Sunday afternoon on a fair day. A minimum watch was posted and Jared had two more hours until his turn for duty.

"You're relentless, I'll give you that," said the captain as he stared at the chessboard, "but shortsighted."

The captain blocked Jared's attacking knight with a bishop; Jared would have to back off or lose his knight. Since the knight was one of the few mobile pieces he had left, Jared pulled it back to safety. He sighed in exasperation.

"You have good instincts," said the captain, sliding his other rook along the king's file, "and an imaginative sense of strategy. However. . . ."

The captain paused while Jared repositioned the same knight. He smiled. In two moves he would have checkmate.

". . . you fall woefully short in your basic philosophy. It's your undoing," the captain finished his thought.

"Not this time, sir," said Jared. "I've got you in two moves."

The captain squinted at the board and scratched his chin. "So you have." He scratched his chin again. "That is, if you *had* two moves." The captain moved a bishop. "Check," he said.

Jared took his bishop with a pawn.

The captain took the pawn with a rook. "Check," he said again.

Jared took the captain's rook with his rook.

The captain slid his second rook down the rank and took Jared's remaining rook. "Checkmate!"

Jared sat back and shook his head. This was the way the games usually ended. Jared had defeated the captain only once.

The captain grinned. He enjoyed winning. "You play individual pieces," said the captain. "That's your weakness." He picked up a piece at a time and placed it back on its original square. "The secret to chess is to know the relative strength of each piece and then to utilize each piece's strength in concert with the other pieces."

"I do that," Jared protested, "and you still beat me."

The captain shook his head. "You don't do that," he said. "You attack with one piece. All the other pieces are merely used as support for that one attacking piece. I'm talking about every piece on the board united in action with one common goal, one common purpose; each one contributing as he is able and depending on the strength of the other pieces so that together they obtain the victory! Take this end game for example. You couldn't stop it because there were too many pieces coming at you with one united effort."

Jared stared hard at the chessboard. He was beginning to see the possibilities.

"Do you have time for one more game before your watch?" Devereaux asked.

"Yes, I think I do," said Jared distractedly, his mind already formulating a strategy.

They were silent as each man made his opening moves. Then the captain sat back in his chair, stretched, and relit his pipe. "We'll be in port tomorrow."

Jared looked up. That meant that sometime tomorrow he

and Shaw would settle their differences.

"Have you ever shot a pistol?" the captain asked.

"No. A musket, but not a pistol." Jared moved his queen into an attacking posture.

"It's time I told you something, son."

Jared glanced at the captain. It was the first time the captain had called him son.

"You don't have to fight the duel with Shaw."

Sitting back in his chair, Jared left the game momentarily to focus on what the captain was telling him. "I don't understand. According to the ship's articles I have to fight him."

"The articles of discipline apply only to men who are members of this ship."

"But I'm a member of this ship."

"No, you're not."

Jared couldn't believe what he was hearing. He stood up, his anger rising along with him. "Are you suggesting I desert this ship when we reach port just to avoid fighting Shaw?"

"Sit down, Morgan!" The captain put on his commanding voice to issue the order, battling Jared's rising emotion with some of his own. "There is something I need to tell you and now is the time to do it."

Jared took his seat.

"Pirates don't purchase men from crimp gangs. There are more sailors wanting to join us than we can accommodate. Every time we board a merchant vessel there is a key moment of confrontation when we call out for those who would join us to drop their weapons. In many cases, at that moment the battle is won, because so many sailors are fed up with the tyranny of life aboard a merchant ship. At times there are so many of them we have to sail to port where they can be dispersed to other ships."

"Then why did you buy me and Magee and Wier from crimps in Boston?"

Devereaux stared past Jared, his pale eyes seeing something or someone who wasn't in the cabin with them. He pulled hard on his pipe twice before answering the question.

"You were about to be sold to a merchant-ship captain named Barlow. I once served under Edmund Barlow. He's a tyrant and a sadist. A long time ago I swore to do everything in my power to thwart Captain Barlow and the merchant who pays him to run those slave ships."

"You bought us to rescue us?"

"The men you're tangled up with are a dangerous sort. They have no regard for life or property other than their own. I ought to know. The crimp who sold you to me is employed by Daniel Cole."

"Cole?" Jared's teeth and fists clenched until they hurt. "I should have known! I should have known!" he shouted. To the captain: "You're certain Cole is behind this?"

Devereaux nodded grimly. "The crimp who works for him is my brother."

Jared was stunned.

"Mister Tracy tells me that you believe my brother and his Indian partner killed your father."

Cautiously Jared nodded.

The captain bowed his head. He spoke softly. "My sincere apologies. I didn't know until after you were onboard. My brother and Seekonk—his Indian partner—have been doing Cole's dirty work for years. They're thugs, hired killers. When I ran into him in Boston, he was bragging about how much money he was going to make on this deal. Cole paid him to get rid of you and Magee, he didn't care how. At first my brother was going to kill you. Then he had a better idea. If he sold you to Barlow, he could make a double profit. That's when I ran into him. I gave him twice the amount of money Barlow had offered him. I knew he'd go for it. He's my brother." Devereaux paused to clear his throat. "I figured the best thing I could do for you would be to take you far away from Cole and Barlow and my brother. The Bahamas are a nice place to live. Once we make port, you're free to go. You don't have to fight Shaw."

Jared was dumbfounded by the captain's revelation. The chess game spread out in front of him was meaningless now. "What about Magee and Wier?"

"Magee is free to go too. As for Wier . . ." the captain's voice trailed off. "If only he could have held on a little longer."

"Can we stay on if we want?"

The question seemed to please the captain. "It's up to you. You'd have to fight Shaw."

"I'll talk it over with Magee. Will we be raiding any of Cole's ships?"

Devereaux grinned widely. "As many as we can find."

Jared grinned with him. "I think I'd like that."

"Be careful, Jared. Revenge is a fickle mistress. She has a way of turning on you."

"I just want to flirt with her a while, not marry her."

The captain pushed away from the table. There was little chance either of them would be able to concentrate on the game. "If you choose to join us," he said, "you can have the satisfaction of knowing that you're serving on a ship that once belonged to Daniel Cole."

"You bought the *Dove* from him?"

"Not exactly. Barlow was the captain then. We were in Glasgow when several of us decided we'd had enough of old Captain Barlow." Devereaux grinned mischievously. "So, we stole his ship! And that's how I became a pirate."

James Magee lay in the sand squinting in the bright sun. "You mean we can just go home if we want?"

Jared sat beside him, running his fingers through the warm

sand; the *Dove* lay careened on Cat Island. A tiny inlet of crystal blue water stretched into the ocean at their feet, just one of the many lagoons made by the coral reefs in the Bahamas. While the residents of Boston were bracing for the first winter storm of the season, these two young men sunned themselves in the subtropical climate. The sun was high in the sky and so bright that even with his eyes closed, it was light to Jared.

"That's what the captain said," Jared said. "We can find our way home, or stay here, or go with the ship—whatever we want to do."

Magee sat up and looked down at his friend. "So we weren't kidnapped to be pirates."

Jared smiled. It wasn't that his friend was hard of hearing; like Jared, he was having a hard time believing they had a choice. "Devereaux was protecting us."

Magee humphed. "I didn't need anybody's protection. I liked what I was doing."

Jared propped himself up on his elbows. "If I remember correctly, we were doing a less-than-first-rate job of protecting ourselves. We could be dead, or enslaved on a merchant ship! Devereaux saved our hides."

"I know." Magee picked up a handful of sand and threw it at the water. "It's just that I liked my job. It was good steady work. I was going to find a girl and settle down; build a name for myself and all that kind of stuff."

"But it was Cole who sold you out."

"The question is why. Why? I thought he liked me!"

"Maybe he just used you to get to me. He had you lead me into the trap, and when it sprung you were caught in it too."

"What does he have against *you?*"

Jared shook his head. "I don't know. But I know this: someday I'm going to ask him—face-to-face I'm going to ask him—and he'd better be real good at explaining it to me."

Magee hugged his knees. "So you're going to go back to Boston?"

A few moments passed before Jared answered. He gazed out over the smooth blue waters. His eyes caught sight of a sail just barely visible on the horizon. His instinct was to cry out, "Sail ho!" Then he remembered he wasn't on watch. "I'm staying with the ship," he told Magee.

"If you're caught you could get hanged."

"Or I could get washed overboard, or killed in a fight, or hit by a falling block, or eaten alive by sharks, or any other number of tragedies that are part of a life at sea. It's the right thing for me to do right now. For one thing, by raiding Cole's ships I hope to sour his business until I can deal with him more directly. Besides, I like being a pirate."

"We haven't done anything but sail down here yet! How do you know you like it?"

"I like sailing, I like the men we're sailing with—with one exception, of course—and I want to see other parts of the world. As for raiding other ships, well, we'll just have to see what that's like. How about you? What are you going to do?"

Magee screwed up his face. "I don't know. . . ."

"Sure you do!" Jared stood up. "Do you remember what you told me back in the tavern just before we got suckered?"

Magee shook his head even as he tried to remember the conversation Jared was referring to.

"You were telling me about a man who was sent to Barbados and you got all excited that he was going to recommend that you should get sent to Barbados too. Well . . . ?" Jared spread his arms toward the open sea. "You made it! Here it is! Somewhere . . . it's around here . . . somewhere . . . I think." Jared laughed at his geographical ignorance.

Magee laughed with him. "I have to admit, you certainly picked the right location to make your sales pitch. But *you* don't have to live with Shaw."

"That will all be taken care of tomorrow," Jared said, "when I shoot him." He said it in a casual way, making light of the duel in a way that hid his real concern.

"In that case," Magee said, "I guess we're brother tars!"

Gunner Rudy Shaw looked awful. His patchy salt-and-pepper beard together with red blurry eyes, yellow teeth, and rancid breath made Jared conclude that he was sick.

"If this isn't a good day for you to duel," Jared said, "we can do it some other day."

"You scared, boy?" Shaw drawled. Anger lit his eyes. He leaned into Jared, his nose working up and down as if he was sniffing for fear.

"Are you sure you want to do this?" first mate Tracy asked Jared.

Jared shrugged. "Why not?"

"Why not?" Tracy echoed. "Because you might get killed! That's why not!"

The first mate's intensity sobered Jared momentarily. He hadn't thought of that. Death wasn't something a young man thought about happening to him. It only happened to older people or the unlucky. And Jared was neither of those things. Jared was young and frisky, like a wolf pup. And, like a wolf pup, fighting to him was yipping and snapping and rolling in the dirt while at the same time your tail was wagging. This duel with Shaw was nothing more than him and Chuckers and Will scraping with one another on a Saturday afternoon. Occasionally tempers flared when someone got hurt; but everyone knew it was unintentional. For Jared, this was just another Saturday afternoon with a different set of friends. At least it was until Tracy brought up the subject of death. Was it the thought of death that made Shaw look as bad as he did?

"I have to do this," Jared said, "if I want to remain on the ship."

His answer seemed to satisfy the first mate.

Tracy stood between the two duelers. The three of them were in the middle of a vast expanse of sand on one of Cat Island's many lagoons. In the distance *Dove* lay careened at an awkward angle. Welshman Bardin, the ship's carpenter, was in command of the maintenance that was underway on the ship's hull. The ship had sailed into harbor at high tide. When the tide went out, the ship settled on the sand. It was then pulled over on its side, exposing the hull below the water line. Barnacles and various kinds of marine life were removed, and the boards and seams were caulked with a mixture of oakum and pitch that was then fired so that it stuck firmly to the wood.

Those sailors who weren't repairing the hull of the ship were scattered around the edges of the sandy expanse, spectators of the duel between the ship's gunner and the would-be pirate.

First mate Tracy handed each contestant a loaded pistol and allowed them time to inspect the weapons. Once they were satisfied, Tracy stood them back-to-back.

"The rules are simple." He pointed to two swords stuck in the sand, one in front of Jared and one in front of Shaw. "The swords are ten paces away. You walk ten paces on my count, turn, and fire. If, after firing, blood has not been spilled, you will grab your swords and begin fighting. The first man to draw blood wins. Agreed?"

"Agreed," said Shaw.

"Agreed," said Jared.

Tracy backed away to a safe distance. "On my count!" he yelled. "One! Two! Three!"

Jared stepped with each count. James Magee was perched on a rock along with several other sailors to Jared's right. Jared made a mental note to tell his friend about how the captain had expressed regret over Wier's death. He thought Magee would like to know that.

"Four! Five! Six! Seven!"

It was funny, the things he was thinking about in the middle of a duel. He remembered wondering what people thought about when they knew they were dying. He'd always assumed they would think about their loved ones or their regrets or something like that. If he followed their example, he'd be thinking about Anne right now. And although he loved thinking about him and Anne, it just didn't seem appropriate to involve her in a duel.

"Eight! Nine!"

Maybe the fact that I can't think about her is proof I'm not going to die, he thought.

"Ten!"

Jared whirled around and aimed his pistol; he was already turned and looking down the barrel of his pistol while Shaw wasn't yet halfway around. Jared waited for him. Shaw raised his weapon. Jared knew he should pull the trigger. The gun was aimed at Shaw's chest. If he pulled the trigger now, he might seriously hurt the man!

From his viewpoint down the barrel of the pistol, Jared saw a flash, a puff of smoke, and heard the explosion of powder the same instant a searing pain burned his left shoulder. He winced and lowered his pistol. It felt like someone had touched his arm with a hot fireplace poker. Jared grabbed his shoulder.

"Are you hit?" Tracy called to him.

"I think so," Jared called back.

Tracy ordered Shaw to remain in place while he came to examine the wound. The first officer pulled Jared's hand away. "Here's where the ball went," he said. His finger poked through one hole of his shirt and out another. Lifting the sleeve, Tracy examined the shoulder. "You've been branded," he said. "Nothing more. The bullet just grazed your shoulder."

To Shaw and the others, Tracy yelled: "Just a graze! No blood!"

Tracy resumed his position. "All right, Jared," he yelled. "Your shot."

Jared looked at the man standing twenty paces away from him. Shaw's shoulders were slumped, the spent pistol dangled at the end of his limp right hand. Never before had Jared seen the bully Shaw look so pathetic. He raised his weapon and placed the sight on Shaw's nose. No, he couldn't shoot there. He lowered the site until it rested square on Shaw's chest. Jared didn't want to shoot him there either. What about a leg? Or maybe an arm. *No, what if I damage some muscles? A gunner is no good without strong arms and legs.*

Rudy Shaw screamed a string of curses. "Shoot me! Shoot me! What kind of a cruel animal are you to put me through this kind of agony?"

Jared lowered the pistol. "I don't want to shoot you!" he yelled.

"You have to shoot!" Tracy yelled at him. "It's the rules."

"Even if I don't want to shoot?"

"You have to shoot!"

"Fine! I'll shoot!" Jared pointed the pistol in the air and pulled the trigger. The gun made a deafening roar. Smoke billowed around him. The tang of burned powder filtered through the air.

"Swords!" Tracy yelled.

"First man to draw blood is the winner!"

This is much better than guns, Jared thought. He grabbed the sword that was stuck next to him in the sand and bounded toward his opponent.

Sword ready, Jared waited at step zero for his shaken opponent to collect himself. Shaw had dropped his pistol in the sand. With shaking hand he reached for the sword and pulled it out of the sand. He gripped it several times, each time tighter, with increasing resolve. Slowly he turned toward Jared. Shaw had regained his anger. Furious was the word that came to Jared's mind when he saw the man's face dripping with sweat, his yellow teeth clenched in a wicked grin.

"If it comes to swords," Tracy had coached Jared, "stay well out of his reach. He's not a good sword fighter and he knows it. So he fights dirty, but then in raids and duels pirates don't have rules of etiquette. You should be able to take him. Even though you've not been fighting as long, you're a better swordsman." Jared enjoyed this compliment since it came from his teacher. "You have several advantages," Tracy continued, "longer arms, you're younger, more agile, you have quicker reflexes. Use these things to your advantage. Whatever you do, don't let him in close!"

"Aaaaahhhhhhhh!" Shaw lunged toward Jared, his sword extended in front of him.

Jared deftly sidestepped the rushing bull. To his surprise though, the bull circled quickly and was right back. *He's too close! Too close!* The warning sounded in Jared's mind.

Metal clashed against metal as Jared blocked several wicked slashes. The force of the blows jarred him. Shaw had massive arms from hauling and loading heavy guns most of his life. Jared couldn't just trade blows with him and win. He had to use his agility, his reflexes, to his advantage. Jared waited for him to coil for another thrust, then, at the last second, he stepped aside again. Shaw missed cleanly. The force of his blow unblocked sent him reeling. He attempted to keep his balance but landed facedown in the sand.

A cheer went up all around.

"Finish him! Finish him!" they cried.

Jared could have easily killed or wounded the fallen gunner. He didn't. He stepped away while Shaw scrambled to turn around and face him. He sat in the sand looking up at his opponent.

"Why didn't you finish me?" he shouted.

"I don't want to hurt you," Jared replied sheepishly.

"Your misfortune!" Shaw threw a handful of sand at Jared's face and at the same time lunged with his sword at Jared's legs.

The sand hit Jared's eyes and caused immediate stinging and watering. He blinked several times. If felt like he had a whole field of rocks under his lids! Between blinks he saw a sudden movement followed by a swish as Shaw's sword barely missed him. Another movement. Another step away. The swish was near his face.

With much rubbing and pain, Jared was able to restore sight to his right eye. The left one still had too much sand in it. Squinting, he followed Shaw as the older sailor came after him. There were several more wild swings. Each sound of an empty swish was a temporary victory.

All around them pirates were yelling and screaming. Some for him, some for Shaw, but mostly just because there was a fight.

Little by little Jared regained the use of his left eye as he managed to keep the pursuing gunner barely out of harm's reach. The salt and sand stung his eyes so much, it made him angry. He became aggressive and now it was Shaw who was backing up, dodging thrusts and slashes. Still, Jared found himself holding back. Several times he could have drawn blood, but he didn't. Several times Shaw was an open target and Jared didn't hit. Not that he couldn't, he just didn't.

Shaw was tiring. The older combatant had sweat pouring down his temples, his breathing was labored, and his point tip began dropping regularly. It became evident that Jared could strike him at will; however, Jared never willed it. Shaw continued lunging while Jared jumped and romped and played.

"Blood! We need blood to stop the contest!" Tracy yelled.

Jared stepped back and turned toward the first mate. "I can't!" he yelled.

SWISH! Shaw's blade came within an inch of his cheek.

Jared drove him back with several thrusts, still not taking advantage of several openings the tiring gunner gave him. The last shove sent the gunner tumbling in the sand.

"You don't have to kill him! You don't even have to disable him! Just cut the skin!" Tracy yelled.

The thought distracted Jared. *Cut him, but don't hurt him. Where? The cheek? The shoulder? The chest? Leg? Where would it hurt him the least?* Staying low to the ground, Shaw had scooted toward Jared, crawling on his hands and legs like a crab. The first indication Jared had that his opponent was in striking distance was when the toe of the man's boot caught him in the back of the knee. Jared's leg buckled underneath him. He hit the ground on his back just as the point of Shaw's blade plunged toward his ribs.

Jared rolled over. Shaw's blade slipped into the sand where Jared had fallen. The blade came again and again Jared rolled out of the way just in time. This time he kept rolling. Shaw was on his knees. The last thrust was as far as he could reach without getting up. Jared managed to get to his feet first. His blade was at Shaw's throat before the gunner could move further.

"It's time to end this," Jared said.

The exhausted, sweaty gunner looked up at him and awaited his fate.

Jared's blade nicked the gunner's chin. A drop of Shaw's blood splatted in the sand.

Although Jared won the duel, it wasn't a complete victory for him. There was something about a pirate not wanting to hurt anybody that didn't sit well with his shipmates. Jared assured them that in a life-and-death struggle with a real enemy, he would have no hesitation about killing. His argument was not readily accepted.

Even the defeated gunner expressed doubts. "You may have won the duel today, boy," he said, "but if you don't learn to kill you won't live past your first raid."

First mate Tracy was enthusiastic about his student's skill with the sword and presence of mind in battle, with the exception of the one distraction that almost got him skewered; still, Tracy had reservations too.

"Just wait until our first raid," Jared said. "Then you'll see how much killing I can do!"

Captain Devereaux had watched the fight from a distance. The moment it was over, he returned to the ship to check on the progress of the hull repair. He never mentioned the duel to Jared.

Jack Devereaux had survived five years as a pirate because he was cautious, always prepared for every contingency, a brilliant strategist, and a good sailor. He refused to join forces with other pirates as was the habit of some. "Too many captains lead to indecision and death," he said. He insisted his ship was always in the best condition possible, that his crew was well-trained, drilled, and equipped to handle any situation; and that his fighting strategy was based on his men's strengths and his enemy's weaknesses. And he never, never, never allowed revenge to be his guiding force.

This philosophy of pirating had earned Jack Devereaux a reputation as a gentleman pirate. Of course, that didn't mean merchants hated him any less or wouldn't love to see him dangling at the end of a rope on the Waping gallows in London or Boston or any number of other cities. But the men who sailed the seas, especially those on his ship, respected him.

While the ship was aground, the sailors had little else to do with their time than to get into trouble in any number of ways. Many of them did it by finding their way to New Providence Island where they could indulge themselves in ways they'd regret for days and weeks afterward. Two indulgences occupied most if not all of their time—drinking and women. And the seasoned sailors always took it upon themselves to introduce the new generation to the rituals of shore leave.

Magee and Jared went along willingly. While James Magee had some experience in the world of liquor and women, Jared had never been much attracted to drink and the closest he'd come to spending the night with a woman was when he suggested to Anne that she arrange for them to be bundled together.

After the first couple of drinks, Jared got bored. The last time he drank heavily, he ended up in a Boston alley with a knot on his head; so, in spite of the endless urging by his shipmates—Michael Dalton, Jeremiah Lee, and Richard Derby especially—Jared tried to excuse himself. Dalton would not hear of it. With a lady draped on each of his arms, he insisted that Jared take one of them, the one named Minuet. She was already paid for, Dalton told him. His gift to Jared for humiliating the unpopular Shaw in the duel.

With a little coaxing from Minuet, Jared followed her upstairs. After she closed the door, Jared felt more than a little reluctant. Her perfume couldn't conceal the bodily odors that lingered in the room. All Jared could think about was getting out of there. He felt like he was in someone's mother's bedroom.

He made several attempts to excuse himself and leave. Minuet thought he was just shy and needed some coaxing. She tried to remove his shirt. He insisted he had to keep his shirt on, which she thought was cute. The harder she tried to seduce him the more revolted he felt, until finally he escaped out a window, slid down the roof, and jumped into an alley eight feet below.

One good thing came from his brief experience with Minuet. It made him long for his Anne. The remainder of his time in New Providence was spent thinking of her. He had to get word to her, to let her know that he was coming back to her someday. Strange, he'd never thought of the fact that Anne Pierpont would possibly consider marrying someone else. It had always been Jared and Anne. She had never shown any interest in other boys, a fact that Jared now realized he took for granted. He was confident that she would wait for him if he asked her to. But she didn't know if he was dead or alive. How long would she wait for someone who was missing? He had to get word to her!

Jared purchased some paper and ink from a print shop, borrowed a pen and, with the permission of the owner, sat in the back room and penned a letter to his beloved Anne. It read:

November 21, 1728

My dearest Anne,

This letter will undoubtedly be a surprise for you since the last words you heard from me came from a tree outside your window. That night seems so far in the distant past. This letter is to inform you that I am alive and well. During my trip to Boston I was taken against my will onto a ship. Although I can't tell you where I am, I can tell you I am a sailor. It hurts me that I can't explain more fully. However, I am confident that when I see you again and am able to explain at length, you will understand what I am about to tell you next.

Although I am now free to return home, I have chosen to stay onboard ship for the time being. There are several reasons for this which I dare not put into print. I only ask that you trust me in this.

I don't know when I will see you again. It may be a year, or two years, maybe more. This is not fair to you, I know, but believe me, this is something I must do. Please wait for me. I know it's asking a lot, but when it comes to you I'm selfish. What I wouldn't give right now for just a few minutes with you. I'd even be willing to sit in your parlor with all the children and the noise. I'd even speak to you through that ridiculous tube if only I were able to see you again. Right now I'm closing my eyes and imagining how you look—your soft skin, kind gray eyes, your beautiful long red hair, the way your lower lip looks like it's pouting. Words cannot express how much I love you and long for you.

I'm not even sure this letter will reach you. But I had to try. My dearest Anne, please wait for me. It's asking a lot of you. I only hope that someday I can make it up to you.

All my love,

Jared

P.S. Please tell my mother I'm all right. And tell my sister something for me, something I never thought I'd ever say. Tell her I miss her. I only wish I could have told my brother that before he died.

Jared walked the docks of New Providence until he found a ship that was headed for Boston. Identifying himself as a sailor aboard the merchant ship *Levant*, which was also in New Providence but headed for Africa, he convinced the quartermaster to carry his letter to Boston and deliver it.

It was a curious feeling for Jared; his heart ached for Anne and was excited about the letter all at the same time. He rejoined his shipmates and they made their way back to Cat Island and their ship. As the water lapped the sides of the shallop and the *Dove* came into view, Jared took stock of his situation in relationship to his drunken crewmates. He felt fortunate. At least *his* heartache wouldn't give him a hangover in the morning.

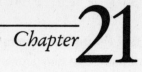

Chapter 21

S AIL ho!" The watchman's cry brought Captain Devereaux from his cabin, spyglass in hand. "Starboard bow, sir."

Devereaux raised the glass to his eye in the direction of the ship whose sail was barely visible to the naked eye. The *Dove* had been at sea for six days, the crew having completed its repairs at Cat Island. They sailed without colors, trolling the sea for fat merchant ships. This was their first contact with another vessel since leaving harbor. Jared had just come on deck. Eight bells had sounded and the watch had been called just as the sail was spotted.

The sun was directly overhead in a nearly cloudless sky, momentarily blinding Jared when he emerged from the ship's dark interior. With his first step on deck Jared tensed; the air was charged with anticipation. It was like the ship was holding its breath waiting for the captain's pronouncement regarding the fate of the ship sitting in the distance. Sailors stood frozen, their eyes fixed on the starboard horizon; those whose tasks would not permit a distraction worked in hushed silence, their ears cocked in the captain's direction.

Jared trained his eyes on Devereaux and wondered what was going through the man's mind. The captain looked like a nautical statue, the kind seen in town squares. The only movement was that of the wind whipping through the black and gray curls that fell from beneath his cocked hat, and the flapping of his coat beneath the bottom button. Jared's heart pounded wildly in contrast to this stone figure peering through the glass.

Just when Jared thought he would burst from waiting, the captain lowered the glass. "Come about, Mr. Tracy!" he shouted. "Look's like we've got one, men!"

A cheer went up on deck. No one cheered louder than Jared.

Moments later the bow of the ship swung through the wind into a larboard tack. The vessel leaned heavily to the right, rolling mightily as the ship beat into the wind; the water rushed by madly just a few feet beneath the starboard railing. It was exhilarating. Everyone moved with a heightened sense of purpose. Even the ship felt determined as it knifed through the sea swells. The prey had been spotted. The hunt was on.

Jared soon discovered that like other forms of hunting, the initial thrill of going on the hunt is soon followed by the agony of waiting. Although the *Dove* raced toward its prey, closing the distance between the two ships would take time. And time meant patience—a quality Jared did not have in abundance. He did his best to content himself with scraps of news he picked up from conversations between the captain and first mate. He learned that the ship was a three-masted East Indiaman, a large ornate vessel designed to haul an enormous cargo. It looked like she was alone, somehow separated from other ships in her convoy. The other ship hadn't spotted the *Dove* yet; she'd made no course changes and she wasn't running under full sails. Still, Captain Devereaux didn't think they'd overtake the slower ship until after nightfall. When Jared heard that, he did his best to rein in his feelings of anticipation lest they exhaust him well before the time of battle.

"They've spotted us," Tracy informed the captain.

The hunt was several hours old when the East Indiaman changed course. The *Dove* adjusted its intercept course. The hunted ship changed course a second time. Again the *Dove* responded in kind. Minutes later the East Indiaman put up every available canvas, including extra studding sails, using oars for yards in an attempt to outrun the *Dove.* But they were only delaying the inevitable. The square-rigged, bulky East Indiaman could not outrun the faster, two-masted schooner.

By sundown they'd closed the gap considerably. The merchant ship ran without lights, hoping to slip away in the inky darkness. At dinner, conversations among the crew members of the *Dove* were subdued, as they were below deck. There was nothing to do now but wait. All day they hauled rigging and shot and powder in preparation for the battle. All they needed now was someone to fight.

When not on watch, men lay silently in their hammocks staring at knots in the wooden beams. The impending battle loomed over them like a black storm cloud. Most of the sailors had survived storms and battles alike. Still, there was no guarantee they would survive another one. How many hammocks would hang empty tomorrow night? Would theirs be one of them? Of course, the watch schedule would have to be set again to accommodate for both losses and gains in the crew. Tomorrow would bring changes, and the kind of changes that took place on the high seas were always unsettling.

Jared moved mechanically from one task to another, constantly aware of the merchant ship somewhere off their bow. That night he stood watch aft. Leaning against the taffrail on the aftermost deck of the ship he stared into the thick, heavy blackness of a moonless night. Having lost visual contact with the merchant ship at sundown, *Dove's* sails had been reefed to slow her to a moderate speed. It was assumed the captain of the hunted ship would change course not long after dark, but which way? The best the pirate crew could do, given the circumstances, was to wait for morning and hope the merchant ship was still within sight. Jared stretched and yawned, still feeling the effects of the built-up tension that had no outlet.

Just then he saw a light flickering in the distance. It was below the horizon, at least he thought it was. On a moonless night the horizon was nothing more than a nebulous line where the stars stopped. He stared hard into the darkness to make sure. Yes! It was definitely below the horizon. Then it went out.

"Mister Tracy!" Jared called to the first mate who was standing by the helm.

"What is it, Morgan?"

"Sir, I just saw a light."

The first mate bounded aft. "Show me," he said, glass in hand.

Jared pointed into the blackness. The first mate lifted the glass in that direction.

"Nothing," he said. "Are you sure it was on the water?"

"Yes, sir."

The first mate cursed. "He could have doubled back," he said to himself. "That would put the most distance between us and him." To Jared: "Go get the captain."

Jared awoke the captain and told him what he saw. The captain joined them at the taffrail, taking his turn peering into the darkness with the glass. "And you're sure you saw a light?" he asked Jared without lowering the glass.

Every time Jared was asked that question, he was less sure, but this was no time for self-doubt. "Yes, sir. It was a flickering light below the horizon."

The captain gave the order to double back. As the bow of the ship swung around, the captain and first mate moved forward, still looking for a light to justify the course correction. As they left Jared at his post, neither officer congratulated him, neither did they warn him. But he knew what was at stake. If the light he saw wasn't the merchant ship, the course correction was sending them farther and farther away from their intended target.

The night watch dragged on. No further light was seen and the captain returned to his quarters. With each passing hour, the dread welled up inside Jared, fueled by mounting doubt. If he was wrong, he would have single-handedly ruined his first mission. *What do they do to a sailor who says he sees something that turns out to be nothing?* At the end of his watch Jared remained on deck, moving to the bow, hoping that he would spot the light again. He didn't.

Ever so gradually, shade by shade, the eastern sky grew lighter. Gray streaks stretched along the horizon, throwing an uncertain light upon the boundless sea. Jared strained tired eyes as he scanned the gradually appearing ocean in front of the ship's bow. It was harder and harder for him to focus. He rubbed his eyes with the backs of his hands.

"SAIL HO!"

Dalton of the larboard watch held a rigid arm over the bow. The captain and first mate emerged from their cabins. Jared searched eagerly in the designated direction just as the first rays of light broke over the horizon, hitting the East Indiaman's square sails so that she virtually popped into view.

The captain viewed her through the glass. "That's her!" he said. "Same ship. Good work, Jared!"

"Yes, well done!" the first mate added.

A blurry-eyed Jared Morgan accepted their praise with a grin of relief.

By midmorning the *Dove* was closing fast on the merchant vessel. She'd been identified as the *Duke of York*, out of England, a regular in the triangular trade route. She sat low in the water, indicating a full cargo. When Devereaux ordered the show of colors and the Jolly Roger was hoisted aloft, the merchant vessel conceded the chase and turned to fight, pointing her port beam toward the pirate ship. Moments later, puffs of white smoke spewed from her beam and Jared got his first taste of cannon fire. The battle was on.

Devereaux set a course dead-ahead toward the merchant vessel. On this heading the *Dove* couldn't return fire, since the ship's guns lined the beam of the ship; however, the straight-ahead course reduced the profile of the attacking ship, giving the merchant vessel less of a target to shoot at. The sound of the shot whizzed past them and over their heads and they continued their pursuit of the vessel. Geysers of water flew up in front of them and beside them, each one a missed shot, each one getting closer and closer to the target. Devereaux ordered the helmsman to hold a steady course.

By now Jared could make out the details of the ship. It was a heavily ornamented craft with the visage of a stern English male for a figurehead. Jared wondered if it had been carved in the likeness of the ship's namesake. The stern was just as ornate, with busts of women on the vertical beams, surrounded by carvings of leaves and a variety of symbols—the moon, a mermaid, a cross, and on and on. Jared had once heard that some shipbuilders spent as much on the ship's ornamentation as they did to build the whole ship. Looking at the *Duke of York*, he would have little trouble believing that fact to be true. On deck, frantic sailors scurried in all directions. Jared could see the anxiety on their faces.

Captain Devereaux ordered the helmsman to fall off onto a broad reach. The helmsman responded as did the sailors manning the lines. The bow of the ship eased over, the sails eased off, and the *Dove's* cannons came to bear on the merchant ship. Jared felt each cannon blast as it rattled the deck. It was a masterful barrage, scoring several hits on the *Duke of York*, but inflicting little damage against its thick hull.

The *Dove* then beat into the wind and swung around behind the merchant ship, attacking its unprotected stern. Rudy Shaw's guns were ready. Several direct hits slammed into the stern. Debris and splinters flew everywhere. Smoke rose from somewhere below deck. The clumsy merchant ship was at their mercy.

One more course change maneuvered the *Dove* into boarding position. The bow swung back toward the starboard stern at an angle that protected them from the merchant vessel's guns.

"Prepare to board!"

Jared grabbed his sword. Shoulder to shoulder with his crewmates, he stood ready to leap aboard the *Duke of York*. Grappling hooks catapulted through the air, gripped their prey, and pulled the ship toward them. With a wild cry Jared jumped aboard the merchant vessel. All the sailors on the poop deck were engaged, so Jared ran amidships. There were merchant sailors on deck, on the yardarms, coming down the shrouds, enough to keep him busy, but still it seemed like a lot fewer than he'd been told to expect.

A dark, mustachioed sailor appeared from the hold swinging wildly at Jared with a cutlass. Jared blocked one blow, deflected another, and blocked still another. The sailor was slow and clumsy, leaving himself open to Jared's thrust. The ease with which Jared defended himself began to worry the sailor. His eyes grew fearful, his brow furrowed. The carelessness of his blows told Jared the sailor was beginning to panic. With all his might he slashed. Jared stepped back and all the sailor caught was air. His next slash came from over his head. Jared stepped aside and when the sailor's cutlass hit the deck, Jared pinned the blade down with his foot while the tip of his blade floated less than an inch from the man's throat.

The merchant sailor said nothing. Brown eyes bulged from a frightened face that was drenched in sweat. Jared remained motionless.

"W . . . w . . . why don't y . . . y . . . you s . . . s . . . strike?" he asked.

Jared remained motionless. His own voice haunted his

memory: *You just wait until our first raid! Then you'll see how much killing I can do!* It was just like in the forest with Chuckers and Will when the wolf was in his sites and he couldn't pull the trigger. Here he had a man at his mercy and he couldn't make the final thrust.

Seeing Jared's hesitation, the sailor knocked the blade away and the fight resumed. He jumped in a completely unanticipated direction and Jared's blade skewered the man's sword arm. His sword clanked to the deck and the defeated sailor dropped to his knees before Jared. "Strike, you demon! Strike!" he yelled.

Jared looked at the red stain on his blade. The sight sent a shudder through him. He wanted to wretch, but he had this little matter of a sailor kneeling in front of him. If he couldn't kill the man, what was he going to do with him?

"Jump overboard!" Jared ordered.

"What?"

"You heard me!" Jared touched the sailor's throat with his blade. "Jump!"

The sailor looked at the railing, then back at Jared. With two bounding steps he was gone, over the side. The sound of a splash told Jared he'd hit the water.

Jared Morgan didn't kill anyone that day. He knocked them unconscious, locked them inside the hold, threw them overboard, but he didn't kill them. After a while it became quite a game for him as he figured out different ways not to inflict mortal harm. Jared defeated fifteen men in all before the fighting stopped.

The battle was over when Tracy succeeded in capturing the captain. A deal was quickly struck. In exchange for the ship's cargo, the captain would be allowed to live, along with his men. Once the cargo was transferred to the *Dove*, the ship and crew would be free to continue on their way. It wasn't your typical pirate strategy of plunder, kill, and destroy, but then the captain and crew of the *Dove* weren't your typical pirates. The defeated captain agreed to the terms, though he didn't believe them. More than once he prophesied that once the pirates had everything they wanted, they would break their word, kill him, and scuttle the ship.

Sailors from both ships loaded tobacco, furs, rice, silk, and indigo along with a tidy sum of gold onboard the *Dove*. Much to the merchant captain's surprise, once the loading was finished, the grappling hooks were released and the *Dove* sailed away.

"Did you see the way Smilin' Jack Tar was fighting?" Derby cried.

"I told you he couldn't kill anybody!" Shaw said. The gunner's voice was slurred with antagonism. "He's gonna get us all killed someday!"

The captain had declared a holiday following their victory. It was a first for the *Dove*. They suffered no substantial ship damage and not a single loss of life. Devereaux said in all his years at sea he'd never seen anything like it. And he was lavish with praise on the crew's performance—the speed with which commands were executed, the accuracy of Shaw's gunners, and special recognition to Jared for his watchful eyes that kept them in the hunt after the merchant ship had doubled back on them in the dark. Following their victory they retreated to a hidden lagoon where they celebrated, took inventory, and prepared to market their goods. At the moment, they were celebrating with a cask of captured rum.

Richard Derby rose to unsteady feet and held an imaginary sword in his hand. "I had just dispatched this pock-faced, skinny tar when I looks up and sees Smilin' Jack Tar." He pointed his imaginary sword at Jared. "With his sword at this one fellow's neck, he commands the man to jump overboard! And the bloke obeys 'im!" Guffaws broke out all around. Some of the men closest to Jared punched him good-naturedly. Enjoying his audience's response, Derby continued: "So I keeps my eye on Smilin' Jack, right? I mean, why not? What's this tar gonna do next? So what does he do to the next fellow? He bonks him on the head with a block!" More laughter. "He sends one below deck and padlocks the door! If we're not careful Morgan's gonna give us pirates a respectable name! Now, we can't have that, can we?"

"No!" a number of them chorused.

First mate Tracy leaned toward Jared. "You really do those things?" he asked.

Jared grinned and shrugged.

"Look at him!" Derby yelled. "Like I said—Smilin' Jack Tar!"

Rudy Shaw shook a drunken head. "He's dangerous! Stinkin' dangerous, I'm tellin' ya. Run the rascals through, that's the pirate way! Mark my words. He's gonna get one of us killed with his coward fightin'."

Captain Devereaux appeared from his cabin to address the men. Everyone quieted down. "Enjoy your victory, men," he said. "You deserve it. It was a job well done." Cheers went up. "But let me caution you. This was an easy victory. Too easy. More than half their crew had either consumption or scurvy, including their gunner teams, which explains their poor shooting. They were in sorry shape when we came upon them; that's why they were separated from their convoy. They couldn't keep up. It was because of the sickness we didn't offer to take any sailors who wanted to join us. I didn't want them bringing the sickness aboard my ship. So enjoy your victory. The next one won't be so easy."

Two days later the *Dove* set sail for Bristol, England, where they would unload their goods. Actually, the goods were unloaded a good distance from Bristol at a cove near Baggy

Point, just north of Barnstaple Bay. It was too risky for them to sail into Bristol Channel; the Royal Navy was constantly patrolling the waters and there was the chance they could be bottled up in the bay. Following the sale of the goods, the profit was divided among the crew members on the share system: the captain, first mate, and quartermaster each received a share and a half; the gunner, boatswain, and carpenter each received a share and a quarter; all other crew members received one share each.

On the way back to the colonies, the *Dove* intercepted a ship carrying whale oil, ginger, and iron to Boston. Although the goods still reached their colonial destination, they did so through a new distributor off of Long Island, a friend of Captain Devereaux. Sailing south, the pirates collected fish, grain, and lumber from the colonial vessels bound for Guadelupe. In each instance the crew of the *Dove* demonstrated superior seamanship to their merchant counterparts. Jared, who was now known exclusively as Smilin' Jack Tar to everyone except the captain, continued his unorthodox approach to fighting. Men jumped overboard, were knocked overboard, tied each other up, were hit over the head, or incapacitated in any number of ways, but were never killed.

The *Dove's* crew wasn't without losses of their own. Bos'n Whitmore was lost at sea when a thirty-two pound cannon ball ripped away a part of the ship's poop deck. Jeremiah Lee and George Cabot were killed in sword fights. Seven new crew members joined when the captain gave his usual invitation to captured ships during the initial confrontation. The losses weighed heavy on Jared's mind. He couldn't seem to shake off the effect of death like the other sailors.

The *Dove* and Jared's exploits were fast becoming local legends. Favorably in the Bahamas among the pirate ports, unfavorably in Boston, Bristol, and London. Rewards were posted in taverns at all major seaports for the capture of any member of the *Dove's* crew. The merchant who put up the most money for their capture lived in Boston. Two out of every three ships the *Dove* hit belonged to him. His name was Daniel Cole.

Following a brief holiday in New Providence, the *Dove* set sail for the open sea and more hunting. As they sailed through the Northeast Providence Channel, a fully loaded brig came into view just off the Cherokee Sound on the Great Abaco Island. It flew English colors and the *Dove* altered its course to "help" them distribute their English goods to island ports.

The merchant vessel saw the *Dove* at almost the same moment and altered course in a heading that moved them away from the island. Although they put up a full complement of sails, it didn't seem to Captain Devereaux that she was making a very determined effort to get away. He plotted an intercept course. The faster *Dove* started closing on her.

No sooner had they cleared Cherokee Sound than two Royal Navy ships came roaring out of a cove on the island. It was a trap!

The *Dove* swung around and headed south with the two Navy ships in hot pursuit. The *Dove* followed the island coastline past Southwest Point and then turned north again toward Mores Island. The west coast of the Great Abaco Island was dotted with hundreds of small islands and coves and lagoons. Devereaux decided that if he was going to play cat and mouse with two Royal Navy ships, he wanted to do it where there were plenty of places to hide. For four days, the *Dove* ducked in and out of harbors, sailed circles around islands, and hid in lagoons attempting to get away from the pursuing Navy ships.

It was during this chase that Jared learned to appreciate the two-masted schooner. It was the perfect pirate ship. She had speed, a shallow draught, and a broad beam—everything a pirate ship needed. Speed enough, of course, to overtake a victim or run from the Royal Navy; a shallow draught so that it could slip into inlets where large fighting ships couldn't follow; and a generous beam so that there was plenty of room to store stolen cargo.

Captain Devereaux played the pursuit masterfully. Although some tense moments ensued, they were never in any real danger of getting caught. After a few days of hide-and-seek, the *Dove* slipped past the northern edge of the island out to sea. The Royal Navy was nowhere to be seen.

"Looks like we've got a convoy, men!"

Three sails in staggered position lay upwind. Up until now the *Dove* had avoided convoys and concentrated on lone ships. This time, however, Devereaux ordered the helm into the wind "with all due speed." He also ordered the colors hoisted before there was any indication the convoy saw them coming. The captain had been on deck without his glass at the initial sighting. He'd sent Jared to his cabin to get it and ordered him to stand by his side once it was delivered.

"Three East Indiamen," said the captain. He leaned toward Jared as he spoke, indicating that the information was for him. "How many lines of guns do you see on each ship?"

Jared squinted in the direction of the ships. The bow of the *Dove* heaved upward, paused, then slammed into the sea as it cut its way toward them. The violent motion made it difficult for Jared to focus; still, he thought he could see two lines of guns on the beams of each of the vessels.

"Use this and look again." The captain held out the glass.

Jared peered through the instrument. With the restricted vision it was even harder for him to site his target. Just when he'd get a ship in the field of vision, the *Dove* would buck and he'd lose it. It seemed like it was taking him forever to hold the target in the field.

"Don't fight the ship, roll with it," Devereaux said.

Jared complied by feeling the movement of the ship with his legs while letting his arms float. There. He found a ship and held it. "It still looks like two lines of guns on each . . . wait a minute!"

"The lower row on each ship is nothing but paint," Devereaux confirmed his discovery. "My guess is they're Cole's ships. He uses that scare tactic a lot. Some ships carry two lines of guns; Cole's too greedy to give up the cargo space."

"Still they outgun us three to one," Jared said.

"Intriguing strategy, isn't it?" Devereaux grinned at his chess partner.

Jared knew the captain well enough to trust the man's naval instincts and his strategy. Still, they'd never attacked a convoy before.

"It helps to know your enemy," Devereaux continued. "Merchant captains do not rise to their position by being creative strategists. They are strict 'by the rules' men who are obsessed with laws and regulations. Most of them are tyrants who spend most of their waking hours making sure everyone on their ship obeys the rules. Those who don't are severely and publicly punished as a lesson to any other sailors who might be thinking of being lawbreakers. So what do you think these three captains will do when they see a threat off their port bow?"

"Do whatever the rule book tells them to do," Jared answered.

"And rule book strategy is the line-ahead formation." The captain used flat hands to simulate two of the ships. "The three ships will form a line, bow to stern and perpendicular to our approach."

"So that all three can bring their guns to bear on us at the same time," Jared concluded.

"That's half-true. What other advantage do they gain with this formation?"

The captain held his hands in position while Jared studied them. "They protect their weak points—the bow and the stern!"

"Good! Exactly right!" Devereaux grew animated in his excitement. It was the same kind of excitement Jared had seen on the opposite side of the chessboard following their games as they reviewed each other's strategy. But, unlike their Sunday games, now the chess pieces were ships, the board was the Atlantic Ocean, and defeat was fatal.

The captain pointed to the ships off the bow. "They're getting into formation," he said. "Get to your post. We've got to move fast."

Jared acknowledged the order. His post was the starboard halyards amidships on the mainsail. When the captain said they had to move fast, he knew he'd be called upon shortly. No sooner had he reached his post than the order sounded to trim the sails. Jared took his place on the mainsheet line and pulled it in. The bow of the ship edged closer into the wind and the *Dove* picked up speed. There is a point just off dead center into the wind where the ship runs fastest. Fall away from that point and the ship loses speed. Cross that point and head directly into the wind and the ship rights itself, the sails luff, and all forward momentum is lost. It's a critical heading when your life depends on speed. First mate Tracy was at the helm, his eyes constantly checking the sails for signs of luffing as he pressed the ship ever closer into the wind.

Just as the captain predicted, the three huge merchant ships moved into line, bow to stern. *Outgunned three to one,* Jared thought as the ships grew larger the closer they came. *What do you do when you're outgunned three to one?*

The *Dove* charged straight at the line. Puffs of white

smoke appeared simultaneously from all three ships. A pop, pop, pop sound followed a moment later. A barrage of thirty-two-pound shot flew all around them. Some whizzed overhead, some hit to larboard, others to starboard, still others fell short. The first volley brought no damage, but from his discussions with Magee, Jared learned that the first volley establishes the range, the volleys that follow are the most deadly.

More puffs appeared. One shot hit the larboard side of the *Dove*. There was a sudden jolt, then a shudder as the ship reacted to the impact and righted itself back on course into the line of fire. Another series of puffs. Jared heard a whizzing sound close overhead. Then a snap. The mainsail flopped over. It looked like a duck with a wounded wing. The ship stood upright, losing speed. "The most dangerous point is when we just come within range of the guns," the captain had said. And that's exactly where they were.

Jared sprang upward along the shrouds, scrambling to the top of the mainmast. The shot had hit the sail and ripped it away from mast. The mast itself was undamaged. The entire rigging needed to be replaced, but there wasn't time for that. He'd have to figure out a way to repair it.

Jared saw the merchant ships lined up against them. From his vantage point atop the mast he felt like he was sitting on the bull's eye of a target. Suicide. That's what it looked like. Sailing right into the line of fire of three merchant ships. With the *Dove* on this tack they couldn't even return fire! Their chances of survival looked mighty slim; and unless he repaired this sail quickly, they wouldn't have any chance at all.

He grabbed the broken line. As quickly as his hands could move he threaded, tied, and spliced the line. "Try it now!" he yelled to the crew below. Jared clung to the mast. The line was pulled tight. The ship leaned responsively to starboard.

They picked up speed again. Jared started down the mast, grateful to be climbing out of the bull's-eye.

Just then he heard a violent flapping sound. One of his splices hadn't held! Jared scrambled back up on top. "Give me some slack!" he yelled. The line eased. Frantically he worked to splice the line again. Again he yelled down and again the ship leaned over in response.

White puffs of smoke appeared once more off the beams of the merchant ships, followed by the roar of heavy cannon fire. The whoosh of passing shot was frighteningly close. There was a direct hit on the poop deck. The ball slammed through the deck and exited the stern; the taffrail exploded in a shower of splinters. The mast jerked violently, smacking Jared in the cheek, nearly knocking him senseless. It was all he could do to keep from falling.

The *Dove* was closing on the end of the line, on a course between the middle and last ship. They were close enough now that due to the angle of fire, none of the first ship's guns were effective nor were the forward guns of the middle ship nor the aft guns of the last ship. However, the remaining guns of the two ships were at point blank range. Still *Dove* did not turn to fire; her course was full speed into the line. Jared clung to the mast as they drew closer and closer.

The report of the cannons sounded like thunder. Flame and smoke spit from their barrels. The starboard fo'csle flew to pieces, sending quartermaster Wendell into the air and over-board. The mast shook violently; Jared felt as if he was being beaten with a giant stick.

The bow of the *Dove* pushed forward into the accumulated smoke of the battle, cutting off the last angle fire from either ship. While just a few hundred yards away, *Dove* made its run through the line between the two ships. There was a sound of thunder and a shudder through the ship that was nothing like Jared had ever felt before. The guns on both sides of the

Dove fired and fired and fired. The larboard guns demolished the stern of the middle ship while the starboard guns ripped into the bow and fo'csle of the trailing ship. The third ship of the line suffered the most damage. Round after round slammed through her decks and into the gun chambers below. Fire and smoke belched from the gaping holes in the decks. One shot hit the mainmast directly. It was almost majestic the way it slowly leaned, then fell against the ship's beam; the bottom portion thoroughly smashed part of the deck while the top mast and sails splashed in the ocean.

On both sides of the *Dove*, the merchant crews scrambled to recover. The scene was chaos, but there was more to it than that. The look Jared saw on many of the crew members' faces was one of bewilderment. With the *Dove* breaking though their line, it did more than damage them, it demoralized them.

Once *Dove* was clear, she was ordered to fall off and concentrate on the last ship in line, the one with the fallen mainmast. The jumble of mast and lines and sails blocked more than half of its guns from firing. First mate Tracy held the *Dove* in this protected area while Shaw's gunners pounded away at the crippled ship. The other two ships rigged to full sails and fled. A few minutes later, the remaining ship hoisted a white flag of surrender.

It was a reunion of sorts aboard the captured ship. The ship was the *Lloyd George*, Edmund Barlow captain. Barlow was the previous captain of the *Dove*, until Devereaux and a few other disgruntled sailors appropriated it. He was also Richard Derby's former captain, until the sailor deserted the ship in Philadelphia to become a pirate onboard *Dove*. The man's presence lived up to all the horror stories Jared had heard of him. His face was thin, as was his pinched nose and the line that formed a mouth; the man looked like he didn't have any lips at all. His eyes were rock hard and when he spoke his voice sounded like a low, menacing rumble.

"You'll hang for this, Devereaux," were the words Barlow chose to greet his former crew member.

"Not today, Barlow." Devereaux was a head shorter than Barlow as the two captains stood toe-to-toe. "Today, we're going to relieve you of the burden of goods in your hold. Are you still the petty tyrant you were when you were captain of the *Dove?*"

"It was arrogant of you not to change the ship's name after you stole her," Barlow said.

"You think so? I never cared much for the typical pirate names—*Revenge of the This* and *Revenge of the That.* I rather liked the name *Dove,* saw no reason to change it. And now I like it even more. Rather humbling, isn't it, Barlow, to be bested by your former ship?"

The captain of the *Lloyd George* showed no reaction at all. From his eyes Jared could see that he wasn't one to react emotionally; he was a person who stored everything away until just the right moment, when he would return it in kind with added measure.

Captain Devereaux made his customary offer to the crew of the *Lloyd George.* Those who wanted to leave the ship and join the *Dove* were welcome to do so. The number of men that stepped forward was astonishing. Under normal circumstances Devereaux would then limit the number he could accept. But because this was Barlow's crew he said he understood how much they wanted to leave. Although there were too many to join the crew of the *Dove,* he offered to take everyone who wished to a port where they could join the crew of another pirate ship.

For the next several hours cargo and crew members formed a steady procession from the merchant ship to the pirate ship. Several members, including Richard Derby, joined forces to request permission to try, convict, and hang Barlow for his offenses against sailors. They argued with Devereaux passionately and at length, but he refused their request.

"At least let us do the sweat," Derby pleaded. He was referring to a form of retribution whereby men form a circle around a mast. The culprit enters the circle and is forced to run around the mast while the sailors in the circle prod him by sticking swords, penknives, forks, and whatever else they can get their hands on into his posterior.

The captain refused that request too. "Derby," he said, "don't let your vengeance consume you. Don't give him," Devereaux motioned toward Barlow, "that kind of control over your life. We've defeated him, taken his men and cargo. Let it go at that."

His talk had only a partial effect on Derby. The sailor bowed to his captain's decision, but he didn't agree with it, nor did he like it.

The transaction between the two ships complete, the pirate captain and crew prepared to disembark the *Lloyd George*. Jared stayed with the captain until all the other sailors had left. Devereaux tipped his cocked hat at Barlow. "It's been grand," he said. "We must do it again some time." He turned to walk down the plank joining the two ships. Jared turned to follow him. Out of the corner of his eye Jared saw Barlow pull a small, one-shot pistol from the back of his waistband.

"I think not," Barlow replied, leveling the pistol at Devereaux's back.

Jared grabbed his sword and lunged at Barlow, at the same time shouting at Devereaux to get down. His blade sunk into Barlow's shooting shoulder just as the pistol fired. The lunge had brought Jared's face close to the miniature pistol, so close the discharge sounded like a cannon. Gunpowder punched the left side of his face; the blow felled him to the deck. His left ear felt like it was punctured; a droning echo of the shot drowned out all other sounds.

Barlow lay on the deck a few feet from him, screaming

curses, holding his limp arm and wincing in pain. The pistol had clattered to the deck.

Devereaux! Was he safe? Jared looked toward the plank. His left eye, feeling the effects of the gunshot, showed only blurred images, but what he saw out of his right eye wasn't good. The splatter of blood on his captain's back told Jared he'd reacted too slowly. Devereaux had fallen to his knees. Derby was trying to help the man to his feet. It was a solo effort. The captain's arms fell limp. His head fell backward at an awkward angle.

Barlow's shot was a signal to his crew. A wave of armed sailors poured onto the deck racing toward the fallen captains. Jared struggled to his feet and fought off one, then two sailors while Derby assisted Devereaux onto the *Dove*.

There were just too many coming at him at once! Four sailors stood between him and the gangplank. Just then small arms fire erupted from the *Dove*. Two sailors close to Jared crumpled to the ground. It was enough of a distraction to give Jared the opening he needed. With his exit cut off, Jared jumped onto the shrouds and climbed toward the yardarms. Two sailors followed close behind him. Jared was skilled at this game of chase, having played hours of tag aboard the *Dove* during some of the carefree hours in port. But this wasn't a game and Jared wasn't about to let himself be tagged by the sailors who chased him.

Below him the plank between the two ships fell to the water as the *Dove* began to push away from the merchant ship. He'd reached the yardarm. A musket ball splintered the wood next to his foot. He scrambled across the yardarm, found a secure line, grabbed tightly, and jumped. The air rushed past him as he catapulted down toward the deck, swinging over the heads of shouting sailors and across the beam of the *Lloyd George*. When the rope reached its full length, he let go and stretched for the *Dove's* starboard shrouds. Grasping and clawing, his hands snagged the shroud, but his momentum continued forward and he couldn't hold on. He tumbled down to the deck, knocking sailors over like they were bowling pins.

Small arms fire was exchanged between ships, then cannon fire. The last Jared saw of the *Lloyd George* she lay listing to starboard, her mainmast fallen, a gaping hole in her bow.

Captain Devereaux's body was committed to a watery grave almost immediately after he died. It was bad luck to have a dead body onboard; besides, there was no way one could be preserved and the stench would soon be unbearable. It was a somber gathering at the mainmast as sailor after sailor took his turn recalling memories of Captain Jack Devereaux. The ceremony ended with a gun salute to their leader. Throughout the ceremony Jared said not a word. Not publicly, not to anyone individually. He kept to himself. And when the ceremony was over he walked to the bow of the boat and stood there alone and silently wept.

The crew elected the red-bearded Irishman, Patrick Tracy, to be the next captain of the *Dove*. Richard Derby became quartermaster. At the recommendation of the new captain, Jared Morgan—Smilin' Jack Tar—was elected first mate, although the smile hadn't been seen since the captain's death. Rudy Shaw argued that he was best suited for first mate, but Tracy said there was no one onboard that could handle the guns as well as he. The flattery soothed him a little. Still, it probably would have set better with him if anybody other than Jared had been elected first mate. As for Jared, he was pleased that Tracy wanted him for his first mate. But there was no elation. The price of his promotion was too high. As he walked the decks of the *Dove* he was a different man. Maybe he'd been childish too long. It was time he grew up and viewed reality. Things weren't always fun. Life wasn't a game. As he looked out over the endless sea he saw nothing but a large expanse of water. There was no thrill, no romance. Only the pain of knowing it was the final resting place of Captain Devereaux. He wondered how many others onboard the *Dove* would soon join the dead captain.

Two weeks later the crew held the final ritual associated with the passing of Captain Devereaux. The captain's goods—his chest, bedding, clothes, books, and other personal items—were auctioned off at the mainmast. It was the pirates' way of honoring their dead. The goods were usually purchased at an extremely dear rate and the money was given to the deceased man's family. In Devereaux's case, it was a younger brother in Maidstone, south of London. Jared watched the proceedings with disgust, thinking it was crass to bid on a dead man's personal possessions. But he felt differently when the captain's chessboard came up for bid. When the bidding stopped, he paid an extravagant price for the board and pieces. To him it was worth it. It was the one remaining physical link he had with his captain, and he treasured it.

The *Dove* spent much of the hurricane season at Cat Island training a new crew and repairing the damage done by the *Lloyd George*. When the pirates' hunting season came again, the new crew and repaired ship were ready for action.

Rumors along the waterfront taverns had it that the *Brixton*, a merchant brig out of Boston, was making a run for Martinique with a sizable load of fish, grain, lumber, and gold to finance the season's enterprises in the West Indies. For weeks *Dove* trolled off the coast of Florida hoping to pick her up, and at last their patience was rewarded.

The crew of the *Brixton* saw the *Dove* coming and put up every sail they had to try to outrun her. With Jared at the helm, Captain Tracy gave the orders for pursuit. With the wind out of the east, the ships were reaching on a larboard tack. *Dove* was gaining steadily.

Just then a fog bank was spotted on the horizon. The *Brixton* was heading straight toward it. "If they go in there," Tracy said, "we'll never find them. Are we within gun range?"

"I can reach 'em," Shaw said.

"Let's fall off and hit her with our larboard guns," Tracy said.

"Wait!" Jared cried. "Captain, I may have a better idea."

"Let's hear it."

"First I need to see a chart."

A chart was brought and their position located.

Jared nodded as he studied the chart. "I think it will work, sir," he said. He pointed to the chart as he spoke. "We're here. The *Brixton's* here. And the fog bank here. Right?" There was general agreement. "Now, just inside the fog is an archipelago that cuts across the bow of the *Brixton*; she's going to have to change course, heading south, southeast. Once she's in the fog bank she's going to want to do two things: first, lose us; second, get out of the fog. I believe that if we convince her we're chasing her into the fog, she'll tack into the wind, then tack again on a northern heading to get out of the fog. My suggestion is that we let her think we're following her, but instead of doing that, we'll be sitting on this side of the fog bank. When she tacks north to get out of the bank, we'll be right here waiting for her."

"That's if she does what you say she'll do," Shaw said. "Pure guesswork. There's no guessing with my guns. Either we hit her or we don't."

"The guns are at extreme range," Jared said.

"It's better than sitting around and doing nothing!" Shaw shouted.

Captain Tracy rubbed his beard. "If I were the skipper of the *Brixton*, I'd probably do exactly what Jared predicts they'd do . . . still. . . ."

Jared and Shaw waited for the decision to be made.

"Let's do it Jared's way," he said. "Keep pressing after her until she's completely in the fog bank. Then, bring her about and we'll wait for her to come out. Rudy, prepare the starboard battery. We want to give her a big surprise when she jumps into our lap."

For an hour the *Dove* sat outside the fog bank waiting for the *Brixton* to appear. There was nothing. At Jared's suggestion, the ship was heading into the wind parallel the fog bank. For if Jared had anticipated the *Brixton's* strategy, the longer it took her to come out, the further east she had tacked before heading back out of the fog. Another half hour passed with no sight of any ship. Jared had taken a calculated guess and it looked like he'd guessed wrong.

Tracy raised his big bushy eyebrows as he looked at Jared as if to say, "What do we do now?"

Then a ship emerged from the fog several hundred feet in front of them. The *Dove* was in perfect position. Her guns were aimed directly at the ship.

"Fire!" Captain Tracy ordered.

Only one volley of shot was needed. In reality, it was a lucky shot, but James Magee's cannon hit the mainmast squarely and as it tumbled into the water, the ship was completely disabled. The deck of the *Dove* erupted with cheers. Captain Tracy looked at his first mate. "You're as good a strategist as Captain Devereaux!"

The gale came up suddenly and by the time they realized it was a hurricane, it was too late—as if they could have done anything about it had they known. In an instant the sea was running higher and higher. Hail and sleet fell harder than Jared had ever felt them. The sails were furled and the *Dove* was sailing on a minimum of canvas. Since Tracy was the most experienced helmsman aboard, he manned the helm, sometimes needing help just to hold course into the wind.

Everything above deck and below was soaked. The winds blew dreadfully; whitecapped waves slapped the bobbing ship around with every intent of tearing it to pieces. The cargo below deck shifted and tumbled, casks rolled from side to side. Rigging lines strained and groaned in the pulleys and tackles. The bow plunged so deep into the sea it disappeared completely; then, several heartstopping seconds later, it would emerge again as white foam drained from its deck.

In order to reduce the risk of capsizing and lower the ship's center of gravity, Captain Tracy ordered two seamen to cut away the foretop mast and the ropes that held the bowsprit. Only one of the sailors returned; the other was tossed overboard and quickly swallowed by the angry sea.

Jared clung tenaciously to the shrouds. He'd tied a rope around his waist just in case he was washed overboard. The howl of the wind was deafening and it was all he could do to cling to the ship as it was so mercilessly tossed around.

There was a nerve-shattering, creaking-cracking sound, the sound that haunts every sailor's nightmares, as the mainmast bent backward. It was a shuddering thought even to think, like imagining one of your fingers being bent backwards. But this was no mere thought. The mainmast ripped its shrouds out of the ship's beam and teetered precariously. Just then the bow slammed into a wave and shot upward, the force of which sent the mainmast crashing backward. In horror, Jared watched as Captain Tracy and Richard Derby tried to jump out of the way. But there was too much mast and sail and rigging. They were both crushed. The laughing Irishman lay lifeless under the mast.

Just as suddenly as the storm began, it subsided. It was a temporary reprieve. They were in the eye of the hurricane. Jared hated every second of it. It was as if the hurricane was mocking them, giving them time to assess the damage, lick their wounds, and bury their dead before the assault began all over again.

As the senior officer, Jared took charge. The dead were unceremoniously dumped into the sea. Jared dropped the red-bearded captain overboard himself. There was no time to mourn him. That would have to come later. If they survived.

The mainmast was severed from the ship with all her lines. It too was thrown overboard. The *Dove* would have to sail with the foremast alone. The shifting cargo was tied down and secured again. They had to work fast with little time to dwell on their losses. And at the end of their reprieve they were exhausted, just as the second half of the storm hit.

Jared took the helm; Magee stood with him. It would take both of them to hold a steady course. The sky grew black, the wind howled, the waves rose to twice the size of the foremast and the *Dove* was at nature's mercy once again, slapped about by the waves, battered by the wind until she could take no more.

The stress exacted upon her was too great. She began to come apart at the bow. Huge chunks of wood broke away as she pounded into the waves. Water poured into the steerage and hold until one time when the bow submerged under a wave, she didn't come back up.

Jared yelled for the crew to abandon ship. The angle of the deck grew steeper and steeper. Jared untied the rope from his waist and, together with Magee, dove into the water just as the wooden vessel that had been their world sank beneath the waves.

James Magee had surfaced several hundred yards away, clinging to a large plank. Jared had managed to find a wooden box to hold on to. He felt himself lifted hundreds of feet into the air as he rose with each swelling wave, then he'd fall into the trough of the wave and the force would nearly knock him out. All around him was debris from the ship. But he could see no other men, only Magee and then only for a brief time. Then even Magee was swept out of sight and Jared was alone in the Atlantic Ocean, clinging to a wooden box in the midst of a hurricane.

Several hours later the storm subsided and an exhausted Jared Morgan draped himself over the top of the wooden box, hoping that it would support his weight because he couldn't hold on any longer. He fell asleep.

For four days and nights Jared drifted on the surface of the ocean. There was very little debris scattered about and no other survivors that Jared could see. The sun beat down on him mercilessly. He was thirsty, hungry, and tired. He wondered how long he could last like this before he died.

On the fifth day he spotted a ship. An ornate East Indiaman. It nearly passed him by until he took off the rag which was once his shirt and waved it frantically. A watchman on the starboard beam saw him and a small boat was sent to retrieve him. Once onboard he was taken to the captain's quarters. From the men who pulled him from the water he learned that the ship was the newly commissioned *Mary-Woodley* out of Rhode Island. They were on their maiden voyage to the Bahamas.

The captain sat at his desk, head lowered as he scratched an entry in his log. Jared assumed the entry was about his rescue. Finished, the captain lay down his quill and looked into the face of the shipwrecked sailor.

Jared found himself staring at none other than Edmund Barlow.

Chapter 22

THE staff and students at Harvard College treated Philip like he was Lazarus returned from the grave. Their reception was hardly surprising. For three years they hadn't heard a word from him. They all thought he was dead. Philip, however, couldn't help but feel chagrined at the analogy. Lazarus was absent three days, not three years. The world of Bethany to which he returned was virtually unchanged. Philip was not so lucky.

Harvard had changed. His former classmates had graduated and moved into careers all over New England, some to the continent. His father was no longer a member of the staff. In his place, his ghost haunted the halls. It was true Benjamin Morgan had been dead for three years. But Philip hadn't returned to classes since the death of his father. Everywhere he went former colleagues and coworkers expressed their condolences and shared their favorite memory of Benjamin Morgan. The way they spoke, it sounded like he died only a week ago.

As for classes, Philip was readily accepted and given a schedule that would allow him to complete his course work in a year. Available staff positions following his graduation was an entirely different matter. As expected, the positions were already filled. Lazarus was the lucky one. He didn't have to live with the people who had replaced him.

On campus Philip's exploits captured the imagination of the student body. He was regarded as a living legend. The students' ignorance about Indians made him uncomfortable. He was constantly pumped for stories of what it was really like to live among savages—how did he sleep at night knowing that at any moment he could be scalped? What devilish ceremonies was he forced to witness? Was it true that some Indians, in an attempt to inject themselves with new life, ate their own babies? And the questions Philip hated most of all: "How did you capture the savage called Wampas, and how long did it take you to convert him from his murderous ways?"

Philip visited "the savage called Wampas" on regular occasions. It was the only refreshing pleasure he had in Cambridge. Wampas had been accepted into the Indian school and was their top student. His capacity for retaining knowledge was extraordinary. The two men grew to be the best of friends, especially now that they had so much in common. They studied together often, which many would conclude was to Wampas' advantage. But the Indian had a keen mind and a fresh way of looking at things. Whenever they parted, Philip felt like he had benefited the most from their discussions.

Off campus—in Cambridge and Boston—there was little left for Philip. Penelope wanted him back, but he didn't want her back. She waited for him for a year before concluding that he would never return. After that she flitted from one relationship to another. It wasn't that she was picky; it was that after her suitors got to know her they decided that no matter who her father was, the benefits of having him as a father-in-law did not outweigh the misery they envisioned in marrying her. It wasn't that Penelope was evil or difficult to live with, it was her constant whining. For some reason, Philip had developed a high tolerance for whining and it never bothered him that much. But if Penelope's difficulty in finding a husband was any indication, Philip's high tolerance for whining was a rare gift. After several failed attempts to let romance have a chance, her father arranged a marriage to a man five years younger than her. Penelope couldn't stand the boy, but her father never asked her opinion and the wedding was announced. Shortly thereafter Philip returned.

In spite of Edward Chauncy's order for him never to return, Philip returned anyway. He felt he at least had to explain about his missing correspondence. He chose to leave out the part about Daniel Cole and put the blame on the tavernkeeper. The expression on both father and daughter's face told Philip neither of them believed him even while they were assuring him they understood. Engagement or no, Penelope wanted to take Philip back. Her father objected; he said it was out of the question. Philip didn't argue with him.

That night as Philip left the house, Penelope manipulated the situation so that she could have a few moments alone with him. She plunged into his arms and kissed him so hard his teeth cut the inside of his upper lip. Philip pried her off, reminding her that she was promised to another man. She began whining: "It's not fair! Why did you have to go away in the first place? I don't care what Poppa thinks, I can't marry Reginold! I don't want to and I won't! I won't!" Philip argued that it was too late. What could they do? The wedding was already announced. With a twinkle in her eye and a fast peck on his cheek, she said, "We'll just have to see about that. I haven't given up on you yet, my darling." Philip's hopes of an easy break from Penelope vanished. He left the house that night determined to avoid the Chauncy household the same as he would if they were carriers of the plague.

He lodged at the Harvard campus like previous years. Still, this too was different. Before he'd spend weekends or an occasional get-away-for-a-while night at home on the Charles

River. There was no retreat for him now. Not on the Charles River. Not in Cambridge. Not in Boston. He didn't stay a single night at the Cole house despite his mother's pleas. He stayed long enough to catch up on the news of Priscilla's marriage and Jared's disappearance. When the conversation turned to staying overnight, Daniel Cole offered Wampas lodging in the slaves' quarters and Philip insisted they couldn't stay. Upon visiting Priscilla he learned about his letters being misdirected. Then the situation grew awkward. Other than their general distrust for Cole, they found little to talk about, so Philip and Wampas went back to Cambridge that night. It had been nearly two months since, and Philip hadn't returned.

What was keeping him here? He had come back to pull his family together. How could he do that when there was nothing left to pull together? His mother was the wife of another man. His sister was off on her own. Jared was missing. If he had known this earlier, he never would have left the reservation. Of course, there was school and his degree, but he had lost interest in these. A scholastic degree would do him no good on the reservation. As Wampas so aptly put it, "Not many people speak Latin and Greek on the reservation." So what *was* keeping him here?

It was late afternoon. The leaves of the trees blazed with autumn colors as the sun lay low in the sky. Unable to find interest in his studies, Philip set out for a walk. He soon found himself standing at a distance from the old Morgan family house. He just wanted to look at it for a while—the front four columns, identically matched windows both upstairs and down, the expanse of yard that separated it from the river. He leaned against a tree and sighed. The past is past. He wouldn't go back to it even if he could, except maybe for bringing his father back to life. The memories he had of the place weren't always pleasant. So why was he drawn here?

He left the house and walked a ways upriver, found a pleasant patch of grass, and sat down. The gentle flow of the river calmed him. He looked over the surface, then beyond at the distant forest. If he were a bird he could fly that direction over the river, over the forest, south to a clearing with scattered huts, a schoolhouse, lake, and a cornfield. If he were a bird, he'd stay away from the cornfield, though; the cornfield's protector was deadly accurate with her sticks and rocks.

He wondered what Weetamoo was doing at this moment. Probably grinding corn for dinner. He could see her thin fingers at work, her slender arms, graceful neck, brown cheeks, black, black eyes—and it made his heart ache.

Philip had learned a song that he memorized and sang when he was feeling like this. He heard it sung by a group of half-drunk Harvard students in a tavern. They, of course, sang it in the spirit of gaiety. He sang it in low times and in earnest and always alone. Nobody ever heard him singing this song. He sang it to Weetamoo in her absence.

> As I was a-walking for pleasure one day,
> In sweet recreation I careless did stray.
> As I went a-walking all by the seashore,
> The wind it did whistle, the water did roar.
> As I sat amusing myself on the grass,
> Oh who should I spy but a young Indian lass.
> She came, sat down beside me, took hold of my hand,
> And said, "You're a stranger, and in a strange land.
> But if you will follow you're welcome to come
> And dwell in the cottage where I call it my home."
> Together we wander, together we roam,
> Till we come to the cottage where she calls it her home.
> She asked me to marry and offered her hand,
> Said, "My father's the chieftain all over this land.

My father's a chieftain and ruler is he,
I'm his only daughter, my name is Mohee."
"Oh no, dear maiden, that never can be,
For I have a sweetheart in my own country.
I will not forsake her, for I know she loves me;
Her heart is as true as any Mohee."
It was early one morning, one morning in May,
I broke her poor heart by the words I did say.
"I'm going to leave you, so fare you well, dear;
My ship's sails are spreading, over home I must steer."
The last time I saw her, she knelt on the strand,
As my ship passed by her she waved me her hand,
Crying, "When you get over to the girl that you love,
Remember the Mohee in the coconut grove."
My friends and companions around me I see;
But none can compare with the little Mohee.
The girl I had trusted proved untrue to me;
I turned my course backward far over the sea.
I turned my course backward, and backward did flee
To spend my last days with the little Mohee.

Priscilla's marriage to Nathan Stearns lasted less than a year. He took sick and died of smallpox shortly after their ten-month anniversary. Life with Nathan had not been nearly as unbearable as Priscilla imagined it would be. In spite of his awkwardness and social shortcomings, there was no one more devoted to Priscilla than her husband. He encouraged her suggestions in money matters and gave her free rein to do whatever she wished. Whatever once was his was now theirs. Not everything, however, was divided equally. If there was any passion in their relationship it was all his. For her part, she was a dutiful wife and came to have genuine feelings of fondness for her husband. When he died she wept because she had lost a friend.

The widow Stearns consoled herself with the aggressive management of the fortune she inherited from Nathan. For companionship she invited Anne Pierpont to live with her in the spacious north Boston mansion. The young poetess would be free to pursue her art under Priscilla's sponsorship.

The two women soon became the talk of Boston society as a seemingly endless line of suitors lined up at their door—to court Priscilla for her money or Anne for her youthful beauty. It took the suitors longer to prepare to call on the ladies than it did for the ladies to turn them away. Anne was determined to remain faithful to Jared, more so upon receiving the letter he wrote her from the Bahamas; and Priscilla had no interest in romance. Her passion was investments.

Priscilla had become a savvy businesswoman. Shrewd enough to know that most businessmen would never deal seriously with a woman, she conducted her business through third parties while she stayed quietly in the background. Priscilla began by investing in Daniel Cole's competitors with enough capital to increase their competitive edge against the prominent merchant. In some of the companies her financial involvement was so substantial she eventually absorbed all other investors and owned the company outright. She picked up several companies this way, always protecting herself by hiding behind a cloak of anonymity. Her financial successes satisfied her greatly. She didn't know if she was more pleased by the fact that she was good at what she was doing or by the thought of the agony she must be causing Daniel Cole. Still, no matter how much her accounts grew, or how much aggravation she caused her principal competitor, her success didn't bring her the fulfillment she thought it would. Her ledgers were cold comfort to her late at night.

Anne lowered her book and sighed. The sigh was of sufficient intensity to distract Priscilla from her work. She paused from recording figures in a large bound ledger and looked at her younger companion. The girl was sitting in a rocking chair next to an enormous multi-paned window that looked out over the garden. Beyond the window yellow and red roses bloomed, and green hedges lined a walkway that led to a fountain with a small trickling waterfall. The idyllic outdoor scene seemed a fitting backdrop for the poetess. She was youthful, hopeful, always pleasant and sweet. *So different from me*, Priscilla thought. Soft sunlight highlighted fair skin, merry blue eyes, and a lower lip that was full enough to be mistaken for a childish pout. Priscilla envied her the thinness of her waist, her small wrists and delicate hands which cradled an open book. She thought that Anne couldn't look more innocent than if instead of a book she were holding a stuffed doll.

"Did I disturb you? I'm sorry, Priscilla."

Priscilla waved a hand over her ledger. "This is just tedious work. It doesn't require any thought." She lay down her quill pen and stretched. "I welcome the interruption." The stretch finished, she asked, "Is there something disturbing *you*?"

Anne looked down at the book in her hands. "Yes," then back at Priscilla, "well, no."

Priscilla smiled, amused at her young friend.

"A little . . . I think . . . though I shouldn't be."

"You certainly have a way with words," Priscilla joked.

Anne laughed with her. "It's Anne Bradstreet . . ."

"The poet you like so much?"

Anne nodded. "Every time I read her poetry, I find myself wishing that I'd written it first! She puts into words exactly what I'm thinking! And she does it so well. I think to myself, 'Why should I even try?'"

"Nonsense! Your poetry is beautiful!"

"You're very kind, but . . . well . . . listen to this." She held the book closer to her eyes and read aloud:

The mariner that on smooth waves doth glide
Sings merrily and steers his bark with ease,
As if he had command of wind and tide,
And now become great master of the seas;
But suddenly a storm spoils all the sport,
And makes him long for a more quiet port,
Which 'gainst all adverse winds may serve for fort.

Priscilla smiled. "You've been thinking of Jared."

"It's been so long and only one letter. I wonder if he ever thinks of me. I'd like to think that in a storm he'd wish he were home with me."

The faraway look in her eyes showed that she was seeing Jared in her mind, out at sea, longing for her.

Anne's voiced changed to a matter-of-fact tone. "So you can see my dilemma. Mistress Bradstreet has already written what I feel."

In truth, Priscilla couldn't understand her dilemma, but then she wasn't a poet. Her world consisted of facts and figures, profits and margins, gains and losses. Her world was tangible, while Anne's universe was that of thought and ideas and imagination. "If you're asking my opinion, I think your poetry is just as good as Mistress Bradstreet's and that you shouldn't allow yourself to feel intimidated by her writing." The look on Anne's face told Priscilla she was unconvinced. "Read me the poem you were working on last night."

"I'm not sure it's ready to be heard yet."

"Let me be the judge of that. Read it to me. Please."

Anne placed the book with Mistress Bradstreet's work in it on the lamp table beside the chair. She retrieved a sheet of paper from a small personal desk. Her voice had a soft innocence to it as she read:

Oh, child, hold out
for rainbows!

Wish for wells
in desert places!
Plant your feet on slopes
that go on rising.

Oh, child, believe me—
Never day was born
beyond redemption.
Never night has lingered
past its time,
But that we drew the curtains
To contain it.

Speak softly to the
universe—
Sing freely to the churning earth!
Every echo rings
into tomorrow.
Every prayer comes winging
back
With Hope.

For Priscilla the words of the poem were spring raindrops falling on parched earth. "How do you do it?" she asked. "Write poetry?"

Priscilla shook her head, fighting back tears. "Remain optimistic in a world like ours. You write of rainbows and hope. I wish I could believe in those things."

There was a knock at the door. With a sympathetic pat on Priscilla's shoulder, Anne fell in line behind the black manservant to answer the door while Priscilla dried teary eyes. "We'll talk more of this later," Anne whispered.

With pursed lips, Priscilla fought back her sentiment with anger. She was annoyed with herself for allowing her emotions to get out of control. In the entryway she could hear the door open. A man's voice said something about chimneys. She jumped up. She had hired him to clean the chimneys *yesterday!* Well, she was going to let him know that being a day late was entirely unacceptable. Priscilla marched to the entry ready to do battle.

"Priscilla, dear, look who's come to clean our chimneys!" Anne said.

Standing at the doorway was a tall, well-built man with curly hair that showed traces of reddish-brown through the soot which covered him head to foot. He carried an assortment of brooms and brushes that were as black as he.

"Don't you recognize him?" Anne said. "It's Master Peter Gibbs! You know, the man who tried to save Jared, the one who owns the tavern."

"Owned. Past tense," the man covered with soot said. "You're Mrs. Stearns?" he asked, pointing to Priscilla.

"Widow Stearns," Anne corrected him.

"I'll handle this," Priscilla said to Anne. She waited for Anne and the servant to leave. Then she said: "Where's Foster? He's the one I hired and he was supposed to be here yesterday."

A white grin burst from beneath the soot. "And it's nice to see *you* again," he said.

"You didn't answer my question."

The grin faded. "Foster fell off a roof two days ago and broke a leg. Please, don't get overly emotional for him. He'll be fine. And don't mind me, I've been doing both our jobs. Got here as soon as I could."

His sarcasm fell on deaf ears. "You should have sent word to that effect yesterday as a matter of business courtesy," Priscilla said. "If you want to be my chimney sweep, you'll remember that in the future."

"That makes it easy," Gibbs said angrily, "because I don't

want to be your chimney sweep, Mrs. Stearns! I don't want your business or anything else that has anything to do with you!"

"Well! You can be assured, Master Gibbs, that Master Foster will hear about this! If I have my way, he'll terminate you!"

"Fine! It's because of you I lost my tavern; you might as well be the cause of me losing this job too! Who knows? God willing, in a couple of weeks I'll have another job you can get me terminated from! Good day, Widow Stearns!" Snatching up the brooms, he turned to leave.

"How dare you accuse me of causing you to lose your tavern!" Priscilla shouted after him. "I never told anyone that the information came from you! So don't try to lay that blame on me, Master Gibbs!"

Gibbs whirled back around showing no signs of concession. "Did you tell anyone that the information came from a tavernkeeper, Mrs. Stearns?"

Priscilla thought back. She remembered her mother angry with her for taking the word of an unknown tavernkeeper over that of a respected businessman like Daniel Cole. "I may have used the term tavernkeeper," Priscilla conceded, "but there are hundreds of tavernkeepers, how . . ."

"Only one of them was indebted to Daniel Cole for his tavern," Gibbs said. "A debt from which I was relieved when Cole sold my tavern."

"Master Gibbs, I'm so sorry."

"Good day, Mrs. Stearns."

"Aren't you going to sweep my chimneys?"

Peter Gibbs walked away without another word.

That night Priscilla and Anne sat on a bench in the garden. It was the first day of the year that was comfortable outside at twilight. The air was fresh, scented by the blossoms surrounding them.

"He likes you," Anne said.

Priscilla pretended not to know who she was talking about. "Master Gibbs. He likes you."

"Don't be ridiculous. Have you seen the white rose near the fountain? It's quite lovely."

"Why don't you give him a chance? He seems like a good man."

Priscilla acted perturbed at Anne's persistence with this topic. She frowned and straightened her dress. "You couldn't be more wrong in your assessment of Master Gibbs' feelings for me. He hates me. I'm responsible for him losing his tavern. So that's the end of it."

"Master Cole found out it was him who told us about the letters?"

Priscilla nodded. "I'm confident we'll not see Master Gibbs again. It's getting chilly. Let's go inside."

Anne rose with Priscilla but didn't follow her. When Priscilla realized she was walking alone, she turned to see Anne still beside the bench deep in thought. "Are you coming?" she asked.

"Priscilla, I have no right to suggest this. After all, it's your money, not mine."

"Suggest what?"

"Why don't you buy the tavern?"

"Why would I want to do that?"

"Then you could sell it to Master Gibbs and he can have his tavern back."

Priscilla shook her head. "It wouldn't work. Cole would never sell it to me and Master Gibbs would never agree to it."

Anne thought for a moment. "You're always using third parties. Why not do that in this case too so that neither Master Cole nor Master Gibbs knows you're the one doing it?"

It was Priscilla's turn to pause and think. "It would put

things right," she mused. "All right. I'll do it, but only because I feel responsible for Master Gibbs losing the tavern in
the first place. I don't want you reading anything else into
this, understand?"

"I understand," Anne said with a smile.

When Priscilla's agents looked into the matter, they encountered a reluctant seller in Daniel Cole. Under Priscilla's
orders, they were instructed to purchase the tavern at any
cost. Cole yielded when he saw the investors were willing to
pay twice the current market value for the property. Circulars
were distributed advertising the tavern's new ownership and
seeking someone with experience to run it. Several qualified
applicants were turned down until finally Peter Gibbs showed
up for an interview. The owner's representative told Gibbs
the owner didn't want this to be a long-term investment and
that, if Gibbs was interested, arrangements could be made so
that he would eventually own the tavern himself. As expected, Gibbs responded favorably and papers were drawn up
selling him the tavern over a period of ten years at the tavern's current fair market value.

Philip walked slowly up the steps to the Stearns mansion.
A childhood memory flashed in his mind as he surveyed the
imposing edifice. He remembered Priscilla as a little girl arranging a corner of the sitting room into her own little house.
She would spend all day arranging everything so that it was
just right—the two chairs that formed her doorway, perfect
rows of cups, utensils, and a stack of plates on an overturned
box, everything three in number. She wanted more, but for
whatever reason that's all Mother would give her. Looking
around him Philip saw that Priscilla now had more than three
cups to arrange, much more. The same meticulous care she
used in the corner of the sitting room was very much evident
in the garden walkway leading to the house.

A black manservant answered the door followed immediately by Anne Pierpont. "Philip! How grand to see you! Please, come in." She embraced him like family.

Was this the little girl that used to chase Jared and Chuckers and Will around the house? She was lovely. Her eyes sparkled with excitement; her smile was warm and genuine. Looking at her a Bible phrase popped into his mind, one that Jesus used to describe Nathaniel—"without guile." The same could be said of the young woman greeting Philip. She was innocent and gracious, there was no cunning in her; she was without guile.

"You've come to see Priscilla," Anne said, taking him by the arm and leading him into the sitting room. It too was immaculate and orderly, with wood-paneled walls and polished furniture. They sat facing each other on a sofa. "I'm sorry, Priscilla's not home." Without asking if Philip wanted any, Anne asked the manservant to bring Philip some tea.

"Have you heard any more from Jared?" he asked her.

Anne smiled sweetly with no trace of her hurt anywhere evident. "No. Thank you for asking. You're very kind."

Philip found himself wondering what his brother did to instill this kind of devotion in such a remarkable woman. "If it's any comfort," he said, "I know what it's like to write letters that never reach their intended destination. If nothing else, I'm sure Jared spends a great deal of time thinking about you."

Anne pressed her palms together, praying fashion, and brought them up to her lips. Her eyes grew moist. "What a wonderful thing to say." There was a pause. Then she said, "You love your brother very much, don't you?"

This was the first time anyone had ever accused Philip of loving his brother. He found himself liking the indictment.

"Well, look who escaped from the monastery!" Priscilla stood in the doorway. Her blazing red hair was gathered up and tucked under a wide-brimmed straw hat in businesslike fashion, unlike the typical mobcap of most colonial women. She wore a fine fichu of spotted gauze; a dress with fitted bodice and full skirt split at the front, with a quilted petticoat. Every inch of her proclaimed her to be a woman of wealth.

Philip rose from his seat.

"Doing missionary work in north Boston?" she said sarcastically as she removed her hat and handed it to the manservant who appeared dutifully.

"Actually, I came to see *you*. I'd like your help."

This pleased Priscilla. "My help? This is a first. I can hardly bear the suspense. In what way do you want me to help you?"

Priscilla sat down in a chair opposite him as Philip retook his place on the sofa. The manservant came in with the tea Anne had ordered. He'd already compensated for the late arrival; there were three cups on the silver tray. Anne poured while brother and sister talked.

"I was thinking," said Philip, "it would be nice if we were able to keep our old house in the family. I've been by it a couple of times and it just doesn't seem right that somebody else is living it. It seems to me that it's something Father would want us to keep in the family, to pass down from generation to generation."

"What is stopping you from buying it?" She knew the answer to the question before she asked it. The only reason she asked it was an attempt to annoy Philip.

"I've already tried to borrow the funds to buy the house. I've not been successful."

Priscilla just looked at him. She wasn't going to give an inch. She was going to make him say it.

"I was wondering if . . . well, if you would loan me the money to buy the house, seeing that you have a family interest in it as well. I'd pay you back."

Priscilla sipped her tea. Peering over the edge of the cup

she said, "Do you have any collateral?"

"Priscilla!" Anne exclaimed. "Really! This *is* your brother!"

Philip stood up. His face was warm. "I should have realized it was a mistake coming here. Please forget this conversation ever took place." His voice was low and resigned to the fact that there was no good reason for Priscilla to share his concerns, let alone be willing to help him. He changed the subject. "Have you spoken to Mother recently? Is she well?"

Priscilla set her cup down on the tray and made the transition to the new topic with seeming ease. It was as if she felt Philip was trying to manipulate her into offering her help by withdrawing his request. She wasn't about to do that. "Mother and I don't speak to one another," she said.

"Really!" Anne said. "The two of you are impossible!"

There was a knock at the door followed by a verbal altercation. A moment later Peter Gibbs burst into the room. He acknowledged no one but Priscilla. He stomped across the room shouting, "I don't want your charity, Mrs. Stearns! You can take your tavern and burn it to the ground for all I care, but I'm not going let you buy me off just to soothe your guilty conscience!"

Priscilla acted the lady in the face of the tavernkeeper's rage. To Anne she said, "I think Master Gibbs has discovered I own the tavern."

"And you can keep it! I want nothing to do with it or you! Our agreement is off, null and void! Do you understand me?"

"How did you find out?" Priscilla asked.

"Oh no, I'm not going to let you ruin someone else's life for a little slip of the tongue! What matters is that you covertly baited the hook, dangled it in front of my nose, and like a brainless fish I jumped at it! Well, no thank you, Mrs. Stearns!"

"Maybe it's time I leave," said Philip.

"Did she dupe you too, pal?"

"More than once, I'm afraid. I'm her brother."

"My condolences."

"That's enough!" Priscilla was on her feet. "I'll not be spoken of in that way in my own house! And as for you, Mr. Gibbs, the only reason I didn't approach you directly was that I knew you'd reject my offer to help you buy back the tavern!"

"You got that right!" Gibbs said.

"Wait a minute!" Philip cried. "You helped a stranger buy back a tavern without him knowing it and you won't help your own brother buy back our family house?"

"Master Gibbs," Priscilla yelled, "you signed a contract and I'm going to hold you to it. Either you fulfill your end of the contract or I'll have you placed in the pillory for refusing to honor your commitments!"

"Ah, the pillory!" Gibbs exclaimed. "At least now we're talking about something with which you have some familiarity!"

Priscilla slapped him.

"Everyone! Please!" Even in a shout Anne's voice was soothing. She stepped in the midst of the arguing trio. One at a time she looked at them directly, silently appealing to them for calm. The sweetness of her presence seemed to be working. "Master Gibbs, won't you sit there and join us for some tea?"

"I really must be going."

Anne placed a hand on his arm. "I'd so enjoy it if you could stay for just a while. Priscilla, Philip, won't you join Master Gibbs and me for some tea?"

Like chastened children, the three combatants took their seats.

"Master Gibbs, my only intent in purchasing the tavern . . ." Priscilla began.

Anne cut her off. "Please, Priscilla dear, I think all three of you have expressed your feelings quite clearly. If you don't mind, I believe it's my turn to speak."

Priscilla sat back in her chair. The two men sat with lowered eyes.

Anne stirred her tea leisurely before beginning. "It is my opinion," she said, "that your anger is misdirected at one another. It is only natural that each one of you is angry; after all, each one of you has been deeply wounded, but not by each other. You have a common enemy—someone who is not in this room. The person who has hurt you, the man who is your mutual enemy, is Daniel Cole. It is Cole who has been trying to get his hands on your family's shares. It is Cole who seduced your mother into marrying him. It is Cole who manipulated Master Gibbs into misdirecting Philip's letters and who took away the tavern when Master Gibbs graciously tried to make matters right. And I have not been immune to this evil man's schemes. He has taken my beloved Jared away from me. And, God forgive me, I don't know if I'll ever be able to forgive him for that."

She paused to retrieve a handkerchief with which she dabbed moist eyes.

"In all these ways this evil man has triumphed. But his greatest victory came today in this room. For those he has hurt are now concentrating their efforts on hurting each other, while he stands safely in the distance. Untouched and unharmed."

No one spoke for several minutes. Priscilla, Philip, and Peter stared at the floor.

"Well, I feel like the town idiot," Peter said.

Priscilla started to say something in response, then thought better of it.

"You are a wise woman, Anne Pierpont," said Philip.

"So what are we going to do?" asked Peter.

"We're going to work together to battle back against Master Daniel Cole," Priscilla said.

"God won't honor revenge," Philip said.

"Not revenge," said Anne. "Redemption. Surely we're not the only ones who have been hurt by this man. There must be hundreds of people in Boston alone who have been victimized in one way or another by Daniel Cole. Why can't we do something to redeem the victims? Master Gibbs is a perfect example. Buying the tavern and selling it to a man she can trust is a good investment for Priscilla, and it helps Master Gibbs get his tavern back! Why can't we do the same thing for others who have been victimized by Cole?"

"I never would have borrowed money from Cole in the first place if I'd had an alternative," said Gibbs. "If we combined efforts, we could give people an alternative to Daniel Cole."

"The Redemption Company," Philip said.

"I like that name," said Anne.

Philip looked at his sister. "Priscilla, you're the key to this. The plan doesn't have a chance of succeeding without you."

All eyes turned to Priscilla. Philip was right. She was the key.

"It won't be easy . . . it will take a decade at least," she pondered.

No one said a word. They realized the futility of trying to force Priscilla into a decision.

"The first project of The Redemption Company," she continued, "will be to buy back the family house in Cambridge. I think it's something Father would want us to do."

There were smiles all around.

Constance Cole sat at the breakfast table, a single boiled egg on her plate. Mechanically, she went through the motions of cracking it. It was part of her daily routine, a routine that made her a virtual prisoner inside the Cole residence. She was never allowed out; she was rarely allowed visitors and then only when her husband was present. With no one around to talk to or care for, Constance felt like she was drying up inside. There was no reason for her existence. She wasn't allowed to do any work around the house; that was the responsibility of the servants. Since she was not allowed a social life, there was nothing to plan for. Philip busied himself with his studies in Cambridge; Priscilla was alienated from her; and Jared was missing. This morning, like every morning, it was her and her egg. Sometimes Daniel would join her for breakfast, but he'd never talk to her. He always read the newspaper or business reports or ledgers or something related to his enterprises. This morning he had an early morning visitor. Constance wasn't introduced to the visitor but she could hear her husband talking to him in the next room as she tapped her egg with a knife.

"What do you have for me?" Cole asked the unidentified visitor.

"It boils downs to this: you've suffered heavy losses this last year. Higher than usual losses at sea due to pirates. We're hoping that trend will reverse itself with the news from Captain Barlow that the pirate Devereaux is dead."

Cole cursed. "What about the local investments?"

"Floundering."

"Floundering?" Cole shouted. "What kind of evaluation is that?"

"Your competition is making headway in every area of your investments — trade, warehousing, retailing, you name it. At first we thought the reversals were nothing more than a series of random setbacks. When we started looking into it more deeply, we discovered that there is one company behind all of it. The company hides behind a myriad of third parties."

"What company?" Cole shouted.

"It's called The Redemption Company."

"Never heard of it."

"Neither had we and it's very mysterious. We've tried to uncover the names of the owners. Apparently they're big on anonymity. They've protected themselves well."

"The Redemption Company. The Redemption Company." Cole said it over and over as he paced.

The smell of cigar smoke drifted into the breakfast area. Constance knew her husband was greatly disturbed. He didn't normally light a cigar until lunch unless something was upsetting him. Here it was, early morning, and already he was smoking.

"I want to know everything there is about this Redemption Company. I want to know who owns it, what their goals are, and especially their weaknesses! Do you understand me?" he shouted.

Constance finished shelling her egg. She laid down her knife beside her plate and folded her hands. She didn't want to rush breakfast unduly; it would leave her nothing else to do the rest of the morning.

Chapter 23

CHARLESTON, South Carolina had established itself early as a city that would not tolerate pirates. In 1718 the courts outlined the official view of piracy in the trial of Major Stede Bonnet, gentleman pirate. Bonnet was a wealthy plantation owner from Bridgetown. It's difficult to say why he became a pirate. In later years friends and family recalled his fascination with Sir Henry Morgan, the buccaneer who was later appointed governor of Jamaica, and William Kidd, one-time pirate who was made governor of the Bahamas. Some people speculated he was hoping to earn a West Indies governorship in similar manner.

Giving no hints of his plans to take up piracy, Bonnet ordered a sloop built to his specifications, hired an oversized crew of seventy men for the ship, paid them regular wages, and went a-pirating. After a streak of fantastic luck, considering the Major was ignorant of navigation and seamanship, and after a short collaboration with the infamous Blackbeard, Major Bonnet was captured and tried for his acts of piracy. The trial was held in Charleston.

Vice-Admiralty Judge Nicholas Trott presided over the trial of Bonnet and thirty-three of his crew members. The judge declared that the sea was given by God for the use of men and is subject to dominion and property, as well as land. For those who violated this God-given property, he surmised that no further good or benefit can be expected from them but by the example of their deaths. Major Bonnet was hanged at White Point near the water's edge on December 10, 1718. His trial set the precedent by which pirates were tried thereafter.

Captain Edmund Barlow turned Jared over to the Charleston officials fully aware of their pirate policy. His prisoner, known only as Smilin' Jack Tar—for Jared refused to answer to any other name while onboard Barlow's ship or during the trial—was delivered to the authorities bruised and bloodied. Barlow explained the prisoner's condition by describing how, after pulling the man from the sea and learning his identity, his crew rose up "almost as one man" and attacked the pirate for the senseless atrocities he and his *Dove* crewmates had inflicted on merchant ships over the years. Smilin' Jack Tar would have been strung up then and there, Barlow explained, had he not interceded. According to Barlow, his motives were civic-minded, preferring this man's execution be an example for an entire city of sailors rather than just for one ship's crew.

Jared's trial was brief. The exploits of Smilin' Jack Tar were embellished to include a total count of thirty-seven sailors killed by his sword, not to mention the loss of goods and ships. Barlow himself testified that the accused maliciously turned and pierced him in the shoulder for no reason. The *Lloyd George* had already surrendered, the hold was empty, and there was nothing else that could account for the man's actions other than his insatiable thirst for blood. Barlow testified that the only thing that prevented Smilin' Jack Tar from killing him was the valiant intervention of his crew members. Jared's defense was the shortest part of the trial. He admitted to being a crew member aboard the *Dove*. Other than that he said nothing. The jury took less than a half hour to find him guilty of piracy. The judge sentenced him to be hanged.

Alone in his jail cell, Jared crouched in a corner and closed his eyes. In his mind he escaped from the damp squalor of his cell, the false accusations, and the impending death sentence by thinking of the past. Of the way Anne would rest her hand on his arm, of the last night he saw her from the tree outside her window, the night he played Romeo for her, the night they kissed. His mind wandered to his father. He wondered if all that stuff in the Bible was true about heaven, if his father would be waiting for him when he died. He wondered what his father would say about his method of dying, of being a pirate. Then he thought of his mother and brother and sister. He was glad his mother wouldn't know he died by hanging; it was better she thought he was lost at sea or something. Priscilla would probably say she wasn't surprised at the way he died if she knew. He thought it funny how much things change when a person is near death. For instance, he'd never much cared for the way Philip and Priscilla treated him as they grew up together; but now that he was dying, he wished he could see them one more time. He chuckled nervously. By this time tomorrow, should all go as scheduled, he would see his brother again. In heaven.

Philip had never liked traveling. So he was in a surly mood as he sailed into Charleston harbor. The Redemption Company was experiencing unprecedented success, the merchant business especially. Priscilla quickly learned Cole's strategy — eliminate the competition, then control the prices. In keeping with the goal of The Redemption Company, their counterstrategy was equally as simple: provide people an alternative to Daniel Cole. Priscilla had purchased several ships — a sloop, two brigs, and a snow — and had no trouble manning them with sailors willing to sail for a merchant other than Cole. However, she was having trouble finding qualified captains for the ships. That's where Philip came in. Women were bad luck to sailors. No captain would ever sign on to a ship knowing a woman owned it. So, reluctantly, Philip took a short leave of absence from his studies to recruit captains. They thought it best to avoid recruiting directly in Boston. It would make them too visible and Cole might figure out who was behind The Redemption Company. So far, Philip had been to Philadelphia, New York, and Plymouth. Charleston was his last stop. While Philadelphia provided him with two captains, and New York one, Plymouth had been disappointing. Philip was hoping he'd find at least one eligible captain in Charleston. He'd hate to have to return to Boston and face Priscilla with only three captains for four ships.

The sloop docked at the wharf near White Point and Philip disembarked. The bay was filled with an assortment of craft from heavily armed Royal Navy brigs to little fishing smacks. The skyline of Charleston rose before him. A Master Cooper was supposed to meet him to show him where to lodge and where the interviews would take place. However, there was no Master Cooper on the docks so Philip began walking toward the city alone.

The first landmark he passed was the gallows, two ten-foot beams sunk into the earth and braced, with a sturdy horizontal beam stretched across the top. Several pieces of paper were nailed to it announcing the hanging of a pirate called Smilin' Jack Tar one week hence. Philip shuddered. He thought the gallows was an odd way to greet people entering the city.

The next day Philip sat behind a heavily scarred table on the dock while a succession of sailors sat opposite him and described their sailing experiences using crude language and even cruder jokes. At present a tall, thin man with a foul mouth and equally foul breath was telling in horrid detail how during a storm his captain's arm was pinned beneath a fallen mast and how he cut off the man's arm to save his life. Philip distracted himself with the activity on the docks behind the man at the table. The scene was abuzz with business—

shallops shuttling personnel and goods back and forth from ships harbored in the bay, men loading and unloading ships tied to the pier, horses and carriages and the widest assortment of people you would ever want to meet milling around the docks.

Philip's heart froze when he first saw them. A sailor and an Indian carrying on a conversation with a well-dressed man in a carriage. Their back was to him so he couldn't be sure it was them, but that didn't stop his hands from turning to ice and his breath from becoming shallow.

"Then there was the time we was jumped by three pirate ships out of Sierra Leone. The cap'n was real scared, until I told him we could outrun 'em if we ..." the thin sailor droned on.

The gentleman in the carriage was irate with the sailor and the Indian. He was shouting something, but Philip was too far away to make out what was being said. His eyes were fixed on the sailor and the Indian, waiting for them to turn around. If he saw their faces, he'd know if it were them.

"Do you wants to hear how I saved us from the pirates or not?"

"No," Philip said absentmindedly, not taking his eyes off the duo. "I mean ... I think I've heard enough ... umm, Master ..." Philip had to look down at the paper in front of him to remind himself of the man's name. "... umm, Master Roberts. ... Thank you for coming. I'll be making my decision in about a week."

"Yeah, well I don't knows how you're gonna decide when you didn't hear a word I said."

Philip shot a quick glance behind Roberts. The gentleman in the carriage was sitting back in his seat ordering the driver to move on. The sailor and Indian stepped back. If they were going to turn around, it would be any moment now.

"Believe me," Philip said, "you made an impression on me.

Again, thank you for your time."

Philip rose from his seat and broke eye contact with the
duo in the distance long enough to shake the interviewee's
hand. The man wore a sneer. He cursed at Philip, called him a
liar, and—to put it politely—told Philip where he would
spend eternity if it were the sailor's choice to make.

The sailor spat and turned away. Philip quickly glanced in
the direction of the duo again, hoping he hadn't lost them.
He hadn't. They were looking right at him! Philip could feel
his chest begin to constrict. He dropped into his seat and
shuffled the papers on the desk, pretending to write something on them. Had they recognized him? What should he do
if they came over to the table? Should he yell for help? He
couldn't stand it anymore. He had to know if they were
coming or not. Slowly he raised his head and looked out of
the tops of his eyes. They were gone! He lifted his head fully
now and looked more carefully. There was a lot of traffic. He
couldn't see them.

"Are you Master Morgan?"

Philip started. Several papers fell to the ground. He looked
to the person asking the question. It was a stocky young man
with black hair.

"Name's Parris . . . Samuel Parris. I'm here to talk to you
about the captain's position. Are you all right?"

Philip's breathing was shaky as he spoke. "Fine. I'm just
fine." He managed to retrieve the papers from the ground
and make a pretense of arranging them in order; in reality he
was shuffling them meaninglessly to hide his shaking hands.

The young man took the seat on the opposite side of the
table. Philip couldn't help but glance behind him to see if the
sailor and Indian had reappeared. They hadn't.

"Your name *is* Morgan, isn't it?" the young man asked.

"Yes. My apologies for seeming somewhat distracted. I'm
Philip Morgan."

"Philip . . . Philip. . . ." The man squeezed his eyes shut as he repeated Philip's name. "I think that's right." He opened his eyes again. "Excuse me, Master Morgan, but this is important to me. May I ask you a personal question?"

"If you don't mind, I'll ask the questions," Philip responded.

"Do you have a brother named Jared?"

Parris had leaned forward and almost whispered the question. He watched intently for Philip's reaction. Apparently Philip gave the man the reaction he was looking for.

"Do you know my brother?" Philip asked.

The young man leaned even farther over the table. "Yes," he whispered.

Philip matched the man's posture and tone. "Master Parris, do you know where Jared is? Where I can find him?"

"My name's not Parris," said the young man. "It's Magee, James Magee. Me and Jared were shipmates. When I heard that a Morgan was here, I had to take a chance that you were related to him."

"I don't understand," said Philip. "Take a chance? What chance? And why a phony name?"

"Can't use my real name anymore. It could get me hanged. That's what they do to pirates."

"Are you telling me my brother's a pirate? I don't believe you!"

The man across the table didn't take Philip's reproach kindly. "Whether you believe me or not, I'm speaking facts," he said sternly. "We were brother tars aboard the *Dove* before she went down in a storm. That was the last time I saw Jared."

Philip thought it best to assume the man was telling the truth for a moment to see what he was up to. "You said that was the last time you saw him. Do you think he perished in the storm?"

Magee shook his head. "He survived."

"How do you know?"

"Have you seen the bills posted all over town about the Smilin' Jack Tar hanging?"

Philip nodded. "What does that have to do with Jared?"

"That's your brother. Smilin' Jack Tar is Jared."

Philip sat there, struck dumb.

"Look, I'm sorry to have to tell you. I just thought you should know."

"You must be mistaken," Philip said finally. "You've confused my brother with another Jared. They can't be the same person."

Magee looked long and hard at Philip. "It was a situation much like this when I first met your brother," he said. "Only Daniel Cole was the one doing the interviewing and Jared was looking for a job. I already worked for Cole—thought I had a good future with him. Following the interview, Cole told me to take Jared to a tavern to celebrate his hiring."

"The Good Woman Tavern," Philip said. The pieces of Magee's story were falling into place.

"How did you know that?"

"I know the tavernkeeper—not a friend of Cole's." Philip read Magee's reaction.

Magee accepted the statement without challenge. He continued, "At the tavern we were drugged by some crimps, a sailor and an Indian. . . ."

The look on Philip's face stopped Magee midsentence.

"They're here," Philip said. "I saw them just a few minutes ago. Over there."

Philip stood and pointed; Magee joined him and looked. After scanning the area for any sign of the duo, they took their seats and resumed their conversation.

"They killed our father," Philip said.

"I know. Jared told me."

"So what makes you think this Smilin' Jack Tar is Jared?"

Magee smiled. "It was his nickname. Given to him because no matter what we were doing, he was always smilin'. He loved bein' a pirate. Never saw anything like him! He's accused of killing thirty-seven men. There's no truth in that. He never killed nobody. Never." Magee chuckled as he thought about it. "He had them jump overboard, threw them overboard, hit them on the head, but he never killed them. It was fun to watch him work." The smile faded as Magee's thoughts were brought back to the present and Jared's impending execution. "From what I've been told, nobody here knows his real name. Those like me who know it, aren't sayin'."

"Do you have any idea why the sailor and Indian are here?" Philip asked.

Magee rubbed his nose with a forefinger, shaking his head. "All I know is they work for Cole."

"Daniel Cole! They work for Daniel Cole?" Philip shouted.

Magee seemed surprised Philip didn't know that already.

Philip slammed his fist on the table. Again. And again. The anger and frustration that welled up within him overflowed with tears. "You wouldn't believe it if I told you everything that man has done to my family," he cried. "O God, keep me from the doing the things I'm thinking right now!" It took him several minutes, but eventually Philip regained his composure. Wiping away tears he asked, "Do you have any idea why the sailor and Indian are here?"

"They could just be crimping."

Philip weighed the possibility in his mind. He took a ragged breath, still fighting to gain control of his emotions. "Do you mind if I ask you what you're doing now?" he asked.

"I'm first mate on a snow. We run coastal routes mainly."

Philip added this piece to the plan that was forming in his

mind. "First things first," he said. "I'm going to rescue my brother, then I'm going to get Cole. Do you want to help me?"

"What do you want me to do?"

"I need to get a message to Boston immediately. Is your ship going there?"

"No." Magee thought a moment. "But I know one that's leaving today for Boston. A tar named Shaw is on it. I can get him to deliver the message. He was on the *Dove* too."

"A friend of Jared's?"

Magee grinned. "Not exactly."

"But you think he'll deliver a message? It's important."

"I think he'll do it."

Philip searched for a clean sheet of paper. He scratched hastily on it. "Tell him to deliver this to my sister, Priscilla Stearns, at this address. It's vital she get it. Are you sure Shaw will do this?"

"I said he would, didn't I?" Magee sounded irritated.

Philip paused his writing momentarily. "You'll have to forgive me, my brother's life is at stake here. There's one more thing. How long will you be in Charleston?"

"We're here for a couple of weeks."

"Excellent. Can you round up a couple of men from your ship who would be willing to help?"

"What do you have in mind?"

Philip outlined his plan to James Magee. Everything depended on Priscilla getting Philip's note in time. This was such a crucial point that he wanted to ask again if Shaw would deliver it promptly. Philip felt uneasy about Magee's vague description of Shaw's relationship with Jared. He had seven days to pull everything together. He prayed it would be enough time.

The sun shone brightly for Jared's execution. As he was led from the darkness of his cell outside to a waiting cart, the bright light hit him with a force that made him turn his head away until his eyes could adjust.

He'd spent the night and morning alone in his cell. No visitors were allowed, not even clergy, since as a pirate he was regarded as a brute and beast of prey. Jared preferred it that way. He hadn't prayed in years and didn't want to make a pretense of doing so now just because he was about to die. The way he figured it, he was about to be sent to God. Anything that he wanted to say to God or God to him could be said better face-to-face anyway.

His hands tied in front of him, he was helped into a cart pulled by a single horse. He thought it strange the misconceptions he had about being this close to death. He'd imagined that during the last hour of his life, physical sensations would somehow be heightened—the sky would be bluer, the air fresher, flowers more fragrant, that sort of thing—knowing that it would be the last time he'd experience such things. But that wasn't the case. In fact, if anything, his senses were dulled by a head cold he was suffering. He was congested and his breathing was labored.

The cart rumbled slowly through the streets of Charleston, streets that were lined with hundreds of residents—men, women, and children who came out to see the hanging and to taunt him as he journeyed to the gallows. There was not a sympathetic face among them. They jeered and cursed. Some threw rotten vegetables or fruit. Others threw stones. At first he was grateful that most of them missed their intended mark; with the velocity of some of the projectiles he could get hurt. Then he had to chuckle to himself. As if getting hurt mattered. In a short while he wouldn't be feeling anything.

The gallows at White Point loomed before him as the cart rolled toward the docks. The horse circled the gallows and then proceeded to pass underneath it like it was some sort of street arch. However, the cart pulled to a stop just as Jared's head came directly below the gallows' horizontal beam. A rope with a noose dangled from the beam, head high.

A burly man with a hairy chest and shaved head stepped into the cart with Jared. He moved Jared half a step sideways until the noose was directly in front of his face. He opened it wider, slipped it over Jared's head, then pulled it snug. Before him was a sea of unsmiling faces; his death would be the highlight of their day. Sailors lined the bulwarks of ships in the harbor looking on; some had climbed the shrouds or masts to get a better view. Jared couldn't help but think it would have been better if he'd died at sea. The clouds and wind and waves would have been much friendlier witnesses to his death. The burly man placed small bunch of posies in Jared's bound hands.

"Flowers?" Jared asked.

"Tradition," was the response.

The charges were read aloud as a warning to all others who might be tempted to consider a life of piracy. The burly man stepped from the cart and awaited the signal for the cart to be pulled from beneath Jared's feet.

Suddenly, there was a commotion near the front of the cart. Jared turned his head to see what it was. Out of the corner of his eye he saw a sailor and an Indian! The sailor, with his Monmouth cap pulled down low, yanked the driver of the cart from his seat and grabbed the horse's reins. At the same time the Indian jumped over the side of the cart and threw a linen bag over Jared's head. The last thing Jared saw was the Indian's intense black eyes and the flash of a knife blade, then everything went dark.

The noose around his neck fell limp. Jared was pulled down to the bed of the cart, his shoulder taking the full impact of the fall. He winced in pain as the cart jolted forward. A shot rang out. Then another. Shouts and screams echoed all around him. He heard the Indian grunt once or twice, pushing people away from the cart, he imagined. The sailor whooped frantically at the horse, urging him on faster and faster. The cart bounced wildly across the uneven dirt road. Then it hit a bump, sending Jared about an inch in the air. Now the cart wheels made a hollow clattering sound. *The wharf? Possibly the pier.*

Jared's mind raced. *Why would the sailor and the Indian want him saved from hanging? It didn't make sense. Maybe Cole wanted to sell him into slavery aboard a merchant ship somewhere. Maybe Cole wanted him put to death some other way. No matter, he was free for the moment. His next course of action would be to escape from these two renegades.* He remembered that the sailor was Captain Devereaux's brother. Maybe he could use that to his advantage.

He tried to sit up and was pushed violently back down to the wooden bed of the cart. "Stay down!" the Indian shouted at him.

The cart made several wild turns. From what little Jared could see under the sack, it suddenly got darker. Had they entered a warehouse? The cart pulled to an abrupt stop. First the Indian pulled him by the arms to get up. Soon a second pair of hands grabbed his other arm. Jared tried to pull free. He shook off the sailor's hands momentarily. An instant later they returned with an even tighter grip.

Jared was dragged across a wooden floor, then what seemed to be a threshold of a small room. The Indian placed a hand on Jared's head and pushed it down. When Jared tried to straighten himself, he hit his head on the low ceiling. Suddenly, the door closed and it was pitch dark. There was a rapid sound of hammers. This wasn't a room, it was a wooden crate! He was being nailed shut in a wooden crate with the sailor and the Indian!

"Hey! What's going. . . ?"

That's all he got out. The Indian's hand slipped under the sack and clamped down on Jared's mouth.

"If you want to live, shut up!" the Indian whispered.

Just then there was a loud commotion all around them. Men shouting orders at one another to search everywhere for Jared and his accomplices.

"There they are!" someone shouted.

Another man cursed. "How did they get out there?"

"Out where?"

"There! In that shallop! They're headed toward the mouth of the bay!"

"John! Go to the end of the pier and keep an eye on them! If they board any ship in the harbor I want to know which one it is. Charles, you and Henry get a shallop and follow them. The rest of you come with me!"

Someone standing next to the wooden crate cursed and slammed it with his fist. The sound of the blow echoed in Jared's ears.

A few moments later all was quiet. Still the Indian kept a tight grip on Jared's mouth. For what Jared estimated to be about ten minutes, the three of them sat in silence in the crate.

Then there was a sharp blow striking wood, followed by the creaking of nails. The side of the crate was being removed. Jared formulated a plan of escape. If he could break away from his two captors, maybe he could lose them in the warehouse or jump off the pier and escape that way. He waited for his chance.

The moment came as they were climbing out of the crate. For just an instant, Jared felt the sailor's grip on his arm loosen. Jared lowered his shoulder and charged into the sailor, sending him sprawling. Reversing his momentum, he tried to do the same with the Indian. His effort met only partial success. He succeeded in knocking the Indian off balance, but the Indian was able to maintain his grip, pulling Jared to the ground with him.

"Jared Morgan! Stop that this instant! We're trying to save you!"

That voice! He knew that female voice. *No, it couldn't be.*

A moment later the bag was lifted from Jared's head. Standing over him was his sister, Priscilla!

Now he was really confused. *Why was Priscilla in league with the sailor and the Indian?* Jared looked at the Indian. There was something different about him. Then he looked at the sailor who was still on the floor, removing his Monmouth cap.

"Hello, little brother."

"Philip!"

"I'd like you to meet a good friend," Philip said, pointing to the Indian. "His name's Wampas. Wampas, this is my brother Jared."

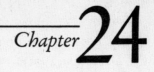

Chapter 24

WHILE the authorities concentrated their pursuit of Smilin' Jack Tar in the direction of the fleeing shallop, the real escapee and his three accomplices sneaked back into town just two streets from the gallows. Philip, the one who masterminded the escape, gambled that Charleston authorities would assume Jared would head south toward the Bahamas where he could live freely in any number of pirate havens. From all indications, his gamble had paid off. After the initial excitement, life returned to normal in the port city. As each day passed and Jared supposedly sailed farther and farther south, the discussion on the streets and in the taverns turned to other things. The plan now was to wait several days, and return to Boston aboard *Salvation*, a brig recently purchased by Priscilla for The Redemption Company. It had brought her and Wampas to Charleston, transferring a load of merchandise to a company warehouse. It would leave as scheduled four days later and return to Boston. This time, however, its cargo would be an escaped pirate.

"I can't believe you were a pirate!" Philip said.

He was lounging in the sitting room of a modest house. It was owned by a friend of Peter Gibbs, another tavernkeeper who was away visiting relatives in Philadelphia. There were four chairs in a circle; Wampas and Jared sat in two of them. Priscilla entered carrying a tray of refreshments.

"It's not like you think," Jared said. "At least not aboard the *Dove*. The captain was the finest man I ever knew. We weren't murderous cutthroats bent on revenge. In fact, Captain Devereaux died shortly after refusing a request to exact revenge on a notoriously barbarous captain."

"How did he die?" Philip asked.

"Shot in the back by the captain he protected."

"You're right," said Philip, "it doesn't sound like the pirates I've heard stories about."

Jared sat forward in his seat. "The ship had a society all its own," he said. "And every person was a vital part of the society, contributing to the welfare of the ship with his unique talents. And here's the best part—we voted on everything. There was no king, no dictator; we were a democracy. We drafted our own rules and elected our captain and first mate. It was the most incredible thing I've ever been part of. I only wish colonial government worked as well."

"As a democracy?" Priscilla said. "The colonies would fall into anarchy. It would never work."

Wampas, dressed in breeches and a linen shirt, said, "It sounds to me that pirates are much like the Indians. There is too little understanding about who we really are."

"I can attest to that," Philip replied.

At Jared's request, Philip explained the details of the escape plan as the four of them sipped tea and nibbled on pumpkin bread.

"Why the hood?" Jared asked. "All I could think about was escaping from the people who were rescuing me."

"I was afraid that if you saw it was me rather than our sailor and Indian, you might call out my name in surprise. That would have been unfortunate. So I thought it was better you didn't know who was rescuing you. We were hoping to bag you before you saw either of us."

Jared chuckled. "All I saw were brief glimpses of an Indian

and a sailor. A deadly combination, as you know. But why disguise yourselves as them?"

"I spotted them in the area a few days before. They had made their presence known and I wanted to take advantage of that."

"Weren't you worried that the real sailor and Indian would show up?"

Jared smiled. "We knew they wouldn't. They weren't feeling very good that day, thanks to a friend of yours—Parris, no that's not right, Magee, James Magee."

"Magee is alive?" Jared shouted. "The last time I saw him we were both swept overboard during a storm. I didn't know if he survived."

"If it weren't for him, you'd be dead. He's the one who told me you were Smilin' Jack Tar. It was Magee who arranged to keep our sailor and Indian out of the way. Some of his friends drugged them."

Jared slapped his hands in delight. "Just like they did to us!"

"About now," Philip continued, "they ought to be waking up to find themselves suspects in Smilin' Jack Tar's escape!"

"Do you know where Magee is now? I'd like to see him."

Philip shook his head. "I don't even know the name of his ship, although he said it was a snow. Magee is also the one who planned the misdirection in the warehouse. If anybody ever caught up to the shallop that was heading away from the pier, they'd find three sailors—one wrapped in an Indian blanket—who were heading out to fish."

"I have a lot of people to thank for my life," Jared said.

"Priscilla brought Wampas down to help us. Yours is the second Morgan life he's saved," said Philip. "If it weren't for him, I would have been a bear's breakfast."

"I can see we have a lot of catching up to do," Jared laughed.

"Who's this Shaw fellow?" Priscilla asked.

"Shaw? Rudy Shaw?"

"That's him."

"How do you know him?"

"He's the one who delivered the note to me from Philip," Priscilla said. "He was all excited and said we had to move fast. Then he said, 'Your brother's a rare bird. I'd hate to see him hang.' He turned to leave and muttered, 'But if he doesn't hang and turns to piratin' again, he won't last long the way he fights.' What does he mean by that?"

Jared held his stomach as he laughed. "I had a duel with him once. He doesn't think I'm cut out to be a pirate."

The four of them sat back, enjoying their success. It dawned on each of the three Morgan children that this was the first time they were together since Philip left in his quest to find the family Bible. Philip promised to tell them all about his quest and show them the Bible when they reached Boston. He'd shown it to his mother when he first returned, but not to Priscilla. She gave no indication of being interested in seeing it.

"How is Mother?" Jared asked.

Philip and Priscilla exchanged grim glances. Jared guessed what they didn't want to tell him.

"She married Daniel Cole, didn't she?" he said.

Philip nodded, confirming his suspicion.

Jared sighed heavily. "That man is evil. I'm sure Mother has no idea what kind of man he really is."

"She knows," Priscilla said bitterly. "She knows because I told her. I told her a hundred times, but she wouldn't believe me. She's just as guilty as he is for all the things that have happened to us!"

"That's not fair, Priscilla," Philip shouted. "Daniel Cole has the whole city fooled into thinking he's a good, honest merchant. Somehow, he's fooled her too."

"How can you say that? She lives with the man! She *has* to know what's going on; she'd be blind not to see it! As far as I'm concerned, she's a traitor!"

"That's ridiculous!" Jared shouted. "We're talking about our mother! She wouldn't do anything to harm us!"

"But she lets him do whatever he wants!" Priscilla shouted.

The shouting lasted for nearly half an hour. Jared defended his mother against Priscilla's attacks while Philip tried to mediate, but his defense of his mother was on shaky personal belief. Wampas excused himself after the first few minutes. The three Morgan children had not been together for almost three years, yet they were fighting like they had never been separated.

The trip back to Boston aboard the brig *Salvation* was more amiable for the Morgans. Jared was sneaked aboard in a wooden crate. Philip and Priscilla, dressed in fine clothing befitting the owners of the ship, boarded as they normally would. Wampas was no longer with them. He chose to travel back to Cambridge by land, planning to stop briefly at the reservation on the way. When Philip learned of his plans, he offered to accompany him on the trip; it would give him a chance to see Weetamoo. Priscilla argued against it. A land trip would take too much time and Philip's presence was needed in Boston immediately. Already they were behind schedule. She needed captains to man the merchant ships she had purchased and she needed them now.

The *Salvation* unfurled her sheets and sailed with the tide. The new crew had been confined to ship while they were docked in Charleston. Officially, they were told the trip to Charleston was a training cruise and they stood watch as if they were at sea. However, the real reason for keeping the sailors onboard was so that they couldn't attend the scheduled hanging. Priscilla didn't want to take any chances of

Jared being recognized. His identity would always be a random element of risk for them. Still, it was prudent to take precautions.

Once they were at sea Jared was uncrated; Philip and Priscilla were astonished at how their younger brother came alive on the deck of the ship. He insisted on exploring its every inch. With his older brother and sister in tow, he gave them a tour of the ship, pointing out where repairs were needed. Philip and Priscilla watched in amazement as he scrambled up the shrouds, nimbly walked the yardarms, adjusted the rigging, and hauled in sheets at the first mate's command. At the captain's table he swapped sea stories with the captain and first mate and demonstrated his knowledge of shipping routes. The captain, an elderly man who had agreed to remain captain only until a new crew was trained, offered to let Jared sail the ship the rest of the way to Boston. Jared accepted the offer in gentlemanly fashion; only Philip and Priscilla recognized the way his eyes lit up with excitement, the way they used to when Father would give in to Jared's pleading and let him do something he'd been begging to do.

At the morning watch Jared assumed acting command of the ship. He barked orders, double-checked navigational readings, took the helm when needed, and sailed *Salvation* into Boston harbor without incident. Philip and Priscilla had found their fourth captain.

Jared Morgan and Anne Pierpont took the ferry from Boston to Cambridge to visit Anne's parents, brothers, and sisters. It was a happy reunion; Anne didn't get across the Back Bay as often as her mother wanted her to. As one would expect with eleven brothers and sisters still living at home, the house was alive with noises of all kinds. After dinner Jared and Master Pierpont took a walk together. The elder Pierpont was impressed that Jared was now the captain of his own ship, *Salvation*, and wanted to hear all about Jared's life at sea aboard a merchant vessel (that was the story Jared was using, since people would not understand his being a pirate). Jared had his own agenda for the walk. He asked Master Pierpont for permission to marry his daughter and permission was gladly granted.

Earlier that day Anne and Jared had stopped by her father's bakery where Jared was reunited with Will. The big-eared boy had taken the apprentice position Jared had passed up. According to Master Pierpont, Will was a hard worker and would make a fine baker. Chuckers and Millie had married and were parents of a one-year-old boy with another baby on the way. Chuckers was currently working at a blacksmith's shop, having had a series of unsuccessful starts. He confided with Jared that his present and former bosses were all imbeciles and that all he needed was someone to lend him enough money to start his own blacksmith shop. According to Anne, Millie told her that the kind of shop he was going to open changed every month—one month it was a cooper's shop, then a furniture shop, then a cobbler's shop. Jared found his former friend to be insufferable—a braggart, a hard drinker, and a know-it-all. He was glad when it was dinner time and they had a ready excuse to leave for Anne's house.

The next morning they returned to Boston by water. Jared borrowed a little shallop with a small mast and sail. They boarded at Watertown, upriver from the Morgan home which was now back in the family. Philip lived there when he attended classes; Priscilla used it as an occasional retreat; and Jared, though he hadn't had occasion to use it yet, knew it was available to him too. A caretaker lived there year-round to see after its upkeep.

"Jared! The boat's tipping! Don't lean so far over the edge!"

Anne, sitting in the bow of the boat facing Jared, was

hugging the far side, trying to balance Jared's weight as they sailed past the house.

The four front pillars of the white house came into view with the vast expanse of green spread before them. With hungry eyes Jared studied every detail of the house, the surrounding trees, and the stable behind it as they drifted slowly by. Satisfied, he plopped back into the center of the shallop. The boat corrected itself, then leaned the other way with Anne's weight. She let out a little yelp and sat upright, perfectly in the center with a hand gripping each side.

"Don't move around so much, it'll tip over!"

Jared didn't hear her. He was still reveling in the past. "You don't appreciate those days until they're past," he said. "Chuckers, Will, and I spent countless hours swimming here."

"If you don't sit still, you'll be swimming today!" Anne cried.

Jared laughed at her. "Relax. The boat won't tip over."

"What if it does?"

Jared shrugged. "We get wet."

Anne pretended to be angry, but they both knew she was playing.

"Come here," he said.

"No! The boat will tip over."

"The boat won't tip over!" he said. "Hold on to the mast and step around it."

She looked at him warily. He held out his hand to her.

With unsteady legs, Anne maneuvered herself around the mast. The boat tipped precariously with her shaky movements. Jared steadied her with his hand and she half-fell into a sitting position between his legs, her back against his chest. With his left hand on the tiller he guided the craft, leaving his right arm free to circle around her waist.

"Now I understand your intentions, Master Morgan!" Anne

cried in mock protest. "I thought you just wanted to show off your sailing skills by returning to Boston by water. When all the time it was your intention to get me alone!"

Jared lay his chin on her shoulder so that they were cheek-to-cheek. "That's the way it is with us pirates," he said. "Once you see us coming, it's too late."

She snuggled contentedly against him as the scenery drifted lazily by. "This is nice." She intertwined the fingers of her left hand with his right.

"Do you remember the last night I visited you at your house three years ago?" he asked.

Anne giggled. "You scared me nearly to death hanging in that tree outside my room!"

"Before that."

She thought a moment. "Oh, yes! That awful courting stick!" she exclaimed. Looking back at him she said, "This is much better."

"You'll get no argument from me." He leaned forward and pressed his lips to hers. "If I remember correctly, you refused to tell me you loved me."

"If I remember correctly," Anne's eyes sparkled with the recollection, "I said you didn't need to hear something you already knew." She lowered her eyes. "I was embarrassed to say it in front of my parents, even with the courting stick. I said it later, didn't I?"

Jared nodded. "It's hard to describe how much those few moments meant to me these last three years. When I'd be standing watch on deck late at night I'd think about hanging onto that tree limb with you at the window. It was that memory that kept me going. I knew that the girl in that window would be waiting for me when I returned."

He kissed her again, pulling her against him tightly. She reached up with her free hand and caressed the back of his head.

"Jared? Can I ask you a question?"

"Sure."

Anne was clearly embarrassed. "It's not an easy question to ask." She looked down into her lap. "But I feel I have to know."

"Would you feel more comfortable if, when you ask the question, I stepped out of the boat?"

"Jared!" She slapped him on the leg. "Don't make fun of me."

"I'm sorry," Jared laughed. "What do you want to ask?"

"Well . . . you were gone a long time. And you weren't at sea all the time. Sometimes you were in port . . . and, well, I know what sailors do in port, especially when they're far away from home and lonely. My question is . . . well, while you were gone . . . in port . . . did you . . . well, did you see any girls?"

"Girls? Lots of them!" Jared exclaimed enthusiastically. "There were girls all over the place. I'd see them walking down the street, and going to market, and. . . ."

She slapped him on the leg again, this time harder. "Jared! Don't be cruel! You know what I mean."

Jared leaned forward until his lips touched the soft red hair that fell over her ear. "I know what you mean," he whispered. "And the answer is, no. Some crewmates took me to a whorehouse. But I couldn't. One thought of you and I knew I couldn't do it."

"So what did you do?"

"I jumped out a window and ran away."

"Jared Morgan! How rude!"

Jared pulled away. "What are you talking about?"

"Imagine how that poor girl must have felt—you jumping out of her room like that and all! You hurt her feelings!" A smirk crossed Anne's lips and Jared knew he'd received the same kind of teasing he had just given. In a more pedantic tone she said, "I think the Bible says somewhere, 'He that teaseth much will himself be teased.' "

Jared growled playfully and poked her in the ribs. Anne squealed and the boat rocked recklessly. "Don't, Jared! Don't! We'll tip over!"

"I love you, Anne Pierpont," he said. "I love you more than anything else in this world."

They had entered Boston's Back Bay. Boston Neck, the only land route to the city, was off to their right. Ahead of them was a strait with Graves Neck on one side and Beacon Hill on the other. Beyond that they would pass the ferry landings on both shores before landing themselves.

"I wrote a poem while you were gone," Anne said.

"Only one?" She shot him a warning glance and Jared quickly raised his hands in surrender. "Sorry, it just slipped out," he said.

"Do you want to hear it or not?"

"Of course I want to hear it. Did you bring it with you?"

Anne laid her head back against his shoulder. "It's always with me." She closed her eyes and recited the poem from memory.

The gentle ocean breeze
releases to my ear
the sweet memory of your voice.
Night courses through my window,
the moon is emblazoned with your eyes.
Slender branches
arching precariously
awakens memories of your tender lips
lingering on mine.
Then the dreary call of reality
makes my body tremble
frightening the fantasy away.

Until the day the finger of God
blends the cruel line separating
fantasy from reality
making the two
one.

There was moment of silence when she finished. Then Jared whispered, "That's lovely, Anne. It really is. Will you write it down so I can have it too?"

Her reply was a kiss.

Priscilla's carriage stopped on King Street near Cornhill. She got out and walked under the figure of a headless woman which led into The Good Woman Tavern.

"Master Gibbs," she said immediately upon entering. "That headless woman outside your tavern is revolting. When are you going to get rid of it?"

"It's good to see you too, Mrs. Stearns," Gibbs replied. "And as for my lady, I've been thinking of commissioning a wood carver to shape a head for her. Would you care to model for it?"

"The last thing I want is for my head to be prominently displayed above a Boston tavern."

Gibbs helped her off with her overcoat and she sat down at the nearest table. He joined her.

"And what brings you to my humble tavern?" he asked her.

She produced several sheets of papers. "Nothing much," she said. "There are just a few more papers to sign."

Peter Gibbs looked them over, then peered at her.

"Is something wrong?" she asked.

"You brought these yourself?" A mischievous smile appeared.

"I fail to see what you're getting at, Master Gibbs."

He laid the papers on the table. "It's just that you could have sent these by way of messenger; yet you chose to bring them yourself. I'm flattered."

"You needn't be," she sniffed. "I happened to be passing by and wanted to get this matter settled, that's all."

Gibbs sat back in his chair. His head cocked to one side as he appraised Priscilla. "It's always business with you, isn't it? Don't you ever do anything just to enjoy life?"

She produced a quill and a bottle of ink from her bag. "I enjoy life just fine, thank you," she said. "Now if you'll sign the papers."

"No."

"No? What do you mean, 'no'?"

"No, I won't sign the papers. At least not until you agree to take a walk with me."

Priscilla put on her tough business demeanor. "Master Gibbs, refusing to sign these papers is no trifling matter, one that jeopardizes our entire agreement. I must insist you sign them!"

Peter Gibbs leaned forward, resting his arms on the table. Giant dimples appeared on his cheeks. They were Priscilla's weakness. She bit her tongue and looked at the papers. "Don't get me wrong," he said. He reached out and touched her hand. Her instinct was to pull away. She didn't. "I'll never be able to repay you for all you've done for me. Monetarily, yes; but not the gesture itself. You didn't have to help me like you did and I'm grateful. Let me show it. Take a walk with me. If for no other reason than to prove to me that you can do something that isn't business related."

She looked up at him.

"Please," he said.

It was the dimples that did it. "All right," she said. "A short walk."

They rode in Priscilla's carriage down to Ship Street. Gibbs helped Priscilla out of the carriage. He offered her his arm and the two walked along the street with the bay on one side and the city on the other. It was late afternoon. Everything was tinted with an orange hue. Shadows were long. They stopped a moment and stared out at the variety of ships bobbing on the water. The Long Wharf stretched into the bay.

"The *Salvation* will be sailing in a couple of months," Priscilla said. "It will be Jared's first voyage as captain. We stumbled into a terrific deal on lumber. He'll be taking it to London where. . . ."

"Excuse me," Gibbs interrupted. "But that's business. There's no business allowed on this walk. If you want to talk about something, tell me about yourself."

Priscilla looked up at Gibbs. "I'd rather not," she said.

"All right, then tell me you like the deep color of the bay at this time of evening or the exaggerated shapes the shadows make. Anything but business."

She nodded in agreement and they resumed their walk in silence. A couple of times she thought of something to say, only to realize that it was business related. A growing realization disturbed her. *Was Peter Gibbs right? Did she think of nothing but business?*

"Look over here." Gibbs turned her toward the city. The sun had just passed beneath the city skyline leaving the sky a blue so pale it was almost white. The steeple of the North Church was the most prominent silhouette in a rather bizarre collection of shapes and forms. The pale-blue sky gave way to bright yellow and orange.

"It's lovely," Priscilla said.

Peter Gibbs slipped his hand into hers. She didn't pull away.

A few minutes later they bumped into Jared and Anne who had just completed their trip from Cambridge. The two couples laughed at the coincidence and Anne excitedly told Priscilla about their trip home, especially the part about her father giving his permission for her to marry Jared. Congratulations were passed around. Peter invited everyone back to his tavern where he hosted a celebration dinner. The foursome laughed and talked late into the night.

Philip was reading when Jared, Anne, and Priscilla returned home rather loudly. The three, still in a festive mood, described their evening to Philip and apologized for not thinking of sending for him to join them at the tavern. Philip told them he hadn't felt like going out anyway. He congratulated Jared and Anne and excused himself to retire to bed. He ascended the stairs to the laughter and good-natured kidding Jared and Anne were giving Priscilla over Peter Gibbs' more than obvious feelings for her.

Philip lay on his bed in the dark and stared at the ceiling. He reviewed the night's events. While the foursome was celebrating at The Good Woman Tavern, he was talking with Wampas who had just returned from the reservation bearing a letter from Weetamoo. The letter remained unopened for the remainder of the Indian's stay as he answered all of Philip's questions. Yes, Weetamoo was fine. She was teaching five children now in the wigwam and was looking forward to getting copies of the printed primer. Wampas said the press at the Indian school at Harvard told him it would be finished in a couple of months.

Wampas expressed concern for Weetamoo. She's not the same, he said. There's something different about her since he saw her last. She insists everything is fine and that she is doing well. Her words are right, he said, but her spirit is suffering. Wampas pleaded with Philip to go see her as soon as possible. Maybe a visit from him, even a brief one, would do her good.

After Wampas left to return to Harvard, Philip read Weeta-moo's letter. It only served to confirm Wampas' assessment of her. The words were right—she told him about the church and her pupils—but her spirit was suffering. It was what she didn't write, or couldn't write that bothered him. She didn't think he would ever return. She'd given up on him.

Maybe she's right. She always seemed to have special insight into things. Maybe she saw this long before I did, Philip thought. It was hard to argue with facts, and the facts were these: even with frequent absences, he was excelling in his classes. There was talk of making a position for him on the staff even if there wasn't an opening when he graduated. *That way we'd at least have our hook in him,* the president had said. Then there was Penelope. True to her word, she'd convinced her father to call off her engagement to Reginold Burns. Powerful board member Edmund Chauncy was once again chumming with Philip, and Penelope nearly tackled him every time she saw him. At first it was easy to avoid her. But lately, as the memory of Weetamoo dimmed and the reality of life at Harvard as one of the elite was dangled daily before him, Philip found himself encouraging her advances "just in case something happens and I have to stay," he told himself. And then there was his position in The Redemption Company now that the Morgan family was back together again. It left him no opportune time in the foreseeable future to leave.

Was God using all this to tell him something? Everything was coming together for him in Cambridge and Boston. Everything he had lived for, except for his time on the reservation, which actually was just a small piece of time in his life.

He had written a letter in response to Weetamoo, and after reading it over, he came to the conclusion that his letter sounded just like hers. The words were right, but the spirit was gone.

Philip closed his eyes and tried to stop the thoughts of

Harvard and Weetamoo and Penelope and The Redemption Company from circling round and round in his mind. Laughter drifted up from downstairs. Jared had Anne. And from what he heard tonight, it sounded like Priscilla had finally found someone to love in Peter. But what did Philip have? Who did Philip love? Where was Philip supposed to be?

The questions were many, but he had no answers as he finally nodded off to sleep.

"Don't stand there looking like an idiot, Watkins. Tell me what you've got."

Timidity perturbed Daniel Cole. Hesitation was a sign of weakness and Daniel knew that in Boston the timid did not inherit the earth.

"I think you're going to like it, Master Cole." The male secretary inched forward and extended a report. Cole snatched it from him and peered over it with ice-cold eyes. It was another morning briefing. Constance sat in a sunny alcove just off the parlor eating breakfast. She spread some apricot jam on a half-slice of bread, seemingly oblivious to Cole's morning business report.

Daniel Cole cursed, flipped a page, and cursed again.

He was reading a complete listing of The Redemption Company's property purchases. It not only included The Good Woman Tavern, the Morgan residence, and four ships, but also several of his competitors, their ships, warehouses, and inventories. Plus there were rumors of several more purchases, which would make the estimated value of the company's holdings exceed his own.

"Watkins, you're a bigger idiot than I gave you credit for if you think this is good news."

"The good news is on the third page, sir. We've discovered the owner of The Redemption Company."

Cole ripped a corner off page two in his haste to get to the third page. A wicked smile spread across his face. He lowered the papers and looked at the plump woman having breakfast in the alcove. "So the harmless flounder has spawned a shark," he muttered. To Watkins: "Is this confirmed?"

Watkins handed him two other pages. "We obtained these last night," he said. They were contracts with Priscilla's signature at the bottom.

Cole leaned forward in his seat. His whispered orders were punctuated with a finger jabbing the contracts he held in his hand. "I want operatives on every ship this woman owns, in every business, and in her house. I want to know her every move, her every word. Do you understand?"

"Yes, sir." The male secretary left immediately.

Daniel Cole sat back in his chair and pulled out a cigar and lit it as he stared at Mrs. Cole sitting alone in the alcove sipping her morning tea like she did every morning. He watched as his cigar smoke swirled across the room toward her. Constance's nose twitched, then wrinkled at the odor. She looked at her husband. "You know I hate it when you smoke this early in the morning, especially while I'm eating breakfast."

"I know," he said, taking another puff and blowing it in her direction.

Within the month Daniel Cole had his harpoons lined up. He was going shark hunting in the business waters of Boston and his target was Priscilla Morgan Stearns. His blood rushed like that of any other hunter in anticipation of the kill. He had stalked his prey, knew her habits, her weaknesses, and where she could be found. He was ready for the hunt.

Cole not only had a list of all The Redemption Company's holdings, but he also knew their future plans. From private discussions in Priscilla's sitting room, he learned that Jared would soon be sailing for China. It was an ambitious venture, to be sure. While Cole had profited greatly with pewter, the growing wealth of Bostonians established a market for finer tableware. An established trade route to China would be worth a fortune.

He learned that Philip was leaving to return to the Narragansett Indian reservation. The discussion apparently sparked a great deal of angry discussion. The decision pleased Cole; it was one less Morgan to worry about. But should he stay, Cole was ready for him.

An ordinary tar aboard *Salvation* was a former crew member of the *Lloyd George*. He recognized his captain as being the infamous Smilin' Jack Tar. This fit the other report Cole received from his sailor-and-Indian crimp team upon their return from Charleston. After being held and questioned by authorities, they were released based on two key facts: first, they had several patrons of the tavern vouch that they were face down on their tables during the escape; and second, during the escape, the "sailor's" Monmouth cap almost flew off. The "sailor" caught it before it did, but not before a witness saw a scar on the left side of his forehead. A scar just like Philip Morgan's. It didn't take Cole long to guess that the Indian of the escape was the very one that was in his house the night Philip returned from the reservation. All the pieces fit.

The hunter had in his sight an escaped pirate and the men who aided in his escape. But the key to the victory was Mrs. Stearns; how could he use the information about her brothers against her? As bait? Possibly. Blackmail? Daniel Cole smiled the smile of a hunter about to corner his prey.

Joseph, Priscilla's black manservant, stood just outside the sitting room listening carefully to every heated word of the fight going on inside.

"Let him go!" Priscilla shouted. "He disappeared for three

years when the family needed him most; this is no different. We'll get along fine without him."

"Philip," Anne said, "why don't you bring Weetamoo here to live? We'd love to meet her."

Philip stood in front of the fireplace, his arms folded defensively. He was the only one standing. "She would never come. Her life is tied to the work at the reservation. Look, the only reason I returned was to make sure the family was all right. Now that I know everybody is fine, it's time for me to return."

Peter Gibbs was seated next to Priscilla. "I'm not a member of this family," he said. "So I can speak from an objective point of view. The way I see it, you're throwing your life away. I mean, look at what you have—offers from Harvard to teach, a successful family business with your sister and brother. What are you going to do at the reservation? Harvest maize? Build huts? If you ask me, it's a terrible waste of a brilliant mind."

"Peter's right," Jared said. "We're finally all together again. Why do you want to leave when you have everything here?"

"The woman I love isn't here."

"What about Penelope?" Priscilla said. "She adores you. I don't know what this Indian squaw looks like, but you could do a lot worse than Penelope Chauncy here in Boston. And with her family connections, she's perfect for your profession at Harvard."

"Don't you think I've struggled with this a hundred times?" Philip's hands formed scales that weighed invisible weights back and forth as he spoke.

"We're all making sacrifices," Jared said. "Anne doesn't want me sailing to China because the trip can take up to two years and I don't want to be away from her for that long either. But I'm going anyway because it's best for the family. I know how you must feel about Weetamoo. And maybe you and she are destined to be together. But we need you here now. Stay in Boston until I return. After our first shipment from China we should know better where we stand financially."

"I can appreciate the sacrifice you're making," Philip said, "but I can't see how my staying in Boston will make any difference at all. Nothing you have said has changed my mind. I'm leaving in the morning."

"Just like Mother!" Priscilla shouted. "He hasn't heard a word we've said. He's going to do what he wants to do regardless of how it affects the family! All I can say is, good riddance!"

Priscilla stormed out of the sitting room, frightening Joseph who was lurking in the hallway shadows with her unexpected appearance.

The next morning, before anyone else was awake, Philip left for Cambridge where he would pack a few things and say good-bye to Wampas before beginning his journey to the Narragansett reservation.

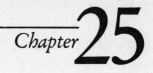

Chapter 25

P RISCILLA was the first to encounter the winds of revival sweeping across the New England colonies when she encountered shops closed at midday for the purpose of prayer. She began to notice other signs as well—people she'd associated with for years who were thoughtless and indifferent about religion were suddenly growing religious. They gathered as families or groups of friends in their homes to pray. They attended public worship services eagerly intent on hearing the minister expound on the truths from God's Word. Priscilla could hardly walk the streets without hearing psalms coming from business establishments and homes. The Halfway Covenant generation that had been riding on the coattails of their parents' piety was discovering personal faith in epidemic proportions. Hundreds of communities were affected; stories of personal conversions were rampant. As for Priscilla, she was immune to the fever.

"You're obsessed!" Gibbs shouted.

Priscilla sat behind a a sea of papers spread out all over a table at the tavern. "I didn't get to where I am today by being frivolous in my business dealings!" Priscilla countered.

Peter Gibbs pushed a broom across the floor. It was a slow day for him; there were only two others in the tap room, both old men with nothing better to do than nurse tankards of ale all day long, read the newspaper, and amuse themselves with other people's conversations. Today Priscilla and Peter provided the entertainment.

"Look, business is slow. It's a beautiful afternoon. Why don't we take a walk by the bay?" he said. They had taken several walks by the bay since their first one when they encountered Jared and Anne. It had become their favorite activity. They could be alone, walk hand-in-hand, sometimes arm-in-arm, and feel the fresh salt air against their cheeks. On cooler days Priscilla's cheeks would turn as red as her hair and Peter warmed them with his hands, then with his lips. Their first kiss was exchanged on the wharf beside Boston Bay. Today, however, Priscilla's mind was entrenched in a deep business rut and it would take a lot of tugging and yanking to pull her out of it.

"Not today, Peter," she said. "I have to get these ship manifests ready." She searched under three piles of papers before she found the one she was looking for. Her eyes focused intently on the list.

"I insist," Peter said. "For your own good."

"You're not my mother and I have work to do."

Peter put away his broom, marched over to Priscilla's table, and gathered all the papers up in his arms.

"Peter! What are you doing? Put those back!" Priscilla yelled.

He unceremoniously dumped the papers in a bin behind the tap room counter. "There!" he said, "work's all done for the day."

Priscilla cursed at Peter, ordering him to retrieve the papers immediately. Her reaction took him back. He'd never heard her curse before.

"You're serious, aren't you?" he said, but he knew the answer to his question just by looking at her.

"Do you think Daniel Cole wastes an entire afternoon or takes time off to go for walks? Of course he doesn't! And if

I'm going to keep from being one of his victims, neither can I; he'd eat me alive if he could, but I'm not going to let him. I thought by bringing my work here we could spend some time together, but if you insist on acting childish about this, I'll work at home from now on."

Peter's face flushed as he retrieved the papers from the bin and threw them back on the table. "There you are, Mrs. Stearns," he said. "Forgive me for not realizing that your entire financial empire would fall if you took a walk with me. And, by the way, if I were you I wouldn't worry about Daniel Cole. The two of you are becoming so much alike it's difficult to tell you apart!"

Priscilla was stunned. "I can't believe you'd say something that cruel!"

"It's not cruel to state the facts," he replied. "Ever since your brother left, you have been obsessed with this vendetta you have against Daniel Cole."

"And why not?" Priscilla screamed, tears streaming down her cheeks. "The man has destroyed my family! Why shouldn't I want revenge? I won't rest until I've hurt him as much as he's hurt me."

"Priscilla, listen to yourself! Listen to what you're saying. The man has already won!"

"Oh no he hasn't!"

"Yes he has! He has won because he has succeeded in making you just like him. You're acting just as selfish, just as hateful, just as arrogant! You don't enjoy life anymore. You don't have the faith you once had. You've lost the ability to love. Building a financial empire that is larger than his won't bring those things back!"

Priscilla wept openly. She hated Peter for what he was saying.

Just then the front door of the tavern burst open. It was Scroggins, the fish merchant who did business at the end of

King Street. "Gibbs!" he shouted. "Close the tavern and come quickly! You won't regret it!"

Peter cast a curious eye at the fish merchant. He was red-faced and out-of-breath. Peter would think there was a fire or some other similar emergency if it weren't for the joy radiating from the fish merchant's face. "Scroggins, what are you talking about?"

"Whitefield!" Scroggins yelled. "The evangelist from England. He's at the common preaching right now! Hurry! You'll be sorry if you miss him!"

The door slammed shut. Peter could hear the fish merchant calling out to the cobbler across the way, telling him the same news.

Peter leaned against the counter. His feet shuffled nervously as he looked at Priscilla. "I apologize for yelling at you," he said. "But that's the way I see things."

Priscilla's only response was a sniffle. There was a long silence.

"You know, I've had people from all over the colonies here in the tap room talking about this Whitefield. It wouldn't hurt for us to go and listen to the man. People say he brings a powerful message from God. What do you say?"

In a soft voice Priscilla said, "God and I haven't spoken to each other in years."

"Well, maybe it's time the two of you got reacquainted."

Silence.

Peter cleared his throat and walked toward the front door. "That's where I'll be if you need me."

"Peter?" The tavernkeeper stopped, his hand resting on the door latch. "If you don't mind, I'd like to go with you."

Thousands of people jammed Boston common to hear George Whitefield preach. And although Peter and Priscilla had to content themselves with a place on the edge of the crowd, they could hear the evangelist with remarkable clarity. From their vantage point in Priscilla's carriage they saw a young, slender man with a round face and great energy. When he spoke he gestured vigorously, he jumped, he pleaded. Everything he did served to reinforce the urgency of his message. From his opening words, he captured Priscilla's attention:

> It is a common saying, and common sayings, are generally founded on matter of fact, that it is always darkest before the break of day; and I am persuaded, that if we do justice to our own experience, as well as consider God's dealings with his people in preceding ages, we shall find that man's extremity has been usually made God's opportunity, and that "when the enemy has broke in like a flood, the spirit and providence of God has lifted up a standard against him": and I believe at the same time, that however we may dream of a continued scene of prosperity in church or state, either in respect to our bodies, souls, or temporal affairs, we shall find this life to be checkered, that the clouds return after the rain, and the most prosperous state attended with such cloudy days, as may make even the people of God sometimes cry, "all men are liars, and God has forgotten to be gracious."

Priscilla was mesmerized by the evangelist's words. Of his oratorical ability, there was no doubt—every syllable rang clear and sharp. Every word in every sentence had the proper emphasis. But what struck her most was the way he spoke to people as if he were sitting in the house chatting with them. This was no scholarly treatise of the kind heard on Sundays. This was one person telling another person about the things of God. His comment about God forgetting to be gracious to God's people struck a particularly responsive chord in Priscilla. He struck again when he spoke of the church.

But, my brethren, I will come closer; there are more unbelievers within the pale than without the pale of the church; let me repeat it again, you may think of it when I am tossing upon the mighty waters, there are more unbelievers within the pale of the church than without; all are not possessors that are professors; all have not got the thing promised; all are not partakers of the promise, that talk and bless God they have got the promised Savior: I may have him in my mouth and upon my tongue, without having the thing promised, or the blessed promise in my heart.

Priscilla had never heard anyone dare say in a public forum the things this man was saying about the church. He was unmasking the pretenders, those who hid behind religious cloaks but were no different from those who never claimed to know God. These were her thoughts exactly. She had recorded the same sentiments years ago in her diary. Now this man was speaking them openly.

There are few Christians can live together, very few relations can live together under one roof; we can take that from other people that we can't bear from our own flesh and blood; and if God did not bear with us more than we bear with one another, we should all have been destroyed every day. Does the devil make you say, that will give it all up; I will go to the Tabernacle no more; I will lay on my couch and take my ease; Oh! if this is the case of any tonight, thus tempted by Satan, may God rescue their souls.

I know we had more comfort in Moorfields, on Kennington Common, and especially when the rotten eggs, the cats and dogs were thrown upon me, and my gown was filled with clods of dirt that I could scarce move it; I have had more comfort in this burning bush than when I have been in ease. I remember when I was preaching at Exeter, a stone came and made my forehead bleed, I found at that very time the word came with double power to a laborer that was gazing at me, who was sounded at the same time by another stone, I felt for the lad more than for myself, went to a friend, and the lad came to me, Sir, says he, the man gave me a wound, but Jesus healed me; I never had my bonds broke till I had my head broke. I appeal to you whether you were not better when it was colder than now, because your nerves were braced up; you have a day like a dog-day, now you are weak, and are obliged to fan yourselves; thus it is prosperity lulls the soul, and I fear Christians are spoiled by it.

If Priscilla didn't know better, she would have thought that Peter had staged this entire performance for her benefit. She couldn't help but think of Philip when Whitefield described how difficult it was for families to live together. And his charge that prosperity lulled the soul hit the mark. She had determined not to go to the tabernacle anymore; she had enjoyed a bed of ease; she had exchanged God for gold and was the poorer for it.

O you frighten me! did you think I did not intend to frighten you? would to God I might frighten you enough! I believe it will be no harm for you to be frightened out of hell, to be frightened out of a unconverted state: O go and tell your companions that the madman said, that wicked men are as firebrands of hell: God pluck you as brands out of that burning. Blessed be God, that there is yet a day of grace: Oh! that this might prove "the accepted time" Oh! that this might prove "the day of salvation"; Oh! angel of the everlasting covenant, come down; thou blessed, dear comforter, have mercy, mercy, mercy upon the unconverted, upon our unconverted friends, upon the unconverted part of this auditory.

Lord awaken you that are dead in sin, and though on the precipice of hell, God keep you from tumbling in. Amen! even so, Lord Jesus. Amen!

The crowd dispersed with much weeping and rejoicing. Priscilla couldn't help but notice how different this was from Sunday church services where people attended to show their neighbors they were good people. Others went to reinforce their community status by strutting to their prominent pews. And although the preachers spoke about God every Sunday, they never encouraged people to know Him personally. Priscilla wondered how many of them actually knew God personally.

How different was this fresh spirit that was moving within her and the residents of Boston! The spiritual awakening that was sweeping the colonies through the preaching of men like George Whitefield put the responsibility for one's faith on the individual. Salvation was a personal matter between a man or woman and God. Growth in grace was a personal matter. But most importantly, the evangelist reminded Priscilla that God and personal relationships were more important than the accumulation of wealth. She felt a warmth in her heart that had been long absent; it was the warmth of God's love.

Priscilla reached over and took Peter's hands and held them. "Dear Peter," she said, "my dear, dear Peter. Thank you for bringing me. Will you ever forgive me for this afternoon? In my anger I have wandered so far away from the truth. How can I ever repay you for what you have done for me today by bringing me here?"

Those irresistible dimples appeared on his cheeks. "I can think of one way you could repay me, but I doubt if you will do it."

"Anything I have is yours," she said. "Just tell me what you want."

"I don't want anything that belongs to you."

"Then what?"

"I want you, my dear Priscilla. Not your possessions. You."

Priscilla blushed. "What exactly are you saying?"

Peter repositioned their hands so that hers were encased in his. "I'm saying I love you. I've loved you ever since you led that horse into my tavern. I know it's wishful thinking on my part, but if I could have anything, I'd ask for your love in exchange for mine."

Priscilla freed one hand and held it over her mouth. "Oh my! What a day this has been!" she cried. "Peter, I don't feel worthy of your love," she choked back tears. "And I fear I've forgotten how to love another person."

"Then let me teach you how."

She threw herself into his arms. "Yes, Peter! Teach me how to love again. Please teach me how!"

Upon returning to Priscilla's home they found Jared and Anne talking excitedly about the Whitefield open-air service.

"You were there too?" Anne asked excitedly.

"It was like Mr. Whitefield was talking directly to me," Priscilla said. "He stirred feelings in me that I haven't felt in years."

Anne was in tears.

"Have I said something to offend you?"

"Just the opposite," Anne cried. "God has answered my prayers today."

"You've been praying for me?"

"How could I do any less? You've been such a strong spiritual influence in my life!"

Priscilla must have had a puzzled look on her face, for Anne explained.

"Priscilla, remember the Bible studies you held at your home?"

Peter looked amused. "Priscilla led Bible studies?"

"Oh, she's an excellent Bible scholar, Peter!" Anne exclaimed. To Priscilla: "You'll never know how much those studies meant to me. You helped me realize that God loves me even though I'm a woman and that He has blessed me with a special gift, and that it would be a crime if I didn't use that gift to glorify Him."

"You remember all that from our studies?"

"Priscilla, your courage taught me to trust God. If it wasn't for you, I would have stopped writing poetry long ago."

Priscilla crossed the room and hugged her younger companion. "Considering my disgraceful actions of late, I must really be a disappointment to you."

"Not at all!" Anne cried. "I knew that someday God would complete the work He began in you."

For the remainder of the afternoon the two couples shared their impressions and feelings regarding the preaching of Whitefield and the miraculous spiritual impact God's Spirit was having on the colonies. Jared remembered how his father had always forced him to attend church services and to endure family times of Bible reading and prayer. He said he never imagined the day would come when he would willingly attend a service or look forward to the time when he could sit around with family and read the Bible and pray.

"Why do you have to look forward to that day?" Peter asked. "We can do it right now!"

Anne retrieved her Bible from her room. Jared suggested Priscilla pick the passage to be read. The others watched as

Priscilla mentally sifted through various Scripture passages in her mind. "Got it," she said. "How about Romans chapter eight?"

Peter sat with bowed head and Jared looked steadfastly at Anne as she read the words of the apostle:

And we know that all things work together for good to them that love God, to them who are the called according to His purpose. For whom He did foreknow, He also did predestinate to be conformed to the image of His Son, that He might be the firstborn among many brethren. Moreover whom He did predestinate, them He also called: and whom He called, them He also justified: and whom He justified, them He also glorified.

What shall we then say to these things? If God be for us, who can be against us?

He that spared not His own Son, but delivered Him up for us all, how shall He not with Him also freely give us all things?

... for I am persuaded, that neither death, nor life, nor angels, nor principalities, nor powers, nor things present, nor things to come, nor height, nor depth, nor any other creature, shall be able to separate us from the love of God, which is in Christ Jesus our Lord.

Then they prayed. They prayed for one another. Jared prayed for his mother. Anne prayed for Jared's safety on his voyage to China. Peter thanked God for Priscilla. Their prayers weren't the kind of prayers that are preserved and published; they weren't the one-hour prayers of the preachers on Sundays; they were the fervent prayers of four people who had just rediscovered the love of God.

"If only our father could see us now," Jared laughed after the prayers were completed.

"Especially you!" Priscilla pointed at her brother. "You were always so rebellious."

Jared sat back in his chair and sighed. "I still can't help but feel something's missing. It just seems ironic to me that we're sitting here talking about spiritual things and Philip's not with us."

"I got the Bible, Father, just like you asked."

Philip stood alone in the middle of the dirt road not far from Muddy River Village. It was the exact spot where Benjamin Morgan's life had come to an end. Philip held the Morgan family Bible in his hands and spoke to the air. "Look here," he said. Philip opened the Bible's cover and pointed to the names printed inside the cover. He read them aloud. "Drew Morgan, 1630; and his son Christopher, 1654; my name's here too! Look—Philip Morgan, 1729, Philippians 2:3-4. Nanouwetea—Christopher Morgan—chose the verse for me." His voice faltered. "Weetamoo penned the words."

Philip stared at his name at the bottom of the list. He felt like an impostor. He didn't deserve to have his name on this list. Drew Morgan had risked his life to bring the Bible and his faith to a new world; Christopher Morgan sacrificed his life to spread the Gospel to the Narragansett Indians. What had Philip Morgan done? What had he done to earn the right to be on this list? Nothing! He didn't deserve to be there because he was violating the charge Christopher gave him. He was violating the Scripture reference next to his name. He was putting his personal interests over his family's need.

"Father, I feel so miserable!" he cried to the heavens. "Don't I have a right to be happy too? Don't I have a right to marry the woman I love? Is it wrong that I want to be with her? Is that so wrong? so terrible?" Philip fell to his knees. "Am I evil for wanting to have a son so that I can be a father to him?"

The Bible fell from his hands, landing awkwardly in the dirt.

"Father, I wish you could meet her. I know you'd love her as much as I do. She'll make such a wonderful mother for your grandchildren." Philip stared at the place where a dying Benjamin Morgan spoke his last words to his son. He got down on his belly with his cheek in the dust, just like he had done on that dreadful day, and he pleaded with his father to speak to him again. "Tell me I'm doing the right thing, Father. Please, tell me I'm doing the right thing!"

Philip heard no new message. Mingled with his sobs he heard the sound of his father's voice telling him the same thing he'd said on the day he died: *Family is important, son, probably the most important thing on earth.* He heard the voice of Christopher Morgan: *If you fail at everything else, don't fail at this—bring your family together in unity and love.* He heard his own voice giving testimony against him: *As God is my witness, I will make every effort to complete what has begun here today, the uniting of the Morgan family.*

Philip Morgan lay prostrate on the ground in the exact spot in the road where his father died and wept until he could weep no more.

The garden was festive and the food plentiful at Jared Morgan's going-away party on the eve of his China trip. It was a small family party held behind Priscilla's house. There was a lavish spread of food including wild turkey, roast goose, apple tarts, and candied fruits. Those attending wore their Sunday best even though it was close family. Priscilla had to insist the guest of honor attend. Jared wanted to inspect his ship one last time before he sailed. Fortunately, Anne intervened and somehow manage to talk him into attending his own party. Jared's first mate, James Magee, and his gunner, Rudy Shaw, were in attendance, each accompanied by a female companion. And Peter Gibbs was there, having just posted his intention of marrying Priscilla Morgan Stearns on the church door.

"I wasn't surprised at all by the announcement," Anne said about the news of the impending wedding. "I knew he loved her when he came to Cambridge on the day Priscilla was in the pillory. I could see it in his eyes."

"It just seems strange to me," Jared said wryly. "There has to be something wrong with a man who falls in love with a woman while she's in the pillory."

Peter laughed with him. "I must admit, this family's history of attracting trouble has given me pause for thought. It all started that day she brought the horse into my tavern. . . ."

Priscilla slapped him playfully on the arm. "Aren't you ever going to tire of that story?" she cried.

The conversation turned to China and the things Jared would see there.

"I envy you," Peter said. "I'd love to travel to other parts of the world."

Jared put a hand on his shoulder. "We can arrange that," he said. "I've got space on my ship for one more tar."

"Oh no you don't!" Priscilla cried, removing Jared's hand. "I couldn't bear to part with him for two years." Realizing how insensitive her remark sounded, she turned to Anne, "Please forgive me, dear. I spoke before I realized. . . ."

Anne smiled at Priscilla. "I took it as an expression of your love for Peter, nothing more." She changed the subject. "I can't wait for him to return! Jared promised he would bring me back bolts of silk!"

Suddenly, the whole garden party turned eerily silent. Everyone stopped what they were doing and stared in the direction of the house. Standing in the doorway was Philip Morgan, his hair and face and clothes filthy with dirt.

"I hope it's not too late to wish my little brother a safe passage to China," he said.

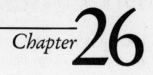

Chapter 26

TWO days after Jared and the *Salvation* set sail for China, Philip sat alone in the sitting room of Priscilla's house with an open Bible on his lap. It was early evening. Anne was upstairs; Priscilla was at the tavern with Peter. He'd been distracted from his reading by the deep hues and long shadows of sunset. The leaves of the tree were greener; the sky was bluer than usual, as was the water of Boston Bay. A handful of skiffs and shallops drifted lazily across the water. An occasional horse and cart or pedestrian ambled down the street. It was as if the whole world were winding down after a hard day's work. The listless scene crept over him like an encroaching fog. Philip yawned.

Mid-yawn, Philip heard a strange noise. At first he thought it was a dog barking in the distance, so indistinct and hoarse was the sound. Then it grew louder. He heard consonants and he realized the sound was that of a human voice—raspy and out of breath, shouting the same thing over and over. Philip leaned forward in his chair and strained his ears to make out what was being said. The sound was getting closer, the consonants harder. Not only did he recognize the word, but he also recognized the voice, as hoarse as it was—it was his mother!

"Priscilla! Priscilla!" she called over and over.

Philip leaped from the chair and ran to the front door. He

reached it the same time as Joseph, the manservant. As the door swung open, Philip saw his mother—her face was red with exertion, her eyes wide with fright. She held a hand against her chest trying to catch her breath, yet still managing to cry out for Priscilla. When she saw Philip, her face registered surprise, then relief. "O Philip! Philip! Thank God you're here!"

"Mother! What's wrong?"

Philip helped her into the house. Anne appeared on the steps from upstairs.

"Mrs. Cole!" she cried. Anne rushed down the stairs and assisted Philip in helping Constance Cole into the sitting room. Joseph closed the door and followed behind.

Constance was helped onto a sofa with Philip on one side and Anne on the other. Philip couldn't believe how much his mother had aged since he'd seen her last. Her skin was ghostly white and sagging with wrinkles; even the spark of fear failed to ignite her dull eyes. She looked like she was drugged. Anne patted her hand and assured her she was safe.

"Philip, thank God you're here." Constance barely had a voice left. "You've got to stop her!"

"Stop who, Mother?"

A motion in the doorway caught Constance's attention. She looked up at Joseph, the manservant. There was fear in her eyes. *Why would she be afraid of Joseph?* Philip wondered.

"Not with him here!" Constance shouted. She pushed herself back against the sofa. "Tell him to go away! Please, Philip, make him go away!"

Philip turned to Joseph. "You may go, Joseph. We'll take care of Mother." As the servant turned to go, Philip saw a glint of fear in the servant's eyes as if Constance had just transmitted a contagious disease.

"Mother, what was *that* all about?"

"Where's Priscilla?" Constance cried.

"Mother, tell me what's wrong!" Philip insisted.

Constance glanced at the doorway. When she was satisfied they were alone, she said, "He's a spy!" Her eyes were so wide as she spoke, her pupils were almost completely lost in a sea of white.

"Joseph a spy? Why? For whom?"

"For Daniel. He tells Daniel everything! That's why I was surprised to see you. Daniel was told you had returned to the Indians."

"I had a change of heart," Philip said.

"Priscilla!" Constance returned to her first cry.

"What about Priscilla, Mother?"

"Don't let her go! It's a trap! Don't let her go!"

"Go where?"

"To the warehouse. To meet Daniel!" Constance blinked several times as tears came.

"Mother, calm down! Tell me what's going on!"

His words had little effect on her. Constance Cole's language was deteriorating. "He's my husband . . . but that's no reason . . . I can't let him . . . not to my little girl . . . I can't let him . . . must stop him . . . stop him. . . ."

Philip watched as Anne pulled his mother toward her to comfort her. She was incoherent.

Constance jerked away from Anne and grabbed Philip's arms. "Stop her! Stop Priscilla! Don't let her go!"

"Priscilla's not here, Mother," Philip explained.

When Constance heard that, all efforts to control herself failed. Her words and actions became totally irrational and disjointed. About the only thing that Philip could make out at all was Priscilla's name.

Anne held Constance Cole with both arms. "I'll take care of your mother," she said. "You've got to go to the tavern and make sure Priscilla is all right."

Philip took a final look at his mother and nodded.

Astride his horse, Philip galloped through the nearly empty lanes of Boston toward King Street. From the moment he recognized his mother's voice, he'd begun to feel his chest tightening, the first signal an asthma attack was immanent. Hearing her raspy voice made his throat scratchy in sympathy. Now, with the pounding of the horse's hoofs, his breaths were growing shorter and shorter. *He didn't need this. Not now!*

Jumping from his mount outside the tavern, he burst through the door, startling the barkeep who instinctively reached beneath the counter for what Philip guessed was a weapon of some sort. Philip quickly identified himself. The worker told him that Priscilla had left a short time ago, but not to worry because Peter was with her.

Outside, Philip mounted his horse. *But where should he go?* His mother had said Cole wanted to meet Priscilla at a warehouse, but she failed to identify which warehouse. Both Daniel Cole and the Morgans had several of them scattered up and down the docks. Philip fought to calm himself so he could think. He reasoned Priscilla would probably not agree to meet Daniel Cole at one of his warehouses, especially at this time of the evening when most of the workers would be gone. She knew Cole too well for that. So they had to be at one of the Morgan warehouses. Philip urged his horse toward the bay. The Redemption Company had three large warehouses on the same pier. It was their largest holding. He'd try there first.

As he rode, the coolness of the damp air settled against his skin and penetrated his lungs. *The chill of death,* he thought. It was an unwelcome thought, but one he couldn't shake. He reached the pier and began to wheeze as he dismounted.

"Lord, keep them safe," he prayed.

Surely Cole wouldn't harm them here, he reasoned. Not on their own property. Besides, Cole wouldn't do anything himself. He hired men to do his killing—the sailor and the Indian. Philip also took comfort in the fact that Peter was with her. The tavernkeeper was healthy and strong, more than able to hold his own against the overweight Cole.

With such thoughts Philip attempted to calm himself, to keep his anxiety in check before it triggered a debilitating attack. He scrutinized the wooden pier. There were two walkways, one on each side of the pier, each about eight feet across from the water's edge to the buildings in the middle. There were three buildings in all on the pier, all of them belonging to The Redemption Company. Additional walkways separated the buildings.

From his vantage point, Philip could see down one side of the pier. There was no movement of any kind, nor could he see any doors open. He walked to the other side of the pier. There was no one on the walkway. But just as he was about to turn away, a movement caught his eye on the water beneath the pier. He took a few steps toward the edge to get a better angle. About two thirds of the way down the pier, at the beginning of the third building, he saw a small barge, its cargo covered with tarp. The barge was piloted by two figures who were navigating it through the pilings.

Philip's breath came up short when he recognized the figures — the sailor and the Indian! The sun was just disappearing behind the city, making the shadows under the pier dark. Philip moved closer to the water to see what Cole's two hired murderers were doing. Why were they under the Morgans' pier? And what was under the canvas?

Just then, Philip had an urge to cough. He tried to hold it, but couldn't. The sound of his cough caused both heads on the barge to snap in his direction. Philip stared in horror as the sailor pointed at him and yelled something that sounded a lot like his last name. The burning in Philip's throat increased as he wheezed and coughed again. A moment later the sailor jumped from the barge to a ladder on the pier's edge. Philip could think of only one reason for his sudden change in course—the man was coming after him!

What to do? Run for help? No. By the time he returned, it might be too late. He couldn't leave without first making sure Priscilla was all right.

When he was sure the sailor was watching, he darted behind the nearest warehouse then stopped, hoping the sailor would take the fake and begin looking on the other side between the buildings. Leaning against the end of the warehouse Philip counted to five, then peeked around the corner. The sailor fell for it! The length of the pier was empty. Philip rounded the corner and ran as fast as he could. He had to get past the break between the first and second warehouses before the sailor got there. And he had to do it quietly so as not to give away his position.

No sooner had he run a dozen steps when it felt like a huge hand clamped around his throat, cutting off his wind. He stopped midstep and threw back his head to gasp for air. All he got was the feeling of liquid fire being poured down his throat, a wheezing sound, and a tiny amount of air followed by a coughing spasm. He was doubled over and helpless, all the while signaling his exact location. Philip was certain his life was about to end.

Priscilla and Peter had arrived at the warehouse thirty minutes before Philip. Daniel Cole was there waiting for them. He held a leather satchel under one arm. With his free hand he brushed the unruly white hair out of his eyes. He was alone.

"What's this all about, Cole?" Peter asked.

"I don't recall inviting you to this meeting," Cole said coldly. "This is strictly a matter between persons of business."

"Peter is here at my invitation," Priscilla said. "I consult him on all matters of business. *Is* this a matter of business, Master Cole? Your invitation was rather vague."

"As I said in my written request that you meet me here, I would like to make a proposal that would be mutually beneficial for me and the owner of The Redemption Company."

Peter and Priscilla looked at each other.

"Oh yes, I know about that," Cole said with a sly grin. "But then, that's my business—to know the competition."

"Why here?" Peter asked. "And why now rather than business hours?"

"Priscilla, dear, is this oaf's presence really necessary? Surely we could do business more quickly without his paranoid interruptions."

"Please state your proposal, Master Cole."

Daniel Cole closed his eyes and shook his head in disgust. "May we at least go inside? It's getting chilly out here. Besides, a portion of my proposal has to do with warehouse procedures that could best be described inside—the one at the far end of the pier has the largest square footage and would suit my purpose best."

"Why these warehouses? Why not your own, Cole?" Peter asked.

"Would Priscilla have come to my warehouse if I'd invited her there?"

Peter had to admit she wouldn't.

"You see my point," Cole said. "May we?" He moved to one side and gestured to the end of the pier. Priscilla looked at Peter and gave a cautious nod.

"The way I see it, Priscilla dear, it doesn't make sense to me that we should expend so much effort fighting each other when we could do so much more by working together. After all, we're family, aren't we?"

The thought of being family with Daniel Cole sent a shiver through Priscilla.

"What I propose is that we form a partnership. Each of us contributes to the partnership, each of us profits from it."

They had reached the third warehouse. Priscilla unlocked the door. She entered first, followed by Peter, then Cole.

"Take warehouse space, for example . . ." Cole continued.

Priscilla passed through a small office that housed the warehouse records and into the warehouse itself. It was dark inside, all except for a light in the side of the warehouse at the far end. There was no door there. No window. Someone had broken in! She had just turned to say something to Peter when he crossed the threshold from the office to the warehouse. Priscilla saw a sailor and an Indian. Her scream came too late. The sailor clubbed Peter with a thick board. Peter dropped to the wooden planks with a sickening thud. An instant later the Indian had grabbed Priscilla and clamped a hand over her mouth.

Daniel Cole stood in the doorway. He stepped over the motionless Peter on the floor and approached Priscilla. He was smiling. "Now the real business can begin," he said.

Peter was dragged to the far end of the warehouse. Priscilla followed, escorted by the Indian. The sailor bound and gagged Peter, leaving him on the floor. The Indian tied Priscilla to a pillar. Then Cole dismissed his associates, telling them to carry out their next unspecified business. Daniel Cole found a chair and set it in front of Priscilla.

"For several years I've been wrong about you," he said. "And when it comes to knowing my competition, I'm seldom wrong. But I must admit you fooled me. It was probably the fact that you are a woman. It gave you the advantage of surprise. You see, I never figured a woman could be much competition." He chuckled. "I guess in that respect you are to be congratulated! Thinking back on it now, I can see my error. Of all the Morgans you are truly the greatest threat. I should have seen it the day I came to Cambridge to do business with your brother. But then there was that woman thing again that threw me off. Even if I had taken you seriously, I would have figured that your interest in financial matters would pass once a young man caught your fancy. But then you've never been one for young men, have you?" Looking over at Peter on the floor he added, "Until recently."

"What is it you want from me, Cole?" Priscilla asked. "You've killed my father, stolen my mother, and hurt just about every person I've ever loved. What have I done to you to deserve such animosity?"

Cole let his head drop back. He took a deep breath, then said, "You got in my way. You Morgans are always getting in my way. First your father. Now you. And I have a firm policy for people who get in my way—I remove them. It's nothing personal really, just business."

"What are you going to do?"

Cole grinned and leaned forward. His fingertips formed a pyramid with the top point touching his lips. He looked like a little boy busting inside to tell his secret. "I've spent a good deal of time working out this little drama for you and your brothers. I needed a plan that would do more than just discredit and humiliate you. Your experience in the pillory taught me that if I just humiliated you, you would come back stronger than before. So I had to devise a plan that would destroy you as well as discredit the Morgan family."

The boyish excitement bubbled as his eyes jumped back and forth, visualizing his plan in his mind.

"See what you think of my plan. Word will get out that your brother Philip has been carrying on covert activities with the Narragansett Indians for years. Together they're planning an uprising greater than King Philip's War. Of course, for such an uprising they'll need weapons and gunpowder. And where will these deadly shipments come from? Why, from his sister's warehouses!"

Priscilla tried to interrupt, but Cole refused to listen to her. He was having too much fun.

"Imagine my shock when I accidentally discovered your covert operations! Naturally, since you're family, I came down to the warehouse to try to talk you out of your wicked scheme. Inadvertently, I arrived just as a huge store of gunpowder was being loaded into the warehouse. I was discovered and you tried to stop me from leaving, but I managed to break free. In the scuffle, a lantern was accidentally knocked over and the gunpowder exploded, resulting in a fire that destroyed this entire pier. Unfortunately, you fell victim to your own wickedness and died in the fire. Philip will be arrested at the reservation for his part in the plot, but unfortunately he will fall victim to a colonial vigilante mob before he ever comes to trial. And so ends the Morgan saga."

Cole sat back with a grin on his face. "How does that sound? It's rather good, isn't it?"

"You're a fool," Priscilla said. "There are two things you've overlooked. First, we don't store gunpowder in this warehouse. Second, when Jared returns he'll expose you for the murderer that you are."

Cole was not disturbed in the least by Priscilla's caveats. "Not to worry," he said. "I'll supply the gunpowder, enough to turn this pier into a giant torch. As for your brother Jared—or should I call him Smilin' Jack Tar—oh yes, I know about that too. A noose will be awaiting him upon his return. And who will the good people of Boston choose to believe? The word of a godly, upstanding merchant or that of an infamous pirate?" Cole rose from the chair. He rubbed his hands together excitedly. "You see, my dear, I delayed our little meeting for a couple of days until after your brother sailed. I *wanted* him to set sail. This way he can make a trip to China before he's hanged. When he returns I'll find a way to acquire his cargo. The way I see it, it's the least the magistrates can do for me since I'm the one who thwarted this dastardly Morgan plot."

Daniel Cole had everything covered. What was worse, Priscilla knew people would believe him. His fabricated story would create a scandal and people loved scandals. Cole moved closer to her. The odor of dirty socks and unwashed underclothes wafted all around him.

"And now, dear Priscilla, it is time to begin this little drama."

Behind him at the other end of the warehouse, a hatchway opened in the deck. Up popped the Indian's head. He nodded at Cole, signaling he was ready.

"Ah, the gunpowder is here," said Cole. "My helper has just floated a small barge of powder under the pier. When it is set off, I figure it will destroy half this warehouse, sending fire and splinters flying everywhere. Don't look so concerned, my dear. The blast won't kill you. No, I want you to spend some time thinking before you die. The explosion will start a fire which will eventually reach here and you will burn to death—a fitting punishment, I think, considering the agony you've caused me. I want you to see all your precious merchandise burn up around you before you go with it."

Cole turned to leave, then came back.

"Oh, one more thing. I nearly forgot." He tied a gag tightly around her mouth. "The explosion should destroy enough of the pier to keep anyone from reaching you—that is, if anyone knew you were here. Your silence is just a precaution. If people think the warehouse is empty, they'll concentrate their efforts on preventing the fire from working its way up the pier toward the city. The end of the pier can burn itself out and fall into the bay and no one will care—unless they hear someone screaming. So, we can't have that, can we?"

Priscilla tried to give Cole a few parting words, but the gag pinned her tongue to the bottom of her mouth. Her words became nothing but muffled sounds.

"Oh," Cole had one more comment, "and please accept

my apologies for not extending a final farewell on your behalf to your mother. Sentiment such as that doesn't fit the drama. Those who plot sedition and anarchy rarely think of their mothers as they are about to die." He chuckled at the added detail to his fabrication.

The clop, clop, clop of Cole's heels against the wooden planking echoed through the warehouse as he walked to the other end. Priscilla watched as he leaned over the opening in the floor to the floating barge below. Something was said from below. Priscilla couldn't make it out.

"Where is he?" Cole shouted.

A garbled response.

Cole cursed, looked back at Priscilla, then all around him. "How long once you light the fuse?" he shouted into the hole. He nodded at the response. "Light it!" he said.

Daniel Cole continued staring down into the hole, apparently watching the lighting of the fuse. As he watched, he reached into the bulky satchel he was carrying. From it he pulled a pistol. He aimed it down the hole.

BLAM!

The pistol's report was deafening. A cloud of gunpowder smoke circled around Cole. He dropped the pistol in the hole, then retrieved a second one from the satchel. He saluted Priscilla and waddled quickly toward the door leading to the office and outside.

Something must have gone wrong, for Daniel Cole no sooner made it into the office when the far end of the warehouse erupted in light and smoke. Instinctively, Priscilla closed her eyes and turned her head as a shower of wood and smoke and splinters flew all around her. The force of the explosion slammed her head against the pole. There followed heat and flying debris. One board hit her forehead, another crashed into the shin of her right leg. The gag around her mouth muffled her screams and whimpers. For a few seconds everything went white and her head felt like it was swirling in pain. She was losing consciousness. Priscilla fought the forces that were attempting to pull her from reality into the dark recesses of her mind. If she blacked out now, she was sure she'd die.

Fighting to keep her senses, Priscilla prayed. She prayed for God to send someone to rescue her. She prayed for Peter on the floor, that even if she died he might live. She prayed for her mother. It was the first time in years Priscilla prayed for her mother. She prayed that her mother would know that she still loved her.

The explosion had ignited fires all around the warehouse. One by one the little fires joined forces into a raging inferno. Before long the entire warehouse would be engulfed in flames—at least what was left of it. Where there was once a hatchway in the deck of the warehouse, there was a gaping hole nearly spanning the width of the warehouse. Through the smoke and fire Priscilla caught glimpses of the water and the pilings of the remainder of the pier below. Those parts of the warehouse that were still standing on each side of the hole were covered with a blanket of flames. Priscilla and Peter were cut off from the rest of the pier and any help that might come from the city.

Behind her, Peter began to moan. She tried to scream at him, hoping to hasten his return to consciousness. But she knew he couldn't hear her. She could barely hear herself above the roar of the flames.

Moments before the explosion, the sailor grabbed Philip from behind.

"Gotcha!" he cried.

Philip was bent over in a coughing fit when the sailor's strong hand grabbed his hair and yanked it backward. He felt the sharp end of a knife jab into his back. His skin offered a slight resistance before the tip of the blade poked into his flesh. A jab of pain followed, then a sticky feeling as his shirt stuck to his back. His head was yanked back so far he was almost bent over backwards. He found himself looking up the nose of a dirty, bewhiskered sailor.

"Looks like it's gonna be a family funeral," he said. "Let's go join your sister."

The sailor had no more completed the sentence when the pier in front of them erupted with thunder and light and smoke. The force of the blast sent Philip and the sailor flying backward onto the deck. The knife flew from the sailor's hand, landing out of his reach. Both men groped to regain their senses and their footing; the sailor used a pier piling to steady himself, Philip lay with his back against the warehouse. They looked like two fighters who had landed simultaneous knockout blows.

The sailor climbed to his knees and spied the knife a few feet away. Philip couldn't let the sailor get to the weapon first, but the sailor was closer to it. So Philip launched himself, not toward the knife, but toward his opponent, hitting the man squarely in the side. The sailor staggered toward the edge of the pier, trying to regain his balance. He reached for the pier piling, but it eluded his grasp and he plunged over the edge. There was an initial cry of surprise as he disappeared. A second later there was a splash.

Turning his attention to Priscilla, Philip ran toward what was left of the end of the pier. The heat of the warehouse fire couldn't begin to match the heat of the fire in his throat. Every breath was labored and the more he exerted himself, the more lightheaded he became. If he wasn't careful, he would pass out and would be of no help to anyone.

"Lord," his prayer was little more that a wheezing whisper, "I didn't react quickly enough to save Father, please give me the strength to save my sister." Philip arched his back, fought for a little air, then pressed forward.

The walkway along the edge of the pier was a wall of flames. He crossed to the other side only to see an identical situation. He'd have to enter the burning warehouse and see if there was a way to get to the end of the pier from inside. Philip pushed on the office door. The bottom of the door scraped stubbornly against the floor planks. The whole door frame had been knocked cockeyed from the blast. Philip pounded against the door with his shoulder until there was enough room for him to squeeze through. He took a quick glance toward the city as he squeezed inside; the sound of the explosion had rocked the sleepy city awake as hundreds of people converged toward the pier. There was no time to wait for help. Philip entered the burning warehouse.

The warehouse office was filled with smoke which burned Philip's eyes as well as his already scarred throat. He bent low and groped his way along. His foot kicked something soft. He bent down on one knee. It was a fat arm, the rest of the body was under a pile of loose debris. A pistol lay nearby. Philip pushed away much of the rubble. It was Cole. His face and arms were gashed and red with strips of blood. There was no sign of life. *A victim of his own treachery*, Philip thought.

Just then Philip heard muffled screams. He pushed aside some planks that blocked his path to the doorway leading to the warehouse itself. Stepping through he could see two fig-ures at the far end of the warehouse, but a chasm separated him from them. He saw his sister tied to a pillar, her face and leg bloodied. Peter lay on the floor; he wriggled like a cater-pillar trying to escape from a cocoon.

Priscilla saw him. Her eyes widened and the intensity of her screaming increased. Philip searched the area around him. He had to figure out a way to cross the chasm. It was too far to jump. He thought of swinging across on a rope, but there were no longer any beams overhead to hold a rope even if he could find one. *What about a plank? Was there one around long enough to span the chasm?* Philip looked around for a sturdy plank. He had to hurry. The heat was intense and groaning wood indicated the entire structure was weakening.

He found a board that looked long enough. He dragged it from under some fallen debris. Coughing and choking, he stood it up on end and pushed it across the span. The edge of the board hit the other side and bounced up. Philip's end of the board jumped in response. As he tried to steady it, the far end slipped by the edge and the plank plunged to the water below. Philip released his grip just in time; a second longer and he would have been pulled into the water.

"No!" he half-screamed, half-coughed. Then to Priscilla: "Hold on! I'm coming!"

A ceiling beam came crashing down behind him, flames dancing up and down upon it.

Another board. He had to find another plank, longer this time. He found one and dragged it to the edge of the chasm. This time just as the far end hit the edge, he put all his weight on this end to deaden the response. It worked! There was now a narrow walkway connecting the two parts of the warehouse.

Philip tried to wipe away the effects of the smoke from his eyes. His efforts served only to make them sting and water even more. He blinked to clear his vision. All it would take was one misstep and he'd be swimming beneath the pier.

He placed a foot on the plank to test it. It seemed steady enough. He walked out over the water. Looking down was a mistake; the movement of the water under the pier threw him off balance. His arms swung wildly and he rocked from side to side to catch his balance. He took another cautious step, then another. His weight made the plank bow in the middle, in effect, shortening the board and pulling the ends of it nearer the edges. *Was the plank going to be long enough?* He took another step and it bowed even more. A cool breeze blew up from beneath him as the water crashed against the pier's remaining pilings. Another step, then another, and another. He nearly ran the last few steps, jumping to the edge. His makeshift bridge held!

Philip ran to Priscilla and removed the gag.

"O Philip, Philip, thank God!" she cried over and over. Then, "Peter? Is Peter all right?"

"Let me untie you first," Philip said, pulling at the knots in the rope.

She was finally free. Just as the last of the rope's support loosened, she slumped and would have fallen to the floor had Philip not caught her.

"My leg," she cried. "It hurts so much!"

"Try putting your weight on it," Philip said. "See if you can walk."

She tried. Her leg wouldn't hold her. Gently, Philip lowered her to the ground. "I'll untie Peter, then I'll be right back."

Priscilla nodded and watched anxiously as Philip ran to Peter.

After the ropes were removed, he was in no better shape than Priscilla. When he tried to stand, he became so dizzy and disoriented, he lost his balance. Philip tried to catch him. The weight of the larger man pulled both of them to the ground.

"Peter! Peter, are you all right?" Priscilla screamed.

"He's wobbly from the blow to his head," Philip yelled back.

"How are we going to get out of here?"

Philip looked at the plank. He had barely crossed it alone, there was no way he would be able to carry or assist someone else across it. "I don't know," he said. "But we have to get out of here. The structure is failing. This whole thing is going to come crashing down!"

Just then a ceiling beam gave way and plummeted to the deck as if in confirmation of Philip's assessment. Sparks flew into the air as it hit.

"We'll go outside to the end of the pier," Philip shouted. "Maybe we can find a boat or something. If not, maybe we'll just have to try to swim."

"I don't think I can swim!" Priscilla yelled, anticipating the worst.

"We've got to try!" Peter said. He'd raised himself up with his arms, became disoriented, and crashed back onto the deck. With his cheek against the plank, he spoke to Philip: "Get your sister out of here."

Philip nodded. "I'll come back for you," he yelled. He helped Priscilla to her feet.

"We can't just leave Peter here!" she shouted.

"Go!" Peter cried. "I'll try to follow."

"I can only help one of you at a time," Philip said. "And the quicker I get you out of here, the quicker I can come back for him. So let's go!"

Priscilla threw an arm around Philip's neck and allowed him to lift her to her feet. Using him as a crutch, they worked their way through flaming debris toward the back of the warehouse that led to the end of the pier.

"Sorry to disturb you, Captain," said the quartermaster, "but I think you'll want to see this."

Captain Jared Morgan was sitting at his table contemplating his log entry when he was interrupted by the quartermaster. The captain was in a foul mood, a fact of which the entire crew was well aware. That's why Jared didn't bark angrily at the quartermaster for the interruption. It must be a matter of importance if he would dare interrupt him, considering how surly he'd been.

There was good reason for the captain's mood. The *Salva-*

tion had been out to sea less than a day when the carpenter came to him reporting excessive leaking in the hull. Upon inquiry, Jared discovered that the carpenter had been negligent in his duties while they were in port making preparations to sail. Because the ship was relatively new, the carpenter's inspection had been cursory; apparently he chose to spend more time at a tavern than he did checking the hull. Now it was discovered that there was extensive rotting. Repairs were needed immediately. In short, the *Salvation* was unseaworthy.

Needless to say, Captain Morgan was furious. He relieved the carpenter from duty and personally guaranteed him permanent retirement once they reached port—*if* they reached port. Jared's anger was compounded by the fact that he allowed himself to be distracted the night before sailing with a send-off party. If he'd been onboard that night, he would have spotted the problem before they set sail. But now he had no choice but to turn the ship around and head back to Boston.

For more than a day he had prowled the ship like a roaring lion. Sailors moved well out of his way whenever they saw him coming. So if the quartermaster was willing to risk his life by poking his head directly into the lion's den, it must be a matter of utmost urgency.

Jared came on deck to see a rising column of smoke coming from the Boston docks. Darkness had just descended upon the city, yet he could clearly make out key landmarks from the light of the fire. His heart jumped when he saw from which part of Boston the fire was blazing. The very area where the Morgans had their warehouses. He ordered his glass. It didn't take more than a moment for his fears to be confirmed. The Redemption Company's inventory was going up in flames!

Captain Morgan ordered a course change and the bow of the *Salvation* swung toward the flames and column of smoke.

Jared looked on intently as they got closer to the blazing pier. There had been some kind of explosion, that was evident from the hole in warehouse three that had almost completely severed it from the rest of the pier. *But what caused the explosion?* There were no explosives in the warehouses that he was aware of. Whatever had caused it, the fire was spreading. Most of warehouse two was engulfed in flames and the fire was continuing its course up the pier toward the city. Jared could see firefighting efforts underway. It didn't look like they were having much success.

Suddenly two figures appeared from the inferno at the end of the pier. Jared raised his glass. "Philip and Priscilla!" he cried. Priscilla looked hurt by the way she leaned against her older brother.

"Mister Magee!" Jared yelled to his first mate. "Bring the ship around. I want a course that will bring us a few feet off that pier. I'm going over the side. As soon as I'm over, you get this ship away from that pier, do you understand?"

"Captain," Magee said. "Let me send some men. . . ."

"James," Jared took his friend by the shoulder, "that's my brother and sister, I've got to go. And until I know what's going on, I'm not going to order anybody to leap into an inferno for me. If I need help, I'll signal you."

"How will you get back?"

"As soon as you clear the pier, send a skiff for me. It looks like that may be our only way off."

"Yes, sir."

"It's going to be a tight maneuver," Jared said. "I guess we'll see what kind of crew we've got."

"We won't disappoint you, sir."

Jared went to his quarters and strapped on his cutlass. Returning to the deck he climbed the larboard shrouds to the yardarm. He selected his line and prepared to swing over the bulwark and onto the blazing pier.

The *Salvation* set a course that paralleled the pier as if they were going to dock on the leeward side. At the last second they beat into the wind. Sailors scrambled on every mast pulling in lines to adjust to the new course. As the bow pinched into the wind, the ship picked up speed. Jared would have to time his jump carefully. The bow swung short of the end of the pier and Jared could clearly see his sister and brother yelling and waving their arms. He grabbed his line and leaped from the yardarm. He flew over the deck of the ship, over the beam, over the water — and let go. He crashed onto the end of the pier and rolled. He didn't stop until he hit the burning warehouse. The boards cracked and fiery beams fell down on him, burning his arms as he instinctively raised them over his head to protect himself. On the water side of the pier, true to his orders, Magee ordered the *Salvation* away from the burning pier. He saw a skiff being lowered into the water.

"Jared! Over here!" It was Priscilla's voice and Philip's cough.

Jared scrambled to his feet and ran toward his brother and sister. "How badly are you hurt?" he asked Priscilla when he saw the blood on her forehead.

"My leg is the worst. I can barely walk," she replied. "Peter's still inside! Please get Peter!"

Jared nodded. To Philip: "Do you know where Peter is?" When Philip indicated he did, Jared told him to go for Peter. He would follow in a minute. To Priscilla: "Can you swim?"

Priscilla looked at her leg. "I think so. I can move it; I just can't put any weight on it. Jared, please help Peter!"

"Listen to me!" Jared shouted at her. "Look there!" He pointed into the water. A sailor was rowing a skiff toward them. "If you think you can swim, I can go help Philip. Otherwise, I'll need to jump first to make sure you get to the boat. But once we're in the water, there's no way to get back up here."

Priscilla understood. Her response was to leap off the pier into the water. Jared waited anxiously at the end of the pier, watching the whitewater and bubbles where she had jumped. One second passed. Then another. Priscilla broke the surface! She looked up at Jared. "Go!" she shouted.

With cutlass in hand, Jared turned and followed Philip's lead into the building, using the blade to clear his way. He ducked under burning beams and through two holes in the walls before entering a larger room. The smoke was heavy and though he tried to stay low, it got into his lungs and clogged his breathing. He thought how Philip must be suffering.

Just as he ducked through a hole in the wall, he saw them. All four of them.

"This is quite a surprise! I was expecting the righteous Mrs. Stearns, but I guess I'll have to settle for the Morgan brothers!" A bloodied and ragged Daniel Cole leaned against a beam, a pistol aimed at Jared. Peter was on the floor; he looked in no condition to offer any resistance. Philip kneeled beside him rubbing the back of his head. The sailor—Captain Devereaux's wayward brother—stood over them with a knife.

"I'm sorry, Jared," Philip said, "I tried to warn you."

The beam Cole was leaning against groaned. The roof of the warehouse was little more than a skeletal frame that would come crashing down any moment.

"It looks like we don't have time for pleasantries." Nodding toward the plank over the chasm, he said, "However, I *am* grateful that you provided us a way out." To the sailor: "Kill them." He motioned to Philip and Peter. "I'll take care of this one."

The sailor raised his knife over Philip.

"Devereaux! No!"

The sailor paused a moment, puzzled that Jared knew his name. There was a loud crack and a fiery beam swung down and slammed into the sailor. For a brief moment Daniel Cole was distracted. A memory flashed in Jared's mind. He was aboard the *Lloyd George*. Barlow pulled a gun on Jared's beloved captain. Jared hesitated and it cost the captain his life. It wasn't going to happen again.

Jared lunged at Daniel Cole with his sword, striking him in the heart. A shocked look crossed the wealthy merchant's face. The pistol fell to the deck. He followed it. Jared pulled burning debris from off his brother and Peter. Philip and Peter were burned but all right. The sailor was crushed beneath the beam.

The two brothers helped Peter through the burning maze to the end of the pier. Jared jumped first. When he surfaced, Peter jumped. Jared pulled him to the surface. Finally, Philip jumped just as the warehouse groaned, leaned to one side, and collapsed in a blaze of flying embers.

Onboard the *Salvation*, the three Morgan children and Peter looked back at the burning pier. Their personal celebration was tempered by the threat of the fire to the city of Boston. The flames had consumed the second warehouse and half of the first. The city firefighters were waging a losing battle as the fire crept steadily inland.

"Looks like the whole city's gonna go up in flames," first mate Magee said.

"Not if I can help it!" Jared cried. "Get me Shaw."

"Shaw?" Priscilla said. "The gunner?"

Gunner Rudy Shaw appeared as ordered. "I need some precision shots," Captain Jared Morgan told him. "We need to knock out that pier before the fire reaches the city. Can you do it?"

Shaw put both hands on the bulwark and stared at the pier for a long moment. "Fixed target. Within range. I can do it."

"Jared!" Priscilla interjected. "Those are our warehouses! Most everything we own is in them. Maybe we can at least save one of them. We've got to try! Otherwise, we're ruined!"

"Priscilla, we can't let the fire reach the city!" Jared cried. "But we'll lose everything!"

"I agree with Jared," Philip said. "The risk to the city is too great."

"Of course you agree with Jared!" Priscilla shouted. "Neither of you have an ounce of business sense. You're not the ones who built this company, I did! And I'm not going to throw it away so easily!"

Peter, who was still feeling dizzy from the blow to his head, held onto the shrouds to steady himself. He said softly, "Priscilla, I agree with your brothers."

She turned on him and opened her mouth to rebut his statement.

Peter reached out to her. "Priscilla, people's lives are at stake! People are more important than things! We can always build again!"

Priscilla started to say something, then stopped. She lowered her eyes in concession. "Of course you're right," she said. Tears filled her eyes. "O Peter, I could have lost you tonight. And Philip. And Jared. But we're all here and we're safe. How could I ask for more?"

The *Salvation* turned its larboard beam to the pier. Two warning shots were fired. Jared monitored the situation through his glass. "They understand," he said. "They're backing away from the pier." He gave the order for his gunner to open fire on the pier.

Philip, Priscilla, and Jared Morgan watched as the Morgan family wealth was pulverized by Rudy Shaw's guns. With each shot a section of the pier exploded and fell into the sea, where the flames were doused. That night the three children of Benjamin Morgan lost nearly everything they had except each other. They counted themselves the most blessed people in Boston.

EPILOGUE

Daniel Cole didn't live long enough to realize the extent of his failure. Not only did he not succeed in destroying the Morgans, his own actions preceding his death proved to be their financial salvation. With the destruction of the three warehouses on the pier, it seemed as though the Morgans were ruined. The resulting loss of income represented in warehouse inventory meant that they would be unable to meet their financial obligations—namely their payroll, properties, and ships. They were rescued by Daniel Cole's estate.

While he was alive, Daniel Cole was a paranoid man. Considering his unethical and cutthroat business practices, he had every right to be. Having no heir, he realized how vulnerable he was to assassination. He figured one of the easiest ways for someone to gain control of his substantial estate would be through his death—much like the way he obtained the estate of Benjamin Morgan. To make himself less of a target, Cole had all of his holdings registered in his wife's name. In this way, his imagined killers would not succeed in gaining his business empire.

Cole's paranoia was the Morgans' redemption. Upon his

death his widow, Constance Morgan Cole, used his wealth to restore the losses suffered by The Redemption Company at her husband's hand. As a result, the Morgans became one of the wealthiest families in Boston.

The summer sun had just risen above the horizon when a discharge of muskets echoed down King Street. An answering volley came from the north part of the city; to be more precise, from in front of Priscilla's house. Emerging from The Good Woman Tavern to the cheers of well-wishers came the two grooms — Peter Gibbs and Jared Morgan. Their best man, Philip, followed close behind. After greeting their friends the grooms set off on foot to the home where their brides were waiting for them.

Halfway to the house the grooms' party was met by male friends of the brides, mostly Anne's brothers and cousins. Each group named a champion to "run for the bottle," a bottle of spiced broth at the door of Priscilla's house. The winner of the race was the one who reached the door first and grabbed the beribboned bottle. He then returned to the advancing grooms and drank a toast to the brides' health, after which he passed the bottle among the celebrants.

When the grooms reached the house, another salute was fired and the two men waited in the garden for their brides. It was a matter of strict etiquette that no other people were allowed in the garden until the brides, led by Philip, assumed their places before the minister. Then family and guests entered and the ceremony began.

The couples were instructed to join hands. They put their right hands behind their backs while the bridesmaid and best man carefully removed the wedding gloves from the bride and groom respectively — taking care to finish their duty at precisely the same moment. Philip assisted Peter first, then his brother Jared. Next, the Scripture passage, chosen by Priscilla and Anne, was read:

> *Two are better than one; because they have a good reward for their labor. For if they fall, the one will lift up his fellow: but woe to him that is alone when he falleth; for he hath not another to help him up.* —Ecclesiastes 4:9-10

Following the exchange of pledges, the couples kissed. At the end of the ceremony everyone kissed the brides and there was more firing of guns and great merriment.

A month after the wedding the family gathered in the garden one more time. Peter and Priscilla Gibbs were there, as were Jared and Anne Morgan and Constance Cole. Philip was the convener of the meeting. With his family seated before him in the shade of the trees, large arching branches forming a cool canopy overhead, Philip stood to address them. In his hands he held the Morgan family Bible.

"As you know," he began, "I will soon be returning to the Narragansett reservation. This time . . ." he smiled, "with your blessing. Two great forces attract me there: the first being my love for Mary Weetamoo. She fills my thoughts and dreams and I cannot think of living my life without her. I only pray that someday each of you will get a chance to meet her. If that day comes, I know you will readily see why I love her so much."

Anne spoke up. "If she loves you as much as we do, she has our respect already."

Philip blushed at the comment. Pulling a sheet of paper from among the pages of the Bible, he placed it on top, using the Bible as a desk. "The second force that pulls me there is the tremendous work that God is doing on the reservation. In this letter from Weetamoo, she writes of the exciting spiritual revival there. A Congregational minister by the name of Joseph Park from Westerly has been preaching in nearby Charlestown. A number of people from the reservation went to hear him. The same kind of spiritual revival that has come to Boston and the surrounding colonies has visited them too. She writes that there is a decrease in the use of alcohol among the Indians, there is less quarreling, replaced by an atmosphere of love and brotherhood. And the Indians are expressing a strong desire to become educated so they can read the Bible and organize their people along biblical principles. That's where I come in. I'll be their teacher. Weetamoo has been using the primer written by our own ancestor, Christopher Morgan, to train the children. I'll instruct the adults."

He paused and looked at his mother.

"It's not Harvard," he said, "but I'll be doing what I love with the one I love."

Constance smiled and nodded in agreement.

"There is one thing I feel I must do before I go." He held forth the Morgan family Bible. "For decades, this Bible was lost to several generations of Morgans. It was our father who learned of the Bible's existence and had the vision of bringing the Bible back into the mainstream of the Morgan family, a task he passed to me when he died. Fulfilling that task has brought me greater hardship and greater joy than I ever imagined. If it were not for my quest for the Bible I never would have met Weetamoo. I never would have known Christopher Morgan—Nanouwetea as the Indians called him." Philip paused a moment as images of the elderly missionary flashed in his mind. "And now," he continued, "I believe it's best for this Bible to stay in the mainstream of Morgan family life, lest it get lost again." He looked at his younger brother. "Jared, would you come stand by me?"

Jared wore a surprised look on his face as he glanced at

Anne. She smiled and patted his hand.

With Jared beside him, Philip said. "I pass this Bible to you. It is my right as the bearer of the Bible. I give you the responsibility of insuring that the next generation of Morgans— your children—follow in the ways of Jesus Christ and keep the Morgan family faith alive."

Philip lifted the cover of the Bible. Beginning at the top, he read the names listed in the front:

Drew Morgan, 1630, Zechariah 4:6
Christopher Morgan, 1654, Matthew 28:19
Philip Morgan, 1729, Philippians 2:3-4

Added to the list in Philip's handwriting was:

Jared Morgan, 1741, John 15:13

"The verse reads: *Greater love hath no man than this, that a man lay down his life for his friends.* I chose it because you risked your life to save Priscilla, Peter, and me. In my opinion you couldn't have expressed your love to your family in any greater way." To the rest of the family he said: "This is the first time that the Bible has been handed from brother to brother. I'll always take special pride in that fact."

Philip handed the Bible to Jared. In front of their mother and family, the two men embraced.

Jared opened the cover of the Bible and looked at the list of names. He shook his head in disbelief. "From what Philip has told me, I feel unworthy to be among the names on this list—Drew Morgan, the man who brought this Bible and his faith to the New World; his son Christopher, the missionary to the Indians; and my brother, Philip, who will always be remembered as the man who went in search of the lost Bible and brought it back to the family. I pray that I will be as faithful as these men."

The rest of the afternoon was spent with congratulations to Jared and farewells to Philip. But before he left his Boston family for his Narragansett sweetheart, Philip fulfilled his responsibility of telling the Morgan family story as it was relayed to him by Christopher Morgan.

"The story begins at Windsor Castle," he said, "the day Drew Morgan met Bishop Laud. For it was on that day his life began its downward direction. . . ."

Weetamoo sat atop the tower overlooking the cornfield. It was a promising crop this year and she was as determined as ever to keep it from being ruined by the blackbirds. As she sat there alone, her mind wandered to her lesson plans for the children. Her wigwam bulged every day with eager minds and restless bodies, and if she didn't keep them busy they got into trouble.

Just then a cornstalk shook. She grabbed a stone and rose to her feet. As she had done hundreds of times before, she let loose a projectile toward the unwanted predator.

"Ouch!"

Though she'd not heard the sound of his voice for what seemed an eternity, she knew it well; she'd dreamed of it often enough to recognize it. The head of Philip Morgan rose among the cornstalks. He was rubbing his left ear.

"Unfortunately for me your aim is as good as ever," he cried.

"Philip Morgan! What are you doing in my corn? Up to your old tricks, I see."

"Well, it worked last time."

"What do you mean by that?"

"I mean the last time you pelted me with a rock you felt sorry for me and I got a kiss."

"That was last time. . . . I'm older and wiser now. Your tricks won't work anymore." Weetamoo made her way to the ladder and descended from her lookout post. She approached Philip in the cornfield. "Are you hurt?"

Philip walked toward her, rubbing his ear.

"Let me see it," she said. She pulled his hand away from his ear. "It's not even bleeding!" Her eyes moved from his ear to his eyes, and it was as if he had never gone.

Philip kissed her tenderly. "I told you I'd come back," he said.

AFTERWORD

Life in America's early colonial days was marked by struggle and transition. One of the fundamental changes came in the area of leadership. Initially, the colonies' leaders were clergymen and devout churchmen whose journals are packed with biblical references describing their early efforts. But by the time of the Revolutionary War, the power of local government had shifted to a growing merchant and patrician class. Hancock, Jefferson, Franklin, and Washington all were among the well-to-do.

One cause of this shift in authority was a decline in spirituality in the late seventeenth and early eighteenth centuries. The early generations of native-born colonists did not share their parents' religious ideals. The result was the Halfway Covenant—an attempt by churches to make members of the unbelieving children based on their parents' faith. In reality, this was nothing more than an attempt to extend the cloak of church authority over nonbelievers. The result was a largely unconverted clergy and church membership marked by apathy.

When the colonists' chief concern turned from the pursuit

of God to the personal accumulation of wealth, abuses and corruption in government naturally followed — the very thing from which the colonists had fled in England. It took a miraculous display of God's grace — the Great Awakening — to call them back to their spiritual roots. This is the historical setting for *The Colonists*. The Morgan family, swept up by these colliding forces, learns that self-seeking results in conflict and misery, but selflessness brings joy and love.

In *The Colonists* I have attempted to represent the major elements of this colonial period as follows:

Philip represents the burgeoning academic world of Harvard. It is left to him to discover, upon encountering the faith of the Narragansett Indians, that a person's spiritual depth is not synonymous with his academic accomplishments.

Priscilla represents the major struggle between spirituality and the allure of merchant wealth and the power that comes with it.

Jared represents the strong development of the individual, which becomes a hallmark for Americans. It is Jared who is exposed to elementary forms of democracy while he serves as a member of a pirate crew. His experience will greatly affect his children as they do battle in the Revolutionary War.

Daniel Cole represents the merchant class out of control, unchecked by religious faith, ethics, or concern for human life.

One lesson to be learned from the early colonists is that true Christianity is not limited to a particular culture or ethnic group. The number of stories about Native Americans whose lives were transformed by Jesus Christ is inspiring. Most of them paid a high price for their faith. Caught between two feuding factions, they were abused and murdered by both sides. Their only consolation was best expressed by the Apostle Paul who was not unfamiliar with the nature of their struggle: *But our citizenship is in heaven. And we eagerly await a Savior from there, the Lord Jesus Christ.* —Philippians 3:20 (NIV)

The Great Awakening was the first "national" movement uniting the extremely individualistic colonies. God's Spirit proved to be no respecter of colonial boundaries. Nor was the moving of God's Spirit a respecter of persons—moving among English, Dutch, Germans, Quakers, Narragansetts, Wampanoags, and on and on. The account of revival on the Narragansett reservation as described in the Epilogue is fact.

The Awakening's emphasis on individual faith in Jesus Christ made it a truly evangelical revival. The results were far-reaching. Greater emphasis was placed on a converted clergy and church membership. The positive social changes were so prominent, Benjamin Franklin commented on them in his autobiography. The Great Awakening united the colonies in spirit, and the Bible once again became the most prominent book in New England. This resurgence of Christian faith explains the many references to God and the Bible that appear in America's founding documents.

Regarding the origins of democracy, the Congregational form of church government certainly served as the early model, but the colonists still had not made the break from rule by aristocracy. The annual kowtowing to the social elite while the church's seating arrangements were determined is evidence of this. Penalties were enforced for sitting in a pew higher than your social status. The formative practice of democracy actually took place in the settlements on the fringes of society and, to my surprise, aboard pirate ships. It was this discovery that prompted me to place Jared on a pirate ship rather than aboard a merchant ship which had a rigid classification of personnel.

Regarding the pirate ship *Dove*, there was a merchant vessel by that name which sailed a Mediterranean route during this time period. According to her records, the crew mutinied in

1736. For my story, I borrowed only the name, not the history of that vessel. All other ships' names were taken from records of this time period with the exception of the *Salvation*, which is fictitious. The *Dove*'s captain, crew, and adventures are fictitious.

The brief account of Major Bonnet Stede in Chapter 23 is a historical account, as is the court rendering dated 1718.

The account of King Philip's War—its personalities and events—sadly, is fact. Both sides must share the blame for this tragedy.

It is the nature of a historical novel to tell a fictional story within a historical setting. Among the historical settings and cultural practices I used are these, from actual records: the custom of funerals (gloves, rings, headstones, expense, procedure); the supplies of the larder; the ever-present danger of wolves and the resulting rewards for killing wolves; life at Harvard (entrance procedures, speaking in Latin, a typical course of study); church services and buildings (box pews, etc.); the church pranks in Chapter 3 are adapted from historical accounts; courting and marriage practices (bundling, the courting stick, the wedding procession and ceremony); the layout of the Narragansett reservation is based on a map rendered in 1709; for Boston streets and its Back Bay, I used Captain John Bonner's map of 1722; the praying Indian colonies and their locations; the Tree of Witness, a site of gross multiple hangings; and the accounts of cruelties onboard merchant ships.

A note regarding the size of families: the Pierponts and their fourteen children represent the norm for that day. I limited the size of the Morgan family to three children for the sake of narrative clarity and the author's sanity.

Historical characters in this story include: Sachem King Philip; John Sassamon, the first Native American Christian martyr; missionary John Eliot; evangelist George Whitefield;

and, in passing, the much-despised Governor Andros of earlier colonial days.

Fictional characters in the story include: the Morgan family, Weetamoo and Wampas (although these are period names), Daniel Cole, Anne Pierpont, and Peter Gibbs; Penelope and the Chauncys are fictional characters although I used the surname because there was a Charles Chauncy who served as Harvard's second president from 1654 to 1672; the crew aboard the *Dove* is entirely fictional as is the nefarious Captain Barlow.

Historical documents used in the story include: John Eliot's Algonquin translation of the Bible; the Algonquin language was taken from Roger Williams' extensive study, *A Key into the Language of America;* the poems of Anne Bradstreet (America's first recognized female poet) have all been attributed to her; Philip's song, "The Little Mohee" which has been handed down orally from generation to generation and reprinted in the Encyclopædia Britannica's *The Annals of America*, Volume I; John Higginson's work, *The Cause of God and His People in New England* as read by Benjamin Morgan; *The Boston News Letter*, the first newspaper to appear in the colonies; *The Bay Psalm-Book* and the songs sung from it; the Indian song of faith which was sung by the praying Indians in Chapter 7 is titled "The Hymn Heard in the Air"—attributed to Pilgrim times, it is still sung today; and George Whitefield's sermon, which is actually a composite of two sermons—"All Men's Place," and "The Burning Bush."

Anne Pierpont's poetry comes from several sources. The headstone inscription attributed to her was gleaned from records of period inscriptions (it was one of the few pleasant ones); "Oh Child," was used courtesy of a gifted poet and friend, Judith Deem Dupree of Pine Valley, California; and Anne's love poem was written by my talented fifteen-year-old daughter, Elizabeth.

In Chapter 7, I wanted the reader to share Philip's frustration of not being able to understand what the badgering Indians were saying, so I used the Algonquin language without benefit of translation. Like Philip, the reader is left to other clues—facial expressions, body language, and actions—to determine the Indians' intentions. For those who would like to read the translated version of the encounter, I offer this account which can be compared to the original:

"An Englishman!" one Indian yelled, pointing at him.

Philip froze. He thought of running, but what good would it do? He doubted he could outrun them, let alone any arrows they might send his direction. So he stood there, trying to act confident, and watched as the three Indians came toward him, eyeing him suspiciously. Two of the Indians were strong and in their prime, one sporting a feather in his hair. The third was older, possibly in his fifth decade. The younger men were armed with knives, and bows and arrows. The older Indian cradled a musket in his arms. One of the younger Indians stood at a distance and kept watch as the Indian with the feather and the older Indian approached him.

"Who are you?" the older Indian asked.

Philip shrugged apologetically. "I don't speak your language," he said. "Do you speak English?"

"Where dwell you?" the Indian with the feather shouted at him as if that would help him understand.

"I wish I could understand you," Philip said. "I'm looking for the praying Indian town. Can you tell me where it is?"

The older Indian shook his head and sneered. "We understand not each other!"

Philip shrugged his shoulders again. The third Indian, the watchman, stood with arms folded and head lowered, hateful eyes peering at the intruder.

"Speak!" the Indian with the feather shouted, striking Philip on the shoulder.

Philip recoiled and stood his ground. "I mean you no harm," he said evenly. "Just let me go on my way."

With one quick swipe, the Indian with the feather snatched Philip's broad-rimmed hat from his head. He looked it over, removed the feather from his own head, and tried on the hat. The Indians laughed—even the angry one standing far off—as the Indian wearing Philip's hat modeled it for his companions.

Philip kept a straight face but made no attempt to retrieve his hat. *Let him have the hat,* he thought to himself. *It's hardly worth dying for.*

Then the Indian with the hat had another idea. Taking his feather, he placed it in Philip's hair. This brought a fresh round of laughter. Philip stood motionless and straight-faced. His cheeks burned with anger.

The Indian wearing his hat seemed to take offense that Philip wasn't joining in the fun. He punched Philip in the shoulder again and shouted, "Let us fight!"

As much as Philip hated the sting of humiliation when the Indians were laughing at him, now that they had returned to anger, he realized how much he preferred them laughing.

"Are you afraid?"

Philip was hit with a third punch, same place. He held up both hands, palms open to his opponent.

"Kill him!" The words came from the third Indian, the one standing far off. His words were low and guttural, dripping with hate. The Indian with the hat looked to his elder as if for some kind of confirmation. Philip had the distinct impression that this tree that once was laden with the bodies of so many dead Indians would now witness the death of a English colonist.

"Let him live," the elder Indian said evenly. Then he turned to leave. "Let us depart!" he said.

"Kill him!" the angry Indian shouted at his elder.

"Let us depart!" the elder shouted back at him.

With the elder Indian leading the way, the other two followed, but not before firing parting shots of hate-filled glances at Philip. With the Indian's feather still sticking out of his hair, the Harvard scholar watched them leave. Halfway across the field the Indian who took his hat flung it as far as he could.

Jack Cavanaugh
San Diego, 1994

The Morgan Family

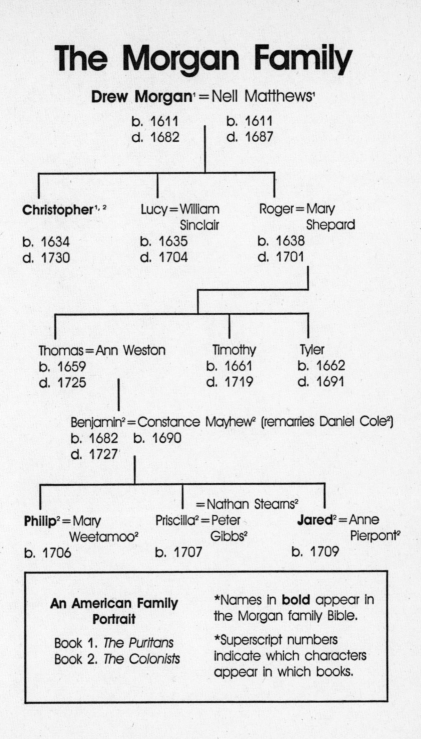

Drew Morgan[1] = Nell Matthews[1]

b. 1611 b. 1611
d. 1682 d. 1687

Christopher[1, 2] Lucy = William Roger = Mary
        Sinclair   Shepard

b. 1634 b. 1635 b. 1638
d. 1730 d. 1704 d. 1701

Thomas = Ann Weston Timothy Tyler
b. 1659   b. 1661 b. 1662
d. 1725   d. 1719 d. 1691

Benjamin[2] = Constance Mayhew[2] (remarries Daniel Cole[2])
b. 1682 b. 1690
d. 1727

         = Nathan Stearns[2]
Philip[2] = Mary Priscilla[2] = Peter **Jared**[2] = Anne
   Weetamoo[2]   Gibbs[2]   Pierpont[2]
b. 1706   b. 1707   b. 1709

An American Family Portrait

Book 1. *The Puritans*
Book 2. *The Colonists*

*Names in **bold** appear in the Morgan family Bible.

*Superscript numbers indicate which characters appear in which books.